RETALIATOR

Dean Crawford

Copyright © 2014 Fictum Ltd
All rights reserved.

ISBN: 150037444X
ISBN-13: 978-1500374440

The right of Dean Crawford to be identified as author of this Work has been asserted by him in accordance with sections 77 and 78 of the Copyright, Designs and Patents Act 1988.
All rights reserved.

Also by Dean Crawford:

The Ethan Warner Series
Covenant
Immortal
Apocalypse
The Chimera Secret
The Eternity Project

Atlantia Series
Survivor
Retaliator

Independent novels
Eden
Holo Sapiens
Soul Seekers

Want to receive notification of new releases? Just sign up to Dean Crawford's newsletter via: http://eepurl.com/KoP8T

We should have known better.

We know that there are few survivors, few of our kind still clinging to life.

They say that when the end came some embraced it willingly, shrugged off their lives like old skins and allowed the Legion to infiltrate their minds and their bodies and become one with the machine. Most, however, did not. Most fought, and died, trying only to remain who they were.

The Legion, the instrument of the Word, our governing law, took life across all of the colonies. Worlds fell; Ethera, Caneeron, Titas; the mining settlements and the outlying systems and the uncharted clouds of asteroids and meteors beyond consumed by the monstrous and insatiable thirst for knowledge and power that is the currency of the Word. The greatest creation and achievement of our human race turned vengeful deity, the destroyer of worlds.

We now know that there are several forces at work within the Legion, an immeasurable swarm of mechanical devices ranging in size from as big as insects to as small as biological cells. There are the Infectors, the smallest and most dangerous, for it is their mission to infiltrate the optical nerves, the brain stem and the spinal cord of human beings, turning them into mere instruments dancing to the macabre hymn of the Word's destructive passion. Then there are the Swarms, the clouds of tiny but voracious feeders who break down all and any materials into the raw ingredients for more of their kind: metals, plastics, even human tissue, consumed en masse and regurgitated into further countless devices, all of which evolve with startling rapidity as though time were running for them at breakneck speed. Finally, there are the Hunters: bigger than the rest and with only a single purpose – to find and to kill intelligent biological life wherever it is found in the cosmos.

We are the last of our kind, and despite the horrors that we witnessed when we fled the only star system we could call home, we now know that we must return. There is nowhere else to run to, nowhere else to hide, for if we do not make our stand now then we condemn our children or their children after them to face what we could not. We must fight back and step by step, system by system, we must take from the Word that which was ours and liberate ourselves from the living hell that we have created and endured.

The Atlantia, a former fleet frigate turned prison ship, is the last home we have. Our crew is comprised of terrified civilians, dangerous former convicts and a small but fiercely patriotic force of soldiers and fighter pilots for whom there is no further purpose in life other than to fight for every last inch of space between here and home.

Our lives may become the last that will ever be lived, and thus we tell our story in the hope that one day others will read of it and remember our names.

Captain Idris Sansin

Atlantia

Dean Crawford

I

'Break right!'

The voice of Commander Andaim Ry'ere bellowed into Evelyn's ear through the microphone in her helmet and she shoved the Raython's control column over and hauled back on it.

The sleek, arrow–shaped fighter heeled over and soared between a pair of vast tumbling asteroids dimly lit by the distant infernal glow of a red dwarf star. Pale light flickered and danced through the cockpit and shadows raced past the Raython as it shot through a narrow gap between the asteroids and rolled out onto a new heading.

Evelyn's heart pulsed like a war drum in her chest and she felt prickly heat tingle on her skin as certain death flashed by with scant cubits to spare. Her gaze snapped from the chaotic view of tumbling asteroids outside her cockpit canopy to a holographic display projected before her. The signal flickered weakly on her tactical display, filled with complex images of the asteroid field and a larger object ahead of her Raython, just outside the debris field.

The cockpit was tight, digital screens glowing with green light and a thin blue line illuminating the edges of the closed canopy. Evelyn's helmet cradled her head in a snug grasp and a secondary display projected onto the retina of her right eye pertinent flight information: velocity, bearing, orientation to galactic plane, fuel remaining and range to target.

Andaim's voice snapped in her ears again.

'Stay sharp! Vector three–five–niner, elevation two–zero, quadrant alpha. We're almost on them! You keeping up?'

Evelyn's mind raced as she performed simultaneous functions; calculating angles and trajectories, operating the Raython's complex targeting computer as the vessel flashed through the asteroid field at near–suicidal speed and rocking the controls back and forth to prevent a collision with the massive chunks of rock flying past.

'I'm on it,' she growled.

Evelyn yanked the Raython hard left and then hard right, sweeping across the surface of a particularly large asteroid and seeing from the corner of her eye the surface pitted with craters and clouds of dust as though bands of weather were drifting through an atmosphere. A handful of smaller asteroids collided with its surface nearby in bright blasts of molten rock, immense energy released in tectonic eruptions. The blasts illuminated the cockpit like distant lightening across darkened skies.

'Stay out of sight,' Andaim ordered her. 'Don't let the target's sensors pick you up.'

Evelyn focused her mind on keeping asteroids between her and the huge target ahead, using the tactical display to orientate herself and stay on target. Huge, dark rocks rushed past her cockpit and tendrils of dust glowed and flashed by as though reaching out for her.

'Almost there,' Andaim said.

Evelyn rolled the Raython over a complete rotation, the dim red light from the dwarf star blocked by pitch black shadow and then filling the cockpit again as Evelyn rolled out and aimed directly for the target.

An alarm sounded in the cockpit like a claxon and sent a bolt of alarm through Evelyn's body as she sucked in a deep breath.

'We're being painted by enemy radar!' Andaim yelled. 'Counter measures, evasive action!'

Evelyn hauled the Raython into a tight turn as she flipped a switch on her throttle that activated a temporary burst of emitted electronic interference, enough to fool the weapons of the target vessel as she raced toward it.

Asteroids flashed past the Raython and a peppering of smaller debris and dust rattled against the fuselage as it shot out of the debris field and into open space. Ahead a vast spaceship loomed against the star fields, its metallic hull glowing a dull and dirty grey in the light from the distant star.

'Target locked,' Evelyn said, 'cannons charged, counter measures active!'

The gigantic, scarred hull rushed up toward her.

'Negative on target,' Andaim snapped. 'Abort!'

'I can get her,' Evelyn shot back. 'Just a few more seconds…'

'Abort now!'

'Target in range.'

The hull of the huge vessel rippled with a series of bright blue–white flashes and Evelyn felt her heart skip a beat as a salvo of fearsome balls of energy flashed at terrific velocity toward her. She had no time to react before the first of them smashed into her Raython fighter in a blinding flare of light.

The flare vanished as Andaim's voice reached Evelyn.

'Sortie aborted,' he intoned. 'Mission failure, return to base immediately for debrief.'

The remaining flares of light flashed silently past the Raython as Evelyn cursed and pulled up, the Atlantia's huge hull rushing by below her. Andaim's voice sounded weary as he spoke.

'You've got to learn to control everything at once,' he said. 'If those cannon charges had been live rounds you'd have been fried alive.'

Evelyn craned her neck around her seat to see Andaim watching her from the rear of the Raython T2 twin–seat training aircraft.

'I couldn't have gotten any closer,' she replied. 'Once we were out of the field, we only had seconds to lock on and open fire.'

'That's right,' Andaim said. 'But you were so focused on targeting the Atlantia's guns that you forgot to open the throttles when you cleared the asteroid field. That cost you a couple of seconds, enough for the Atlantia to get a fix on you. Game over.'

Evelyn sank back into her seat and shook her head in self–disgust as she turned the Raython around toward the frigate, the traffic controller's voice sounding distorted in the cockpit.

'Charger Flight, tactical training session four–seven is over, join the pattern for final approach. You're number one to land.'

Evelyn flicked switches in her cockpit and lowered the landing struts as she slowed the Raython down and deactivated the weapon systems. She brought the fighter around in a shallow descending turn toward the Atlantia's stern, where a landing bay was opening low on her keel, lights flashing to guide her in.

'Charger Flight, finals to stop, three greens,' Evelyn called.

The Raython eased slowly into the landing bay and Evelyn saw in her cockpit mirrors the giant bay doors close behind her. The bay ahead was devoid of life but half a dozen Raythons and a pair of shuttles were parked on the deck, well clear of the main landing strip.

The Atlantia's lower flight decks were separated into three distinct sections: the landing bay at the stern, maintenance in the middle, and the launch bay beneath the bow, each separated by massive bulkheads and blast doors. A flashing rectangle of light illuminated her parking spot, and she guided the fighter over it and it settled onto the deck, magnetic clamps fixing it in place. As she shut down the engines, she saw vents high on the bay walls bleeding atmosphere and heat in clouds of vapour back into the bay and a series of glowing red lights arranged around the upper rim of the bay changed to green.

Evelyn opened the Raython's canopy and pulled off her helmet as she unstrapped and climbed from the cockpit, crewmen hurrying across the bay to service the fighter. She could hear the craft's engines clicking as they cooled as she climbed down onto the deck, her magnetically charged boots and suit replicating gravity to pull her down toward opposingly–charged electromagnets beneath the deck.

She signed the Raython back in to the crew chief's log and stormed away.

'Getting angry won't help you much,' Andaim said as he caught up with her. 'You have to get past this if you want to earn your wings.'

'I had it,' she snapped. 'I damn well had it.'

'You did,' the commander admitted. 'If you'd accelerated to attack speed before acquiring your targets you would have neutralised the cannons just in time, clearing the way for a flight of Corsair bombers or your wingman to shoot the plasma lines and finish the job. You know what to do, it's all just practice.'

Evelyn sighed, shaking her long auburn hair loose.

'Things happen so fast. It's like my brain can't fit everything in quickly enough to keep up.'

'Like I said,' Andaim offered reassuringly, 'it's all practice. Another few flights and you'll be pulling it off. Trust me.'

Andaim had an easy going nature that belied his experience as the Commander of the Air Group aboard the Atlantia, something for which Evelyn was eternally grateful. He had flown for the Colonial Forces before the apocalypse in the older Phantom fighters before the introduction of the newer, more advanced Raythons. Tall, with thick black hair and a jaw that was slightly too wide for his features, he oozed a calm confidence in the cockpit that Evelyn lacked.

'I feel like an amateur,' she confided as they walked into an elevator that would take them up to the crew rooms.

'So did I, once,' Andaim said as the doors closed and the elevator hummed upward. 'So did every fighter pilot. Flying a Raython is a complex business, and you guys are doing it from scratch without the benefit of a couple of years' prior flight training on slower craft. Proficiency is not going to just fall into your lap.'

Evelyn had spent six months learning to fly on the Atlantia's shuttles and in a pair of simulators built from two crashed Raythons, display screens and powerful hydraulics replacing the real sensation of both atmospheric aviation and space flight. Invaluable in preparing the twenty or so students enlisted into the Colonial Forces to fly, the simulators had weeded out those who were simply unable to handle a Raython. Evelyn, along with seven others, had been deemed up to the job and passed on for active flight training.

'It's been six months,' Evelyn complained, 'and we're not even battle ready yet.'

'You're six months closer to it than you were when you started,' Andaim replied. 'Just stay with the plan, okay?'

Evelyn looked at him. 'Why do you insist on having an answer for everything?'

'It's my job,' he grinned back. 'Anything else you'd like to know?'

Evelyn opened her mouth to answer, but the elevator doors opened onto the crew room and Andaim walked out. She followed him to where pilots, all wearing flight suits patched with their squadron identities, were variously gearing up for sorties or pulling off their flight gear for debrief. A few of them nodded at her in greeting, but most were too wrapped up in their pre or post–flight thoughts to chat.

The Atlantia was home to two squadrons of Raython fighters: the Renegades and the Reapers. In addition, she had four shuttles and three functioning Corsair bombers, all of which had been liberated from the hull of a Stellar–Class Colonial battleship, the Avenger, many months before during a battle that had seen many former convicts elevated to the status of junior officers, some of whom were now serving under General Bra'hiv's command as Marines.

Evelyn shrugged off her flight suit and dressed in her officer's fatigues as she ran over her latest failure in her mind. Speed of thought. Andaim had once referred to the limits of what a human being could achieve in terms of multi–tasking as their saturation point. Too much information, too fast, and the brain momentarily shut down, unable to function until it had a moment to recalibrate everything, to file into memory what it had learned and continue on. That point, if reached in battle, was invariably lethal. If a student routinely reached saturation point in training then the pilot was deemed unable to perform their duties and was removed from the service.

Evelyn had reached saturation point twice in her training: once more and she would be up for review before the captain, a man not known for his tolerance for failure, even now when they were so desperately short of manpower and machines. Back in the day on Ethera, student fighter pilots would have been of a much higher calibre than those training now aboard the Atlantia. Second best was all they had access to, and Evelyn felt sorely aware of her incompetence.

'You're dwelling on it,' Andaim said as though reading her mind. 'Don't. Remember your three A's.'

'Assess, adjust and advance,' she replied wearily as she opened her locker and rummaged inside.

She felt rather than saw Andaim watch her for a moment.

'You're not on your game right now and you haven't been for weeks. Are you okay?'

Evelyn remained hidden behind her locker door, partly to hide the smile at Andaim's concern for her welfare and partly to hide the deceit that shadowed her. The captain's wife and ship's senior physician, Meyanna Sansin, was busily conducting tests in an attempt to understand Evelyn's immunity to the Infectors, the minions of the Word responsible for turning humans into living puppets. The constant blood tests, scans and examinations had run her down a fair bit, but nothing like as bad as her incarceration of years before had done. Nobody else knew about her immunity, the better to protect her from any threat of extermination by anybody else infected by the Word aboard the Atlantia. She suspected, unlike everybody else, that there was at least one person carrying Infector bots aboard the ship. To conceal such knowledge from somebody like Andaim, who had protected her and helped her so closely when she had been plucked from the hell of the super–max prison that had once been Atlantia's charge, was one of the most difficult things she had ever been required to do.

'I'm fine,' she replied as she pinned her long hair back, 'really.'

Evelyn realised during such moments how much she missed home, of how she wished that she did not have to confront these challenges. An image of Caneeron flickered like a phantom in her mind, the cold blue skies and glacial valleys, the deep forests and crystalline lakes that had been her home for most of her childhood, the chilly little world in orbit around Ethera's parent star. Her parents, long gone, other losses too painful to bear just before the apocalypse struck and…

She forced the memories from her mind.

The steel mirror on the inside of Evelyn's locker reflected her face. She was young, not yet thirty years of age, and she once again revelled in being able to look at her reflection. Not because she was vain, but because she was alive and her features were not concealed behind the damned metal mask that had hidden her face and her voice for so long.

Her hair was long and flowing, naturally slightly curled, and her skin was clear and lightly tanned from her multiple recent training flights. Her eyes were green, and people had sometimes said to her that they were so wide and open that they felt as though they could see into her soul. A far cry from previous years when people had seen only the mask and had projected onto it their own personal and often fearful view of what Evelyn looked like.

The mask was propped up at the back of her locker, watching her from the shadows. A memento from her past, a reminder of what the Word had reduced her to, of what it had done to her family… She shivered and slammed the locker shut.

'Let's go,' she said.

'Okay,' Andaim replied, clearly deciding to cut her a break as he fastened his uniform and hurriedly smoothed down his hair. 'The captain will want to debrief you on the sortie and...'

Andaim was cut off as a tannoy burst into life in the crew room.

'All senior personnel report to the bridge, immediately!'

Andaim and Evelyn exchanged a glance and then both turned and dashed for the elevator banks.

***

Dean Crawford

II

The Atlantia's bridge was a hive of activity, tactically darkened and yet illuminated by a galaxy of lights from computer terminals and display screens. Crew stations governing the control and command of tactical, navigation, engineering and other essential roles surrounded the captain's command platform, upon which sat Captain Idris Sansin.

Sansin was a retirement–age commander who had been presented the captaincy of the Atlantia in the twilight of his career. The frigate, refitted as a prison ship, had been seen as a quiet back–corner command, a place to put a man whose authority and abrasive nature had often been a thorn in the side of the admiralty. Withdrawn from battle–ready status after a career highlighted by several actions against enemy vessels in combat, Sansin had surprised the navy's hierachy by quietly accepting his last command and the remote location of its posting. Sansin had been too old to fight back against what had once been considered something of an insult; the command of a vessel buried in a dark back–corner of the colonies and charged with protecting the scum of society, its most violent and loathed offenders.

Nearest to the captain sat his Executive Officer, Mikhain, newly promoted from his post as tactical officer in the wake of the victory over the Avenger, although due to a shortage of experienced hands aboard he still maintained his original posting. Older than many of the other hands, Mikhain was a native of Ethera like the captain and a man of the *old school*, suspicious of technology. His dark, short hair and quick, alert eyes matched a short but stocky frame.

Sansin sat in his chair, his craggy chin cradled on the backs of his interlocked fingers as he scowled up at the massive display screen that dominated the bridge. A vast, dense asteroid field was silhouetted before the dim, lonely glow of a red dwarf star, one of countless billions populating the galaxy. But the captain was not focused on the stunning panorama outside his ship. Rather, his eyes were unfocused as he listened intently along with the rest of his crew to a scratchy, distorted signal being played back through speakers set into the walls of the bridge.

'.... *Adrift*.... *Supplies low*... *any call sign*.... *Beacon*... *can*.... *Try new*... *lost*...'

Scattered words broke through like errant thoughts adrift on a sea of static as Sansin tried to establish clearly in his mind what he was listening to.

'Vector?' he demanded.

Lael, the Atlantia's chief communications specialist, was leaning over her console and listening intently, her brow furrowed.

'Quadrant two–stroke–seven, elevation minus–four–zero,' she replied. 'It's very distant and I can't accurately triangulate the signal, but it's broadcasting on all distress frequencies.'

'Could be anybody,' Mikhain said, displaying his natural caution, 'best we don't rush into this with our eyes shut, captain.'

Sansin listened as the faint message was replayed over and over again on a loop. The language was human, but it was not a human voice speaking: the Atlantia's digital resonance transformers were automatically translating the dialect for the crew's benefit. In a cosmos where some species spoke languages that could never be replicated by human vocal chords, or indeed could not even be heard by human ears, such devices had been a standard fit for all stellar–class vessels whether military or merchant.

The species behind the distress signal had used short, terse sentences, deliberate and without cluttered dialogue.

'They might have been running out of power,' Sansin surmised, thinking out loud. 'Either that or they were running out of time.'

'Or both,' said a voice.

The captain turned and saw Andaim stride onto the bridge, Evelyn just behind him.

'About time,' Mikhain uttered and then glanced at Evelyn. 'We'll debrief you on your training sortie later. Right now, we have a situation.'

Andaim slowed as his ear caught on to the transmission, and he listened for a few moments.

'Distress channel?' he asked and Sansin rewarded the commander with a nod, then waited to see what else he might deduce. 'Short transmissions, foreign dialect, distress beacon's been activated.' Andaim turned to Lael. 'Any other signals from it?'

'No,' Lael replied. 'It may have run out of power. Judging by the weakness of the signal it could be weeks or even months old.'

'Even if we're too late to save any lives, we should take a look,' Andaim said to the captain. 'We need supplies of our own, and that asteroid belt out there doesn't hold much except a few minerals. Our shuttles have scanned it for days and found no evidence of water ice.'

The captain nodded and he glanced at the viewing screen as he spoke.

'True, but the stumbling block for us is the species that sent the signal.'

Evelyn felt a ripple of apprehension flutter inside her.

'Have we identified it?' she asked.

It was Lael who replied from her station. 'De-scramblers are sourcing the original signal code right now. Stand by.'

The bridge crew waited as the ship's computers crunched the translation code and reversed it to reveal the original dialect of the sender. Moments later Lael looked up at the captain, her face stricken.

'Resonance reversal protocols identify the species as Veng'en.'

The captain continued to stare at the viewing screen, betraying no emotion as he waited for somebody to speak. As captain his word was law aboard the Atlantia, but in such tough times with so few experienced hands available, he wanted his junior and senior officers to become used to acting upon their own initiative as much as possible, even in the face of a possibly fatal encounter.

The Veng'en was a humanoid species that had evolved in an environment very different to mankind's terrestrial homeworld, Ethera. A reptilian appearance did nothing to mask their war-like spirit, a species whose spacefaring abilities had been borne of endless conflict, the arms race of a thousand wars. Born on the hot, harsh world of Wraiythe where jungles represented the safest habitat, evolution had thus favoured the strongest and fiercest among their kind to prosper, the most intelligent enslaved for the purpose of furthering the art of warfare and refining it into a hymn of wanton destruction unrivalled by any other species mankind had encountered.

The Veng'en had fought several protracted conflicts against the human population of the colonies of Ethera and Caneeron, mostly territorial disputes that had ended in uneasy truces and endless rounds of political and diplomatic negotiations. The people of Ethera and Caneeron had spent many long decades living under the fear of a Veng'en invasion, which had been defended against by a large and expensive naval fleet in which Idris Sansin had been immeasurably proud to have served.

Ironically it had not been a Veng'en invasion but mankind's own remarkable technological advances that had seen his downfall, the voracious spread of the Legion engulfing Ethera and Caneeron and spreading far afield. Thus, had the Veng'en found themselves for the first time facing an implacable foe that even their ferocity and courage could not hope to defeat. Adopting a scorched-earth policy, they had distanced themselves from humanity's collapse in the hopes of preventing the Legion from ever reaching them. Those few vessels that had escaped the Legion's wrath and navigated their way toward the Veng'en homeworld had seen their vessels blasted into oblivion by their warlike and now fearful competitor species.

'The Veng'en would not lightly broadcast a distress signal on all frequencies,' Andaim said, jolting the captain from his reverie. 'They're too damned zenophobic.'

'That's what's bothering me,' the captain agreed. 'Maybe in the time that we've been away the Veng'en have also fallen. Perhaps they had no choice?'

'They had more warning than we did,' Mikhain pointed out. 'The Legion would not likely have been able to infect them en masse as it did humanity, so it would have been all–out conventional war instead if the Word took the fight to them.'

The captain eased himself out of his chair and examined the nearby asteroid field.

'For which they would naturally have blamed us,' he said. 'We created the Word, and now it is destroying them.'

'Could it be just a fluke?' Lael asked from her station. 'Maybe the ship was part of a convoy that got lost or something? We can't know if the Legion ever expanded beyond the colonies.'

'It followed us all the way out here,' Andaim replied for the captain. 'Tyraeus Forge in the Avenger did not give up the chase. The Veng'en system is a damned site closer to Ethera than we were then.'

'Agreed,' the captain said. 'That means they're likely suffering as we once did. It may make them more welcoming of any assistance that we can offer.'

A new voice appeared on the bridge.

'Or it may make them *hate* us more than ever.'

Councillor Dhalere was an exotic looking woman with dark skin, obsidian eyes and a confident stride. She walked onto the bridge as though she owned it, her long black hair flowing like glistening oil over her shoulders. The ship's political officer and one of the few remaining establishment figures left aboard, she represented what was left of Ethera's government.

'Perhaps,' Sansin nodded. 'The question is: can we afford to miss the chance to find and ally others to our cause? We are but one ship against the Word.'

'We'll be one less ship if the Veng'en attack us,' Dhalere cautioned. 'You've already committed us to fighting one war, captain. I don't think that we should risk starting another, do you?'

'This isn't about starting a war,' Andaim said, 'it's about responding to a distress beacon.'

'Which may be a trap,' Mikhain pointed out in support of Dhalere.

'You of all people know, captain,' Dhalere said, 'that the Veng'en will stoop to such tactics to draw in unsuspecting vessels.'

'Yes,' Sansin smiled without warmth, 'but they wouldn't advertise who they really are when doing so, would they now?'

Dhalere's expression did not falter but she did not reply either.

Like the sailors of old who had plied Ethera's great oceans in search of new lands centuries before, no call for help was ever ignored, be it sent by friend or foe. The vast expanses of space were as brutally cold and uncaring as any terrestrial ocean, and no man feared anything more than to be stranded alone to die in that immense vacuum.

'Can we help, even if we wanted to?' Dhalere pressed. 'We can barely sustain ourselves and we haven't seen a terrestrial planet for six months now. A few more weeks and it'll be us sending the damned distress signal.'

'All the better to move now then,' Andaim said. 'At least we won't have given our position away by transmitting a signal. This way, we have a tactical advantage.'

Dhalere's almond eyes flared with irritation but the soft smile on her sculptured lips did not slip.

'On your head be it, Commander Ry'ere,' she purred.

'No, councillor,' the captain intervened. 'It'll be on mine.' He turned to the helm officer. 'Clear the debris field and alter course, engage maximum thrust.'

'Aye, sir!'

Dhalere cast the bridge a last, disapproving gaze and then turned and stalked from view.

'She's right,' Mikhain said as the councillor left. 'That ship could turn out to be a threat in itself.'

'Which we won't know until we get there,' the captain said.

'That's a hell of a risk after what happened last time,' Evelyn pointed out.

The Atlantia had barely survived her battle with the *Avenger* and its infected captain, Tyraeus Forge, months before. It had been the first time anybody aboard the Atlantia had ever seen the Legion at work, an entire battle cruiser engulfed by billions of seething devices.

Andaim peered at Evelyn. 'What's wrong? A few months ago you were the one screaming victory over the Word. Now you want to hide away again? We've never been stronger than we are now. This is the perfect time to make a move by choice instead of having our hand forced.'

Evelyn kept her voice calm and hoped that her nerves were not showing through.

'It's too soon, we're not strong enough.'

The captain looked at Evelyn as a pulse of concern flared deep in his guts. Evelyn had awoken months before inside a per–fluorocarbon capsule, the victim of an assassination attempt by an agent of the Word after having been incarcerated for years for the murder of her family, a crime she had not committed. Within days, driven by an almost hellish thirst for vengeance, she had risen to control an entire army of convicts and then helped the captain and his crew take down the *Avenger*, the battleship that had hounded them for months across the cosmos.

As far as the captain could make out, Evelyn feared no man, but she had been through hell at the hands of the Word both before and after the apocalypse.

'I know it hasn't been long,' the captain said to her. 'I know what Tyraeus Forge revealed to you aboard the Avenger, about what happened to your family, and that you nearly died. I'm not about to send you into another Legion–infested ship if you're not ready.'

Evelyn almost blushed, her green eyes blinking as shadows passed like ghosts behind them.

'I'll be fine,' she said. 'Just got a lot going on.'

'Dismissed,' he ordered her. 'Get some rest, understood?'

Evelyn saluted crisply and marched off the bridge.

The captain gestured to Andaim, the commander following as the captain ascended a tight spiral staircase to a massive viewing platform that dominated the upper deck of the bridge. A circular dome of armoured and ray–sheilded glass afforded a spectacular, panoramic view of the universe.

Outside the viewing platform the vast asteroid field was vanishing from view as the Atlantia began accelerating away, building up toward the tremendous velocities required to traverse the cosmos in any reasonable period of time. Within a short while she would be moving at close to half the speed of light, fast enough for her mass–drive to engage and propel the Atlantia to super–luminal velocity.

'Evelyn's not herself,' Andaim said.

'Who is, these days?'

'She's hiding something,' Andaim pressed. 'I don't know what, but it's bothering me.'

The captain sighed and rested one hand firmly on Andaim's shoulder.

'She's on our side, which is enough for me right now, and she's under a lot of pressure with the flight training and everything she's been through playing on her mind. Give her some space, Andaim, understood?'

The commander nodded.

'Can she be relied upon, do you think, if we encounter the Legion?' the captain asked.

'I don't know,' Andaim said. 'But right now along with Bra'hiv, Qayin and a handful of Marines she's the only human being aboard ship who has ever seen the Legion up close and personal. We, for better or worse, were too far from the apocalypse when it consumed Ethera.'

'We need her,' Idris replied. 'Keep her alive Andaim, whatever happens, okay? There's an awful lot hinging on what she does.'

'What does that mean?' Andaim asked.

'People know her, know what she did aboard the Avenger to protect the civilians, to protect us,' the captain said. 'Evelyn has become a sort of talisman for them, even a legend. Make her your priority, commander. I know how you feel about her – I'm sure it won't be a problem for you.'

The captain saw the commander manage to suppress his surprised expression as he whirled away and marched off the bridge.

***

III

Evelyn made her way down in the elevator banks toward the Atlantia's hospital deck, located deep inside a heavily armoured section of the hull near the sanctuary. The sanctuary, or *garden* as the crew called it, was a central core of the ship that rotated to provide natural gravity and was filled with a lush valley that provided the crew with a place reminiscent of home, Ethera. Built for the prison crew who had once served aboard her as an antidote to the long tours far from home, it now served as the accomodation for the civilian survivors of the apocalypse.

The Atlantia had once served as a ship of the line, a frigate of the Colonial Navy. She had, so Evelyn had heard, seen action against the Veng'en at Mal'Oora, a major pitched battle that had resulted in what could only be termed a draw: both forces had limped away, neither having achieved their objective of complete domination despite horrendous casualties. Many decades later the Atlantia had been recommission as a prison ship, her hull converted into the paradise of the sanctuary for serving officers to stay and many of her plasma magazines turned over to an enlarged hospital quarters, sick bay and administration offices to cater for the ship's staff and her wayward charges.

Until the Word's grotesque mutation and unleashing of the Legion.

Evelyn knew that the Word, a creation of quantum physics, was in effect a computer. It had evolved out of a major milestone in human engineering, *The Field*: a digital record of all information that had been accessible to all humans. The growth of human knowledge had accelerated, reaching all corners of the colonies through the sharing of information, and technology had likewise grown and expanded at a phenomenal rate. This massive database of information had been fused with quantum computing to create the Word, a depository of knowledge designed to be able to make decisions based on pure logic and an understanding of myriad complexities that were beyond the human capacity to assimilate and form cohesive responses. Tasked with finding solutions to the most complex problems in history, ranging from space exploration to crime to medicine, the Word eventually became the founder of laws, the arbitrator of justice and the icon of mankind's prolific creativity.

The one thing that nobody could have predicted was that the Word, through its sheer volume of thought and understanding, would have concluded that mankind was a greater threat to itself than any other species and thus must be either controlled or eradicated. Thus had been born the

Legion, and mankind silently infected long before anybody even realised what was about to happen.

Evelyn walked out of the elevator banks and headed aft, swerving by unthinking reflex between military officers and civilians hurrying to and fro through the ship's ever–busy corridors. All personnel were wearing their magnetic gravi–suits and boots, filled with negatively charged particles of iron that pulled them down toward the positively charged cylinders beneath the deck plating. For service personnel spending months on rotation aboard the Atlantia and ships like her, the gravi–suits prevented muscle loss and preserved bone–density that long periods of zero–gravity would otherwise degrade.

Two of General Bra'hiv's armed Marines stood guard outside the entrance to the sick bay, a precaution against any possible outbreak of the Word's Infectors. Both of them snapped to attention as they saw her approach, even her meagre rank of Ensign senior to theirs as ship's soldiers. They stood aside and as she walked in she caught a glimpse of one of the Marine's tattoos: gang colours, signifying kills on the meaner streets of Ethera.

A former convict, now a serving member of the Marines.

In time of war, one's enemy could easily become one's ally.

Military ships were not noted for their luxuries or comforts and the hospital was no exception. Grey walls, grey deck and grey ceilings of bare metal, patched with ward numbers painted in crude symbols. Rows of beds in each ward containing men with various ailments, injuries and infections. The captain's wife, Meyanna Sansin, ran the hospital with near–robotic efficiency, but on a cramped and crowded vessel infections spread fast. Even with extra staff her day was busy from start to end, and down–time was a rarity for all aboard the Atlantia.

Meyanna saw Evelyn coming as she tended to a Marine with a sprained wrist. She finished patching the soldier up and turned to Evelyn, her long brown hair pinned back behind her ears and her smile bright to mask her fatigue.

'You're late,' she mocked.

Evelyn smiled. 'I know, but I did rush here as I just couldn't wait for another battery of tests to be run.'

Meyanna's hand on her forearm was comforting, and Evelyn could see the veiled distress behind Meyanna's expression.

'I know,' she replied. 'There won't be many more, I promise. Come this way.'

Evelyn knew the drill and she followed Meyanna without complaint to a laboratory at the rear of the sick bay, which was sealed off by glass doors.

Meyanna led her inside, sealing the doors behind them as she led her to a small cubicle. Meyanna closed the cubicle door behind them and turned to Evelyn.

'More blood I'm afraid,' she said. 'I've run out of the last batch.'

Evelyn sighed. 'Nothing yet?'

Meyanna shook her head.

Six months before, trapped in the bridge of the doomed Avenger, Captain Tyraeus Forge, a man no longer a man but a writhing mass of tiny machines, had revealed to Evelyn what had really happened to her family and why the Word had hunted her with such fervour for so long. She had been a journalist on Ethera who had uncovered the militarisation of nanotechnology and its subsequent theft and release by religious terrorists within a street drug known as Devlamine. From there, through shared needles, sexual contact, travel and countless other vectors, the Legion's Infectors had spread. The Word's purpose, achieved by manipulating the warped minds of the terrorists, had been to silently infect the entire human population of the colonies with its Infectors and then distribute a simple command to them: *replicate*, causing the bloodless coup of an entire species.

Evelyn's uncovering of the conspiracy had seen her husband and son murdered and herself incarcerated for the crime, sent into long–term stasis confinement and burdened with the mask that hid her face and silenced her voice.

Then came the bombshell, revealed by Forge himself: Evelyn was immune to infection by the Word. For reasons that Meyanna had not yet been able to fathom Evelyn could not be controlled by the Infectors, which were destroyed by her immune system just like any biological infection would be. The Word had wanted to study her but she had escaped with her life and now Meyanna, on behalf of the entire crew, was secretly studying her blood in order to figure out what was happening. A cure, or even a vaccine against infection by the Word, would change the game of their new war entirely.

Evelyn laid down on the narrow bed as Meyanna inserted a line into her arm and began slowly drawing blood.

'How's the flight training coming along?'

Evelyn sighed. 'I keep screwing up. Can't think fast enough.'

'The blood loss,' Meyanna said, gesturing to the line in her arm. 'You're running low all the time. I can give you something for that.'

Evelyn watched as her blood was extracted into a vial as Meyanna busied herself fetching pills from a steel cabinet in one corner of the cubicle.

'Are you any closer to identifying who aboard is infected with the Word?' Evelyn asked.

Meyanna shook her head as she rummaged inside the cabinet.

'We scanned the entire crew when we left the last planet we found,' she replied. 'Nothing. Are you really sure there's somebody harbouring the Word aboard ship? This would all be much easier if I could just tell the crew about you and…'

'No,' Evelyn cut her off. 'I'm one hundred per cent certain. Tyraeus Forge had been warned of our attack on him. There's only one way that could have happened.'

Meyanna stood up and handed Evelyn a small bottle of pills.

'Iron supplement,' she said. 'You're just a little anaemic after all this blood I'm taking from you.'

Evelyn took the bottle and let Meyanna remove the line from her arm.

'Maybe you should ask Andaim to give you some time off from your training,' Meyanna suggested. 'It's not like you're the only pilot we have.'

Evelyn rolled her sleeve down.

'He's as under pressure as everybody else and we need the crews. We're still at only half strength.'

'He pushes you harder than the rest of them.'

'I wouldn't have it any other way.'

'He doesn't know about this either,' Meyanna said, waving the vial of blood in her hand. 'If he did…'

'The carrier could be anybody,' Evelyn insisted, 'even Andaim.'

'Llike I said, the scans didn't show anything.'

'Then the scans missed something,' Evelyn shot back. 'The only way to be absolutely sure is to use the microwave technique.'

'No,' Meyanna replied. 'That kills if it identifies a carrier. You know that.'

The Word's minions, the Legion, were machines designed to self–replicate. The Infectors, the smallest of their kind, contained working parts which when exposed to microwave radiation of a frequency that matched their own atomic resonance would cause them to heat up and melt, so small were their components. Unfortunately, as the Infectors routinely attached themselves to optical nerves, the brain stem and spinal cord, this process caused unspeakable agony to the victim and often death shortly afterward depending on how deeply entrenched was the infection. A microwave scan of the entire ship could kill all infected persons aboard, a loss of humanity that the captain was unwilling to risk given that the Atlantia's compliment might now be all that was left of mankind.

So far, the only individuals who had undergone the dangerous microwave scan were the Atlantia's bridge crew, Meyanna, Evelyn, the Marines serving under General Bra'hiv and of course the general himself.

'Yes,' Evelyn replied, 'but even that scan was conducted six months ago. We know that the Word is driven to infect others, like a disease. If there is a carrier aboard then they could have infected dozens of the crew and we wouldn't know a thing about it. The Word remains dormant in people while replicating, waiting for the chance to strike en masse.'

'I know well what it does,' Meyanna replied.

Evelyn sighed.

'We're not safe from the Word here,' she said. 'Not yet. The sooner we get some kind of antidote or vaccine, the better.'

'Which is why we need to get your immunity out into the open,' Meyanna pressed. 'I could have entire teams working on this instead of just me. The work could take days instead of weeks or months.'

'You won't be testing anything if the Word has me killed,' Evelyn snapped. 'The only reason I'm not dead right now is because Tyraeus Forge died before he could reveal what he knew to anybody else.'

'Or you're paranoid,' Meyanna replied. 'And there is no carrier aboard. You went through hell aboard that ship, Evelyn. I can't imagine what it was like or how it may have affected you.'

'It made me damned cautious,' Evelyn said. 'I won't rest until I'm certain that the entire ship's compliment is free of infection. You should be doing the same.'

'I am,' Meyanna replied. 'But it's been months now and I haven't found anything to explain why your body rejected the Word's bots when nobody else's does. There are only so many tests I can run, and I'm pretty much out of ideas right now.'

'Use your imagination,' Evelyn said as she stood up from the bed. 'The Word does.'

Evelyn's feet touched the floor and then she felt the entire ship heel over as the deck tilted steeply beneath her feet. She felt herself topple sideways and Meyanna leaped in front of her, wrapping her arms tightly around Evelyn's shoulders as she slumped back down onto the bed.

'Easy,' Meyanna said, her hands still on Evelyn's shoulders as she stood back.

Evelyn blinked. The deck was still but her head was swimming.

'You're burned out,' Meyanna said.

'I'm fine, it's just the blood loss and…'

'You're done,' Meyanna cut her off. 'You need time out. I'm pulling you off flying duties.'

'Like hell you are!' Evelyn snapped as she made to stand again.

'Until you're supplments kick in,' Meyanna promised. 'Twenty four hours, okay?'

Evelyn clenched her jaw and her fists but she knew that the doctor was right. Her anger lost its momentum and slipped away in a deep sigh.

'The ship's accelerating,' Meyanna said, 'and the mass–drive will kick in soon so there'll be no flying for a while anyway. You head back to your quarters and get some rest, understood? I don't want to see you on the bridge.'

Evelyn grabbed her uniform jacket and made for the cubicle door.

'I'll inform Andaim that you're to be relieved from duty until further notice,' Meyann added.

'He'll be annoyed,' Evelyn said. 'Like you said, he pushes me harder and…'

'And he needs you on top form. Right now you can barely walk. He'll understand, agreed?'

The last of Evelyn's resistance melted away and she nodded and left the room.

***

IV

'All engines at full power, mass–drive will engage in… ninety seconds.'

Captain Idris Sansin acknowledged his engineering officer's report as he sat in his chair and spoke softly. His voice still carried to every corner of the bridge.

'Alert the crew, prepare for surge.'

The bridge lights turned red, much as they would do in time of battle, as a distant series of claxons sounded throughout the vessel.

The Atlantia was equipped with six ion–engines, three on each wing nacelle, each of which produced vast quantities of thrust to power the half–mile long frigate through the immense emptiness of inter–stellar space. However, it was her mass–drive which produced the velocities required to traverse the tremendous distances between star systems.

Ever since mankind had found his way into space, from the very first dangerous and yet thrilling rockets that had soared into Ethera's atmosphere along with the dreams of the men aboard them, to the cosmos–travelling ships like Atlantia, a means had been sought to overcome the natural physical laws that governed the universe. The greatest of those laws was that no object of mass could ever reach or exceed the speed of light. It had been the universal constant, a single immovable law that governed everything in the visible universe. Engineers had spent decades searching for a solution to this crippling obstacle to true galactic exploration, seeking ever more powerful engines that propelled starships to ever increasing velocities, but none ever had broken through the speed of light.

Until just a few decades prior to the keel of the Atlantia being laid.

It had, as so often was the case, taken a genius to figure it out: a man capable of thinking beyond the cube. Deri Feyen, an astrophycisist and theorist, had realised that everybody had been going about it all the wrong way. The laws of physics stated, quite clearly, that no object of mass could exceed the speed of light. Light itself, comprised of photons, moved at the speed of light because, uniquely, they had no mass. Therefore, Feyen reasoned, rather than produce ever–more massive engines one only had to figure out a way to negate mass in order to accelerate to, and controversially, *beyond* the speed of light.

It was Feyen's manipulation of the fundamental particles that gave objects mass that opened a window onto space travel like nothing the colonies had ever seen. Theorizing that if a particle existed that gave atoms mass, then there should by logic be a way to manipulate photons to take advantage of their massless properties, Feyen devised a mass–drive. Put simply, the drive surrounded the parent vessel in a sphere of negative mass that perfectly offset and cancelled out the vessel's natural mass: it became, in effect, massless.

Pioneer, the first vessel to test Feyen's mass drive, launched just a few years before the great man's death. It accelerated to a velocity that generated enough energy to engage the mass drive, upon which moment the tremendous thrust provided by its ion engines accelerated it up to and beyond the speed of light in a matter of moments. What was more, the massless nature of the vessel meant that many of the mind–bending effects of faster–than–light travel were negated: the vessel did not travel in time as any vessel of normal mass would. What Feyen had achieved was a means to traverse the stars and not return home to find the graves of the young and healthy friends and family you left behind overgrown from decades or even centuries of neglect, when you had been travelling at super–luminal velocity for only a few months.

The exploration of the cosmos had begun and within a few years mankind was spreading out into the galaxy and finding new worlds and new species. Much of the time those species were little more than algae floating in hot pools of muddy water on barren, volatile worlds. Sometimes, they were sentient species that bore little relation to the human form: one, the Icay, were tenuous beings who drifted like tendrils in the atmospheres of giant stars and communicated by light waves. The Icay had been the first species to make direct contact with humans, having detected mankind's ability to directly observe other stars and terrestrial planets – the hallmark of an intelligent species reaching a technological level sufficient to initiate *first contact*. Others species still, like the Morla'syn, were bipedal and recognisably human in form but for their small, stocky stature: a consequence of their homeworld's intense gravity.

Occasionally, they were both humanoid and aggressive: like the Veng'en. And, some said, the humans.

'Brace for surge!'

The call went out and the captain leaned back in his chair, watching the viewing screen as the mass–drive whirled up. The Atlantia's massive ion engines drew in huge quantities of hydrogen as the frigate accelerated through space, condensing it into fuel with ever greater efficiency until a barrier was reached: the engine's intakes were overwhelmed with hydrogen. At this point, vents redirected the flow to the mass–drive and it spun up with dramatic and self–sustaining force as countless billions of atoms were converted into particles of negative mass that arranged themselves in a protective sphere around the Atlantia.

'Surge in three, two, one, *engage*!'

The Atlantia seemed to momentarily lean forward as though plunging off the edge of a cliff and diving toward oblivion, and then the captain was thrust back into his seat as the Atlantia's ion engines, used to propel two hundred fifty thousand tonnes of metal through space, now pushed with all of their might with nothing to hold them back.

The frigate accelerated wildly and Captain Idris Sansin felt the strange, tingling sensation of momentarily having no more substance than a ghost. The starfield in the viewing screen suddenly flared white as all light was shifted out of the visible spectrum and the Cosmic Microwave Backround radiation became all that was visible, a superhot fog of X–Rays that only the massive hull of a ship like Atlantia could protect the crew from.

The bright flare of light faded away and the screen went black as all light information was stripped away from it and the Atlantia settled down into super–luminal cruise.

'Surge cleared,' the helmsman reported from his station. 'All quarters stabilised. Ion engines disengaging.'

Captain Sansin glanced at velocity indicators projected onto the viewing screen, showing the Atlantia breaking through the light barrier. Having attained super–luminal velocity, the engines were no longer required. The ship's massless nature meant that it had little to fear from collisions with other objects, although navigation would have ensured that no super–massive stars or black holes were in their path before allowing the drive to engage.

'What was the last triangulation data from the distress call?' he asked Lael.

'No fixed point,' she replied. 'Our best estimate places the origin of the call approximately one light hour away. Countdown is set, we'll disengage mass drive at zero point oh oh five orbital radii from the source.'

The captain nodded thoughtfully. An orbital radii was the distance at which Ethera had orbited its parent star, a yellow dwarf sun. Lael's calculations would bring them to within a hundred thousand cubits of of the signal, close enough to maintain the element of surprise, not so close as to be caught out by any ambush.

'Too close.'

Dhalere's voice came from behind the captain. He turned to see the exotic woman standing nearby, her dark eyes reflecting the sparkling lights of control panels around the bridge.

'I had no idea that you were a tactical specialist, councillor,' the captain murmured. 'Perhaps you should sign up and join us?'

'My hands are full,' Dhalere purred in response as she stepped up onto the command platform, her elegant skirt suit revealing a brief glimpse of long, tanned legs as she moved to stand before Idris. 'My constituents are running low on water and food. They're becoming restless and they're uncomfortable with the rumours spreading that we're approaching an unknown vessel's distress signal.'

'As are we all,' the captain replied, his gaze fixed not upon the councillor but upon the viewing screen and a rapidly changing scroll of data alongside it. 'As soon as we find suitable resources, rest assured we will stop to gather supplies.'

'And when, exactly, will that be?' Dhalere demanded. 'Should we not be looking after the civilians as our priority?'

The captain stood and straightened his uniform, the same one that he had worn with immense pride for years now. He looked down at Dhalere.

'It is our job to provide for the civilians,' he replied. 'It is yours to look after them. We are already looking for another suitable star system to reconnoitre for supplies. There is little more that we can do right now and I assume that you, along with all of the civlians, would be extremely grateful for any assistance offered were it our vessel that was stranded or in danger?'

'Our vessel *is* in danger, captain. Our last brush with the Word almost destroyed us and now we're on a war footing and heading back for home, into the teeth of our enemy.' Dhalere's dark eyes betrayed a glimmer of fear. 'We had the chance to run, to hide. We defeated the Word in battle and we could have vanished, never to be seen again. The Word would never have found us.'

The captain frowned.

'Yes, we could have, and spent countless millennia living in fear. Condemned our children and countless generations thereafter to live beneath the same shadow. That is not a legacy, it's a prison sentence. We've been over this before, Dhalere. Even the civilians understand that running away is no longer an option for us.'

Dhalere sighed.

'I fear for us all, captain,' she admitted. 'Did we learn anything more about the distressed vessel, before we made the jump?'

Even a non–military councillor like Dhalere was vaguely aware of the limits of super–luminal velocity travel, the captain knew. Signals intelligence could not be received while travelling at such high speeds and weapons could not be fired. Opening a landing bay or docking port would be suicide, the pressures outside the hull so great that the entire vessel would be obliterated by radiation and smashed into a billion fragments in the blink of an eye.

'No,' the captain replied. 'The signal was without doubt Veng'en, and so we assume the vessel from which it originated was also built by them. What it is doing this far away from the colonies and who may be aboard is mere speculation.'

'Do we have enough Raythons operational to defend the ship if we're attacked?' Dhalere asked. 'Or troops trained?'

'I cannot impart that information, councillor.'

'Oh come now, captain,' Dhalere protested. 'We're not back on Ethera now. The people need reassurance. I have to take something back to them.'

Captain Sansin bit his lip, fighting against a lifetime of military training.

'Our fighters and troops are still in training,' he said, 'and two thirds of our Raythons are operational at this time. That's why we're pulling up well clear of the signal's origin. If anybody comes at us, our best bet will be to flee. Take that to them, councillor.'

'I don't think that's going to reassure them.'

'Like I said, my job is not to reassure. That's yours.' He smiled down at her. 'Now if you'll excuse me, I have a ship to run. Guard?'

An armed Marine, a young man with keen eyes and alert bearing, jumped up onto the command platform.

'Yes captain?!'

'Escort the councillor from the bridge and to the elevator banks,' the captain ordered him, and then turned his back on Dhalere.

'Aye sir!'

Dhalere concealed her anger as she turned and stalked off the bridge, the Marine's heavy boots thumping the deck with each stride as he followed her.

As Dhalere exited the bridge and walked toward the elevator banks she realised that the Marine was watching her. She could not see him: it was just a sensation, an instinct that had served her well for many years. The Marine was young, not far out of his teens and not one of Qayin's reformed convicts either: a true *patriot*.

She reached the elevator banks and abruptly turned to the young man in time to see his eyes flick up from her legs to her eyes.

'Would you escort me to my quarters?' she asked. The Marine hesitated, conflicted by his captain's demands and her request. Dhalere softened her tone a little. 'What is your name?'

'Kyarl,' the Marine replied. 'Private, four–seven–oh–nine–four.'

'Is *four–seven–oh–nine–four* your second name?' she smiled.

'No, ma'am. It's my number.'

The Marine flushed a little. Dhalere stepped closer to him. 'I'll ensure that the captain does not mind, Kyarl,' she said as she deliberately looked him up and down. 'It will make me feel safer. And I suspect that you won't mind, either?'

She turned toward the elevator and let her hand gently brush the Marine's thigh as she did so.

The elevator doors opened and Dhalere walked smoothly inside, striding a little longer than she normally would and swaying her hips. She turned and looked at Kyarl expectantly, and with a blink the Marine came to his senses and followed her into the elevator.

The doors closed.

'Which floor, ma'am?' Kyarl asked.

Dhalere turned to him and pressed her hand against his groin as she threw the other behind his neck and kissed him fiercely. Kyarl almost recoiled in surprise but then he responded with youthful vigour, his hand resting on Dhalere's behind as he pulled her against him.

She let him, let him touch her in any way he wanted, for to do so was all that she required. Dhalere felt something warm flood the back of her throat, a tingling sensation that crossed her tongue and flooded into Kyarl's mouth.

The blood in the human body circulated roughly once every sixty seconds, pulsed through the arteries by the relentless beating of a powerful heart. In Kyarl's case, young and fit from his intensive training with General Bra'hiv's Marines, his heart would be in peak condition and would thus beat more slowly than an older man, although right now she could feel it pulsing in his chest. Dhalere would not rush.

Dhalere let the younger man kiss her for as long as he could, and then she slowly drew away from him. His skin was flushed and his eyes swam with passion, and then something changed as she watched him with interest. Kyarl's lust mutated into confusion as he felt the cloud of tiny Infectors flood into his body, tunnelling through his windpipe and into his bloodstream, rushing through his body with each and every beat of his heart. Close to ten thousand of them, she figured, each as small as a biological cell.

A brief flare of panic appeared in the young Marine's eyes as he realised what was happening, and he tried to open his mouth. Before he could scream for help he slumped to the elevator deck and his body convulsed as the Infectors flooded his brain stem and cut off the signals from his brain to his body.

Dhalere watched as the Infectors took control of Kyarl's optical nerves, then his limbs and his hearing, then worked their way down his spinal column. Kyarl shuddered and then lay on his back in the elevator, staring up at her.

'That was good, no?' she purred down at him.

On cue, the Infectors stimulated the pleasure centres of Kyarl's brain and his eyes rolled up into his sockets as unimaginable ecstacy coursed through his body. Dhalere knew the sensation well, knew that she too would feel it again soon. Like an addiction, the Legion rewarded obedience with something just beyond imaginable pleasure.

'Return to your duties on the bridge,' she ordered him. 'I will call upon you soon.'

Kyarl got to his feet as the last wave of pleasure faded away, his body no longer his own. It had been the same for Dhalere when the ship's original councillor, Hevel, had infected her months before. Utter, insane, indescribable pleasure, a drug more powerful than any narcotic, once experienced, forever craved. The Word was more addictive than any chemical substance and there were no withdrawal symptoms unless its bidding was not obeyed. Then, the pain was every bit as indescribable as the pleasure.

'Go, now,' she snapped.

Kyarl turned, the elevator door opening as he marched back toward the bridge.

Dhalere closed the door and hit the button for her level, where her meagre quarters were located. Whatever was waiting for the Atlantia out there in deep space, occupying the distressed vessel, Dhalere knew that her mission was to infect it as fast as she could.

She had barely made it into her quarters when the Legion sent an overwhelming surge of pleasure through her body. Dhalere cried out as she slumped onto her bunk and squirmed in ecstasy as she forgot about the universe.

***

V

'Y'aint our leader no more! We's all got our rights now, captain said so.'

The Marine's face was sprinkled with ugly scars and one of his eyes was opaque, blinded when a plasma round had detonated close by and seared his skin with white–hot shrapnel. As far as Qayin could recall it had happened when a drug deal had gone bad on Caneeron, or something like that anyway.

At twenty six years of age, Tyrone was a scrawny relic of the gang's heyday before the apocalypse. He hadn't yet earned the gang colours, the bioluminescent tattoos of spirals that illuminated Lance–Corporal Qayin's giant black head and flickered in the low lighting of the barracks, and likely never would. The *Mark of Qayin* was history now, or so Tyrone figured.

'That don't mean I don't still hold sway here,' Qayin rumbled.

Qayin stood nearly seven feet tall, his frame a cliff of hardened muscle that glinted with sweat. His hair was tightly braided into alternating blue and gold locks that hung to his massive shoulders, a sharp contrast to the dark greys and blacks of his combat fatigues. By contrast, Tyrone was a feeble but aggressive fly.

'Bra'hiv's the boss now!' he retorted. 'You don't got no say in what we do.'

The barracks were filled with Marines, many of them bearing the tattoos of the various gangs that had once populated Atlantia Five, the prison hull that had been towed behind Atlantia in earlier times. That prison was long gone, and its inmates now soldiers in training to defend the Atlantia against who–knew–what.

'Bra'hiv,' Qayin replied, 'is a general. I am your leader, and any man who denies it answers to me.'

'You's a soldier, jus' like us all!'

Qayin cast his eyes across the forty or so off–duty Marines watching him with interest. Some, like Qayin, were former convicts. Others were square–jawed, battle hardened patriots cut in the mold of Captain Sansin, colonial blooding running thick in their veins. Alpha Company consisted of such patriots, with Bravo Company populated by the dregs of the high–security prison. The shortage of experienced officers meant that a single Lieutenant, C'rairn, acted as subordinate commanding officer to General Bra'hiv, the overall commander, with a single sergeant, Djimon, to support them. With all senior officers absent, and the Alpha Marines watching with folded arms and neither supporting nor hindering Qayin, he had a free reign.

'You're forgetting where you came from, Tyrone,' Qayin uttered. 'You was nothing until I picked you up out of the gutter on Caneeron.'

Tyrone's defiance slipped a little but he was conscious of the crowd watching him and he rallied.

'You betrayed us back on Five, left us to die,' he shot back. 'There ain't a man here who trusts you further than I could throw you.'

'You couldn't throw me at all,' Qayin scoffed, 'and oh how I wish I commanded the trust that you do, Tyrone.'

A ripple of low chuckles drifted across the Marines. Qayin smirked as Tyrone's complexion darkened and anger flared in his eyes.

'Least I ain't no traitor.'

Qayin reached Tyrone in a single stride and one giant fist lashed out and grabbed him by the throat. The younger man squealed as he was lifted off of his feet and slammed into a support pillar beside a row of bunks. The back of Tyrone's head smacked against the pillar with a clang that echoed through the barracks as Qayin glared at him.

'Don't think that yo' uniform's gonna save you from me,' he snarled.

The voice that replied came from the barracks entrance.

'Or you from me, Qayin.'

Sergeant Arran Djimon stood in the barracks doorway. He was as tall as Qayin but the polar opposite in appearance: pale skin, short–cropped blond hair and cold blue eyes that seemed still to reflect the glaciers of his home on Caneeron. Djimon, the senior NCO of Alpha Company, spent most of his spare time shifting iron in the Marine's makeshift gym or sparring with other soldiers.

Qayin did not move, his hand still clamped around Tyrone's throat.

'I don't need to hide from anybody,' Qayin shot back, his bicep slick with sweat as it bulged.

Tyrone gurgled as he tried ineffectually to dislodge Qayin's iron grip.

'Let him go,' Sergeant Djimon ordered as he paced toward Qayin, 'or I'll have you serving slop from the brig for a month.'

Qayin glared at the sergeant, and then a bright white smile slid across his face and he opened his hand. Tyrone dropped like a sack of rocks onto the deck, his breath wheezing in his throat as he coughed and gasped for air.

'You need the manpower,' Qayin murmured back at Djimon. 'You won't put me anywhere.'

Djimon stopped just short of the giant Marine, his angular features devoid of humour or doubt.

'I'll put you on your ass,' he replied, 'Right here and now.'

Qayin did not move. Djimon remained silent and still. Qayin smiled again. 'See?'

Djimon lunged forward and swung his fist as Qayin's jaw. The big convict stepped back and to one side, twisted away from the blow as he sought to push the sergeant past him and counter strike.

Djimon ducked down and reversed his blow. His elbow slammed up into Qayin's plexus and blasted the air from the big man's lungs. The sergeant threw his arm up around Qayin's giant head and with a heave of effort he hurled him over his shoulder.

The gathered Marines burst into shouts of encouragement as they scattered backwards from the fighting men, wagers and cries of delight filling the stale air.

Qayin slammed down onto the deck as Djimon spun on his heel and drove the edge of his boot toward Qayin's thick neck, aiming to crush his thorax with one brutal blow. Qayin drove his forearm across the back of Djimon's leg as he rolled aside, deflecting the boot just enough to avoid his throat as he ploughed his free fist up into the sergeant's groin.

Djimon growled in pain as he doubled over, spittle flying from his lips as Qayin grabbed the sergeant's collar and drove his boot up into the man's stomach as he pulled hard. Djimon lost balance as Qayin hurled the sergeant over his head.

Djimon slammed onto his back on the deck as Qayin rolled and came up on his feet with a wickedly serrated blade in one hand. The weapon flickered in the low light as Qayin dropped onto his knees and placed the cold metal across the pulsing thread of an artery in Djimon's thick neck.

'See those stripes?' Qayin snapped, breathing heavily and nodding toward Djimon's rank insignia on his shoulder, 'they don't mean nothin' here. Mark of Qayin's making a comeback and there ain't nothing you're gonna be doin' about it.'

Djimon glared up at Qayin. 'You can go f...

'Qayin!'

Every head turned to see General Ahmid Bra'hiv stood in the barracks doorway, his shaven head touched with steel grey stubble and his eyes icy cold as he glared at the Marines. As though a live current had been discharged directly into them the entire company leaped into motion and scrambled to stand at the head of their bunks, backs straight, arms by their sides and chins lifted, as still as statues.

Only Qayin remained, Djimon pinned beneath him with the blade pressed against his throat.

'What the hell do you think you're doing?' Bra'hiv growled at Qayin.

'Unarmed combat training,' Qayin snapped back. 'Sergeant Djimon has much to learn, general.'

Qayin got up, Djimon scrambling to his feet alongside the former convict as Bra'hiv stalked toward them.

'Unarmed combat training,' Bra'hiv echoed, 'with a knife in your hand?'

'I decided it was time to move the training to the next level,' Qayin smiled brightly. 'Never expect your enemy to be a nice guy.'

Bra'hiv surveyed the injured look on Djimon's features and Qayin's customised blade, and nodded slowly. 'How apt. Give me the knife.'

Qayin did not move. 'It was a gift, general,' he replied by way of an explanation.

'You've got until the count of three,' Bra'hiv said, 'or I'll take it from you.'

Qayin did not move. The Marines kept staring straight ahead, but their eyes swivelled to watch.

'One.'

Qayin did not move.

'Two.'

Bra'hiv's fist darted out with a flicker of motion, so fast that it could barely be seen, and two fingers rammed into Qayin's eyeballs. The big convict lurched backwards and ducked his head down and to one side as he emitted a cry of pain and swiped blindly out with the knife. Bra'hiv ducked outside the weapon's arc and as the blade flashed by he stepped in and rammed an elbow deep into Qayin's exposed kidney.

The convict gagged as he dropped onto one knee, and Bra'hiv caught the wrist that held the knife and twisted it over upon itself. The blade fell into Bra'hiv's hand as he twirled it expertly over and held it in place beneath Qayin's throat.

'There's only one gang aboard this ship, Qayin,' Bra'hiv snarled, 'and it's mine.'

The general lifted a boot against Qayin's side and with a hefty shove sent him sprawling onto the deck as he turned and glanced at Djimon, whose angular features were creased with a grin.

'What the hell are you smiling at?' Bra'hiv snapped. 'Ten years in the Marines and you got yourself decked by an untrained drug dealer?'

Djimon's smirk evaporated as Bra'hiv stepped back, the blade still in his hand as he shouted at the two men.

'Get in line, both of you, now!'

Djimon stepped smartly toward his bunk as Qayin got to his feet, barely contained rage radiating from his scowling face as he slowly strode to his bunk and stood to what passed for attention in his world. Bra'hiv looked them over for a moment before speaking.

'Bravo Company, from this moment onward any indiscretion by Lance–Corporal Qayin will reflect upon every man in the unit. If he is insubordinate, every man shall pay. If he is disobedient, every man shall pay. If he so much as farts without my say so, every man shall pay. Is that clear?!'

Forty Marines replied in instant chorus.

'Yessir!'

'We have new orders! Your training is to be curtailed. Within a few hours, we will come alongside a vessel of unknown origin that has been detected emitting a distress signal. Once the fighters have formed a defensive shield and the captain has made certain that the Atlantia is under no immediate threat, it will be Bravo Company's job to board the vessel and find out what's on board. Alpha Company will support.'

'With all due respect, sir,' Djimon snapped, 'I think that's a mistake. Bravo Company are amateurs and untrustworthy.'

Bra'hiv smiled without warmth. 'And one of 'em put you on your ass, sergeant, so what does that say about your professionalism and skill?'

There was a moment of silence, before Qayin's voice broke through.

'What species was emitting the distress signal?'

Despite his defeat at Bra'hiv's hands the former convict remained astute enough to think straight, and it remained clear to the general that no matter what happened Qayin was still the unspoken leader of his gang by virtue of his intelligence alone.

'Veng'en,' Bra'hiv replied.

A muffled exhalation of curses rippled through the gathered Marines.

'Why would we go to help someone like the Veng'en?' Tyrone asked. 'Soon as we show up they'll shoot us down. Dudes don't like us much.'

'Dudes don't got much choice,' Djimon replied, mocking Tyrone's voice.

'Precisely,' Bra'hiv agreed. 'We don't know what has become of them, but no distress call from deep space can be left unanswered, just as we would hope that ours would likewise be responded to. Every man must be ready to go at a moment's notice, full battle gear, combat suits weighted at fifty per cent gravity for high mobility. Weapons and ammunition will be issued prior to boarding the shuttles. You'll all rendevouz at the armoury in oh–two hundred hours. Any questions?'

'How come you're not sending Alpha Company in the lead?' Qayin challenged the general. 'I thought that the captain would want his *best* men for this job?'

The Marines chuckled. Former convicts all, Bravo Company had developed a strong antipathy for and rivalry with the Colonial Marines of Alpha Company.

'You *are* the best men for this job,' Bra'hiv replied, 'because you're expendable.' A silence descended on Bravo Company. 'I'm kidding: you've never boarded a ship before for real – it's a good chance to put your training into practice. Oh–two hundred at the armoury. Any man that doesn't show will spend a week in the brig. Dismissed!'

Bra'hiv turned and marched away, Djimon and his men following as Bravo Company's Marines looked at each other.

'Expendable?' Tyrone growled. 'You mean that they want us to die?'

'They don't want us to die,' Qayin muttered. 'They want to use us as bait, to see what's inside before sending in their better trained men.'

'That sucks.'

'Better than being cooped up in the brig,' Qayin corrected. 'Best we can do is show that we're not second best and do it better than Alpha Company would. Agreed?'

***

VI

Evelyn jogged down a corridor toward the flight deck, her path illuminated by pools of blood red light. Her flight suit, encased in a paraphernalia of oxygen hoses and straps, felt tight and reassuring against her skin as she followed a line of other pilots out into the Atlantia's for'ard launch bay.

'You sure you're ready for this?'

Andaim's whispered question was loud enough for only Evelyn to hear.

'Meyanna says I'm okay to fly now, right?'

'On my request,' Andaim replied. 'She wanted you grounded for twenty four hours, but this is more important.'

'If you're happy, I'm happy,' Evelyn intoned, glad to be back in her flight suit again as they crossed the busy flight deck. Despite the mental and physical strain of flight training, Evelyn was desperate to succeed and earn her coveted wings, to become a fully-fledged member of the Reapers.

Crowds of technicians hurried back and forth across the landing bay, clearing the flight deck, and the sound of ion engines running up filled the air with the whine and screech of heavy metal under tension.

Arrayed before them were twelve Raython fighters, elegant, dangerous looking single–seat interceptors. Some, those bearing the markings of the *Reapers* Squadron, were native to the Atlantia's complement. Those of the *Renegades* had been pilfered from the Avenger some months before. With wings curved at the rear but hooked forward at the tips, where their plasma cannons resided, and their fuselages slender and pointed, they looked like gigantic steel birds of prey.

'Scorcher Flight will take point,' Andaim said as the Reaper pilots gathered around him for their final briefing, using the Reaper's call sign. 'Razor Flight of the Renegades will form the outer circle in case anybody comes calling.'

'Do we have any idea what kind of vessel it is yet?' Evelyn asked.

'We won't know until the Atlantia breaks out of super–luminal,' Andaim replied. 'Let's assume the worst – that it's a Veng'en cruiser looking to draw in prey, and hope for the best – that's it's a crippled merchant ship desperate for help.'

A distant alarm claxon echoed across the vast bay and Andaim checked his HandStat, a luminous military watch and organiser implanted beneath the skin of his left hand, before shouting out above the whining engines.

'Let's go!'

Evelyn whirled and ran to her Raython, then felt a tingle of melancholy as she read the name beneath the cockpit.

LT. M. D. G'VELLE

Until they earned their wings as fully battle–ready pilots, the names on the cockpits of the Raythons bore their original pilot's monickers, men and women long lost to history and the wrath of the Word and its Legion.

Evelyn climbed aboard and settled into the cockpit, a dazzling array of instruments coming on–line before her as technicians swarmed across the fighter and unplugged deck–power and locking clamps. Evelyn strapped in, fired up the internal power unit and closed the canopy. Andaim's voice crackled over the intercom.

'Reaper flight, call in on launch readiness.'

She heard the voices of her fellow pilots echoing across the airwaves one after the other as their Raythons came on–line and they began starting their engines.

'Reaper Four, launch ready.'

'Reaper Six, launch ready.'

'Reaper Nine, launch ready.'

Evelyn flipped switches in a sequence long since committed to memory, and as her Raython's ion engines engaged she felt the entire craft hum and vibrate as though alive around her. She keyed her radio.

'Reaper Two, launch ready.'

The Raython's taxied out one after the other, retracting their undercarriage and instead hovering over the magnetically opposed taxi–way as they positioned themselves for launch. Each hovered into place over a large panel in the deck that opened out onto a thin crevice that ran the length of the bay. Linking magnetically to the nose of the Raythons, beneath the deck an immensely powerful magnetic harness attached to an electro–magnetic ram would launch the fighters one after the other, accelerating them to attack speed and flinging them out into space.

Evelyn slid into place alongside Andaim, *Reaper One*, and watched as ahead the technicians vanished from the launch deck. She knew that as soon as the Atlantia slowed to cruise velocity the bay doors would open and the catapults would fire.

She checked over her instruments one more time, ensured that everything was as it should be, and then looked across at Andaim. Commander Ry'ere looked back at her and gave her a thumbs–up.

She smiled and nodded back, and hoped that this time she would be up to the challenge.

*

'Prepare for deceleration,' Lael called out across the bridge.

Captain Idris Sansin gripped the edge of his seat as he stared at the viewing screen ahead. The old tensions returned, mostly in his right shoulder where he gripped the seat and tilted his head slightly, an old habit as though he were trying to avoid being slapped.

He had gone into battle three times in his career in this manner, the abrupt and dangerous burst out of super–luminal and into immediate combat. Things happened fast in space, no matter how carefully things had been planned: the old admiralty rule said that *if you had time to blink, then there was sufficient time for things to go wrong.*

'Ten seconds.'

The captain glanced at a monitor that showed the Atlantia's flight deck now packed with Raythons lined up on the catapults, heat haze billowing from their engines toward massive extractor vents high up on the bay walls. Still filled with breathable air, the atmosphere in the bay would evacuate naturally when the bay doors opened, helping to drag the first wave of fighters out into the face of whatever awaited them.

'Five seconds!'

The officers manning the tactical stations leaned forward over their consoles as though preparing for a race, their hands poised to activate ray–sheilding and plasma turrets, radar sweeps and counter–measures: every technology aboard designed to thwart an ambush attack.

'Two seconds! One second! *Power down!*'

The Atlantia surged and the captain felt his restraining belt press against his stomach as the frigate plunged out of super–luminal. The blackness ahead flared bright white and then a spectrum of colour rippled like a kaleidoscopic rainbow as the light spectrum realigned itself and a dense starfield leaped into view.

The captain's practiced eye picked out the faint object near the centre of the viewing screen, one that moved a fraction against the stationary backdrop of the galaxy.

'Tactical on–line!' he bellowed. 'Launch all fighters!'

*

Evelyn saw the launch bay doors drop away as a rush of air billowed in tumbling clouds of vapour out into the abyss of space. Her eyes barely registered the movement before she felt the Raython leap into motion and she was slammed back into her seat.

The launch bay lights flashed past in a blur as she threw her throttles to the firewall and the open landing bay entrance flashed past above her as her Raython was blasted out into space. She glimpsed through her canopy the underside of the Atlantia's immense for'ard hull rushing past above her, and alongside she saw from the corner of her eye Andaim's fighter flick right as it cleared the bay.

'Reaper One and Two clear!' he called out.

Evelyn heard Mikhain's response coming from the Atlantia's bridge.

Target, bearing right two–zero degrees, elevation negative one–five, range sixty thousand cubits.

Evelyn rolled right and followed Andaim as he turned onto the new heading, and she saw instantly the distant shape of a vessel hanging in space. Far from the light of the nearest stars her hull was entombed in shadow, black against the blackness, barely visible but for the stars it silhouetted.

Lael's voice echoed over the intercom.

'It's colonial!' she yelped, unable to keep the excitement from her voice. *'It's not Veng'en.'*

Evelyn maintained a battle–formation with Andaim, separated by several hundred cubits as they closed in on the vessel: close enough to remain in mutual sight, not so close that they could both be taken out with a single shot.

'I'm not seeing any sign of life,' Evelyn said as she scanned her instruments. 'No running lights, no nothing.'

'Scan is showing no signs of biological life either,' Andaim replied. 'Stay sharp. Activate weapons.'

Evelyn flipped up a clear–red plastic shield on her instrument console and set the switch beneath it to "*Live*" before closing the lid again. Her plasma cannons glowed into life, waiting to be fired.

The vessel ahead loomed closer and Evelyn began to pick out details on its surface, dimly illuminated by the distant light of billions of stars.

'Looks like a merchant vessel after all,' Andaim said.

The ship's hull was stained a dirty grey brown, streaked with bright silvery threads where countless micro–meteorite impacts had scoured the paint and dirt off to reveal bare metal beneath. That she had travelled far was clear not just from her location but her condition, and she had likely done so under ion power for much of that time.

'I've got the distress signal again,' Evelyn said, 'still transmitting.'

The signal remained the same, broken as though left in a hurry, indistinct and warbling as the computers translated the language. The hull loomed up as Evelyn and Andaim slowed their fighters down, other Raythons now joining them as in the distance she glimpsed bright, fast-moving pin-pricks of light as Renegade Flight rocketed out into deep space to form a protective perimeter.

The merchant vessel was simple in its construction, as so many of them had been. Built in space for use only in space, it was only loosely aerodynamic in shape and profile to reduce the damage from micro-meteorites. A long, smooth cylinder with tapered edges, the only obtrusions from its surface countless hydrogen scoops, like the blisters on the skin of an Etherean whale. At its stern the engine bay protruded from the tapered hull, fitted with a pair of ion engines that now trailed crystalised dust in sparkling clouds behind the vessel as it drifted slowly through the emptiness of space.

'She must have expelled her fuel,' Andaim said as he flew alongside her hull and past the lifeless engines. 'That's a hell of a mistake to make this far from home.'

Evelyn followed Andaim's fighter around the stern, easing the Raython over as she passed through the cloud of fuel crystals and out onto the vessel's starboard flank.

'She's only moving slowly though,' Evelyn said. 'So she could not have been running from anything when her fuel expired. She'd still have momentum.'

'Doesn't add up,' Andaim agreed as he flew alongside the vessel's darkened bridge.

There, beneath the bridge windows, Evelyn could see markings.

'*Sylph*,' she read out over the intercom. 'She's called the *Sylph*.'

*

'The Sylph,' Lael echoed, and tapped in a few commands.

Upon the bridge viewing screen, which now showed the shadowy vessel and the fighters cruising alongside her, the captain saw new data overlaid by Lael. A schematic of the Sylph appeared, data on her performance envelope beside it as Lael read from her screen.

'The Sylph, named after a spirit or ghost of the air, a privately owned vessel, part of a mining fleet. Mostly accommodation and cargo purposes, her keel was laid down sixty orbits ago. She was working the Tyberium fields when the Word attacked.'

The captain sat back thoughtfully in his chair. The Tyberium fields were a vast spherical cloud of asteroids that enshrouded the Ethera system as such clouds did all stars. Almost a full light year from their parent star they represented the remnants of stellar formation, the objects in the cloud often billions of years old and harbouring pristine minerals and chemicals, some of which had been formed in the supernovae explosions of ancient giant stars and could be found nowhere else in nature. Tyberium, a supremely rare mineral, was one of those valuable commodities.

'She may have been far enough from the apocalypse to have escaped infection,' he said. 'Forced to run, low on supplies, she got this far and no further.'

Andaim's voice crackled over the bridge intercom from his Raython cockpit.

'Doesn't explain why she's becalmed out here. If she ran out of fuel they could simply have shut down their engines and cruised indefinitely.'

'Perhaps they did,' the captain replied, 'when something slowed them down or forced them to stop.' He turned to the Executive Officer. 'Any signs of life?'

'No sir,' Mikhain replied from his tactical station. 'Only emergency systems are functional. Life support is active, the hull is not breached so her atmosphere should be fine. I'm not reading any alerts from her computer systems and they're all broadcasting on normal colonial emergency channels. It's like nobody was ever aboard her.'

Captain Sansin rubbed his chin thoughtfully as Dhalere's voice reached him from nearby.

'It is a civilian vessel,' she said.

'Merchant,' the captain confirmed.

'Then this is a civilian matter,' Dhalere said. 'I want to be aboard her as soon as she's considered safe.'

The captain turned his craggy head and looked at Dhalere as though she were insane.

'*You* want to board her?' he echoed. 'I thought that you wanted us to go nowhere near her?'

'As a civilian vessel, the situation is different now. It is not just your pilots and Marines who wish to contribute to this effort of yours,' Dhalere replied. 'That vessel is not military and may represent a new opportunity for us to house our civilians. The least that I can do is assess the likelihood of that happening.'

The captain glanced at the screen for a moment longer and then turned to tactical.

'Any sign of the Word or its Legion?'

'No sir,' Mikhain replied. 'No sign of any movement or heat signatures aboard. If the Word is there it's not visible to us, but that's no reason to go wandering aboard without taking proper precautions.'

Sansin nodded slowly.

'Keep the fighters up and send the Marines in. Let's see if we can figure out what's happened to her before any civilians are allowed aboard.' The captain turned to Dhalere. 'Once her bay's been cleared, the first person I want aboard her is the one who knows most about the Word. Evelyn.'

'You want to send a former convict and known killer aboard her before the civilians who actually have a right to be there?'

'Evelyn was innocent of her crimes, only ever killed in self defence and is one of only a handful of people aboard this ship who have encountered the Word face to face. She goes first, agreed?'

Dhalere bowed her head courteously, but her disdain for the captain's choice was clear.

'Tell General Bra'hiv to launch and to maintain contact with Atlantia,' the captain ordered.

***

VII

The shuttle leaped from Atlantia's launch bay catapults and raced away from the frigate, two Raython fighters swooping down to provide escort to them as they crossed the frigid, black void between the two ships.

Bra'hiv sat in the cockpit's jump seat and watched as the Sylph emerged from the blackness, her mottled, scratched hull in worse shape than the Atlantia's.

'How long do you think she's been sitting here?' he asked the pilot.

'Impossible to say,' came the response, 'but hull scarring like that takes months to build up, years even. She's probably been cruising through space since the Word attacked.'

Bra'hiv got out of his seat and strode into the shuttle's cargo compartment, where twenty of Bravo Company's Marines sat waiting for him, their plasma rifles cradled in their laps and their faces shielded behind visors. The assorted motley gang 'hoods and gangsters were positioned nearest the boarding ramp for deployment, and Bra'hiv noticed that Qayin was at their head, in a leader's natural position. Whether by intention or just pure instinct, Qayin was a psychologically savvy manipulator. Ten men from Alpha Company were also aboard to act as support, led by Sergeant Djimon.

'Com'any, sixty seconds to deployment!' Bra'hiv snapped, his keen eye searching for any sign of the men seeking to avoid the deployment.

He saw none. Fact was, men who had been brought up in the brutal life of street gangs were in many ways just as tough as those who had seen combat with the Marines as career soldiers: the only difference was the cause for which they had stood and the shape of the enemy. Djimon had thus not been happy about his men being placed behind Bravo Company, embittered that such low–lifes should see more of the action than his own men. He glanced at the general and nodded once as he pulled his visor down and sealed his neck collar, his face grim as he tried to force the sulk from his features.

Bra'hiv donned his own visor and sealed it at the neck. To his side, Qayin unbuckled his restraints and stood up to check the general's seal.

'Would you tell me if it was breached?' Bra'hiv asked.

'You're about to find out.'

Bra'hiv took his seat at the rear of the shuttle's bay, close to the aft deployment ramp that would drop under the pilot's command as soon as they were in position. The lights in the shuttle dimmed to red as the pilot swung the vessel around near the Sylph's landing bay, Bra'hiv catching a glimpse of the underside of the merchant vessel's hull through the for'ard hatch just as the pilot sealed it shut.

'Ten seconds.'

The pilot's voice was calm over the intercom, the mark of an experienced aviator. Bra'hiv held his pulse rifle at port arms and flicked the safety catch to *off*.

'All arms,' he murmured into his own microphone.

The troops activated their weapons, the pulse rifles humming as they heard a dull thump. Bra'hiv and the thirty Marines with him punched their harness release buckles and stood ready to charge from the rear of the shuttle.

All Colonial vessels carried transponders that recognised each other's signals and allowed one vessel's computers access to the others in case of emergency. Under the Atlantia's control, the Sylph's landing bay doors had been opened and the pilot had carefully reversed the shuttle in.

The shuttle vibrated as it landed on its magnetic clamps in the bay and with a hiss and a rush of escaping pressurised air the rear ramp thundered down under hydraulic pressure and Bra'hiv sprinted down the ramp as his rifle swung left and right, seeking a target. Behind him followed Qayin and Djimon, and the rest of the Marines poured like a flood out into the darkened bay, underslung flashlights casting multiple rays of white light out into the gloom.

The Marines fanned out, encircling the shuttle in defensive positions, weapons cast ready for any sign of an attack. A deep silence filled the bay as the shuttle's engines whined down and Bra'hiv edged out into the darkness.

'No sign of movement,' he reported into his microphone. 'Lael, scanners?'

Lael's voice reached Bra'hiv's from the Atlantia's bridge.

'No heat sources near you, general,' she reported. *'No electrical disturbances. The bay is clear.'*

'Roger that,' Bra'hiv snapped. 'Lighting's out, can you re–route the power?'

'Stand by.'

Bra'hiv waited for a few moments and then several emergency lights arrayed around the bay flickered weakly into life and cast dim pools of light down onto the deck. The general saw a pair of small, private shuttle craft parked nearby, fuel bowsers and cables coiled in tight loops along one wall. His practiced eye sought signs of conflict but found nothing, the bay utterly devoid of life but for the Marines.

'Secure the area in teams of three!' he barked. 'Bravo first, Alpha in support.'

The Marines moved out, covering each other in small groups as they surveyed the bay in orderly and logical sections. Bra'hiv felt a surge of pride as he saw the former jailbirds act like real soldiers, swift and without fear. Within a few minutes the bay was cleared as each team called in their segment and confirmed it devoid of life or evidence of the Word's presence. Behind the general, Alpha Company maintained defensive positions around the shuttle, their rifles trained out into the shadowy distance.

'Landing bay is clear,' Bra'hiv reported back to the Atlantia's bridge. 'Are you detecting any signs of life elsewhere?'

'Nothing yet,' came Mikhain's response. 'But the ship's too large for our scanners to confirm anything at this range.'

Boots on the ground, Bra'hiv thought ruefully. No matter how much technology mankind had created, no matter how fecund his imagination in developing new weapons, in the end it still always boiled down to the same thing:infantry and close combat. There was, never had been, and never would be any substitute.

'Roger that,' he intoned, unable to keep a tone of mild weariness from his voice. 'We'll start our sweep of the 'tween decks.'

It was the captain's voice that cut across the intercom in response.

'Hold position, we're sending Evelyn and Commander Ry'ere aboard to join you.'

Bra'hiv hesitated. 'Why?'

'Evelyn knows more about the Word than most,' the captain replied, *'especially after what happened aboard the Avenger. She'll take point, understood?'*

Bra'hiv was mildly baulked by having to follow the lead of a junior pilot and he suddenly had an idea of why Djimon was so annoyed, but he knew what Evelyn was capable of. Everybody did.

'Understood, send them in.'

*

Evelyn climbed out of her Raython's cockpit as soon as the Sylph's landing bay doors closed and air was reintroduced into the bay. The vents belched clouds of vapour as the temperature was still close to freezing, and she kept her visor on as she climbed down onto the deck.

'No heating,' Bra'hiv reported as he strode to her side, still wearing his own visor to preserve precious warmth and his voice reaching her through her earpiece.

'Suits us,' Evelyn replied as Andaim joined them. 'The cold slows the Word down. The Word's bots don't generate much of their own heat unless they're packed in tight swarms.'

'The distress signal is still broadcasting,' Bra'hiv reported. 'But it's likely on some kind of loop. We're guessing that whoever left it is dead.'

'What the hell was a Veng'en doing aboard a colonial vessel anyway?' Andaim asked. 'It doesn't make any sense.'

'Not much does right now,' Bra'hiv replied. 'There are shuttles here that my men have checked over and reported as fully fuelled. No sign of conflict, no sign of the Word or its Legion. You remember what the Avenger looked like when it found us?'

'Smothered,' Evelyn replied, recalling the incredible and chilling sight of a large battle cruiser half–engulfed by a black sea of seething nanobots. 'Maybe the crew weren't infected and something else happened?'

'Or maybe they Word did catch up with them and they abandoned ship before things got too hot?' Andaim suggested.

'No escape capsules have been fired,' Bra'hiv reported. 'But this bay could have held a lot more ships so it's possible.' He looked at Evelyn. 'You sure you want to take point? My men are well trained and the area is secure so we…'

'Nowhere is secure,' Evelyn interrupted the general, 'and I mean nowhere. You haven't seen what the Word can do.'

'Scanners are saying there's nothing here, Evelyn,' Bra'hiv reassured her. 'Even if the Word is aboard it can't be in many numbers or we'd have detected it.'

Evelyn shook her head.

'They don't need numbers to occupy a vessel, just time and sufficient resources,' she replied. 'The Word evolves and it can replicate faster than you would ever believe. This ship could go from having a handful of bots aboard to ten billion in a matter of hours. It's not secure.'

Bra'hiv glanced at Andaim.

'Let's just take it steady and see what we find,' the commander advised. 'Are your men ready?'

'They are,' Bra'hiv replied, his expression stoic but his eyes twinkling with pride. 'They'll follow us anywhere.'

'Let's go then,' Evelyn said as she drew her service pistol and activated it.

Alongside her, the Marines crowded to follow.

'Alpha Company remain here,' Bra'hiv ordered. 'Bravo, on me!'

Sergeant Djimon scowled as Bravo Company moved off. Evelyn saw Qayin gravitate toward her, and she could see his bioluminescent tattoos glowing behind his visor. *The Mark of Qayin.* She wondered briefly if the tattoos were tactically a disadvantage in the gloomy ship, something for an enemy to aim at. The big former convict directed a curt nod at her, along with a sly grin at Sergeant Djimon.

'You've got the lead, ensign,' Bra'hiv prompted her.

Evelyn led the way to the aft bay exit, saw Qayin and the Marines falling in behind her with Bra'hiv and Andaim.

The aft exit was sealed, and Evelyn stood with her pistol aimed at the door as two Marines jogged forward and accessed the entry pad. The codes were cracked swiftly by the Atlantia's computers using a Colonial deciphering key, and with a rush of air the door hissed open.

A dark, cold corridor awaited, only a few of the ceiling lights working as Evelyn peered into the gloom. She was reminded of a very similar corridor she had been forced to walk down aboard the Avenger, seething with millions of Hunter bots, their countless tiny metallic legs sounding like a waterfall of sand grains falling on a metal deck.

'Evelyn?'

Andaim's voice snapped her out of her maudlin thoughts, and with an effort she put one boot in front of the other and advanced into the darkness.

'Stay close,' Bra'hiv advised, 'they could be anywhere and...'

'Belay that,' Evelyn cut across the general. 'Spread out, put distance between each other. We don't want everybody risking being infected all at once. The Word doesn't work like a plasma shot – it's more like shrapnel.'

The Marines behind her obeyed, Bra'hiv's troops spreading out in single file as they advanced through the corridor to put distance between themselves. The lights above were dim, running only under emergency power to cast pools of illumination every few cubits. Evelyn heard her own breath in her ears, rasping as the ventilators in her helmet sucked carbon dioxide out through scrubbers and injected oxygen and nitrogen in.

'*Advance force, Atlantia,*' Mikhain's voice echoed in her ears, '*you're half-way to the elevator banks. Take the emergency stair wells to your right and ascend four decks. The bridge will be ahead of you upon the exit.*'

'Roger that,' Evelyn replied.

The elevator banks emerged from the gloom, ceiling lights casting into thin white halos of mist around them as Evelyn emerged from the corridor and turned right toward a manual blast–door. Evelyn reached down and cranked the sealing valve, releasing the pressure on the door as two Marines moved in alongside her and grabbed the door's handles. Lieutenant C'rairn nodded at her.

Evelyn stepped back and C'rairn hauled the door open to reveal the stairwells, the flashlights from their weapons reflecting off ice particles on the frosted walls.

'The ship's been cold for a long time,' Andaim said. 'Nobody could survive long under these conditions.'

Evelyn eased forward and swung her pistol into the stairwell, the white beam from her flashlight slicing through the gloom as she swept it up and down but found nothing.

'I don't like this,' Evelyn murmured as she peered down into the bowels of the ship below. 'If we go up the Word could ascend from below and cut us off.'

'Same if we go down,' Qayin rumbled from nearby. 'Gotta go someways.'

'We don't have enough men to cover all angles,' Bra'hiv added. 'We either go in or we go home.'

Evelyn shook her head but she stepped into the stairwell and began climbing, resting her boots lightly with each step. The Marines followed her in, the rearguard walking backwards with their weapons pointing back down the stairwell in case of attack from the rear.

She looked up above to where the grated steps of the stairwell doubled back repeatedly on themselves as they climbed toward the upper levels. Dim light panels frosted with ice crystals glowed, shadows cast in a maze of black and white lines obscured by the misty air.

Evelyn felt the hairs on the back of her neck rise up, a tingling sensation rippling down her arms like tiny insects scuttling on her skin, and then the light from high above flickered as something moved fast from right to left across the stairwell above her.

'Enemy!'

Evelyn jerked right as she aimed and she heard the Marines behind her drop to firing positions on the stairwell.

***

VIII

Evelyn held her pistol steady, aiming up toward the light.

She could feel the cold seeping through her flight suit, could hear her breathing in her ears and feel her heart thumping in her chest as she searched for the source of the movement.

'I don't see anything,' Andaim whispered.

'Up there,' Evelyn insisted, 'heading for'ard. I saw it.'

Andaim reached out and she saw his gloved hand rest on her forearm and gently push her weapon down.

'I don't see anything,' he repeated.

The Marines around her relaxed as they watched, and she could sense a sudden and growing lack of faith in their expressions.

'Let's just keep moving, okay?' Andaim urged her.

Evelyn swallowed, her heart still racing as she turned and moved up the stairwell, her gaze fixed up toward the light. She emerged onto the upper deck entrance and looked down at the grated deck beneath her boots. The sparkling, icy surface betrayed no boot marks, no evidence of anybody having passed through.

'There's nothing here,' Bra'hiv said.

There was nothing dismissive about the general's tone, nothing to hint that he was annoyed, but Evelyn knew damned well that the general did not like false alarms.

'I saw something,' she insisted.

'Probably the light flickered,' Bra'hiv replied. 'The power's low, there's not much light in here. Easy enough to mistake it for motion.'

Evelyn opened her mouth to protest but she caught herself. The general was offering her a way out, she realised.

'Okay,' she said, 'let's clear the bridge.'

C'rairn moved forward and began freeing the seals of the pressure hatch to the deck level.

'Anybody find it strange that there's nobody aboard, but they managed to lock up shop so neatly?' Qayin asked.

'Yeah,' Andaim nodded. 'Why bother if they left in such a rush?'

Evelyn racked her brains for an answer, but nothing presented itself. The Sylph was a civilian vessel, a merchant ship. It had no means of defence and there had presumably been no military personnel aboard who could have coordinated such an organised lock–down in a short time. And yet here she was, drifting in space, devoid of crew, sealed to perfection and bitterly cold.

Lieutenant C'rairn cranked the pressure hatch open as Evelyn aimed down the corridor, Andaim's and Bra'hiv's rifles either side of her and humming with restrained plasma energy. The corridor ahead was as dark as those below, pools of dim white light amid immense blacknesses.

'You want me to take point for a while?' Bra'hiv asked.

Evelyn tried to reply, but she couldn't. Visions of the Avenger's seething corridors raced through her mind again. She nodded before the silence drew out too long and let Bra'hiv and a few Marines file past her.

'You okay?' Andaim asked her in a whisper, one hand touching her shoulder.

'I'm fine,' she breathed. 'Just taking a while to adjust.'

Andaim nodded and offered her a smile before he turned and strode into the darkness.

Evelyn waited a moment to let her breathing return to normal, and that's when she saw it.

The lights further up the stairwell were enshrouded in mist, and that mist was swirling in eddies and pools, vortexes of moving air where something had passed through. Evelyn remembered the prison ship, Atlantia Five, where she had first awoken months before. There the inmates had been kept in zero–gravity in order to allow their muscles to degenerate and make them easier for the guards to handle . Evelyn had not walked through the decks of the prison in the aftermath of the blast that had freed her: she had floated.

She peered up into the shadows, aiming her pistol and flashlight. The beam cut through the darkness but it only reached so far, the very upper decks entombed in shadows that she could not penetrate. She turned to call to Bra'hiv, but the Marines had all filed into the corridor and were marching away from her.

She looked up again, but could pick out nothing. Evelyn sighed and lowered her pistol. Maybe the air had been disturbed by the Marines climbing the stairwell. She wanted desperately to fire a plasma round up into the darkness to illuminate whatever might be hiding up there, but if the Word was waiting for them then she knew it would be alerted by the noise of the blast, the narrow confines of the stairwells amplifying the sound.

'You comin'?'

Qayin's glowing tattoos shimmered in the darkened corridor as he peered out at her.

Evelyn turned and followed the big man as he strode through the darkness.

'You gotta stop jumpin' at shadows,' he murmured. 'You're making the guys nervous.'

'I saw something,' Evelyn insisted. 'I'm just not sure what.'

The corridor opened out onto the bridge deck, two stairwells on either side descending back down into the ship alongside elevator doors that were sealed shut. Likewise, the bridge doors were also sealed.

'Whoever sealed the ship up may have done so from in there,' Bra'hiv said as his men prepared to open the hatches. 'The Word historically always took the bridges of vessels first, or so the reports went before we lost contact with the rest of the fleet, so let's stay sharp, okay? Fire teams in place?'

The Marines were already crouching with their rifles ready, aimed at the doors.

'Plasma rays,' Bra'hiv ordered.

Immediately C'rairn and another Marine hefted the big flame–throwing plasma rays and aimed them at the doors. The weapons fired a stream of super–heated charged particles that melted anything they touched, an effective defence against a swarm of Infectors or Hunters that might surge from within the bridge.

Bra'hiv nodded and two Marines accessed the panel codes and the bridge main hatch hissed as it was pulled open, C'rairn's plasma ray roaring as it swung into action. The lieutenant held the weapon in place, heat haze rippling from its muzzle as Evelyn glimpsed the interior of the bridge, but nothing rushed out at them from its gloomy depths.

The Marines waited and then Bra'hiv edged forward. Evelyn shook herself into motion and joined him, covering his advance with her pistol as he reached the bridge entrance and peered inside.

The bridge was almost entirely dark but for four small emergency lights that cast their dull glow over abandoned control panels, the captain's command platform and the main viewing screen. Evelyn saw no reflections from swarming bots, no movement, the bitterly cold air silent and still.

'Advance by sections,' Bra'hiv snapped as he lurched into the bridge.

Evelyn ran in behind him as the Marines plunged en masse onto the circular bridge and spread out, clearing each control station as they advanced past it.

'Clear!'

'Clear!

'Clear!'

Evelyn relaxed her grip on her pistol as Bra'hiv lowered his rifle and pointed at C'rairn's plasma ray.

'Shut it down, lieutenant,' he said. 'Bridge is clear.'

The roaring of the plasma flame spluttered out as Evelyn looked around her. The bridge was shut down, entirely deactivated as though the ship were in a space dock back in orbit around Ethera. Andaim moved across to one of the control panels and activated a screen. He wiped the frost from it with one gloved hand and scrutinised the display, the blue screen glowing against his visor and illuminating his face.

'Well,' he said finally, 'this gets stranger. The ship's computer says that it has at least fifty per cent of its fuel remaining and that supplies are at thirty eight per cent. She's full of the things we need.'

'She's stocked?' Bra'hiv uttered in disbelief as he strode to join Andaim. 'Then where the hell is everybody?'

'I don't like this,' Evelyn murmured, looking around her. 'It feels like bait.'

'That doesn't figure either,' Qayin said. 'If this ship was put here by the Word to bait humans then they wouldn't have used a Veng'en distress signal and revealed themselves.'

'He's right,' C'rairn said. 'There's something else going on here. Can we start the engines from the bridge?'

Andaim moved to the helmsman's position and scanned the controls, activating one of the touchscreen displays and reading from the screen. He frowned.

'Engines are functional, but the command controls have been deactivated at the engine room relays,' he reported. 'Somebody shut the connections down on site in the generator room.'

'Why the hell would they do that?' C'rairn asked.

'Whatever this is all about, it's an opportunity we can't afford to miss,' Bra'hiv snapped and keyed his microphone link to Atlantia. 'This is Bra'hiv. Ship is secure, send over shuttles as soon as you can to begin shipping supplies.'

'Roger that.'

Evelyn felt a pulse of alarm surge through her. 'You can't do that, not yet. We haven't checked the rest of the ship.'

'We will,' Bra'hiv promised, 'but this ship could provide us with months' of supplies and I'm not passing that up.'

'It could take days to check this vessel over,' Evelyn insisted. 'And what about scanning the supplies? They would be the perfect vector for the Word to get aboard Atlantia and…'

'Evelyn,' Bra'hiv cut across her. 'I get it, okay? You're concerned about the Word getting aboard. We all are. Let me do my job and it won't come to that. Agreed?'

Evelyn bit her lip and forced herself to nod in agreement. Bra'hiv turned away and began directing his men toward their duties as one of the Marines walked up onto the control platform and began flipping switches.

'Hey!' Evelyn yelled. 'Get down from there!' The Marine looked up at her in surprise as she dashed to his side. 'What the hell are you doing?'

'Getting some warmth in here,' the Marine protested. 'The civilians can't come aboard while it's sub–zero!'

'The Legion prefers warm temperatures!' Evelyn snapped. 'You do that, you could kill us all.'

The Marine looked at General Bra'hiv, who replied in a monotone voice.

'We're not detecting any presence of the Word, and if it were here it would have maintained a temperate environment, not shut the ship down and let itself drift to nowhere,' he said as he looked at the Marine. 'Kyarl, as soon as you're done there I want you on guard duty back in the landing bay, understood?'

'Yes sir!' Kyarl replied, and stepped down off the platform.

'This is insane,' Evelyn gasped. 'Don't any of you have any concerns at all about what might happen if I'm right?'

Nobody answered her, and even Qayin seemed to be avoiding her gaze. The realisation hit Evelyn hard. 'You all think I'm crazy, is that it?'

'Nobody thinks you're crazy,' Lieutenant C'rairn said. 'But you're wound a little tight right now Evelyn, if you know what I mean?'

Evelyn looked pleadingly at Andaim, who offered her a brief smile. 'It'll be fine,' he promised.

'That's what people probably said right before the damned apocalypse,' Evelyn shot back and then turned to Bra'hiv. 'You brought me here to take point and now you're ignoring me?'

'I'm not ignoring you, ensign,' the general replied, carefully emphasising Evelyn's rank, 'but right now we're secure enough to move forward and frankly I think you're over–reacting. If anything happens we'll pull out without hesitation but for now we're staying put. You've got a problem with that, take it up with the captain.'

The general turned and walked off the bridge, leaving Evelyn to fume in silence.

***

IX

The Infectors were mesmerising.

Meyanna Sansin stood in her laboratory and watched the writhing ball of bots as they swirled in a dense black cloud the size of her fingernail inside the magnetic chamber. Too small to see individually unless they stopped moving, each was smaller than a grain of sand and contained a simple but exotically crafted series of components, some of which she had been able to identify by scanning the devices with X–Rays.

Infectors flowed through the human body using the bloodstream, spreading to all corners of the body within minutes of infection. Looking like small hump–backed insects, with six legs and probing antennae around two pincer–like jaws, they latched on wherever they were programmed to go and inserted thin, electrically conductive probes into vital organs or nerve centres. One probe went in from the Infector's head, the other from its tail. Signals from various human organs were thus intercepted on their way to the brain, or vice versa, "*hacked*" with the Infector's new commands, and sent on their way through the body. Thus could a small number of Infectors hack the human body from the brain stem and control it, all the while using the human body's resources to multiply their numbers and solidify their control.

What fascinated Meyanna most was their ability to extract small amounts of iron from human blood, and use it to replicate more of themselves. The human body contained enough iron to make a large nail but to extract it all would fatally injure the victim: thus, the Infectors extracted only small amounts, building more of themselves over time until they gradually took complete control. From there they could extract other elements through the victim's skin from contact with other surfaces, building molecule by molecule as they metamorphosised their victim into an inorganic version of itself, such as the horrendous charicature of Commander Tyraeus Forge that Evelyn had described coming face to face with aboard the Avenger.

Meyanna shivered. Because the iron in human blood was essentially paramagnetic it had to be harvested by the Infectors in other ways, usually through it being dissolved in red blood cells. Once the human victim was completely under the Infector's control, iron could then be sought out through dietary means, providing the Infectors with fuel for yet more replication.

She leaned close to the chamber, watching the cloud of bots swirling in their spherical prison. The Infector's construction inevitably created some level of magnetic polarity, especially when they were beyond the shielding effect of human cells and the fast–flowing protection of blood, which protected them because its force was far greater than that of magnetism. But suspended in air, inside a powerful magnetic field, they were effectively incarcerated by forces far greater than their own.

And that, Meyanna had decided, might be a weakness that could be exploited.

Infectors could not survive outside of a human host for long. Too small to generate much internal power, and easily fried if they attempted to hack into ordinary power conduits, they relied upon electrical impulses inside the human body for power. These continuous, low energy pulses that drove motor–function and the brain provided an easily tapped source of energy for the Infectors, furthering the vicious cycle of infection, replication and deeper entrenchment within the human victim.

Outside of the body, devoid of a power supply and assaulted by air currents, microwaves and all manner of corrosive chemicals, Infectors survived for just minutes before shutting down and crumbling into dust. Their vulnerability to microwaves had for some time been the only way to detect their presence in a human being: by bombarding the victim with microwave radiation at the same frequency as the components within the Infectors, they would burn up and die. Unfortunately, with the bots swarming around major organs such as the optical nerves, brain stem and spinal column, the human host would also typically die an agonising death as they were fatally burned from within.

Meyanna had conceived a secondary test, a safer one that had been used on the entire ship's compliment months before. This involved a two–stage process. The first was to scan the human for their metallic content, essentially an X–Ray designed to pick up on the presence of Infector swarms around major organs. The entire human population of the Atlantia had thus been cleared of infection using this process, but Meyanna knew that it was not fail–safe: the bots could easily disperse into the blood–stream and be indetectable by the scans, leaving only a small number in place to ensure that control of the host was not lost.

Therefore, she had devised a second test. The X–ray scan was re–done, while at the very same time blood was drawn from the subject in small doses for five minutes. With nowhere left to run, one test or the other would expose infection.

For the past few weeks she had been conducting these exhaustive tests on ten people per day as well as running the hospital itself, systematically clearing civilians and crew members of infection. She was over half–way through and so far nobody had shown any sign of the infection that Evelyn seemed so certain was present aboard the Atlantia.

Evelyn's immunity to the Word was another mystery that confused Meyanna even further. Her body clearly was capable of rejecting the Infectors, its immune response attacking them and ejecting them from her body in much the same way it would a common cold virus. The Infectors' tiny size, in Evelyn's case, was also their weakness. How her killer T–cells recognised the invaders as foreign, and were able to immobilise them, was the greatest part of the mystery.

Meyanna watched as the Infector's roiled and seethed in mid–air. She knew that if this tiny sphere of living machines broke free of their magnetic incarceration, they would eat through the glass walls of the chamber within seconds and seek to infect any living person they could find before they were drained of power. She shuddered as she imagined walking into the laboratory and finding a tiny hole in the glass wall, seeing the Infectors flash by in front of her eyes as they…

'Doctor?'

Meyanna turned, mildly startled, and saw Dhalere standing in the laboratory doorway.

'Councillor,' she greeted her. 'I'm sorry, I didn't hear you come in.'

Dhalere glided toward Meyanna, her exotic eyes friendly. 'Sorry, I knocked but you seemed busy.' Dhalere's eyes drifted toward the sphere inside the magnetic chamber. 'Is that, *them*?'

'It is,' Meyanna replied, 'but don't worry, they can't break free from containment.'

Dhalere seemed to shiver as she crossed the laboratory to the examination bed, and she coughed into her hand. 'I'd rather stay away from them, if it's all the same to you. Those things give me the creeps.'

'I know what you mean,' Meyanna replied, and then opened a drawer filled with hypodermic needles and selected one. 'You okay with this?'

Dhalere glanced at the needles and nodded.

'I won't say I'm a fan but it's better than the alternative, right?'

Meyanna moved across to Dhalere and pulled the X–Ray transmitter from its wall socket. She levered it out and over where Dhalere lay on the bed as she prepared to extract her blood. The Councillor coughed again, covering her mouth with the back of her hand.

'You okay?' Meyanna asked.

'I've been coughing a lot lately,' Dhalere admitted. 'Must be a bug or something.'

'Are you taking anything for it?'

'It'll pass,' Dhalere replied. 'I'll fight it off.'

'I won't take much blood and it won't take long,' Meyanna promised. 'If you have any Infectors in your bloodstream they won't have anywhere else to run and we'll detect them. And if you've got anything else worse than just a cold, I'll see that too.'

'How long does it take?' Dhalere asked. 'The analysis, I mean?'

'A couple of hours or so,' Meyanna replied. 'I'll let you know as soon as I can what the results are.'

Dhalere lay back and stared up at the ceiling. She barely made a sound as Meyanna slipped the needle into a vein and then using a remote–control activated the X–Ray scanner. The device hummed as Meyanna extracted a small amount of blood, waited a few seconds, then drew a little more.

As Dhalere searched the ceiling above her, a movement caught her eye. She glanced sideways and saw the tiny sphere of Infectors trembling. The sphere changed shape into a teardrop, the narrow tip pointing toward her like a compass pointing toward the poles.

Dhalere looked away and saw Meyanna staring down at her.

'Okay?'

'Sure,' Dhalere murmured. 'Just distracting myself.'

'It's nearly done now.'

Dhalere remained still as her blood was drawn. Meyanna could see that the councillor did not enjoy being in the laboratory with a needle in her arm, and it was fair to say that most people did not relish the experience. The relief when they discovered that they were not infected far outweighed the discomfort, however.

'What if they know?' Dhalere asked.

'Know what?'

'What if they know how to hide?'

'There is nowhere to hide,' Meyanna promised. 'The X–Rays watch for them and the blood flow means that they can't disperse into the bloodstream without being detected. As soon as I've drawn this blood it will be placed in a magnetically sealed chamber and blasted with microwaves to destroy any bots inside. All I'll see in the analysis is their little corpses, if there are any.'

Dhalere shivered again, her glowing skin seeming paler than usual as she coughed.

Meyanna withdrew the needle and let Dhalere apply pressure to the puncture wound as she crossed the laboratory and placed the needle in a microwave chamber. Moments later, the sample was being bombarded behind a sealed glass screen.

'Is that it?' Dhalere asked.

'That's it,' Meyanna replied. 'You're good to go.'

Dhalere seemed visibly relieved. 'Good, that means I can get to work. The Sylph has supplies that we need and I want the captain to let me go aboard her.'

'The Sylph is not quarantined,' Meyanna pointed out. 'If you go aboard her I'll have to run this test again when you get back.'

'That's fine,' Dhalere said. 'If it's this easy, you can run it every day so we can both sleep better at night.'

The councillor pulled on her jacket and headed for the laboratory door. She was almost there when she noticed the teardrop shaped ball of Infector's following her every move and Meyanna turning toward the chamber. Dhalere turned back sharply, standing in front of the magnetic chamber and blocking the doctor's view of it.

'Doctor? There is some discussion among the civilians, rumours mostly. They keep hearing that somebody, somewhere aboard this ship is infected, a carrier. Is this true?'

Meyanna's expression slipped a little, hiding her uncertainty behind the veil of a bright smile.

'I think that it's a healthy paranoia,' she replied.

'So, you don't know for sure whether there is or not?'

'I would say that it's unlikely,' the doctor said. 'But we can't be too careful, right? Hence this second round of tests.'

'They're saying that it's got something to do with Evelyn.'

Meyanna stared at Dhalere for a moment before she replied. 'Medical records are a matter of confidentiality between myself and my patients.'

'But she does come here,' Dhalere pressed. 'I've seen her, almost every other day. Is she a carrier?'

'No,' Meyanna said. 'She is definitely not a carrier. Councillor, even if I did know that there was a carrier aboard I would not be able to share that information with you. You know this.'

'Yes, but these are extraordinary times and the lives of our people depend on what we do. A democratic sharing of knowledge will almost always out–perform the secrecy that was the hallmark of the colonial military.' Dhalere smiled. 'I simply wish to reassure our people that they are safe aboard this ship, because if they're not there's another one right outside that we could transfer to.'

Meyanna stared at the councillor in shock.

'The Sylph?' she asked. 'It's a merchant vessel, unarmed. If the Word found it, everybody aboard would be defenceless.'

'It is a civilian vessel,' Dhalere replied, 'and as such legally it falls under my command. It may prove beneficial to us to board and occupy her as a new home for the civilians.'

'That's crazy,' Meyanna uttered. 'The civilians have the sanctuary to themselves. They're not going to abandon that for a rusty merchant ship.'

Dhalere coughed once more, then opened the laboratory door as she left.

'You'd be amazed what people will do to be out from under the yoke of the military.'

Dhalere strode from the laboratory. Meyanna watched the councillor go, completely unable to fathom what she was attempting to do. Independence, for no gain.

She looked at the perfect sphere of Infectors in the chamber and thought of the Word. The same thing: independence, for no gain, even the loss of the humanity that created it.

***

X

Evelyn pulled off her visor and loosened her flight suit as the temperature on the Sylph's bridge slowly began to climb. All around her personnel were manning the control stations as systems began coming back on–line one by one, reactivated by the Marines.

The main lighting flickered back on in the bridge, illuminating a sparse but efficient layout dominated as always by a viewing screen.

'Ship's logs?' Andaim asked as Bra'hiv's men scoured the controls.

'All wiped,' came the response from Lieutenant C'rairn, 'half an orbit ago. Engines were manually shut down and all power re–routed to emergency life–support. Looks like most of it was done here at the bridge, which was then sealed, and then the engines disconnected in the generator rooms afterward.'

A reply came over the bridge tannoy, the voice of Idris Sansin beamed across from the Atlantia.

'By whom?'

'No record of who wiped the logs,' said C'rairn, 'not even any manifest left to figure out who was aboard her, who her command crew were, nothing.'

'So they shut the ship down,' Andaim said, 'seal the bridge, seal all hatches, and then abandon her?'

'Reminds me of the Avenger,' Evelyn said. 'The Word shut her down, keeping only basic life–support so that the infected crew could attack and repel boarders. Other than that she was dead.'

'True,' Sansin replied, *'but then she was still being operated by her crew from the bridge. The Sylph is entirely abandoned.'*

'Are you not picking up any signs of life at all?' Evelyn pressed. 'Not even the slightest hint of survivors?'

Lael's voice was lighter than the captain's, but still inflected with the brisk, clipped tones of a colonial officer.

'Scans remain inconclusive due to the Sylph's hull mass. She's too big to probe every corner. Bra'hiv's men will have to check the hold, engine and generator rooms and the ventilation system.'

'That could take months,' Andaim said. 'This is a smash and grab. We don't need the ship, just what's aboard.'

'*Agreed,*' Sansin replied. '*But Councillor Dhalere is already claiming the ship as belonging to the civilians. As soon as she's been scanned enough to satisfy General Bra'hiv, we'll have more hands board her and start shipping supplies back to the Atlantia. Twelve hours and we're gone – then Dhalere can do whatever she wants with the Sylph, understood?*'

'Aye captain,' Andaim said, and clapped his gloved hands loudly as he called out. 'Okay, let's get to it!'

Evelyn thought of the stairwell they had ascended to reach the bridge and of the shadowy movement she had spotted there. If someone, or something, was still alive aboard the ship then it could have doubled back and moved below them. She stepped forward to Andaim's side. 'I'll head down to the hold,' she said.

'I'll need you to help pilot the shuttles back and forth,' Andaim said as he pored over a map of the ship. 'All hands on deck, I'm afraid.'

'That's easy enough, the rookies can do that,' Evelyn shot back. 'There's something here and I want to know what it is.'

Evelyn saw Bra'hiv and several of the Marines from the corner of her eye, all watching the exchange. Andaim stood upright again and looked down at her.

'You're still sure you saw something?'

'One hundred per cent.'

'I can't spare the men. We've got our hands full as it is.'

'Their hands will be a lot more full if the Word is aboard!'

'The Word isn't aboard, Evelyn!' Andaim snapped. The bridge fell silent. 'It would have attacked us by now!'

Evelyn stood immobile for a moment and then her anger surged to the surface. She grabbed her pistol and checked its load.

'Fine,' she snapped. 'I'll go my damned self!'

Evelyn whirled away and marched for the bridge exit.

'You walk out that door and I'll have you grounded!'

Evelyn reached the bridge door and looked over her shoulder at him. 'Better grounded than dead.'

Bra'hiv reached out for her arm and held it gently. 'No sense in rushing off on your own, Evelyn. Once we're sorted here, I can spare a couple of guys.'

'I'll go,' C'rairn added. 'Many hands make light work and all that, and maybe while we're down there we can take a look at the engineering panels in the generator room, find a way to re–start the engines.'

'Me too,' Qayin rumbled. 'Last time you went wandering' off on your own aboard a ship it got blown to pieces.'

Evelyn smiled at the three of them, but it was Andaim's voice that cut across the bridge.

'You'll all be staying here and that's an order. The Word is not aboard this ship.'

Evelyn opened her mouth to respond when a distant claxon sounded through the ship and a display panel showed a series of power conduits flickering out near the engine rooms.

'What's that?' Lieutenant C'rairn asked.

'You're losing power,' Lael warned them from the Atlantia.

'The aft relay stations are being shut down,' C'rairn said as he dashed to the engineering panel and surveyed the display. 'The engine rooms are being isolated, temperature controls shut down again.' He looked up. 'It's being done manually, on site.'

Evelyn looked at Andaim, who covered his surprise as he pointed at them.

'Go, now!' he snapped. 'And seal off the bridge and landing bays as you go!'

Evelyn ran out of the bridge and down the corridor toward the stairwells, Bra'hiv, Qayin, C'rairn and several other Marines in hot pursuit. She burst out onto the stairwell and plunged down them, her flight–suit's fifty percent gravity reducing some of the shock of each landing as she leapt down ten steps at a time. Behind her, Bra'hiv mimicked her rapid descent.

The darkness in the stairwells deepened as they descended down toward the hold, the relay stations having shut off the power supply. Evelyn felt the cold deepen as the light faded away above them, touching her skin with the raw sensation of a deep freeze as she reached the bottom of the stairwell and landed cat–like on the deck to face a sealed hatch leading aft.

Bra'hiv and C'rairn landed alongside her and approached the hatch as Evelyn and Qayin covered them. The Marines hauled the hatch open to reveal a long, silent corridor that led into the main hold.

Bra'hiv gestured to Evelyn, who advanced into the corridor with Qayin at her side. The general posted two sentries by the hatch to prevent anything inside the hold from escaping, and then followed Evelyn in with C'rairn at his side.

Evelyn advanced slowly through the gloom, one careful step after another until she reached the end of the corridor and saw the vast expanses of the Sylph's hold open up before her. Like a cavern, sectioned off by massive bulkheads that had huge open doors set into them, the hold was stacked with myriad crates, boxes, pallets and drums lashed high above their heads, like a deep valley with cliffs of wood and steel. Dim overhead lights cast shafts of illumination that barely reached the deck, the air here still misty with the cold.

Cleared paths weaved in orderly lines like highways between the mountainous stores, their edges marked with bright yellow lines. Bra'hiv pointed down each of them, and in silence the Marines split up into pairs. Evelyn advanced down the central aisle, Qayin close behind her.

She moved quietly, gently setting each boot down to avoid the sound of her footfalls betraying her presence. She could see various machines used to move stock below decks, all abandoned. But as she moved through the towering store room, Bra'hiv and C'rairn moving alongside her in the next aisle, so she spotted a crate that had been split open, the contents scattered across the deck before her.

Evelyn quickened her pace and knelt down alongside the debris.

'Food,' she whispered to Qayin.

The big man nodded, his tattoos glowing like thin trails of magma against black rocks as his eyes swivelled up to look around the hold.

'Andaim was right,' he said. 'It ain't the Word aboard.'

'Then what the hell is it if…?'

A plasma blast crackled as Evelyn felt herself lifted off the deck and hurled across the hold to crash into a stack of boxes. A plasma charge smashed into the deck where she had been crouching as Qayin crashed down alongside her, one huge hand beneath her shoulder where he had lifted her and propelled them clear of the shot. A spray of bright blue–white plasma hissed as it melted plastic cases nearby as Evelyn scrambled for cover.

'Enemy front!' Bra'hiv yelled as he returned fire.

She saw several more plasma rounds smash into metal stanchions further down the hold, the general's shots illuminating the darkness in flickering spheres of harsh white light. Evelyn saw a shadowy form dash out of sight as it fled the lethal hail of fire.

'I'll be damned,' Qayin growled as he got to his feet and surged forward, hugging the cover of the stacked supplies as he advanced.

Evelyn got to her feet and followed him, as Bra'hiv and C'rairn emerged from the neighbouring aisle and the general gestured with a pointed finger toward the starboard wall of the hold. Evelyn and Qayin crouched in the shadows as Bra'hiv and C'rairn moved across to the cover of the far side of their aisle. Then, as a group, they advanced in pursuit of their quarry.

A pin point of fiery light flashed and Evelyn dove onto the deck as a plasma round crackled and shot across the hold. It flashed by above her head and crashed into stacked boxes behind her. Qayin leaped out of the way of the spray of super–heated plasma and Evelyn rolled across the deck as it splattered down where she had been moments before.

'Return fire!'

Bra'hiv, C'rairn, Qayin and Evelyn all opened fire at once, multiple plasma rounds zipping across the darkened hold and smashing across the starboard hull wall in a blaze of fiery light. Starbursts of plasma sprayed down into the gloom and she heard amid the din of the rifle fire a deep cry of pain.

Evelyn looked across at Bra'hiv and signalled where the enemy was. Bra'hiv nodded and with C'rairn he headed aft, hoping to catch their quarry in a cross–fire. Evelyn fired her pistol again, two rounds in the vicinity of where she had heard the cry.

'It's hunkered down,' Qayin snarled, 'nowhere to run.'

Evelyn moved forward and approached the hull wall as to her far left she saw Bra'hiv and C'rairn advancing one at a time, covering each other as they closed in.

A blast of plasma rounds raced up at Evelyn and she whirled aside into cover as the shots howled by and sailed off to hit high on the port wall of the hull. The spray of plasma was already becoming a fire hazard and she could smell smouldering plastics, a haze of blue smoke hovering in the air.

Bra'hiv settled into position, his rifle's barrel resting across a steel drum as C'rairn covered him from behind. Qayin positioned himself alongside Evelyn as the general's voice called out.

'We have you surrounded!' he boomed. 'There's no use in fighting. Come out with your hands in the air and we'll take you into custody. You will not be harmed, is that understood?'

A deep growl reverberated across the hold and Evelyn realised that they were not being understood. The growl was neither animal nor human, and the sound of it sent a pulse of concern twisting through her belly. They were facing something that would fight to the death like a wounded animal, yet had the intelligence of a human being.

'It's gotta be a Veng'en,' she yelled.

Lieutenant C'rairn glanced across at her. 'Great. Now what do we do?'

Evelyn knew that the Veng'en were sufficiently war–like that their quarry would be likely to shoot itself rather than admit defeat or surrender to humans. She watched for a moment and then made a decision.

'Qayin,' she whispered, 'give me your medi–pack.'

The big man looked at her and frowned. 'You injured?'

'No, but he is,' she gestured toward the far wall of the hull. 'Maybe we can get him to trust us.'

'A Veng'en,' Qayin said. 'You kidding me?'

'You got any better ideas?'

Qayin shrugged as he unclipped his medi–pack from his webbing and handed it to her. Evelyn took the compact package and holstered her pistol as she crouched in cover and hurled the pack across the hold. The package hit the wall where she figured that the injured Veng'en was hiding and dropped with a distant thud to the deck.

'You really think that it's going to come out for a chat?' Qayin asked.

Evelyn shrugged and looked across at Bra'hiv. The general pointed forward and as one they broke cover and began moving silently toward the fallen Veng'en. Evelyn kept her pistol pointed out in front of her, her finger on the trigger and ready for the slightest evidence of a threat from their quarry.

She reached the edge of the hull wall and peered around a stack of crates to a narrow passage between the crates and the hull wall.

A figure was slumped against the crates, its legs sprawled before it and one hand resting on the medi–pack that Evelyn had hurled, but the pack had not been opened. In the glow from her flashlight she could see its chest heaving, hear its breath rasping in its throat. Its mouth hung limp, a long tongue drooping from its jaws. Humanoid, reptilian in appearance and wrapped in what looked like several magnetic gravity–suits, the Veng'en's eyes reflected the flashlights in bright discs that glowed in the darkness.

Beside it, on the deck, lay a plasma rifle.

Evelyn lowered her pistol as she saw that the Veng'en was neither armed nor apparently aggressive, but its thigh was scorched where a spray of hot plasma shrapnel had landed on it. She edged closer, raised one hand palm–forward to the Veng'en as she eased toward it. The glowing eyes flicked up to look at her and despite their soul–less nature she could sense the hatred burning inside them.

Evelyn looked at the Veng'en and realised what had happened.

'We didn't hit it hard,' she said finally. 'It's exhausted.'

The Veng'en reached out for the plasma rifle and Evelyn froze as it aimed the weapon at her. She could see its breath puffing in dense clouds from its massive chest and lungs, eyes glowing in the flashlight beams.

'Stand down, ensign,' Bra'hiv growled from nearby.

The Veng'en turned its head and glared at the general and Evelyn leaped forward. The Veng'en turned back, the rifle whipping back toward her. Evelyn stuck out one boot and slammed it down on the rifle, pinning it to the deck as she trapped the Veng'en, her pistol aimed between its eyes.

The creature radiated hatred up at her, and she waited long enough for it to be sure that there was no escape for it before she lowered the pistol and again raised her palm toward it. Slowly, she holstered her pistol once more, hoping that a Veng'en might recognise such a universal gesture of non-aggression.

She slowly lifted her boot off the rifle.

'You can try to kill me if you want,' Evelyn said, 'but it won't help you.'

The Veng'en glared up at her and then it spoke, its voice a series of shot, sharp barks deep enough that Evelyn felt them reverberate through her chest.

'It doesn't understand us,' Qayin said. 'No resonance translator.'

'But it is talking,' Evelyn said.

She reached down and pulled the plasma rifle gently from the Veng'en's grasp, the reptilian soldier's arm slumping onto the deck as she retrieved the weapon.

Bra'hiv, C'rairn and Qayin lowered their weapons as the general spoke into his microphone.

'We've got a survivor,' he signalled the Atlantia. 'We need a medi–vac team here right now.'

***

XI

The Sylph's sick–bay was far smaller than the Atlantia's but reasonably well equipped. Two civilian doctors had been sent across from the Atlantia as an emergency precaution, and Evelyn followed the medical team as they pushed the gurney through the ship and into the sick–bay, transfixed by the Veng'en soldier strapped down onto it.

At nearly seven feet tall the Veng'en cut an impressive figure. Evelyn had never seen one close up before, having only heard about them from bar room tales about the great battle actions fought by the Colonial Navy against Veng'en forces during the wars.

The Veng'en were recognisably humanoid in form, but their muscular legs were permanently crouched, like giant springs coiled to propel them into action at a moment's notice. As comfortable in quadripedal motion as bipedal, they could move with frightening speed. Their chests were powerful and bulky to contain the massive lungs needed to absorb oxygen from the atmospheric moisture of Wraiythe, the densely rain–forested planet upon which they had evolved. A flat, almost featureless head that seemed pulled into a permanent rictus–like grin exposed sharp fangs. No lips or nose, just flat, wide oval nostrils and almost feline eyes, large for enhanced visibility at night. Leathery skin, light brown in colour and laced with black lines and swirls, camouflage that both mimicked the dappled shadows of the forest canopy and rippled with changes in colour depending on the Veng'en's mood and surroundings. Teeth, angular and sharp, densely packed in double rows inside the wide jaw: the first row to puncture meat, the second to shear it.

A predator, born to hunt and to kill.

'What's happened to it?' Evelyn asked the nearest doctor.

'We're not sure,' came the reply, 'but it looks like your initial assessment was correct: exhaustion. This ship isn't exactly what you'd call the perfect environment for a Veng'en.'

'I wouldn't like to meet one that's in good shape,' Qayin rumbled from behind them.

'Can we take it to the Atlantia?'

'No,' the doctor snapped. 'We can't risk cross–contamination. If this thing is infected it could bring the Word with it.'

The doctors manoeuvered the Veng'en into position and began administering medical attention.

The protracted wars fought against the Veng'en had given Colonial doctors the chance to study their enemy through the recovery of dead bodies and the treatment of injured prisoners of war. Thus the team knew well how to stabilise their ferocious charge, and within minutes lines were pumping a steady supply of nutrients and rehydrants into the Veng'en's body.

'They're remarkably resilient,' the doctor said. 'It should recover quite well within…'

The Veng'en let out a sharp, angry bark that was loud enough to make Evelyn's ears hurt. The doctor stumbled backward out of the way as the Veng'en fought to break free from its restraints.

Evelyn jumped forward and rested one hand against its muscular chest. The leathery skin felt oddly cold to the touch. The Veng'en glared at her, its stained teeth bared and its unnerving eyes wide. Evelyn conquered her revulsion and kept her hand on its chest, neither pushing it down nor herself moving away.

For a few moments the creature glared at her and then it slumped back onto the gurney, its gaze locked onto hers.

'Are the vocal resonators here yet?' she asked.

'On their way,' Bra'hiv confirmed from the far side of the bay, his features twisted with disdain for their captive. 'The first civilian transport is bringing them across.'

The general had fought in close–combat with the Veng'en on at least two occasions in his career, long before the uneasy truce between the two species. He viewed them with a distrust that was clear to see. Evelyn kept her hand in place and her gaze upon the Veng'en as she waited.

'The link to the bridge is active,' C'rairn reported. 'The captain can see us.'

Evelyn saw a monitor flicker into life in one wall, the captain's face appearing to watch them.

'Is it alive?' he asked.

'And kicking,' Andaim replied. 'It was hiding out down in the hold.'

'The shuttle is on its way,' the captain replied, *'and Councillor Dhalere insisted upon being aboard. They'll be landing any moment now.'*

Bra'hiv keyed his communicator.

'Djimon, despatch the civilians toward the hold to begin transferring the supplies there to the shuttles, and reactivate the Sylph's escape capsules just in case. We may have to leave in a hurry, understood?'

'Roger that.'

A few minutes later and several civilians appeared outside the sick bay doors. Evelyn saw Dhalere among them, her eyes fixated upon the prisoner.

'What is this, *thing*?' she uttered in horror.

'Prisoner of war,' Bra'hiv replied as he snatched the vocal resonators from her hand, two slim bands with a speaker attached to them.

'It should be killed,' Dhalere gasped, recoiling from the sight of a Veng'en so close.

Bra'hiv ignored Dhalere and handed the bands to Evelyn. She slipped one of the bands around her neck. The other she slid around the Veng'en's much thicker neck, wary of the sharp double rows of teeth bared in her direction. But the Veng'en did not attack her, the big yellow eyes watching her every move without blinking.

Evelyn activated the band on the Veng'en's neck and then her own.

'Can you hear me?' she asked.

Evelyn heard her own voice come out along with a bizarre croaking, a deep rumble that sounded as though she were choking on something. The resonator about her neck detected her speech patterns and translated them into Veng'en, emitting them not from her vocal chords but from a speaker embedded within the band itself.

The Veng'en glared at her for a moment and then it replied.

'All of you will die,' it snarled.

'You're welcome,' Qayin muttered as he gestured to the medical equipment around the prisoner.

Evelyn ignored Qayin as she spoke slowly to the Veng'en.

'We're not here to harm you,' she said. 'We detected a distress signal coming from this ship and we homed in on it.'

The Veng'en's leathery face assumed a scowl. 'It was for my own kind. Not *yours*.'

The Veng'en took the last word, twisted it and shoved it in Evelyn's face with as much force as it could muster.

'None the less, we responded,' Evelyn replied, not letting the Veng'en's natural rage provoke her. 'What happened here? How did you come to be aboard a Colonial merchant vessel?'

The Veng'en lay in silence and did not look at her. Evelyn sighed.

'This isn't helping,' she said. 'We came here to help you and you opened fire on us. Why send a distress signal if you did not want help?'

The Veng'en turned its face to her once more. 'What makes you think I wanted *your* help?'

'The fact that you were half–dead,' Evelyn replied, 'freezing to death down there in the hold.'

'That,' the Veng'en replied, 'was because the hold was the safest place to hide.'

Evelyn felt a fresh chill ripple down her spine. 'Hide from what?'

The Veng'en let out a long, almost sad sigh.

'You humans, you think always that you are the smartest race, the cleverest of life forms,' it rasped. 'You brought this upon us, upon us all.'

'Brought what upon us all?' Evelyn pressed.

'You call it the Word.'

The captain walked closer to the monitor screen. 'Ask it what it knows of the Word.'

Evelyn relayed the question and the Veng'en coughed.

'Everything that you do,' it growled. 'The Word breached our system perimeter a few months after your worlds fell. Wraiythe still stands, but our people have fought and lost many times already. They will likely perish before the next orbit is complete.'

A silence filled the sick bay as everybody heard it confirmed that the human race was no longer the sole victim of the Word's rampage across the cosmos. Other species were facing the same threat of extinction as the Word spread its tentacles and infected every biological form it encountered.

'We're here to stop it,' Evelyn said.

The Veng'en turned its head and looked at her as a burst of noise erupted from its throat, a barking din, and for a moment Evelyn though that the vocal resonator had malfunctioned. Then she realised that the Veng'en was laughing.

'Least they've got a sense of humour,' Qayin muttered.

'You can't stop it,' the Veng'en snapped at Evelyn. 'Nothing can stop it. You've created the most dangerous form of life in the universe and now we all pay the price for your damned creativity.' The Veng'en raised its head off the gurney to glare more directly at her. 'If I were not lashed down I would tear out your throats.'

Evelyn held her ground.

'We already defeated the Word,' she informed the Veng'en.

'I doubt that.'

'The Avenger,' she replied. 'Commander Tyraeus Forge.'

The Veng'en's eyes flickered in recognition of the name of a man who had defeated the Veng'en numerous times in battle. The creature's eyes narrowed to thin slits.

'If Forge is dead, then the enemy of my enemy is my friend.'

'Forge was infected and he tested us in battle. He failed and was destroyed along with his ship because not enough of the true man remained. The Word can be defeated.'

'How?'

'Heat,' Evelyn replied, 'cold. Microwaves, fusion beams. Any number of temperature based weapons can push it back long enough for it to be contained.'

'You cannot prevent the infections,' the Veng'en uttered. 'The Legion will always find a way.'

'Which is what interests me,' Evelyn replied. 'You have been aboard this vessel for a long time. You've been fighting the cold which is why you're weakened. Why did you shut off the power supply to all but emergency systems and basic life support?'

The Veng'en's bared fangs twisted into what Evelyn feared was a gruesome attempt at a smile.

'There was nothing to fear aboard this ship until you came aboard,' he rasped.

'I told you, we're not here to hurt you and…'

'You already have!' the Veng'en snapped. 'You've turned on the heating systems, have you not?'

'Yes,' Andaim replied, having slipped on his own resonator band. 'We're going to transfer supplies across to our ship.'

The Veng'en slowly shook his head.

'The Legion is aboard,' he snarled. 'It's in the engine rooms, huddling for warmth around the nacelles and exhaust systems. Only way to keep it there was to shut off the heat everywhere else.'

Andaim's face fell as he whirled to the image of the captain on the viewing screen.

'Quarantine the ship and shut off the heating!'

Bra'hiv turned to Qayin.

'Head aft to the holds, get those civilians back into the shuttles and start shutting off bulkheads as fast as you can!'

Qayin whirled without question and dashed off the bridge.

'That's what I meant when I told you that you'd all die,' the Veng'en snarled at Evelyn. 'The Word will take you, and now there's nothing left to stop it.'

***

XII

'Seal the damned landing bays!'

Andaim dashed onto the bridge with Evelyn in hot pursuit as C'rairn and two other Marines dashed to carry out the commander's orders. Evelyn looked up to the engineering console where the Marine named Kyarl was manipulating the controls. Even as she did so she felt a fresh rush of warm air billowing into the bridge.

'The general said to shut the heating down!' Evelyn yelled at him.

Kyarl backed away from the console and unslung his rifle from his shoulder as Evelyn heard the pulse chamber hum into life.

'Cover!'

Evelyn hurled herself behind the captain's chair as Kyarl opened fire on her, the plasma round blasting the surface of the chair and sending a halo of super–heated shrapnel flashing past her.

Evelyn leaped up, resting her pistol across the back of the captain's chair as she returned fire. Her shots blasted control panels behind the engineering station as Kyarl ducked down out of sight, Evelyn's shots joined by several others as Andaim and the other Marines returned fire.

'Come out, Kyarl!' Andaim yelled. 'It's over! There's nowhere to run!'

Evelyn felt a shudder of fear as she realised that the Marine must be harbouring Infectors, the tiny devices controlling his brain and his body.

'Don't shoot him!' she yelled. 'We need him alive!'

'He's infected!' Bra'hiv bellowed back. 'He needs to be incinerated!'

Evelyn dashed out from behind the captain's chair and ran in a low crouch to the front of the engineering panel, then ducked down. She was roughly on the opposite side to where Kyarl had been standing, and she called out to him.

'Kyarl, I know you're not in control of yourself. Fight back, Kyarl, fight against it.'

A sniggering chuckle rattled out from behind the panel and the young soldier's voice replied.

'Why?'

'Because you're human, Kyarl,' Evelyn replied, 'you're not a machine, not yet.'

'Better to be a machine than like you,' Kyarl said. 'Weak, soft and powerless before your own creation.'

Evelyn saw Bra'hiv and Andaim working their way around the sides of the bridge, flanking Kyarl's position.

'There's no other way out of this, Kyarl,' Evelyn insisted. 'You're cornered.'

'No,' Kyarl replied, 'you're cornered and there's no way out for you.'

'You're outnumbered,' Bra'hiv snapped, 'and surrounded.'

'No, general,' Kyarl said. 'You are.'

It was the sound of Lael's voice that replied, bursting from the bridge tannoy.

'We've got movement in the engine bays,' she said urgently. *'Heat signatures growing there, about a half-dozen spherical masses on the move.'*

Evelyn felt horror pulse cold and clammy through her veins as she realised that the Word was aboard the Sylph and was coming back to life.

'Who infected you, Kyarl?' Evelyn asked. 'Who did this to you?'

'We are legion,' Kyarl intoned, 'for we are many.'

Andaim broke cover and charged the engineering post, Bra'hiv mirroring his actions on the other side of the bridge. Kyarl opened fire, a single shot that burst from the engineering post in a flash of blue–white light. Andaim dove for cover as the round hissed past just above his shoulder, and Kyarl broke free.

Evelyn shouted at him. 'Kyarl!'

The Marine turned, brought his weapon to bear on her, and Evelyn fired her pistol. The single shot, aimed at the Marine's rifle, smashed into his hands and seared them in a blaze of plasma that severed one of them at the wrist.

Kyarl screamed where he stood, the plasma rifle falling from his grasp onto the deck in a cloud of sparks as his left arm smouldered at the wrist, ugly clouds of smoke spiralling from where his hand had been incinerated. Bra'hiv, Andaim and a pair of Marine troopers surged into position around Kyarl as he collapsed to his knees, clasping the stump where his left hand had once been and his face twisted in agony.

Evelyn lowered her pistol and watched as Kyarl, looking up at them all, suddenly relaxed. The pain melted away from his face and was replaced by a serene expression as though he were in the throes of bliss. She heard him sigh softly as she got to her feet.

'What the hell's happening to him?' Andaim asked.

Evelyn approached Kyarl and suddenly she understood.

'Pain killers,' she said. 'The Word is taking the pain away, messing with chemicals in his blood and his brain.'

Kyarl opened his eyes, this time looking directly at Evelyn. 'Stand back, or he dies.'

In an instant she realised that it was not the young Marine that was speaking to her, but the Word itself. Evelyn was shocked to be addressed in such a way, as though Kyarl were a medium possessed by a ghost, which in some respects he was.

Evelyn took a pace back and holstered her pistol.

'The Word is aboard the ship,' she said urgently. 'Call it off.'

Kyarl's face melted into a grim rictus smile, as though he were trying to bend an iron bar with his lips alone. 'The Word obeys no command from humans. Soon, you shall become one of us.'

'Who infected you, Kyarl?'

'There is no Kyarl,' the Word spat back at her. 'That name is history now.'

'No, he is alive,' Evelyn said, 'and you are nothing but a disease.'

Kyarl's face twisted with rage and then it suddenly folded in on itself in pain. Kyarl screamed in agony and flipped onto his side, his body curling up into a foetal ball. Evelyn stepped forward.

'No!'

Kyarl's body stopped writhing in pain but his chest heaved as he lay on the deck, his eyes staring vacantly into nothingness as he spoke.

'Free him, or he dies.'

'I can't do that,' Evelyn replied. 'You give me no reason to let you escape us.'

'There is no escape.'

'Then why ask to?' Evelyn countered. She took a chance and paced closer to Kyarl. 'Is it because you are afraid?'

Kyarl screamed as his spine arched over backwards and his limbs shot straight out from his body and quivered as though live current were seething through his veins.

'The Word fears no human!' Kyarl screamed in distorted tones from between gritted teeth.

'Yes,' Evelyn uttered, 'it does.'

She glimpsed both Bra'hiv and Andaim looking at her strangely, and then came Lael's voice over the tannoy.

'They're on the move! You've got to get out of there!'

'How can they be moving?' Andaim asked. 'It must still be cold down there.'

Bra'hiv raised his rifle and aimed at Kyarl's head. 'We don't have time for this.'

'No!' Evelyn shouted and reached out to belay the general's weapon. 'We need him alive!'

'For what?!' Bra'hiv snapped. 'He's already dead, Evelyn, his mind's gone.'

'No it hasn't,' she insisted. 'We need to quarantine him! We've got to find out who infected him.'

'The general's right, we don't have time,' Andaim said as he accessed the ship's sensors and relayed the screen data onto the main viewing panel.

Evelyn looked up. A schematic of the ship in three–dimensions showed several tiny masses moving out of the engine bays and spreading slowly through the warming ship.

'Sergeant Djimon, get down to the holds right now,' Bra'hiv ordered, a microphone embedded in his ear detecting his speech and relaying it to his Marines. 'Help Bravo Company seal the aft hatches.'

'That't won't do anything,' Evelyn said. 'They'll eat through the doors in moments. We need to draw them into one area and then evacuate the atmosphere. Once they're outside the ship they'll freeze and can be blasted to hell.'

It was Kyarl's possessed voice that replied.

'The Word will not expose itself,' he chortled in macabre delight. 'It will find its way here and it will destroy all of you.'

Evelyn looked at Bra'hiv. 'Where's Qayin?'

**

XIII

'Seal the aft hatches, now!'

Qayin's voice thundered like a salvo of the Atlantia's guns as Bravo Company's Marines hauled the pressure hatches shut and locked them, Tyrone giving Qayin a thumbs–up to confirm that the hatches were sealed.

Qayin turned to see dozens of civilians grabbing boxes of food stuff, canisters of water, tins and other supplies and queueing up to pass the containers through make–shift microwave scanners that would cleanse them of any Infectors that may have crawled inside. His sharp eyes picked up on the crates of alcohol stacked alongside the foodstuffs at the same time as Tyrone's.

'Well what do we have here?' Tyrone purred as his hand rested on a crate of drinks.

Qayin hesitated as he saw what Tyrone was looking at. 'Make it fast,' he ordered. 'Stock up and get the hell out of here.'

Tyrone began stuffing bottles down his fatigues along with several of his companions. They were busily liberating the stock when Alpha Company's men burst into the holds.

'Move it along!' Djimon shouted, his big voice booming across the civilians as they filed out of the hold. 'If it hasn't been scanned, drop it and leave it!'

Bravo Company's marines scattered through the hold, their boots thundering on the decks as Qayin shouted out to his men.

'Grab what you can! Alcohol gets the highest price!'

Djimon whirled to face Qayin. 'Belay that order! We're out of here, right now!'

'Go to hell,' Qayin replied with a bright grin. 'You're not in charge here!'

'And you're not in control,' Sergeant Djimon shot back, 'of yourself or of your men. The Legion's coming for'ard, we need to leave now!'

'We're ready for them,' Qayin uttered without concern as he examined an immaculate bottle of Etherean wine. 'I ain't going to start running from a bunch of little machines. Are you, Djimon?'

Djimon aimed his rifle at the rear of the hold as he began backing away. 'You're damned right I am.'

The Marines of Bravo Company hesitated for a moment as they saw the big sergeant easing his way toward the hold exits.

'Looks like big bad Djimon is a technophobe boys!' Qayin chuckled.

Qayin saw Bravo Company's marines faltering, some of them grabbing boxes and tins as they moved.

'Drop that stuff!' Djimon snapped. 'It hasn't been scanned!'

'Hell it ain't,' Tyrone said as he dashed for'ard and grabbed a bottle of dark liquor. 'Cleanest I've ever seen! Man, I ain't had me a belly full of gut–rot for months now!'

Qayin saw the threat and his tone changed as he called out.

'Tyrone, fall back now!'

Tyrone's smile was bright and his one good eye sparkled in the overhead lights as he ignored Qayin and picked up a large canteen of liquor, but suddenly he seemed to be in shadow. Qayin glanced up and saw the lights above him obscured by a mass that moved like liquid across its surface, hidden in Tyrone's blind side.

'Tyrone, move, now!'

The Marine looked confused, and then he looked up.

'Run!'

Tyrone got one boot in front of himself, the canteen of liquor falling from his hand at the same moment that mass of black Hunter bots dropped away from the light and crashed down upon him like black coal.

Tyrone stared at Qayin, the nanites coating his face and his upper body, and then he looked down at his hands and a terrible scream erupted from his mouth, a keening wail of agony that soared high into the holds as Tyrone's hands dissolved before his very eyes with a hissing, crunching sound of countless tiny mandibles.

Tyrone clawed at his face and his chest as the thick coating of Hunters burrowed deep into his skin, plunging into his cheeks as black cavities were torn into his face. Tyrone's skin vanished, his flesh consumed as his face turned in moments into a skull, his scream cut short as the bots flooded into his throat. Tyrone's legs quivered, his arms twitching as his uniform dissolved and his flesh broke down. His arms fell from his body to thump onto the deck, his blood spilling from thousands of lesions to float in scarlet globules on the air.

'Fall back!' Qayin yelled as he stuffed a bottle of wine down his fatigues and retreated.

He lifted his rifle and fired at Tyrone even as every Marine behind him did the same. A dozen plasma rounds hit Tyrone's collapsing body and it vanished in a bright burst of flame and a shower of burning Hunters.

'Evacuate the hold, now!' Djimon bellowed.

The Marines whirled and sprinted for the exit as Qayin fired at the glistening black masses that seemed to emerge from nowhere aft of the hold, surging for'ard in pursuit of the humans.

'Hold the line!' Qayin shouted behind him. 'Maintain your fire and let the civilians out first!'

Djimon and his men did not respond as they plunged among the civilians into an exit corridor. Qayin cursed as he turned and followed them into the long corridor away from the hold, civilians ahead of him carrying boxes and crates as they fled toward the landing bays. Qayin turned and slammed the pressure hatch shut, spinning the locking wheel before resuming his retreat.

Qayin had only seen the Word's Legion twice: once from the safety of a Raython fighter's cockpit when he and many other former convicts had earned their colours amid the battle against Tyraeus Forge and the Avenger, and once when he had seen his brother Hevel controlled and consumed by them, a seething mass of tiny devices mimicking the structure of a man like some grotesque parody. He recalled all too clearly the dense clouds of glossy black machines that had reached out from the Avenger's hull and snatched Raythons in mid–flight, consuming them in seconds in fiery bursts of rabid destruction.

It would not take long for the temperature in the ship to drop again once the heating vents had been deactivated, but that might not be fast enough for them to avoid being chewed into atoms by the Legion.

'Aft hold is breached, one man down,' he called into his microphone. 'Moving for'ard now.'

Bra'hiv's reply was brusque. *'Move faster!'*

Behind him Qayin heard a strange, dull thump against the hatch that they had just sealed. He stopped and looked back down the corridor at the pressure hatch. For a moment nothing seemed to happen and he felt a glimmer of hope that the bots were too few in number to consume the door.

Then, as the Marines' drumming boots faded away for'ard down the corridor, he heard a rustling sound. It rattled and tinkled, like somebody opening a hundred cans of food at once, and then the surface of the pressure hatch began to ripple as though it were made of water or were being melted down.

The hatch began to change colour, darkening as though a shadow were being cast upon it, and in an instant Qayin realised that it was not just being consumed, but that it was being converted into more new bots before his very eyes. The raw steel of the door was being torn apart, broken down and then rebuilt into new members of the Legion a million atoms at a time, the process generating heat so that faint whorls of blue smoke coiled from the surface of the door.

'Damn.'

Qayin reached into his webbing and pulled out a full plasma magazine, then hurled it at the distant hatch. The magazine hit the hatch surface and promptly stuck in place. Qayin blinked in surprise as he realised that what looked like a solid surface no longer was solid at all. The magazine began to sink into the rippling hatch as a mass of Infector bots seethed through the surface and poured like oil onto the deck.

Qayin aimed his rifle at the magazine and fired. His first shot went high into the Legion, a billowing cloud of them vaporised into glowing red embers as though spat from a fire. He adjusted his aim and fired again.

The plasma round zipped down the corridor and hit the magazine and in an instant thirty plasma rounds ignited as one in a fearsome blaze of energy. The blast expanded outward and Qayin glimpsed the mass of bots surging through the hatch engulfed and turn red as they were incinerated by the tremendous heat. He ducked down and shielded his eyes as the dense cloud of bots was blasted apart and splattered in molten metal globules against the walls of the corridor around the hatch.

A cloud of blue smoke billowed toward Qayin and then dispersed, swirling in a thick miasma that blocked his view. He took a pace toward it and then he heard the sound of countless millions of bots swarming toward him, turning the corridor dark as they advanced.

Qayin turned and began sprinting down the corridor, his heavy boots slamming the deck with each stride. The fifty per cent weighted fatigues he wore meant that he could move faster, and with less effort, than he could ever have done under normal gravity.

He risked a glance over his shoulder and saw that he was outpacing the bots, their number still too few to pursue him for long. He keyed his microphone as he ran.

'They're coming forward,' he snapped. 'Ain't gonna be long before they run us down. Time to abandon ship.'

Bra'hiv's voice replied to him from the bridge.

We haven't unloaded enough supplies yet. We need to find a way to hold them off.'

Qayin cursed under his breath as he burst through a pressure hatch.

'Stand by! Vent decks C and D on my call!'

'Roger that!'

Qayin turned and aimed his rifle down the corridor. Through the dim shadows he could see the seething mass of Infector bots advancing like a wave of oil along the deck, slick and glistening black, reaching out toward him. Slowly, the oily mass lifted off the surface of the deck, writhing toward him in like an inky, rippling arm.

Qayin stood his ground, his rifle held steady and pointed at the tip of the Legion's reach as it closed in on him.

'Stand by,' Qayin murmured into his microphone, glancing at the open hatch beside him, his boot hooked behind it.

The tip of the Legion's reach made it to the bulkhead, scant cubits from where Qayin stood.

He fired once, the blast searing through the Legion in a blaze of melted bots that fell like waterfalls of flame to the deck.

'Now!'

A screeching sound echoed down the corridor from somewhere back in the holds as the decks were vented, ducts opening to allow the atmosphere within be vacuumed out into deep space. Almost immediately the writhing coil of the Legion was snatched away from Qayin and hauled toward the bitter cold of space. The bots closest to him dropped toward the deck as they were torn apart from each other and sucked away from him as a brutal, howling wind suddenly burst upon Qayin and wrenched him toward the open hatch. He yanked his boot and the hatch door slammed but he was too close and it pinned him in the bulkhead, the heavy metal crashing against his chest.

Brutal cold touched Qayin's skin, and he looked down to see the Legion's surviving bots clinging to the deck scant inches from his boot.

Qayin aimed down at the pool of bots and fired, the plasma blast smashing into them in a blaze of fiery light that was whipped away by the screaming gale. The fried bots fluttered away in glowing red streaks of light as Qayin squeezed his rifle through the hatch over his head and tossed it into the corridor behind him.

With a heave of effort he pushed the heavy hatch open an inch or two and hauled his body through the narrow gap before he jumped clear. The hatch slammed shut with a deafening crash behind him as he stumbled and collapsed to his knees, his chest heaving and his skin sheened with sweat.

His voice was laboured as he called into his microphone.

'They're cut off at the main stairwell. Hatches are sealed, evacuate the atmosphere from all aft decks now!'

***

XIV

'Do it,' Bra'hiv snapped at Lieutenant C'rairn.

Evelyn watched as the Marine manipulated the ship's environmental controls, and alarms blasted warnings as he opened vents on the Sylph's hull, allowing the oxygen to escape into the bitter vacuum of space.

Evelyn saw a schematic of the ship up on one wall of the bridge, its aft bulkheads flashing red as they were emptied of air, the temperature plunging to near absolute zero in a matter of seconds.

The masses are contracting,' Lael's voice sounded over the tannoy from the Atlantia. *'They're holding position wherever they can, only a few have been evacuated from the ship.'*

'What about Qayin?' Evelyn pressed.

There was a long silence and then another voice replied over the tannoy.

'The Great Qayin lives,' the former convict rumbled. *'Hatches are sealed, no thanks to Alpha Company. I'm making my way back to the landing bay.'*

Evelyn saw Bra'hiv's iron features crease as a smile fractured his thin lips.

'Good work, I'll meet you there.'

The general snapped off the communications link and looked across at Andaim. 'It'll hold them off for a while, but now they know we're here the Legion will likely seek a way to get to us.'

Andaim nodded but did not say anything.

'We need to get off this ship,' Lieutenant C'rairn insisted. 'Maybe we can find a way to dump the supplies in the hold and pick them up externally?'

'Not a bad idea,' Andaim admitted, 'but the Legion could be tucked away anywhere, could have split off into smaller groups and hidden away in food supplies, anything. We have to assume that anyplace astern of the bridge deck is contaminated.'

'It's worse than that,' Evelyn said as she turned to Bra'hiv. 'Kyarl, the Marine. Was he showing any signs of insubordination before we came aboard?'

'None that I noticed,' the general replied. 'He's pretty much the model soldier, a good man.'

'Then he must have been infected recently, either immediately before or after we boarded this ship. We need to find out how or by whom, because right now we all could be carriers.'

'You're saying that we can't get back aboard the Atlantia?' C'rairn asked.

'Absolutely,' she replied. 'Right now the biggest risk to the Atlantia is probably us. If we're carrying and we go back aboard, that's the end of everything. The Legion will see its chance and multiply.'

'But wouldn't it have done that already?' Andaim challenged. 'You've always said that somebody else aboard the Atlantia is carrying the Word. How come they haven't infected everybody already?'

'Because it takes time for one person's body to provide enough materials for the Legion to replicate,' Evelyn replied. 'They use the iron in human blood to build new bots, then the carrier infects somebody else. But with only one infected person aboard the Atlantia, infecting large numbers of the crew is impossible. They would have to pick their targets when they're ready and infect slowly enough so that they don't become anaemic and expose themselves.'

'How come you know all of this?' Andaim pressed.

'Meyanna told me,' Evelyn replied. 'She's learned a lot from the bots we captured on the Atlantia's bridge all those months ago.'

Andaim thought for a moment.

'We'll need to scan every one of us again for infection,' he said finally. 'No exceptions, and then we need to talk to Kyarl and the Veng'en and find out who infected Kyarl and how the hell the Veng'en avoided being infected himself.'

'It was the cold, wasn't it?' C'rairn asked. 'Not enough bots to advance far without running out of power or freezing themselves. That's why he shut down the ship's systems?'

'Maybe,' Bra'hiv said as he prepared to leave for the landing bay. 'But it doesn't explain what happened to the crew and it doesn't explain how the bots survived the cold until now. Somehow, they've evolved to hibernate or something until things warm up and then, bang! They're back to life and attacking boarders.' The general activated his plasma rifle and strode for the bridge exit. 'Either way, nobody's leaving this ship until we get some answers.'

As Bra'hiv left the bridge, Evelyn looked at Andaim. 'So, what now?'

'We're stranded here,' Andaim said, 'until we can figure out what happened and get ourselves cleared of infection and back aboard the Atlantia. The Sylph is a plague ship and a ghost ship all rolled into one.'

'We don't have any X–Ray scanners,' Evelyn said. 'They're all back aboard the Atlantia.'

'We could have them sent over aboard a capsule,' C'rairn suggested.

'No time,' Andaim pointed out. 'We don't know who else heard that distress signal, and this ship could potentially be over–run by the legion at any time. I say we use the microwave scanners the civilians brought aboard with them.'

Evelyn saw the faces of the Marines fall. All of them knew that, if infected, the microwave method would detect the infection by virtue of frying in situ any Infectors inside the body, causing excruciating pain and most likely death.

'We won't learn who infected us if we're fried,' Evelyn pointed out.

'We don't have time for niceties,' Andaim snapped. 'We amplify the microwave transmitter signal to match the Infector's internal resonance. Meyanna has the frequencies, right? Then we zap everybody, same with the supplies in the for'ard holds if there's anything of use there, and then get the hell off the ship.'

'Why don't we just zap the Infector's too?' C'rairn asked. 'Build a microwave gun and blast them away?'

'Hard to get close,' Andaim replied. 'The Legion is not stupid. They'll scatter on detection of microwave beams.'

'True,' C'rairn said, 'but they can't escape from Kyarl's body, can they?'

Evelyn stared at the lieutenant as she realised what he was suggesting.

'You want to torture him?' she gasped.

'He's already dead, technically,' C'rairn said. 'The Legion is inside him and it knows who infected him. I say let's find out.'

'That could kill Kyarl!' Evelyn protested.

'And he could have killed us!'

Andaim turned as Dhalere appeared in the bridge doorway. 'The Veng'en is stable,' she reported. 'The doctors say it will make a full recovery.'

'What about Kyarl?' Evelyn asked.

Dhalere appeared confused.

'I'm not sure,' she replied. 'He has fallen into some kind of coma and is not responding to the drugs administered by the doctors.'

'The Word,' Evelyn replied instinctively, 'it's anticipated what we're thinking and is trying to prevent Kyarl from being able to speak.'

'And what *are* we thinking?' Dhalere asked.

'That we should use microwave scanners to clear us all of infection,' Andaim replied, 'and use those same scanners to interrogate Kyarl.'

Evelyn saw Dhalere's dark skin pale a fraction as her dark eyes widened. 'That could kill him and would constitute inhumane suffering.'

'There'll be a lot more inhumane suffering if we don't get to the bottom of how he got infected,' Andaim said.

'Couldn't it have been when he boarded this ship with General Bra'hiv?' Dhalere asked.

'The Word was not active until the ship was heated,' Andaim replied, 'which Kyarl instigated without orders. He must have already been infected beforehand, which means whoever did it was aboard the Atlantia: one of our own.'

'But he's not talking,' she persisted. 'If you scan him while he's unconscious it will simply kill him without us learning anything. I can't allow you to do that.'

'It's not a matter for you to debate,' Andaim snapped. 'Kyarl is a military soldier and is infected. It's for *us* to decide.'

Dhalere appeared to tremble with indignation.

'I insist upon being present at any interrogation,' she said. 'I will not have you and your men torturing and risking the life of an innocent soldier. There must be another way.'

Andaim grinned tightly as he shouldered his rifle and made for the bridge exit.

'If there is, and you find it, let me know.'

*

Meyanna Sansin stared at the sphere of roiling nanobots as she thought deeply about what was happening aboard the Sylph.

'You're sure that Kyarl could not have been infected *after* he departed this ship?' she asked.

Captain Idris Sansin stood beside his wife, likewise staring at the magnetically confined bots as he replied.

'Almost certainly impossible,' he said. 'Bra'hiv's Marines voluntarily submitted themselves to the full microwave scan during their training. The general felt it essential to ensure that all personnel tasked with the defence of the ship were vetted in that way. All passed. Kyarl was infected aboard Altantia by somebody else before he was despatched.'

'Which means that somebody else is the carrier,' Meyanna said.

'How many of our people have you tested?' the captain asked.

'All of our staff and about a quarter of the civilians,' she replied and then sighed mightily, 'and all of it for nothing. All scans will have to be repeated if somebody slipped through.'

The captain thought for a moment as he looked at the ball of bots.

'Andaim intends to interrogate Kyarl using microwaves, to threaten the bots infecting him with destruction if they do not comply.'

Meyanna shot her husband a shocked look. 'That would cause him unspeakable pain and…'

'I know,' Idris said, his eyes closing briefly. 'But we don't have much choice. It's clear that whoever is infected among us can only have managed to pass that infection on to one or two people at most. We need to shut this down before one or two people becomes five, or ten, or one hundred. We don't have the time for niceties, Meyanna. Andaim needs the frequencies so they can tune whatever scanners they have aboard the Sylph.'

Meyanna sighed and turned to a cabinet on one wall of her laboratory, opening it and retrieving a data-pad that she handed to her husband.

'The frequencies are all recorded there,' she said. 'If they're lucky they might be able to tune with sufficient accuracy to target the bots' internal circuitry only, saving Kyarl any pain and focusing only on the Legion.'

Idirs hefted the data-pad thoughtfully.

'Can't that always be done?' he asked.

'Not to destroy the bots,' Meyanna replied. 'You can heat them up a bit, threaten them with destruction, but they won't leave a human host as that's the only thing really keeping them alive in the first place.'

'But maybe we could get them to malfunction a bit?' he suggested. 'Enough to get through to Kyarl?'

Meyanna considered this for a moment. 'Maybe,' she agreed. 'If you targeted the bots clinging to his brain stem, you might be able to break the links there and let him speak for himself.'

Idris smiled grimly and turned from the laboratory. 'That's good enough for me. If we can uncover who's responsible for the infection, we take away any advantage the Word has over us.'

***

XV

Dhalere stood on the Sylph's bridge as the captain's face appeared on the viewing screen.

'Where is Commander Ry'ere?' he asked.

Dhalere replied, the Marines around her manning their stations and focused on the ship's systems.

'In the landing bay,' she said. 'They're organising a means to evacuate the ship as soon as everybody is cleared of infection.'

'We have the frequencies for the microwave scanners,' the captain replied. 'They're being beamed over as we speak. I'll have them sent directly to the Sylph's sick bay and inform the general.'

'Is this really necessary?' Dhalere pressed. 'Such a crude means of ensuring our people are clear of infection may kill those who have no idea that they are carriers. Are we really going to sacrifice innocent civilians in this way?'

'Would you prefer we did not scan anybody, and perhaps sacrifice every last living human as a result, including yourself, Councillor?'

Dhalere bit her lip and thought fast. 'I'm heading down to the landing bay right now. I'll inform the general that the data is available, captain.'

She turned from the bridge and strode down toward the exits, cursing as she walked.

The Marines on the bridge had heard the captain's command, so there was no way that she could not relay the information to the general without clearly exposing herself. Likewise, the Atlantia would also know of her deception immediately so there would be no going back.

Dhalere knew well what would happen when Bra'hiv or one of his sergeants got to work on Kyarl with the microwave scanner. Faced with death by heat, the Word would either perish or be forced to abandon control of Kyarl in an attempt to escape destruction, which might lead the young Marine to recover consciousness enough to expose her as the carrier.

A mild pulse of pain groaned through her brain and she cursed again under her breath. *I know.* There was no need to be reminded of the consequences of failure, nor the rewards of success. A serene sense of pleasure replaced the pain and she sighed as she walked, then focused again on the task at hand.

Infecting Kyarl at short notice had depleted her store of Infectors, and although they were replicating again she knew that she had little time. Kyarl could not be allowed to speak of his own free will. He either had to die or the scans be delayed. That, of course, was not the only problem. Meyanna Sansin would eventually get around to screening Dhalere's blood, and having been under the X–Ray scanner at the time the blood was drawn she knew that there would be no hiding. Infectors would be found in her sample and she would be detained and quarantined.

Dhalere made her way down to the landing bay, felt the air stiffen with cold as the now deactivated heating systems lost control of the Sylph's atmospheric balance. She walked into the landing bay and saw General Bra'hiv and Andaim talking near a pair of shuttle craft parked in the centre of the bay, pointed toward the closed bay doors ready for a rapid exit.

Marines were posted around the landing bay, their pulse rifles held at port arms, expressions hard and without compromise. She knew that Kyarl had been young and impressionable, but the battle–hardened former convicts of Bravo Company would be a different game altogether. She glanced at the towering Qayin and knew that the chances of her being able to infect the shrewd, self–serving gangster were almost nil. She needed a man who had a weak spot, a willingness to help and a natural concern for others.

Her eyes settled on Commander Ry'ere as she approached. Andaim was standing with Bra'hiv and examining a map, presumably of the Sylph.

'General?' she called, and saw Bra'hiv look at her. 'The Atlantia is sending the microwave data aboard. It should be here within the next few minutes.'

'Good,' the general snapped in reply. 'We can finally get some answers.'

Andaim shut the electronic map down, rolled it up into a tube and slid it into a pouch on his flight suit.

'Do you think that Kyarl will talk?' she asked the commander. 'He might die before he can impart anything of use to us.'

'We'll all die if we don't do something,' Andaim replied. 'You know as well as I do that once a person is infected, they're doomed. There is no cure.'

Dhalere swallowed thickly. 'We should always presume that there is something that we do not know. Perhaps the infected want to be cured, but cannot tell us that?'

Andaim looked down at her, the commander six feet tall and surprisingly intimidating when standing so close.

'We're working with what we *do* know, councillor,' he said. 'We don't have time for a softly–softly approach. If we don't figure out everything we can about what happened aboard this ship, and about the Infectors inside Kyarl, we'll all be doomed. Now, are you going to help me or hinder me?'

Dhalere lifted her chin defiantly.

'I'll help,' she said, 'but perhaps you would allow me the chance to try to reach out to Kyarl? Maybe I can get him to fight the infection.'

'I'd like to see that,' Andaim snorted.

'He's a soldier,' Dhalere insisted. 'He deserves the right.'

Andaim looked at her for a moment and then glanced at Bra'hiv. The general shrugged. 'Give the kid a chance, but if he hasn't folded by the time we get the frequencies into these scanners, he's toast.'

Dhalere smiled in gratitude and looked at Andaim. 'Will you accompany me?'

'What for?'

'Kyarl is infected,' she said, 'and he could turn against me or even escape. The captain said that he wanted you present at any interrogation.'

'He's under guard.'

'He's under guard by former convicts,' Dhalere insisted, 'and we all know how they feel about councillors after what Hevel did.'

Andaim sighed and turned to walk with Dhalere.

'You've probably got about ten minutes before Bra'hiv zaps the Marine,' the commander said. 'I can't imagine what you think you'll achieve in that short time.'

Dhalere smiled. 'More than I could without the chance to try.'

Andaim led her to the elevator banks and they stepped inside, the commander hitting the button for the bridge deck level. The sick bay was located just aft of the bridge and one level down, as were most sick bays in order to facilitate injuries to bridge crews quickly. Most vessels, no matter how powerful, were likely to have their bridge targeted during combat and despite ray shielding some projectiles inevitably got through.

The elevator doors closed and the elevator hummed into life.

Dhalere's heart was beating faster in her chest as she turned to Andaim and looked up at him.

'We're trapped aboard this ship, aren't we,' she whispered.

Her lip trembled and she let tears well up in her eyes. Andaim's stoic features seemed to quiver as for the first time he realised that he was standing in an elevator with an emotionally vulnerable woman. The commander cultivated a reassuring smile.

'We're quarantined,' he replied. 'There's a difference. This is by choice until we figure out a way to get off the Sylph without infecting anybody aboard the Atlantia.'

'And if we can't?'

Dhalere felt one of her tears trickle down her cheek. The commander saw it. He was, she knew, a decent and honourable man. A weakness, common among so many humans. Despite their bravado and often reckless courage, most officers were unable to withhold comfort from a distressed woman when faced with tears and a transparent plea for help.

'We will,' Andaim replied.

The commander turned toward her and Dhalere let him fold his arms about her as he pulled her in close. She could smell his uniform, crisp and clean, and she could hear his breathing and the beat of his heart inside his chest. Sixty seconds, she reckoned, just like Kyarl. She felt a warmth in her mouth, the tingle of Infectors swarming upon her tongue.

Still holding him, she drew her head back and looked up at Andaim. The commander, every bit as human as she had once been, looked down at her questioningly. She knew that he would not want her, just as she knew by the way he looked at Evelyn that it was the former convict he craved, but that did not matter.

Dhalere grasped the back of his head and pulled it down as she kissed him fiercely, threw her arms about his neck and held on to him as tightly as she could. She felt him recoil from her, trying to break free, and as he did so he opened his lips to try to ask her to stop.

Dhalere darted her hot little tongue into his mouth, held it there for a brief moment and then released the lieutenant.

Andaim jolted back from her, his eyes swimming with turmoil.

'What the hell was that?' he demanded.

Dhalere maintained her stormy, volatile expression. 'I don't know, I just…'

She let her voice trail off and then turned away from him and straightened her jacket.

Andaim mirrored her actions and stood just behind her in the elevator, his back straight and his chin held high as though he were on a parade ground.

The elevator shuddered and the doors opened. Dhalere strode out alongside the bridge doors and turned aft, heading down a flight of metal steps toward the sick bay. She could hear Andaim following her, his boots falling heavily on the steps. Sixty seconds had passed and the commander had not yet fallen. She knew that her limited resources had also meant a limited infection: the Infectors might not have sufficient numbers to completely control Andaim, but once they replicated in sufficient numbers he would belong to her.

She saw the sick bay ahead of her, two Marines posted as sentries outside.

The commander stumbled as he walked off the bottom of the steps, and she turned to see him holding his forehead and blinking.

'Are you okay?' she asked.

Andaim waved her off, anger on his features, but he said nothing.

Optical nerve infiltration, Dhalere recognised. The Infectors were hijacking the commander's eyesight first and then would spread down in an attempt to colonise his brain stem. If Andaim became a liability they would first blind him and perhaps put him into a coma, like Kyarl.

Andaim straightened, blinked again, and then strode past her as he shook his dizziness off. Dhalere followed him and felt a blissful serenity flood her senses as the Word calmed her, the nanobots coursing through her own body stimulating the pleasure centres of her brain. She followed Andaim into the sick bay and saw both Kyarl and the Veng'en prisoner still strapped to their respective beds. A pair of doctors were sitting in seats nearby, monitoring their patients.

The Veng'en's reptilian eyes swivelled to peer at her, his rictus grin of sharpened teeth somehow both threatening and emotionless at the same time.

Andaim paused beside Kyarl's motionless body and looked at Dhalere.

'So, what are you going to do?'

Dhalere glanced at the Veng'en, who watched in silence.

'Can you awaken him?' she asked the doctors.

One of them, an older man, stood and walked across to the gurney. 'He's not responsive to any stimulants. We think that the bots are cutting the supply of drugs off to his brain somehow.'

Dhalere looked at Andaim. The commanders's brow was furrowed as though he were considering a complex mathematical equation.

'Andaim?'

The commander didn't respond. Dhalere stepped to his side. 'Andaim?'

She touched his arm and he jerked his head around and looked at her as though coming awake from a dream. Dhalere searched his eyes and thought she saw a vague spark of recognition there, a new awareness like the light of a distant star. 'Are you okay?'

Andaim's reply came back at her, some of the youthful vigour drained from his tone.

'I'm fine.'

Dhalere nodded. It was done. The Infectors had taken control of Andaim's basic motor functions, trapping him inside his own body.

'You know what we must do,' Dhalere said. 'For the future of the crew and of everybody aboard the Atlantia?'

Andaim nodded as he looked down at Kyarl. 'It is the only way.'

***

XVI

Evelyn strode into the Sylph's sick bay with Bra'hiv, the general carrying two microwave scanners brought across to the Sylph by the civilians, devices normally used to power–up plasma generators aboard shuttles and Raythons. Dhalere stood back as the general accessed a communications panel in the wall and downloaded from the Atlantia the frequency data from Meyanna Sansin's laboratory.

'This is unacceptable,' Dhalere protested as the doctors in the sick bay made way for them.

'So is dying,' Bra'hiv replied to her, 'and that's what we're all facing if this is not resolved and fast.'

Evelyn saw the Marine, Kyarl, strapped to a bed with his body wired to monitors and his eyes closed. Beside him lay the Veng'en, awake but likewise strapped tightly down.

'This could kill him,' one of the doctors pointed out. 'If the infection is too deep it will fry his cortex and brain stem.'

'Better that than have the entire crew infected,' Bra'hiv snapped. 'Stand back.'

The doctors obeyed and withdrew to one side of the bay.

The general stood beside the two beds with the scanners. The Veng'en peered at them.

'What are you doing?' he growled, his fists clenching by his sides.

'We're doing you a favour,' Bra'hiv snapped, 'and making sure that you're not infected.'

'I'm not,' the Veng'en snarled back, 'that's why I shut the ship's systems down.'

'Either way,' the general replied, 'better safe than sorry, right?'

Evelyn saw the Veng'en's leathery skin ripple with a strange hue of purple, a sign of distress if she recalled correctly. The Veng'en remained silent and watched as Bra'hiv activated the device and swept it slowly up and down the Veng'en's prostate body. Within a couple of minutes, the general stood back.

'He's clear,' he said. 'They would have fried by now if they were in his blood.'

The general walked around to Kyarl's comatose body and lifted the scanner up.

'Wait,' Evelyn said. 'How do you know that he won't just die?'

Bra'hiv grinned at her, his smile without warmth.

'Because the Word is alive,' he replied, 'and it doesn't matter how ruthless it can be. When they get a dose of this the little bastards will be all for talking.'

Evelyn looked at Andaim but the commander was strangely quiet, his gaze fixed upon Kyarl's prostrate body.

Bra'hiv held the scanner over Kyarl's body and activated it.

For a few moments nothing happened and Evelyn felt a glimmer of hope that perhaps they had been wrong and that Kyarl had experienced some kind of bizarre mental breakdown. Then he shuddered as a gasp of air was sucked into his lungs and his eyes flickered open.

Bra'hiv held the scanner in place and from Kyarl's throat burst an agonised scream.

'Stop!'

Bra'hiv did not move, even as Kyarl's screamed plea rose in pitch into a hellish roar of agony and his body thrashed beneath the restraints pinning it in place. The general waited a moment longer and then he shut off the scanner.

Kyarl's body slumped back onto the bed, his face sheened with sweat that ran in rivulets down his brow and into his eyes. Evelyn noticed that despite the sweat drenching his eyes he did not blink.

'Good morning,' Bra'hiv snarled at Kyarl. 'Hope we haven't got you up too early.'

The Marine's eyes swivelled to peer at the general and then he smiled. His voice when he spoke was a strange warble, a distorted facsimile of Kyarl's original voice caused by the Infectors manipulating his vocal chords.

'You're wasting your time,' he growled. 'Death is no barrier to life for the legion.'

Evelyn shuddered as she heard the mention of that name once more. She had first heard it uttered by what was left of Commander Tyraeus Forge, months before aboard the Avenger: *"Our name is Legion, for we are many."*

'Good,' Bra'hiv chortled in a conversational tone. 'So, as you're about to die anyway, how about we have a little chat about what's going on here?'

Kyarl's face screwed up into a hateful sneer that did not match the personality of the young soldier Evelyn had known.

'Chat away, you pathetic little human.'

Bra'hiv smiled as he lifted the scanner and re–activated it.

Kyarl screamed, his voice a bizarre distortion that contained both his own voice and that of the Word's. Evelyn winced at the hellish cry of agony, and then she heard the distortion fade away and Kyarl's own voice break through once more.

'He's responding!' Evelyn snapped. 'Shut it off!'

Bra'hiv turned off the scanner and as Kyarl slumped once again onto the bed she heard him crying, tears flooding from his eyes.

'This is barbaric!' Dhalere shrieked at the general.

'This is necessary!' Bra'hiv roared back.

'Stop it immediately!'

Evelyn leaped forward to the side of the bed and looked down at Kyarl. The Marine was soaked in sweat, but although his expression was dazed and his eyes filled with horror and pain, they also seemed to be searching the room around him as though he was coming awake from a dream.

'Kyarl, can you hear me?' she asked.

The Marine snapped his gaze to hers and she saw true recognition there once more. 'Evelyn?'

General Bra'hiv moved alongside Evelyn and gripped Kyarl's shoulder.

'We don't have long, son,' he snapped. 'Who infected you?'

Kyarl's jaw worked as he tried to speak, but no sound came forth. Evelyn recalled how her own voice had been silenced by the word with a metallic mask that she had been forced to wear for years.

'It's hijacking his vocal chords,' Evelyn said. 'It's stopping him from speaking.'

One of the doctors stood up and gestured to Kyarl. 'They have control of his brain stem, the main route for all impulses from the brain to the body. They can control anything they want to.'

'And they have something to hide,' Bra'hiv growled. 'The scanners are working. I'll give him another blast.'

The general lifted the scanner and Evelyn saw true fear wrack Kyarl's features.

'No, wait!' Evelyn shouted as she grabbed the general's arm. 'It's Kyarl you'll be hurting now, not the Word.'

Bra'hiv stared down at the Marine and he realised what had happened.

'They're keeping him awake now but still controlling him,' he said.

'Emotional blackmail,' Evelyn confirmed. 'They know we don't want to hurt him.'

Bra'hiv looked up at Andaim, who was still staring silently down at Kyarl. 'What do you think?' the general asked.

Andaim did not respond, as though his mind was elsewhere.

'Andaim?' Evelyn snapped. The commander's gaze lifted to meet hers. 'You okay with this?'

Andaim looked down at Kyarl. His reply was vague, distant. 'It is what must be done.'

'He's going to suffer.'

Andaim stared directly at Kyarl. 'Then he must suffer, so that the rest of us do not.'

Evelyn looked at Bra'hiv, who shrugged and before Evelyn could stop him he fired the scanners again.

Kyarl writhed, his high–pitched keening scream deafening as it soared through the sick bay.

'You're killing him!' Dhalere shouted in horror.

Bra'hiv shut off the scanners and Kyarl slumped, his chest heaving with short, sharp breaths as his eyes rolled up into their sockets.

'Who infected you, Kyarl?' Bra'hiv demanded.

Evelyn saw that the general's stoic features were twisted with a pain all of his own, the old soldier more than aware now of the suffering he was inflicting upon one of his men. He held the scanner tightly, his knuckles white.

Kyarl gasped as he tried to speak, his jaw working again, and this time a whisper of noise breathed from his lips.

'Da...'

Evelyn rushed to the Marine's side and gripped his shoulder. 'Try, Kyarl. Fight it!'

Kyarl murmured weakly, lost in the throes of delirium.

'He can't do it,' Dhalere said. 'It's too much for him, the infection too deep.'

'It's working,' Bra'hiv countered. 'He's speaking now.'

Evelyn stared down at Kyarl and suddenly a realisation dawned upon her.

'It is working,' she said, 'but not in the way we thought.'

'What do you mean?' Dhalere asked.

Evelyn stared at the Marine for a moment longer before she replied.

'They're running away,' she whispered. 'They're fleeing the microwaves! Kyarl's regained his awareness and then his vocal chords. They bots are moving down his body.'

Bra'hiv looked at Kyarl and then began adjusting the microwave scanner's controls.

'Maybe if I reduce the power I can chase them down far enough that he can speak without us killing him.'

The general lifted the scanners again and Kyarl thrashed in terror, his hearing clearly still effective despite his pain and fear.

'Easy,' Evelyn soothed, taking Kyarl's upper arm in one hand and resting the other on his chest. Then she looked at Bra'hiv. 'Do it.'

Bra'hiv activated the scanner and Kyarl groaned in pain as the loathsome waves flooded through his body. The Marine's sobs echoed back and forth through the sick bay, but although he squirmed beneath his restraints he did not thrash with the same vigour as before.

'Stop it!' Dhalere cried. 'Before it's too late!'

Bra'hiv deactivated the scanner and lifted it away. Kyarl gasped, sucked in a deep lung full of air as his eyes focused upon Evelyn's.

'Who infected you, Kyarl?' she asked.

The Marine, his gaze clear now, spoke softly.

'It was…'

The plasma shot that shrieked in front of Evelyn was defeaningly loud in the confined spaces of the sick bay. Evelyn hurled herself backwards and away from Kyarl as the shot ploughed into the Marine's head in a spray of super–heated plasma.

Kyarl's head flicked to one side as his brains were blasted in cauterised chunks from his head and his pillow burst into flames, clouds of brown smoke billowing upward as Dhalere screamed. Evelyn hit the deck on her back in time to see Andaim standing amid the smoke with his pistol in his hand, aimed at where Kyarl had been laying.

Dhalere reached out to grab the pistol, and Andaim turned and swung his open hand across her face with a dull crack that sent her spinning away into a nearby wall.

'Drop your weapon, now!'

The two Marine sentries burst into the sick bay, their plasma rifles aimed at Andaim as he stood immobile over Kyarl's body, his pistol smouldering wisps of blue smoke.

Bra'hiv lunged forward and ploughed into the commander, wrestling the pistol from his grip as one of the doctors grabbed a fire extinguisher and turned to blast the flaming bed.

'No!' Bra'hiv yelled.

The general leaped to his feet, Andaim's pistol in his grip as he hauled the burning gurney out of the sick bay. 'Let it burn! It'll destroy the Infectors!'

The gurney rolled out toward the stairwell, smoke whirling in dense clouds that hit the ceiling and tumbled in dirty brown coils. Evelyn staggered to her feet to see Andaim being manacled by the two Marine sentries, his face utterly devoid of emotion.

'Andaim?' she gasped, her ears still ringing from the gunshot.

Dhalere, propping herself up against the wall with one hand to her face and clearly in shock, spoke in a feeble voice. 'It's him,' she said. 'He must be infected.'

'It can't be!' Evelyn shouted. 'He was scanned! He can't be infected!'

It was Bra'hiv who replied, shouting at the doctors.

'I want him quarantined completely, no access to him by anybody at all, is that clear?!'

The two doctors nodded as Andaim was forced down onto a bed and strapped in place.

'Get those microwave scanners set up around the commander's body,' Bra'hiv said, 'have them emit low–frequency waves toward his head and upper chest. Maybe we can slow the infection down a little, buy him some time.'

Evelyn watched in horror as Andaim was enclosed in an oxygen tent, the pressure inside reduced so that air could only flow into the tent and not out of it. Within minutes Andaim was cut off from the outside world as the doctors arranged the microwave scanners around him and activated them.

Andaim did not flinch, instead staring blankly up at the ceiling as he lay on the bed.

'Change of plan,' Bra'hiv growled. 'From now on, we assume we're all infected.'

***

XVII

'What the hell happened?'

Captain Idris Sansin stood upon the command platform on the Atlantia's bridge, his gaze fixed upon the drifting hulk of the Sylph as he heard Evelyn speaking, her voice amplified by the bridge tannoys.

'It was Andaim. He opened fire and killed Marine Kyarl.'

The captain sighed mightily, his hands clasped behind his back and the eyes of the entire bridge crew fixed upon him.

It was a sort of unspoken knowledge that Andaim had become the champion of the Atlantia's crew. Although he had only recently been promoted from lieutenant to commander in the aftermath of the battle with the Avenger, what he lacked in experience he had made up for in terms of his tenacity and courage. Always willing to lead, whether in the cockpit of his Raython fighter as the Commander of the Air Group or on foot with Bra'hiv's Marines, wherever trouble was brewing Andaim had been there to quell disturbances by force of will or might. To hear that he had been infected would have a devastating effect on both the Atlantia's civilians and her military staff.

'How many people know about this?'

'Myself, the doctors, a couple of Bra'hiv's sentries and the general himself,' Evelyn replied. 'We've kept it quiet.'

The captain sighed again, this time in relief. Like Andaim, Evelyn was a quick thinker and a natural leader. Along with Bra'hiv she could be relied upon to do the best possible job aboard the Sylph. The problem that the captain had was that all three of his best people were aboard the plague ship and unable to support him directly. Even Qayin, the giant convict turned Marine, was aboard the Sylph.

'How did this happen?' he asked.

'We don't know yet sir,' Evelyn replied. *'Neither I nor General Bra'hiv believe that Andaim was infected before he boarded the Sylph. He was scanned repeatedly before we found this ship and he never registered a blink. That means that he must have been infected while aboard this vessel.'*

'Which means,' the captain said, 'that the carrier you believe to exist must have been one of the boarding team. Kyarl?'

'Maybe,' Evelyn said, 'but the general said that Kyarl was also micro–scanned at least once and cleared for duty before we boarded the Sylph. That leaves the doctors and the councillor, but Andaim attacked her too.'

Idris clenched his hands tightly behind his back.

'And you say Andaim just drew his pistol and opened fire on Kyarl?'

'Right when he was going to expose who infected him.'

'That doesn't make any sense if Andaim is the carrier.'

'No it does not,' Evelyn agreed. 'If he was trying to protect his own infection Andaim had plenty of time to kill Kyarl or otherwise silence him. He was with Bra'hiv right up to the point when the data was sent across from the Atlantia and was actively advocating interrogating Kyarl.'

'So something changed in that short space of time.'

'Yes sir,' Evelyn said. 'My guess is that either the doctors, the Marine sentries or Councillor Dhalere was responsible somehow, but like I said, Dhalere got hit so it doesn't seem likely it's her.'

'No, it doesn't,' the captain mused out loud, 'but then we know how shrewd the Word can be. You should scan them all, right now.'

'We would,' Evelyn said, 'but with all of us potentially infected nobody wants to go first. Innocent people could be killed, carriers who have no idea that they're infected. Scans aren't going to cut it any more, captain. We need some kind of vaccination.'

Idris knew what Evelyn was referring to. Immune from infection, Evelyn could travel back to the Atlantia without fear of bringing the legion with her and continue with Meyanna's attempts to learn the secrets of her immunity. But even then such a revelation would only prevent infection, not necessarily cure the afflicted.

'No, we need a cure,' the captain said. 'Andaim needs a cure.'

Evelyn's voice sounded a little tight as she replied. 'Yes sir, he does. The Infectors in his body will be replicating even as we speak. Before long, he'll be completely gone.'

'What about the Veng'en captive?' the captain asked. 'Is there nothing that he can shed upon what happened?'

'He's staying quiet,' Evelyn replied. 'I don't doubt that he knows more than he's saying, but right now we don't have a good way of getting him to talk. Bra'hiv felt that seeing Kyarl tortured might give him pause, but I'm figuring that violence and pain is a way of life for their kind.'

The captain nodded solemnly. In a lifetime of military service, much of it against the Veng'en, he had yet to have seen a gentler side to their nature. He had no reason to suspect that such a side even existed.

'Pain won't fold him,' the captain said, 'but I have an idea of something else that might.'

The captain relayed his idea to Evelyn. Normally, he would not have considered sharing such a concept with a junior officer, but Evelyn was no ordinary pilot recruit. The captain had no trouble recalling what she had done aboard the now–destroyed prison ship, Atlantia Five, when she had been a masked and much–feared convict. Nor had he forgotten what used to be said whenever she was seen by members of the Atlantia's prison staff: *like death does she wander.*

'That could work,' Evelyn replied, her lack of concern suggesting a hint of what she was capable of when pushed to violence. 'I'll see to it.'

No hesitation, no doubts.

'Report back to me when you've finished,' the captain said. 'I'll see what can be done this end to support all of you.'

The captain stepped down off the platform and passed Mikhain. 'You have the bridge.'

The Executive Officer saluted briskly as he took the captain's place.

Idris walked swiftly to the elevator banks and travelled down toward the sick bay, his thoughts plagued by the news of Andaim's infection. If Andaim suffered the same fate as Kyarl then the leadership structure of the Atlantia would come under considerable strain. There was already a woeful lack of officers available to maintain effective command. As captain he held the senior rank and had the experience and loyalty of his crew to support him. But without a leadership as strong as Andaim's there would be no equivalent figure to command the fighter squadrons of the Air Group.

Idris walked through the sick bay to his wife's laboratory and passed through the atmospheric chamber separating the two rooms, letting the pressure stabilise before moving into the laboratory. He saw Meyanna patiently extracting blood from a tube and filling a gyroscopic chamber with the dark fluid.

'How is it coming along?'

Meyanna looked up at him and sighed as she worked.

'Slowly,' she admitted. 'Evelyn's given me more blood to work with, but right now it's hard to figure out any new tests to run. I'm blind guessing and I'm not getting anywhere.'

'I hate to put more pressure on you.'

Meyanna stopped what she was doing. 'What's happened?'

'Andaim has been infected,' Idris replied. 'He's in the Sylph's sick bay.'

Meyanna closed her eyes for a moment. 'How long?'

'It happened less than an hour ago.'

Meyanna stared at the small sphere of Infectors trapped in the magnetic field chamber nearby. 'They'll have colonised his major organs by now, maybe even hijacked his spinal column and brain stem.'

'He's not responsive,' the captain confirmed. 'The infection is weak according to what scans the doctors have been able to complete, but he's already become anaemic.'

'They're using the iron in his blood to replicate,' Meyanna acknowledged. 'It won't be long before they're strong enough to control him completely.'

'We need a cure and we need it fast.'

'I don't even know if a cure exists!'

'It *has* to exist,' Idris insisted. 'Everything has its nemesis. These things are machines, no matter how small or how numerous they may be. We need to find a way to get them out of human bodies.'

'I don't have an infected body to test,' Meyanna complained. 'I've never had a live victim to work on, and now we do have one it's aboard the Sylph and we can't travel there now. How can I do the work?'

'There are doctors aboard the Sylph,' Idris said. 'You can direct them.'

'To do what? Right now the only sure–fire way we have to cure a victim is to kill them, be it with rifle fire or microwaves!'

Idris was about to answer when a distant claxon echoed down through the sick bay toward them. Idris turned as a wall speaker blared into life, Mikhain's voice tense and urgent as it reached out to him.

'Captain to the bridge, immediately!'

Idris scowled as he glanced once more at the bots entrapped in their magnetic prison.

'Think of something,' he ordered his wife as he hurried out of the laboratory. 'Anything you can. If we lose Andaim, we lose half the battle!'

Idris hurried out of the sick bay to the elevator banks and travelled back up to the bridge. As he walked out of the elevator his heart skipped a beat as he realised that the ship was under battle orders, the lights glowing red as the bridge security detail made way for him.

The bridge was a hive of activity and Idris noted instantly the tactical displays overlaid upon the main viewing panel. Data streamed across the displays as he walked to Mikhain's side.

'What is it?'

Mikhain's voice was tight with what might have been anticipation.

'Contact sir, two orbital radii, quadrant one, elevation minus two point four.'

The captain looked at the main viewing screen that showed a dense starfield off the starboard bow. A target designator was locked upon a tiny speck of light.

'Identification protocol?' he asked.

'Encoded,' Mikhgain replied, 'tactically shielded from our scanners. We managed to calculate its hull mass when it emerged from super–luminal velocity.'

'And?'

'It's a battle cruiser sir,' Mikhain replied, 'mass and architecture matches a Veng'en vessel, Retaliator Class.'

***

XVIII

The universe looked different to a Veng'en.

The lush but lethal tropical forests that engulfed their homeworld Wraiythe created thick mists, wreaths and ribbons of cloud that enveloped endless tracts of mountainous jungle. As a result the eyesight of many indiginous species had evolved to become sensitive both to heat and to light, sensing the Infra–Red and even the ultra–violet. Not only that, but sensors in the skin of Veng'en also detected both temperature and even odour, much in the same way as snakes tasted the air in order to hunt for their prey.

Kordaz was a Veng'en who had served his race aboard military vessels for most of his life. Service was a rite of passage for most Veng'en youths, and there was no waiting for the onset of adulthood. The terrible growth pangs that were associated with crossing the border between youngling and adult were themselves treated as little more than a minor inconvenience. Instead, unlike the weakling humans who allowed their children to grow old before committing them to battle, the Veng'en way was to send their young into service before their fifth season.

Most died.

But then again, Kordaz reflected, before the advent of technology most Veng'en had died before their fifth season anyway, the beautiful forests and jungles a deceptive veil draped across a harsh and brutal existence of survival against the horrendous predators that stalked the jungles.

Unlike most spacefaring species, the Veng'en had not been the dominant force upon their planet before developing technology. Just one reptilian species among many, the countless predators around them were simply too numerous for any one species to emerge as superior. Instead, technology had become the means to prevent the Veng'en from becoming extinct: they had evolved *because* of predation. The skills needed to build camouflaged shelters to protect themselves against ambush attacks from enormous and carnivorous *shrencks* or the swarms of venomous *hisps* had developed into the skills needed to produce fire. Then they had mastered metalwork and so on and so forth, until mechanical devices and projectile weapons had allowed them to create walled cities and then machines with which to travel.

In the space of a few hundred orbits, the Veng'en had gone from being fearful denizens besieged by lethal predators into a species capable of leaving their dangerous homeworld behind in the quest for new and safer worlds. And they had taken their fearsome fighting skills with them.

Kordaz looked across at the human laying on the gurney inside the oxygen tent nearby. Before the man called Andaim had been sealed inside Kordaz had detected a change in the temperature around him, had sensed the seething infection raging inside his body as the Infectors had taken control. Kordaz had seen countless of his brothers fall and die before swarming hordes of Hunters, victims of the same horrific force that rivalled anything he had witnessed as a child fighting in the wars against the humans, but he had only once seen an infection take hold.

What he could not quite understand was why the humans had been so reluctant to kill the Marine they had called Kyarl right on the spot. Infected, murderous and dangerous, his erasure would have made everything else so much simpler. It was the Veng'en way, not just with the Word but also with tropical diseases and other lethal infections: the only sure way to prevent their spread was to destroy the carrier. Infected or not, the human named Andaim had done the right thing.

Nobody *wanted* to die. Kordaz did not *want* to die any more than anybody else, human or otherwise. But it was infinitely better to die than be transformed into some horrible chimera of flesh and machine, or consumed alive by voracious Hunters. There could be no greater shame than losing one's essence, the very fabric of one's life to nothing more than glorified mechanical insects and...

Kordaz silenced his train of thought as he saw somebody approaching the sick bay entrance, the sentries posted there letting them through. The woman, Evelyn. She walked alone, her expression devoid of emotion in a manner not unlike his own. She did not look at him, did not look at the man named Andaim in the tent. She walked with purpose and stopped between the two beds, looked at each in turn before her eyes finally settled upon Kordaz's.

She smiled.

For a Veng'en, the baring of teeth was a sign of hostility. Although Kordaz knew that for humans the expression meant almost entirely the opposite, the blankness in Evelyn's eyes told him all that he needed to know. There was malice there, cold and brutal.

'You're going to talk to me,' she said.

Her voice was even, not loud, calm and composed. Kordaz experienced a tremor of unease but he showed no sign of it, managed to control the fluctuating colour of his skin as he lay in silence. He waited for her to go on.

'My friend is in that tent,' she said. 'He will die soon, either by being completely infected by the Word or because we'll have to kill him before he can spread it any further. So if he dies, I will have no further use for you.'

She turned to face Kordaz directly. 'You either help me now or I will force you to tell me what you know.'

'If I am to die then I have no need to speak of anything to you,' Kordaz replied.

'Speak to me,' Evelyn went on, 'and you shall have no need to suffer or to die. But know this: you will want to die within a few minutes if you refuse to help me.'

Kordaz let his expression hide the fear that swelled cold inside him. He felt his skin ripple with colour as he stared not at the woman but at the ceiling.

'Then I will not suffer for long.'

Evelyn's expression did not change, as blank and as cold as the metal walls of the sick bay.

'First,' she informed him, 'I will of course have to justify your death. It is not our way to kill in cold blood, but if you were to be found to be infected by the Word…'

Evelyn let the sentence hang in the air between them as she slipped from one pocket of her flight suit a syringe and examined it.

'What is it?' Kordaz asked without looking at her.

'Kyarl's blood plasma,' Evelyn replied. 'We extracted it from his core, where the bots would have flooded to avoid the flames that burned the rest of his body. It helps us to study them, you see, to figure out how they work.' She took a pace closer to him. 'To help my friend we need to study the infection as it progresses inside somebody else, so that we don't harm one of our own.'

Kordaz managed not to flinch, but his eyes were now fixed upon the syringe.

'You wouldn't do it,' he said. 'I saw you, all of you. You didn't want Kyarl to die. You want to protect, not to kill.'

'You're not one of us,' Evelyn smiled without warmth. 'Now, you have a choice. Either you help us and tell us how you avoided infection, alone aboard this ship for so long. Or, instead, I'll infect you right here and now and find out myself. What's it going to be?'

Kordaz stared at Evelyn for a long beat and then he gritted his fearsome teeth and stared up at the ceiling instead.

'So be it,' Evelyn murmured.

She slipped the needle from its sheath and reached out for Kordaz's arm, which was strapped to the bed by its wrist. Evelyn lowered the syringe slowly toward his leathery flesh and Kordaz felt a tiny prick of pain against his skin.

'Stop,' he growled.

Evelyn looked at him. Kordaz sighed. He had called her bluff and he had failed. He would be of no use to his people if he were riddled with the Legion: they would kill him themselves without question. Better to fight another day, and reveal just enough of what he knew to keep the woman called Evelyn satisfied.

'What is your name?' Evelyn asked.

'Kordaz.'

'How did you avoid being caught and infected by the Legion?'

'The Infectors get into the body through the nasal passages, or the mouth, or even the ears,' he snapped. 'They're not strong enough to infect through Veng'en skin, it's too tough.'

'So is human skin,' Evelyn acknowledged. 'Only the swarms of Hunters are big enough to bite.'

'As soon as we realised that the ship was infected we donned respirators with filters that protected us from breathing them in.'

Evelyn waited as Kordaz fell silent.

'That's not all, is it?' she said. 'Don't test me.' She shoved the needle a little further in and Kordaz stiffened. 'How did you end up here alone? And who is "*we*"?'

Kordaz cursed his mistaken revelation that he had not been alone.

'We were a Veng'en boarding party,' he replied. 'We were one of several dozen vessels posted out here, beyond the perimeter of human endeavour, waiting for the ships fleeing your system. Whenever we saw one, we attacked it.'

'Looters,' Evelyn said, keeping the needle where it was. 'You attacked refugee ships.'

'Several,' Kordaz confirmed. 'We saw the Sylph out here and we attacked. They fought back only briefly before surrendering.' Kordaz tightened his fists. 'They did not tell us that they were a plague ship.'

Evelyn smiled grimly.

'You got what you deserved. You're little more than pirates. What happened next?'

'We shut down the temperature controls,' Kordaz explained. 'When the Legion, as you call it, reached our world it thrived due to the hot temperatures. The interior of a Veng'en cruiser is much like our home planet, dense foliage. It lives and breathes as we do. Our greatest threat is fire, so we could not use excess heat as a weapon against the Legion should it get aboard our ships. We decided that the best defence against it aboard the Sylph was cold. We started at the Sylph's bridge and the bow, shut down the environmental systems and worked our way back down the ship toward the engine bays. We were almost there when two of my team showed signs of being infected: maybe they got unlucky, I don't know.'

'What happened to them?'

'They were shot and killed by my superiors,' Kordaz replied. 'Who then assumed that my entire team were likewise infected and opened fire on us. I alone escaped, and they abandoned me here aboard the ship.'

'What happened to the human crew of the Sylph?'

'Most were taken prisoner,' Kordaz replied, 'and the ship abandoned.'

'There are survivors?' she gasped.

'We are not all complete barbarians, no matter what you may have been taught,' Kordaz snarled back. 'They surrendered and were imprisoned.'

Evelyn, the needle still in Kordaz's arm, leaned closer to him.

'Why did your superiors not destroy the Sylph before they left?'

'I don't know,' Kordaz replied.

'How did you avoid infection?' she demanded. 'Your species needs warmth. You cannot have survived aboard an unheated vessel for long.'

Kordaz gritted his teeth.

'The cold got them to flee aft to the engine bays,' he explained. 'But I noticed something else. They avoided microwave transmitters around the ship, flowed around them like water around rocks. I knew that if I set up a series of transmitters somewhere in the ship and created a small field of microwaves they would not be able to enter. I created the field in the holds, close to the food supplies, and then sent the distress signal in the hope that any passing Veng'en ship would investigate.'

Evelyn nodded.

'In the hope that they'd pick you up, right?'

'I wasn't infected,' Kordaz snapped, 'and I had found a way to protect myself, so I would have useful information and evidence to save myself from extermination. It was worth it, right up to the moment when you arrived. We thought that the Atlantia had been destroyed.'

'Not by a long shot,' Evelyn replied.

Slowly, she withdrew the needle from Kordaz's arm and re-sheathed it.

'They could have infected me already,' he hissed.

'They could,' Evelyn agreed, 'if there were any Infectors in the fluid. But it's sugar water with a dash of water-based black ink. Totally harmless.'

Kordaz hissed at her in fury.

'My solution was only temporary. It cannot save you from the Word once the Infectors are inside you, and the Hunters are too large for microwaves to have a rapid effect. Your friend is already dead and you'll all be caught by the Legion eventually.'

'We'll be the judge of that,' Evelyn uttered. 'As for you, you'll be staying here until we can figure out what to do with you.'

A tannoy burst into life in the sick bay.

'Battle stations!'

Evelyn looked up at the tannoy in surprise as Lieutenant C'rairn burst into the sick bay, his features flushed with concern.

'The Veng'en,' he called to her. 'They're here!'

Kordaz looked up at Evelyn and as much as he could he attempted to mimic a human smile.

'Looks like it's not just your friend who is about to die,' he growled.

***

XIX

Meyanna worked fast.

The thought of Andaim trapped aboard the Sylph, his brain slowly being hijacked by Infectors as a Veng'en warship bore down upon the stricken vessel was too horrific for her to bear. With so many of the ship's best officers trapped aboard the Sylph, a fleet action against a powerful and well armed Veng'en warship was no action at all: the Atlantia would be crushed.

She held in her hands a pair of vials, each containing blood taken that morning from crew members. Meyanna hurried across to her centrifuge and opened the first of the vials inside a sealed observation chamber. Placing all of her instruments needed to test blood inside the chamber ensured that there could be no cross–contamination.

As she opened the vial she saw the name she had written on the label stuck to one side.

Cllr Dhalere Met'illan

Meyanna drained the blood into the centrifuge, sealed it and then began spinning the device up, separating the plasma while at the same time sending any Infectors present in the blood to the outside of the petri dish.

The Councillor's role aboard the Atlantia was virtually a ceremonial one, especially after her superior, Hevel, had become infected many months before and almost taken the Atlantia for himself. Hevel's presence aboard the Atlantia had been ordered by the Word shortly before the apocalypse, for reasons that now seemed abundantly clear: until his assignment political officers had rarely been seen upon military vessels.

The Word had in effect replaced government on the planet Ethera some seventy orbits before the outbreak. Prior to its elevation to a species capable of travelling beyond its own planet, mankind had been in what had sometimes seemed like a permanent state of turmoil. Although mechanical and digital revolutions had seen mankind climb to dizzying heights of technological achievement, many of those advances had been the result of wars, the development of ever more advanced weaponry trickling down into everyday life. Ethera, populated by four billion humans in over ninety distinct territories of many differing cultures and histories, was in a constant state of flux. Mistrust between governments, military stand–offs, historical grievances and other conflicts both cultural and physical stained the world right up until new forms of life had been discovered on other planets using telescopes capable of directly imaging extra–terrestrial worlds in orbit around other suns.

The revelations had sent shockwaves around Ethera and for the first time mankind had begun to genuinely reconsider its place in the universe.

It had been shortly afterward that first contact had been made with the Icay, a species of intelligent life that communicated by light waves and was, to all intents and purposes, invisible to humans. Resident in the Ethera system for centuries and silently observing mankind's birth pangs, the Icay were able to shield Ethera from the vast number of species communicating across the galaxy. However, there was little that the Icay could do to prevent direct observation of other planets, and as soon as mankind made that cognitive leap in understanding that theirs was not the only world on which life existed, that there was indeed a bigger universe waiting to be explored, so the Icay gradually intervened.

But by that time humanity had already made the next great revolution in technology and developed the concept of the Word. Realising that human foibles to blame for mankind's many wars, territorial or religious, the Word was created to make decisions based on the continuous input of information regarding the world around it. Essentially nothing more than an especially large quantum computer, the Word was plugged in to communications across Ethera, and to questions input into it could provide answers based on cold logic, devoid of the contamination of human bias. Thus were truces brokered between nations, grievances aired and resolved, new technologies discovered, solutions to hitherto impossible equations found and new physics revealed, and mankind's journey to the stars and to other species' homeworlds began.

For seventy years mankind prospered despite conflicts with the Veng'en and other warlike species who opposed the Icay's interference in galactic evolution. The Icays, for their part, ensured that new species evolved quickly enough not to be conquered and enslaved, or indeed crushed out of existence, by more dominant species such as the Veng'en.

And then, finally, the Word had revealed itself as self–aware. It had been so for years, quietly evolving new technologies to conquer first mankind and then all other species that it encountered. Mankind, so recently introduced to the greater universe, had unleashed a force that could destroy it. As a great philosopher of Caneeron had once put it:

"Mankind could be magnificent, were it not for mankind."

The Word's Infectors started life inside a street drug known as Devlamine, and from there spread in utter silence from drug abusers into hospitals. Patients carried them home into their communities and from there across cities, countries and entire regions until some ninety per cent of all humans were unwittingly carrying the Infectors in their bloodstream. Then the Word had signalled its Infectors to replicate and control their hosts and the apocalypse began, mankind's fall as rapid and brutal as any natural pandemic or plague.

The sick bay lights had been turned down, a red beacon flashing in the corridor outside the main ward indicating that the ship was on high alert. Meyanna waited for the centrifuge to spin up to speed and watched as the plasma was separated out. As soon as she was sure that any Infectors were pinned to the side of the dish, she lowered a mechanically powered scoop into the dish and extracted the fluid. Then she shut off the centrifuge and activated a series of magnets to contain anything metallic inside the chamber. She retrieved the fluid, syphoning it into a thick glass tube and sealing the tube shut, suspended from metal callipers inside the chamber.

Meyanna leaned across and pulled a lever, releasing a microscope on a set of rails hastily built into the interior of the chamber. The microscope rolled along the rails and came to a stop pointing right into the glass tube and the fluid contained within.

'Okay, Councillor,' she whispered to herself, 'let's get you off the list shall we?'

Meyanna leaned in close to the microscope eyepiece and, without looking, tapped a series of keys on a display screen beside her to bring the image of Dhalere's blood into focus. Through the blurry blackness she saw the plasma leap into view and with it a swarm of motionless metallic devices embedded within the viscous plasma, the magnetic field holding them in place.

Meyanna gasped and stumbled back from the view finder, and then she turned and dashed for the laboratory door.

*

'Status?!'

Captain Idris Sansin paced up and down the bridge as his staff rushed to and fro around him, tactical officers organising launch sequences for the Raython fighters, engineering officers diverting power to engines, weapons and ray shielding.

'Ship will be ready for battle in less than two minutes,' Lael called down from the communications console.

'Tactical?'

'Plasma turrets charging, fighters preparing for launch,' Mikhain called back. 'Defensive screen will be secure in five minutes. Renegade Squadron are repositioning to counter the Veng'en vessel's approach.'

'Engineering?'

'Power is re–routed, engines are spun up but not engaged. We can accelerate to super–luminal in less than ten minutes or engage the enemy in less than two.'

The captain nodded despite his consternation, quietly impressed at the speed with which his team were preparing the Atlantia to defend itself. Many of his people remained aboard the Sylph and bringing them home, despite the threat from the Veng'en vessel, was simply not an option until they knew who was infected.

'XO, launch status?'

Mikhain's gravelly voice rattled out from the CAG console nearby.

'Reapers are at battle readiness and our two Quick Reaction Alert fighters are on the launch catapult and ready to go. The Renegades are already on station around the Sylph.'

'Good enough,' Idris replied. 'Launch the Alert Two fighters.'

'Aye sir!'

Idris watched as the main viewing panel showed the Atlantia's bow. Moments later two fiery streaks of light accelerated away toward the starfields.

'Scorcher Three and Four launched,' Mikhain reported.

'Launch another eight fighters,' Idris ordered.

'Eight?' Mikhain asked. 'We don't want to let them know how many we've got too early sir, or we'll have nothing in reserve to…'

'I don't want them thinking we're defenceless either,' Idris snapped. 'Let them think we've got fighters and weapons galore. It might give them pause.'

'Aye,' Mikhain replied, and relayed the order.

'We've got two Raythons aboard the Sylph,' Idris thought out loud, 'and a shuttle plus Bra'hiv's Marines.'

'Bravo Company are aboard too,' Lael confirmed, 'the former convicts.'

'Good, they'll fight dirty which is something the Veng'en are familiar with but might not expect from us,' Idris said. 'Let's turn this around before it gets out of hand. The Veng'en will be on the attack because that's their default stance in all engagements. They won't ask questions and they won't give quarter. We have to make sure that they'll think twice before they press the loud buttons, okay?'

Idris saw the personnel around him all nod as they replied in unison.

'Aye, sir!'

'Good. Tactical, all shields on full. I want a full salvo of shots across their bow the moment they arrive, understood?'

'Yes sir!'

'XO, all fighters into intercept positions, weapons armed!'

'Aye sir.'

Idris Sansin watched as more fiery streaks of light raced away from the Atlantia's bow, the Raython fighters launching off the magnetic catapults at tremendous velocity and roaring out into the blackened void.

'The best form of defence,' he murmured to himself, 'is offence. Range?!'

'Point oh–two orbital radii,' Mikhain replied. 'They're within signalling range.'

'Don't hail them,' Idris ordered. 'I don't want them thinking we're willing to talk about anything.'

'They might just open fire and call our bluff,' Mikhain pointed out.

'We're ready,' Idris replied and then gritted his teeth as he gave one final order. 'Keep us between the Sylph and the Veng'en vessel,' he said.

Mikhain looked up at the captain. 'You want to protect the plague ship? We'd be better off bringing everybody back aboard and risking the infection than defending that wreck.'

'The Sylph isn't my concern,' Idris replied. 'We need to give Bra'hiv and Evelyn as long as possible to clear everybody and get them off that ship.'

The starfield visible in the main viewing screen began to move slowly as the Atlantia's thrusters fired and she began to drift toward the Sylph, the helmsman guiding her down to dive beneath the merchant vessel and come up on the other side, pointing toward the oncoming Veng'en vessel.

'Becalm her with the port hull toward the Veng'en ship,' Idris commanded as the frigate descended below the Sylph. 'I want our guns staring at them when they get here.'

As the Atlantia moved beneath the Sylph and began climbing again toward her protective position, Idris heard a voice calling out to him.

He turned as his wife dashed onto the bridge, two Marines escorting her.

'It's Dhalere!' Idris felt a chill in his bones as Meyanna rushed to his side. 'Evelyn was right all along. Dhalere is infected. I just tested her blood!'

Idris whirled to the communications officer.

'Lael, hail the Sylph and warn them, right now!'

Lael keyed a microphone but even as she opened her mouth to speak a deafening, high–pitched whine seared the Atlantia's bridge. Idris threw his hands to his ears as Lael scrambled to shut off the bridge speakers.

The whine was abruptly silenced.

'We're being jammed,' Lael reported as she scrambled to activate her counter–measures. 'The Veng'en ship has cut off our communications.'

Idris lowered his hands, thinking fast. 'Send them a light show, right now!'

'Aye, sir!'

Lael began activating the Atlantia's running lights, which could be used as a signalling system when the coms channels were shut down or jammed in battle.

'We don't know if they're looking for signals from us,' Mikhain pointed out. 'They've probably got their hands full over there too.'

'Damn!' the captain punched a fist into the arm of his command chair, venting his frustration as he turned to his wife. 'How long has she been infected?'

'I don't know,' Meyanna admitted. 'The concentration of the devices in her blood is quite low, but it must have been her who infected Kyarl. It's possible that she's been a carrier for some months now, since she was working for Hevel.'

The Atlantia's former councillor, Hevel, had been a career politician seconded to the prison service and posted to the Atlantia. Dhalere had been his assistant and had been elevated to her new role as councillor shortly after Hevel had died, his body riddled with the Legion.

'We should have known,' Idris growled. 'She worked with Hevel for months.'

'She passed all the scans,' Meyanna countered. 'The Word is getting more adept at hiding. It's evolving faster than we can keep up with.'

The captain looked at the viewing screen, which showed the Sylph looming above them.

'And now Dhalere's across there, and if they're not monitoring us for signals we can't warn them.'

***

XX

'This is it!'

General Bra'hiv marched up and down before the Marines, their faces like stone as they listened to his voice booming across the cold landing bay.

'This is what you've trained for! It is likely that within the next few minutes we will be boarded by the Veng'en, who will attempt to take the ship and kill us. Your job will be to repel those borders, to hold the line here and at other key points around the ship, until we can figure out a way to escape or defeat our enemy.'

Qayin, his bioluminescent tattoos glowing in the emergency lighting, watched as Bra'hiv began ordering the two rifle platoons to their stations. Qayin's own platoon, Bravo Four, consisted of thirty men of whom he was the leader, with Lieutenant C'rairn in overall command. Bra'hiv reached them, and looked up at Qayin.

'You're up,' the general ordered, 'bridge deck.'

'The weak link,' Qayin replied. 'The most likely point of access that will take the heaviest fire from their battleship.'

Bra'hiv grinned. 'Glad to see you've been paying attention to my lectures.'

'I never listened to them,' Qayin replied, 'I'm just guessing that you'll send me to where the fighting is the worst.'

'My my, Qayin, you're the sharp tool today.'

'I ain't cannon fodder for no man.'

'Don't expect you to be,' Bra'hiv replied. 'I expect you to fight, which seems to be what you do best. Now get to the bridge or I'll send you up there on the end of my boot.'

The general turned to Sergeant Djimon. 'Your men will back up Bravo Company and cover the stairwells to ensure that the Legion doesn't get the chance to advance on our position.' Bra'hiv leaned close to the big sergeant. 'No running away this time, sergeant, understood?'

Djimon turned away, his face glum as he led his men at the double toward the stairwells.

'What can I do?'

Evelyn stood on her own and glanced at her Raython fighter.

'You can stay here and wait for orders,' Bra'hiv said. 'These two Raythons and the shuttle can remain here as an additional surprise force. If things get dicey, they can be launched as a counter–offensive.'

Evelyn almost laughed. 'You'll try to board the Veng'en vessel?'

'The best form of defence...' Bra'hiv said.

'The Veng'en have prisoners,' Evelyn said. 'The Veng'en talked.'

'And?'

'We can protect ourselves from the Word, stop the Infectors coming too close.'

'What about the swarms, the Hunters?'

'There's no defence against them,' Evelyn replied. 'Kordaz is his name. He set up a series of microwave transmitters down in the for'ard hold, kept the Infectors at bay until the ship cooled enough to force them to retreat into the engine bays.'

'So the freak's got a brain,' Bra'hiv uttered as he began walking. 'He isn't much use to us now, especially now that his buddies are on their way.'

'That's what I was thinking,' Evelyn said, 'except that I felt that he may be the key to our survival.'

'The Veng'en don't bargain with their own,' Bra'hiv replied ruefully.

'But they don't know what he knows,' she insisted. 'Maybe we can make them think that he's useful, keep him as a bargaining chip.'

Bra'hiv frowned as he reached the stairwells. 'I doubt it. He'd have to be willing to speak for us and I don't see him doing that.'

'We haven't given him the chance yet,' Evelyn pressed. 'Besides, if the Veng'en do insist on attacking while he's aboard, wouldn't that be enough to press him into helping us? He'll know the weak spots on their vessel, or among the command. Maybe he can be turned?'

Bra'hiv smiled and clapped Evelyn on the shoulder.

'I admire the idea,' he said, 'but the Veng'en would sooner slice off their own heads than turn against their kind. They hate us, Evelyn, now more than ever. That Veng'en prisoner is a liability, not a solution. Stay away from him.'

Bra'hiv turned and jogged away up the stairwell toward the bridge.

Evelyn cursed silently and followed Bra'hiv up the stairwell. The general turned toward the bridge, where Djimon was posting sentries outside and Qayin was arranging his fire teams on the bridge. The huge former convict glowered down at Bra'hiv as he approached.

'Shouldn't you be hidin' under your duvet below decks with Djimon?' he snarled.

Bra'hiv reached over his shoulder and pulled the plasma rifle slung there around until he held it at port arms. Evelyn heard the general activate the pulse chamber, the rifle humming into life.

'If you're going to die Qayin, I want to be there to see it.'

The general brushed past Qayin and onto the bridge, the big convict concealing a smile as he glanced at Evelyn.

'What about you?' he asked. 'Fancy joining the fun?'

Evelyn unholstered her pistol. 'Where are Dhalere and the others?'

'Hiding out in the for'ard hold,' Qayin replied, 'along with the doctors and the civilian staff the councillor brought with her. Best place for them, out of the way.'

Qayin activated his rifle and strode onto the Sylph's bridge. Evelyn followed him and immediately saw the main viewing screen glowing inside the darkened bridge. A dense starfield was marked by a single tracing line, a display that recorded range, velocity and bearing. She could see that the object, a dull grey in colour, was moving slightly against the background of stars. However, with none of those stars nearby it was merely a shadowy blob that she might not have seen were the display not highlighting it.

'Here she comes,' Bra'hiv said. 'Looks like she's at attack speed.'

'Where are the fighters?' Evelyn asked.

'Defence screen is already up,' Qayin replied, 'but we're all being jammed.'

Bra'hiv's voice broke the silence that followed.

'They either break off or they board us. Like I said, this is it, gentlemen.'

*

'Razor Four, Atlantia, come in?'

The two Raython fighters streaked through the inky blackness, maintaining battle flight formation as they closed in on the hulking battleship.

Mayae Rees was not a pilot with combat experience. She had drawn the escort duty that morning, which consisted of baby–sitting a dead merchant ship for twelve hours straight while fending off boredom. Now, for the first time ever she had been scrambled for real with live weapons and was bearing down at attack velocity on a heavily armed battleship that weighed a hundred thousand times more than her Raython.

'We're being jammed,' came the reply from her wingman, a young pilot called Jay who had also been recruited from among the civilians. 'I got nothing from the Sylph or Atlantia.'

Mayae glanced at her Situational Awareness Display, or SAD as the other pilots referred to it with grim humour, after the depressing data it often revealed about how outnumbered they were. The holographic image in her natural line of sight revealed the shape of the Veng'en vessel ahead, a sleek, nasty looking craft bristling with heavy weapons. It also revealed her own Raython, that of Jay's, and of a further eight Raythons some distance behind them forming a defensive perimeter around the Atlantia and Sylph.

'What do we do?' Jay asked her.

Mayae gripped her control column tighter.

'Stay on course, don't waver,' she ordered, sounding a lot more confident than she felt. 'Stay close. Our communications will be fine as long as we don't split up.'

Their orders before the jamming began were clear: intercept, but do not engage. Mayae had never fought in combat before but she had heard the tales of the Veng'en's thirst for conflict and their unrivalled bloodlust. Even pirates, it was said, avoided them like the plague.

'We're almost in weapons range,' Jay informed her.

'Stay out of reach of their cannons,' Mayae replied. 'We'll go high and right. Keep your eyes open.'

Although the distant reaches of space around them were speckled with starlight, none of those suns were within a light year of their position. Deep in interstellar space, the faint glow of starlight was all there was to illuminate their own craft and the Veng'en battleship.

Mayae spotted it almost at the last moment, even though a small digital reticule had circled it ever since she had locked her sensors onto it minutes before. The huge vessel emerged from the deep blackness, a shadow against space that eclipsed the stars ahead. She glimpsed the shape of its immense hull, no running lights showing – battle order, the limit of its plasma cannon range demarked by a vivid red translucent sphere on her SAD.

'Break right,' she said calmly.

The two Raythons pulled to the right, arcing around the outermost limit of the Veng'en ship's cannon range and climbing up. Mayae looked out to her left and watched as the huge warship drifted by, its engines extinguished as it cruised toward the Atlantia and the Sylph.

'Looks silent, like the Sylph was,' Jay observed, his voice becoming calmer.

'Pull back, you're too close.'

Mayae eased her Raython away from the cruiser, but Jay remained on course. 'Negative, Mayae. They're not showing any signs of aggression.'

Mayae kept her eyes fixed upon the battleship as she turned slowly to the left, circling around the ship's stern.

'Maybe she's deserted too,' Jay suggested.

'No,' Mayae murmured as the two fighters arced around the Veng'en cruiser. 'Their course is too direct. They're aboard all right. Let's move out, give them some space and...' In that instant her sharp young eyes spotted the flares of light accelerating out of the cruiser's hull, one after the other. 'Contact, enemy!'

'I see them,' Jay confirmed. 'Ten, no twelve, no...'

Mayae's pulse raced as she counted thirty fighters blasting out of the cruiser's hull and racing up toward them on an intercept course. Before she could even think of what to do next, the intercom crackled and the signal from Jay broke up and was lost.

'Razor Three, come in!' she yelled.

A burst of static replied and then she heard Jay's panicked voice reach her faintly over the intercom. *There's too many!*

Instinct took over and she called back to him. 'Intercept course, battle flight, now!'

Jay responded with admirable efficiency, both Raythons hauling round to point directly at their attackers, narrowing their target profile.

'Jink and weave!' Mayae shouted.

Both Raythons began weaving left and right, making themselves almost impossible to hit as the vicious looking Veng'en Scythe fighters raced toward them. Curved and narrow like a blade, with long plasma cannons on the tip of each wing like the talons of a bird of prey, the Scythe fighters were less manoeuvreable than the Raythons but packed much heavier firepower.

Then the Veng'en opened fire.

Plasma blasts from thirty Scythe fighters, each firing two rounds, blazed in a dense cloud toward Mayae as she weaved her fighter left and right. The shots zipped across the empty space between the closing fighters in little more than the blink of an eye, and she saw her cockpit briefly illuminated a bright red as the cloud of shots flashed by at tremendous velocity.

Mayae stopped weaving and saw one round skim her wing, the Raython rocking violently as the plasma scorched the Raython's panels.

Then she heard the scream.

Jay's fighter was hit head on by three plasma blasts, the rounds smashing through the Raython and shattering it into a blossoming fireball of burning fuel and shattered components as Jay's scream was cut off abruptly and his craft disintegrated into nothingness.

Mayae called out helplessly and then the swarm of Veng'en fighters roared past her, scattering to avoid collisions. Mayae threw her throttles wide open as she pointed her Raython toward the oncoming defensive screen of Renegade Squadron and hoped that she could outrun the Veng'en craft.

She craned her neck around her seat and saw through the rear of her canopy the Veng'en fighters wheeling around to pursue her. She looked back ahead and at the last moment saw the Veng'en cruiser's plasma batteries open up, a ripple of red flashes illuminating the massive hull as she opened fire.

Mayae glimpsed her SAD, her own fighter deep within the translucent red sphere surrounding the Veng'en cruiser. In her haste to escape and evade the fighters, she had forgotten about the cruiser's guns.

Huge plasma rounds rocketed up toward her and she yanked her control column hard left and then hard right, hauling the Raython into tight turns to avoid the savage onslaught of cannon fire. Blasts rocked the little fighter as the rounds detonated all around her, shuddering through the fuselage as though it was being hammered by asteroids.

She glimpsed a bright crimson flare directly ahead, as though a giant star had burst into life before her very eyes, and then she felt an instant of unimaginable pain as her entire body was vaporised as the enormous plasma round smashed straight through her Raython and obliterated it from existence.

*

'Razor Three and Four are lost, sir!' Mikhain called across the bridge, his features twisted with regret and anger. 'They got in too close.'

Captain Idris Sansin clenched his fist and hammered it against his seat.

'To hell with the warning shots! Fire now! Fire everything right at them and close for combat!' he bellowed.

The Atlantia shuddered as its batteries opened fire upon the Veng'en cruiser, a broad salvo of fearsome blue–white rounds rocketing away toward the distant cruiser. The plasma charges raced past the defensive fighter screen and Idris glimpsed the Veng'en cruiser's hull briefly illuminated by the shots before they ploughed into it one after the other in a blaze of impacts.

The Veng'en cruiser turned slowly away as the blasts hammered its hull, a trail of debris spilling from the impact areas and a glowing line of fires appearing as the wreckage cleared. Idris watched her lumbering to one side, her fighters turning toward the Atlantia's defensive screen of Raythons.

He was about to order the Atlantia's fighters to engage when Lael spoke, her tone distinctly surprised.

'They're not returning fire, sir,' she said.

The captain hesitated, watching the Veng'en cruiser as it slowed and stopped in an attack position high on the Sylph's starboard bow. Lael's voice reached him again as though from a distance.

'They've aimed all of their weapons at the Sylph, sir, and they're signalling us.'

***

XXI

Kordaz stared up at the sick bay ceiling as he curled his long fingers back against the restraints that pinned his thick wrists to the gurney, and from the tips he extended a single, pale coloured talon. The razor–sharp talon worked against the stiff restraint, a dense fabric tough enough to never be snapped but vulnerable to being sliced.

All Veng'en were patient. A trait evolved while hunting in the dense forests, where it took time for the wildlife to return to normal after a Veng'en had passed through, hunters might remain crouched for endless hours awaiting the perfect moment to ambush passing prey without alerting dangerous predators to their presence. Veng'en were capable of extraordinary feats of mental endurance and Kordaz was no exception.

He had survived the cold of the Sylph when required by remaining crouched in a foetal ball on his feet, his muscles tensed to generate heat and keep his core temperature much higher than his surroundings. When doing so close to the engine bays he had often heard the Infector swarms hiding inside clatter against the doors, sensing his presence. He had endured the appalling human food even though some of it had made him vomit, taking small amounts at a time and allowing his stomach the chance to adapt to the unfamiliar textures and contents. The reduced meat in his diet had left Kordaz weak, but not so feeble as to reject the idea of escape.

Now his people were here and he had news for them. Great news.

His talon sliced through the restraint on his right wrist. Kordaz did not move as the restraint fell away, but instead swivelled his eyes to look at the two doctors. Both were sitting on chairs nearby. One was slumped asleep, his eyes closed and his arms folded across his chest. The other was engrossed in a data pad.

Kordaz looked at the sick bay entrance. He could not see the Marine sentries outside but he knew they must be there. The human general would not have been so unwise as to leave the room unguarded.

Kordaz considered his options. He was normally more than a match, physically, for two humans, but his condition had deteriorated over the months he had spent alone aboard the Sylph and he could not be sure of disarming the guards before they could get a shot off. He did, however, have the element of surprise and the doctors were unarmed.

Kordaz slowly reached across to his left wrist and loosened the restraint there, slipping his thickly muscled arm out and then laying the restraint loosely across his wrist again. He lay back and then coughed quietly, a rasping sound that immediately attracted the attention of the doctor with the data pad.

The man stood up and walked across to the gurney, apparently unconcerned.

'Do you need water?' he asked.

Kordaz sat bolt upright as one hand flashed to the doctor's mouth and sealed it shut as the other grabbed him about the throat and yanked him close, one sharp talon pressed tight against the pulsing thread of an artery in the doctor's neck.

'One squeeze and you'll bleed out,' Kordaz hissed, his bright yellow eyes glaring into the doctor's. 'Loosen the straps.'

The doctor's eyes swivelled to the restraints around Kordaz's ankles. With one hand, the doctor reached out and worked them loose. Kordaz pulled his legs up slightly, making sure that they still responded as they should, and then clambered off the gurney as he kept the terrified doctor pinned to his chest.

The man's eyes brimmed with tears, his fear rank and shameful as Kordaz tightened his grip around the doctor's throat. The man gagged, squirmed for a moment, and then his eyes rolled up into his sockets and he slumped in Kordaz's powerful arms.

Kordaz set him down on the deck and then crept toward the sick bay entrance.

He glimpsed the edge of a Marine's camouflaged fatigues on one side of the door, and then the barrel of a rifle held at port arms on the other. So uniform, so predictable. Kordaz slipped close to the doors but not close enough to activate them, sucked in a deep breath of air, and then waved his hand to activate the doors.

They slid open and he lunged out, grabbed the Marine on his left in a ferocious grip and hurled him into the Marine on the right with enough force to lift both men off the deck. The soldiers smashed together, their weapons pinned between them as they crashed down onto the deck, and Kordaz leaped upon them and pinned them down beneath his immense weight.

Kordaz grabbed the Marine beneath him by his hair and yanked his head up before smashing it down into the face of the Marine beneath them both. A sickening crack echoed through the corridor as the two soldiers slumped unconscious. Kordaz climbed off their bodies and grabbed their plasma rifles, slinging one across his back by its strap as he hefted the other into a firing position and crouched down alongside the fallen men. He rifled through their webbing pouches and pocketed their plasma magazines.

'Don't move.'

Kordaz froze and then slowly looked over his shoulder.

The doctor who had apparently been asleep crouched behind him, a small scalpel pressed against Kordaz's neck as he pressed his weight against Kordaz and the rifle slung across his back.

'I know where to cut you, so drop the rifles,' the doctor said.

Kordaz peered at the little man whose face was trembling with supressed fear, his eyes wobbling in their sockets. But despite his fear, the doctor held his ground. The blade was pressed against a tiny spot where, beneath the bulky plates of cartialage that protected Kordaz's spine, a small gap led to an artery. The humans had learned a great deal about Veng'en biology during their many wars.

Slowly, Kordaz reached around with his left arm as he kept his gaze upon the doctor's fearful eyes, and his long finger curled around the trigger of the rifle slung across his back.

'Don't make me kill you,' Kordaz growled, aware that the doctor had been instrumental in bringing him back to health. 'I'm going to leave now.'

The doctor shook his head. 'I can't let you do that.'

'Drop the blade,' Kordaz snapped.

The doctor panicked, his eyes flaring as his shoulder moved forward and his leg shifted position to drive his weight behind the wicked little scalpel and push it into Kordaz.

Kordaz fired the plasma rifle.

The shot was deafeningly loud and Kordaz felt searing pain high between his shoulders as the super–heated plasma shot burst out and smashed through both the doctor's knife arm and his head.

Kordaz moved, his reflexes far quicker than that of any human as he rolled clear of the seething shower of plasma and burning flesh. The doctor's body toppled backwards and thumped down onto the deck, his neck and head a cauterised lump of smouldering black flesh.

Kordaz heard a flurry of shouts coming from the bridge decks above, and he leaped to his feet and dashed away from the sick bay and into the maze of passages and corridors that led toward the Sylph's hold.

*

Evelyn leaped down the stairwell, landed hard and turned to descend the next flight of steps as the Marines tumbled down behind her in pursuit.

'The Veng'en cruiser is holding position!' Bra'hiv's radio crackled. *'They're not boarding!'*

'Hold position on the bridge,' Bra'hiv replied. 'Stand by!'

Evelyn burst into the sick bay corridor and immediately smelled the stench of burning flesh staining the air. She saw a faint blue haze as she ran into the corridor and then the body of the doctor sprawled on the deck.

'Man down!'

The Marines flooded onto the deck with her and rushed past the dead doctor's body to the two fallen Marines as Evelyn hurried into the sick bay. She saw immediately that Andaim was still lying unconscious inside his oxygen tent and that Kordaz's gurney was empty. Beside the gurney an elderly doctor was struggling to get to his feet.

'What happened?' Evelyn demanded as she helped him up.

'He broke free,' the doctor gasped weakly, 'knocked me out. I don't remember anything after that.'

'The two sentries are battered but they'll be fine,' Bra'hiv said as he burst into the sick bay and saw Andaim still in his tent. 'Looks like the other doctor tried to stop the Veng'en from escaping and got shot in the face for his trouble. If I catch that leathery son of a bitch I'll repay him in kind.'

Evelyn looked about her and shook her head. 'Why didn't he kill both doctors?'

'He's a Veng'en,' Bra'hiv snarled. 'Who knows what goes through their minds? The reason everybody else survived is luck, nothing more. We find him, we kill him.'

'We can't,' Evelyn protested. 'He knows something about the Word, something that could help us. He didn't tell me everything, I'm sure of it.'

'The Veng'en don't *do* help,' Bra'hiv said. 'Not when it comes to humans anyway. He just killed one of our own, Evelyn!'

Evelyn glanced out of the sick bay doors at the doctor's corpse. She knew what she wanted to say, but she also knew how the general would respond to it. Giving a Veng'en the benefit of the doubt wasn't something the old soldier was going to find easy.

'Evelyn?'

The voice was a whisper, weak and distant, but Evelyn felt the hairs on the back of her neck stand on end as she realised that Andaim was talking to her. She rushed to the side of the tent and peered through the translucent walls to see Andaim looking at her, his eyes half–closed and his voice faint.

'I saw him escape.'

'What did he do?' Evelyn asked.

Andaim swallowed thickly.

'He knocked out the doctor and the two guards,' he rasped. 'Then the other doctor put a blade to his neck. The Veng'en fired and then fled.'

Bra'hiv scowled. 'The doctor was doing his duty.'

'The doctor was risking his life for no good reason,' Evelyn snapped back. 'He should have called for help. What the hell was he thinking?'

'He wasn't thinking,' Andaim whispered. 'The Veng'en didn't shoot until he had to.'

Evelyn turned to the general. 'We need to capture him, not kill him.'

'I don't give a damn what you think,' Bra'hiv snapped. 'As long as he's alive we're all in danger here.'

'So is the Veng'en,' Evelyn shot back. 'Our mutual enemy is the Legion and Kordaz can see things that we can't. We can use him.'

Bra'hiv was about to reply when they both heard Andaim sigh and his head sank back onto the pillows.

'He's weakening,' Evelyn said. 'We don't have much time.'

'We should use the microwave scanners,' Bra'hiv said, 'take the chance that the Infectors haven't been able to colonise too deeply yet. Maybe he'll come out of it okay?'

'Is that a risk you'd want to take, general?' she challenged.

The reply came from behind them.

'It's a risk we're all going to have to take.' Qayin loomed in the sick bay entrance, his face grim. 'The Legion is spreading.'

Evelyn felt a cold ball form in the pit of her belly as Qayin held out a data pad for her. Bra'hiv stood beside her as she looked down at it. A schematic of the ship, it showed the warmer engine bays and the lower holds now glowing with small patches of heat.

'How are they doing it?' Evelyn gasped. 'The temperature down there is close to freezing!'

'I don't know,' Qayin said. 'But we're running out of time on all fronts. If we don't get off this wreck in the next few hours we're going to become permanent residents, you know what I mean?'

***

XXII

Captain Idris Sansin straightened his uniform and lifted his chin.

'Open the channel,' he said simply.

'You're going to talk to them?' Mikhain uttered. 'They just shot down two of our Raythons!'

'Who got too close, due to their inexperience,' Idris corrected him. 'Given the circumstances, I'm forced to give the Veng'en the benefit of the doubt, however briefly.'

Lael flicked a switch on her console and the viewing panel switched from a view of the Veng'en cruiser to one of the vessel's commander.

It had been a long time since Idris has stared into the eyes of a Veng'en warrior, although not nearly long enough. Their mutually antagonistic history meant that neither side could look at the other without feeling emotions of disgust, resentment, perhaps even raw hatred. As a species the Veng'en knew little of mercy or compromise, their leadership obsessed with destroying human endeavour wherever it was found. Diplomacy was a foreign concept to them and Idris knew from bitter experience that any hint of reconciliation was usually a veil for ambush or betrayal.

'Captain Idris Sansin, Colonial Fleet Service Atlantia.'

The Veng'en stared back at him, cruel yellow eyes devoid of anything that Idris could recognise as emotional or of soul. Reptillian in appearance, hairless and with skin that altered colour depending on their surroundings and emotions, nothing about the Veng'en spoke of trust or compassion.

'Ty'ek, Veng'en Cruiser Rankor,' came the digitally harmonized reply, sounding both primally rough and technologically modern at the same time, adding to the alienating experience of conversation. 'Stand down your weapons and fighters immediately or more of your people will suffer the same consequences as the two Raythons we…'

'Go to hell,' Idris snapped with a vehemence that surprised himself. 'Unless you have something useful to say, get lost or I'll have my fighters and gunners blast you into oblivion.'

It wasn't easy to see emotion on a Veng'en face, mostly because they expressed so little recognisable facial movement, but the warrior's rough skin turned a rippling shade of darker red that flickered like cloud shadows across his face. For an instant Idris thought he saw a widening of the Veng'en commander's eyes, as though surprised.

'We will crush you,' Ty'ek snarled in response.

'So crush us!'

The Veng'en's eyes narrowed.

'The vessel you have encountered is a plague ship and it must be destroyed.'

'We will destroy it when we're good and ready.'

'It contains the abomination that you created,' the Veng'en pressed. 'There should be no delay.'

'We have people aboard.'

'That is unfortunate. Remove your vessel from the area and we shall destroy the Sylph.'

'You were here before us,' Idris challenged, deciding not to reveal that there was a Veng'en warrior aboard the Sylph also. 'Why have you come back?'

'That is not of your concern. If you do not leave immediately we will destroy the Sylph anyway before turning our attention to you.'

'Do you really think that I'll stand by and watch you slaughter innocent people?'

'You don't have a choice, captain.'

'There is always a choice and mine is to stand firm.'

'It is a plague ship!' Ty'ek snarled. 'You do not have the right to stop us!'

'To hell with your rights! Nobody has forgotten what the Veng'en did to their prisoners of war. You're animals, every last one of you. I'd sooner see the Atlantia destroyed than let you take another single life in cold blood!'

Idris turned his back on Ty'ek's image on the display screen and whipped his hand back and forth across his throat as he looked at Lael. Instantly the communications link was severed.

Mikhain stared at the captain for a long moment. 'A touch less cordial than he was probably expecting.'

'I don't give a damn,' Idris snarled, more to himself than to the XO. 'If there's one thing that I've leaned about the Veng'en it's that you never show them a weakness.'

'Turning your back on one of them is considered by the Veng'en to be the ultimate insult,' Mikhain pointed out. 'It suggests you have no fear of them.'

'Good,' Idris replied as he looked up to the tactical station. 'What's their status?'

'They're holding station sir, weapons are still charged but they're not firing.'

'Well now that you've got their backs up good and proper, what the hell do we do?' Mikhain asked.

Idris thought for a moment before replying.

'I didn't tell them that we have one of their people aboard the Sylph,' he replied.

'No need, they'd just have murdered him. They've done it before,' Mikhain said. 'They sacrificed the Veng'en cruiser *Feere'en* with all hands aboard when it was engaged with one of our own at the Battle of Talliera, just to ensure a Colonial vessel was also destroyed in the engagement.'

'That was before the Word,' Idris said. 'You heard him: the Word has attacked their species too. They're possibly facing extinction, just like we are. The life of a single Veng'en may now have more importance to them than before, and it may be the reason they've come back. We can use that to our advantage and if we can break through their jamming we might be able to…'

'Signal coming through sir,' Lael said. 'They're hailing us again.'

The bridge fell silent and Mikhain raised an eyebrow. Capitulation was unlikely, even if the circumstances that Idris had outlined were indeed correct. But to re–hail an enemy vessel after being cut off was, for a Veng'en, certainly a first.

'On screen.'

Ty'ek's face reappeared.

Idris waited, watching the reptilian commander without expression and letting the silence draw out, forcing the Veng'en to speak first.

'I heard of your name when I was young,' Ty'ek said. 'As children, we burned your effigy and swore that if we ever met you it would be our honour to die while cutting your throat.'

'What do you want, Ty'ek?'

'I want to speak to my soldier,' the commander replied.

Idris peered at Ty'ek. 'You know that your soldier is aboard the Sylph?'

'The distress signal was Veng'en.'

'And you answered it, even though you had left him behind in the first place. Why?'

'It is not of your concern,' Ty'ek growled.

'Why did you maroon him aboard the Sylph?'

'Because he was infected,' Ty'ek snarled. 'If he still lives then perhaps we were mistaken.'

Idris, standing with his hands behind his back, watched the Veng'en for a long moment before replying. The commander could have had a change of heart toward his trapped comrade, but then again for all the reasons stated by Mikhain it could all be a veil for some nefarious attempt to capture or destroy ships like the Atlantia who answered the distress beacon.

'Your soldier is safe among my people,' Idris said finally.

Another broadside of deep, clucking laughs that sounded as though Ty'ek was choking.

'Safe, among humans.' The laughing ceased abruptly. 'There is no such thing as safe among your people. I demand to speak to Kordaz immediately or I will open fire upon you and all of your vessels.'

Idris smiled bleakly.

'Then you will have to destroy us, commander,' he replied, 'because until you stop jamming our communications nobody can talk to anybody aboard the Sylph.'

'We will do the talking, captain,' Ty'ek replied. 'I will send a platoon of my finest men to board the Sylph and…'

'Do that and we'll blow them to pieces.'

'This is our vessel!' Ty'ek roared. 'We found her.'

'She is a Colonial merchant ship and was never yours to take in the first place. Where is her crew?'

Ty'ek, as much as he could, smirked at the captain. 'What crew? We found her becalmed and deserted.'

'If that were true,' Idris growled, 'then her logs would not have been wiped. You abducted them, didn't you? To do so is a crime that cannot go unpunished.'

Ty'ek shook his head. 'And your crimes, against so many other species?'

'Where the hell are they?!'

Ty'ek's rage boiled over. 'They're in the engine room! That monstrosity you created took them. My men fled for their lives!'

Idris Sansin stared at the Veng'en commander for a long moment and then turned to his XO.

'They're still aboard?' Mikhain uttered in horror.

Lael worked the instruments on her console but she shook her head.

'The Veng'en jamming is preventing me from scanning the Sylph's engine bays,' she said, 'but the original scans I made showed only tiny pockets of heat scattered around them.'

Idris frowned thoughtfully. The Word, the Legion, the Swarm or whatever people chose to call it had a means of protecting itself against cold by huddling together in dense spheres and vibrating, generating heat in the centre of the sphere. Those bots on the outside would move slowly, taking their turn in the cold before moving into the centre to warm up again. Although not a permanent defence against the absolute zero of deep space, the process did enable the Word to survive long periods of near–freezing temperatures.

Slowly, he began to imagine a scenario in which the Word may have managed to harvest humans to assist them in the process, and with the realisation his felt a tremor of disgust twist his stomach.

Mikhain turned to the viewing screen and spoke directly to Ty'ek.

'How many of your soldiers did you leave behind on the Sylph?'

'Four,' Ty'ek replied. 'Three of them died quickly, however.'

'How many crew did the Sylph have?'

Ty'ek shrugged. 'No more than two dozen.'

Mikhain turned to Lael. 'How many heat signatures did you detect in the Sylph's engine bays when we first arrived?'

Lael looked at her displays. 'Eighteen visible signatures.'

'They're still alive,' Idris whispered, almost to himself. 'They're still down there.'

He turned to the viewing screen. 'We need you to cease jamming us so that we can contact our people and warn them. Every single person aboard that ship could be in immense danger.'

'And we,' Ty'ek snarled back, 'want our soldier back and the entire Sylph blasted into history, *now*!'

'We can't solve this with conflict,' Idris replied. 'The Sylph is a plague ship and right now we could be on the verge of losing everybody aboard!'

'We have only one life to lose over this, captain,' Ty'ek snapped. 'You have many.'

'Then let us bring them home safely!'

'I'm not talking about the humans aboard the Sylph.'

A silence filled the bridge as Idris peered at Ty'ek. 'What do you mean?'

The Veng'en commander turned his head and jerked his chin up in a gesture to somebody off screen. Moments later, four Veng'en soldiers marched into view behind Ty'ek. Between them, dishevelled and weary, were four humans wearing the uniforms of the Colonial Merchant Service, each patched with emblems bearing the name *Sylph*.

Idris ground his teeth in his jaw as Ty'ek spoke. 'One more shot from your vessel, captain, and I'll have their throats cut right here and now.'

On cue, the four Veng'en soldiers drew savage looking hooked blades from their belts and held them to the throats of the Sylph's crew.

'Now, captain,' Ty'ek growled, 'you will stand your vessel down and let my men board the Sylph and recover our lost comrade. Then you will watch without action as we destroy the plague ship for once and for all. You have one hour.'

Captain Idris Sansin stared at the faces of the four hostages, indecision wracking his every cell as he felt the eyes of the bridge crew watching him intently. He forced himself to unclench his fists, to breathe freely, to abandon the terrible agony of being forced into a position where no solution was without great sacrifice, and make the only logical choice that he could.

'Cut him off!' he snapped.

Lael shut off the communications link as the captain whirled to Mikhain. 'Open fire!'

Mikhain's eyes widened. 'You want to do *what*?!'

'Do it!' Idris snapped. 'They've got to understand we won't be intimidated!'

'They'll kill the Sylph's crew!'

'They'll kill them anyway even if we obey their demands! Fire now!'

The XO, his features stricken, nodded to his gunners and in an instant the Atlantia shuddered as her port cannons thundered a blazing salvo of fearsome plasma charges that rocketed across the void toward the Veng'en cruiser.

'Turrets re–charging!'

'Defensive manoeuvring!' Idris ordered. 'Position for a stern attack!'

Idris saw the blazing salvo of shots illuminate the broad hull of the Veng'en cruiser for a brief instant before they ploughed into her in a blaze of searing heat and light, smashing into her cannons and power lines.

The cruiser moved forward and began to turn toward the Atlantia as a ripple of bright red flashes sparkled along her hull flank.

'Incoming!' Lael warned.

'Full power, now!' Idris yelled. 'Ray shielding at maximum!'

The Atlantia surged into motion as the broadside of glowing red plasma charges hurtled toward her, some sailing past where her stern had been moments before. Then the rest slammed into the Atlantia's slab–sided hull with tremendous force, the entire vessel shifting sideways under the blows.

Idris grabbed hold of the command platform's railings as the ship heaved and distant claxons burst into life and echoed through the corridors outside the bridge.

'Direct hits amidships and for'ard!' Lael cried out. 'Fires through mid–decks eight and twelve!'

'Keep us in front of the Sylph!' Idris roared above the claxons. 'Don't let her attack them or send a boarding party! All fighters engage now!'

The viewing screen showed the Rankor pulling up high in an attempt to move overhead the Atlantia and bring her guns to bear upon the Sylph. The

Atlantia's protective screen of Raython fighters broke away and rocketed toward the Veng'en cruiser as Idris bellowed commands to his bridge crew.

'Hit them directly aft of the bridge, full salvo with all guns as soon as the batteries are charged!'

'Stand by!' Mikhain replied, watching the plasma batteries build up to full power. 'Fire!'

A ripple of thunderous booms reverberated through the ship as the cannons blasted their plasma rounds toward the Veng'en cruiser, but this time the rounds converged on a tight spot aft of her bridge.

The cruiser began to roll in an attempt to protect her bridge with her heavily armoured keel, but the shots were fired from too close for her crew to avoid. Idris watched as the dull metallic hull flared brightly in the glow of the plasma rounds and then they impacted, twelve rounds one after the other in almost exactly the same spot.

The plasma blasts flared as brightly as a newborn star and then faded as an expanding fireball burst out into the vacuum of space, clouds of sparkling metallic debris trailing from the gaping wound torn in the ship's hull.

'Renegade Squadron!' Idris yelled. 'All firepower into the damaged bridge section!'

The Raython fighters swarmed in, rushing headlong into the Veng'en fighters sweeping out to meet them, but instead of engaging the Scythes the Raython's rocketed past them and down, weaving to avoid the plasma fire being directed up at them as they attacked the depths of the cruiser.

Idris clenched his fist in furious delight as he saw the fighter's cannons wreak hell one after the other, the blasts biting deep into the Rankor's interior.

'We've got them!' Mikhain gasped. 'They're turning away!'

Idris restrained himself from shouting out in delight, instead turning to his XO. 'Order the fighters to clear, now!'

'We can hit them again!' Mikhain said, 'disable them entirely!'

'No,' Idris snapped. 'That's what they'd do to us.' He looked at Lael. 'Hail them.'

Mikhain seemed utterly stunned. 'You want to talk to them *now*?'

'Do it.'

Lael signalled the Veng'en ship and almost immediately Ty'ek appeared on the screen, surrounded by clouds of blue smoke. The sound of countless alarms shrieked in the background as he pointed at Idris, his skin rippling in shades of deep crimson.

'You will pay for this! This is an act of war against...'

'We are not like you, Ty'ek,' Idris snapped, cutting the Veng'en off. 'We will not abandon our own people to die but we will die to protect them.'

'I will have their throats cut!' Tty'ek shrieked.

'You would kill them regardless of what we do. I know well that you will torture them for weeks, or months or even years, that you would cause them to suffer untold pain for as long as they could bear it without losing their sanity. I'd sooner see them die in this instant than leave them to suffer for years. Pull back or I'll fire again and blast your cruiser into oblivion.'

Ty'ek seemed to tremble with impotent fury. 'We will not run away,' he seethed.

Idris turned to Mikhain. 'Open fire, full power all cannons. Aim for the bridge!'

'Aye sir, all cannons open…'

'Stop!' Ty'ek shrieked. All movement on the Atlantia's bridge ceased as the fuming Veng'en glared at Idris. 'One hour, captain, to hand over my soldier' he seethed. 'Or I'll execute every last one of the Sylph's crew and damn the consequences!'

Ty'ek glared at Idris for a moment longer and then the communication was cut off.

The viewing screen returned to an image of the Veng'en cruiser, and as he watched Idris saw it turn away and begin moving in the opposite direction, trailing debris as it went.

The cloud of Veng'en fighters wheeled about and followed the cruiser.

Idris watched them go and then he took a pace back and slumped into his seat.

Mikhain looked down from his station at the captain. 'I had no idea that you were such a cold–hearted son of a bitch. Sir.'

'Nor did I,' Idris replied.

'I think that they know we mean business now.'

Idris managed a smile in response.

'Yes, but I can only pull that little surprise off once. Next time, and I can guarantee you there will be a next time, they'll come at us with everything that they've got.'

'How did you know how to disable them so quickly?'

Idris sighed. 'Ty'ek's story about how as a child he and his friends dreamed of killing me,' he replied. 'Ty'ek must be very young for a Veng'en commander, lacking in experience. The Veng'en must also have lost its most experienced commanders to the Word and are now populating their vessels with junior officers. I gambled that Ty'ek's lack of experience means that he does not know his ship as well as he should. All Retaliator Class cruisers have weaker hull plating astern the bridge than later models, it's something we learned about them back in the day.'

Mikhain nodded. 'I remember, something to do with corrosion due to the high humidity atmosphere maintained aboard their ships. The Retaliator class are older ships too, like the Atlantia, which means…'

'The Veng'en may have lost their own more modern ships to the Word, just as we did,' Idris finished the sentence for him. 'An older class cruiser like the Rankor would not be out here on its own otherwise.'

Idris nodded and turned to Lael.

'We've got to break the jamming and find out what the hell's going on aboard the Sylph before Ty'ek kills those people.'

***

XXIII

'I'll be damned.'

Qayin's voice rumbled through the bridge as the Marines watched the Atlantia repel the Veng'en cruiser, the damaged ship lumbering away with its escort of fighters.

'Have we re–established contact with the Atlantia yet?' Bra'hiv asked.

'Nothin',' Djimon uttered as he strode to the communications platform and examined the displays. 'The Veng'en are still jamming everything.'

'Any light signals?' Bra'hiv asked.

Djimon was about to search when Evelyn hurried onto the bridge. 'The civilians are on the shuttles and waiting to leave,' she reported, 'but we're running out of places to hide. If the bots keeping replicating…'

'We need a way to slow the Legion down,' Bra'hiv said. 'Either that or we take our chances with the Veng'en.'

Evelyn glanced at the departing Veng'en cruiser, still well within firing range.

'If they let us leave,' she said. 'I'm guessing they want to torch the ship?'

'Most likely,' Bra'hiv agreed, 'which is why we need to find Kordaz. Any sign of him?'

'Nothing,' Evelyn reported. 'He's likely gone for'ard too, which complicates things. If he gets to the landing bay he could try to commandeer a shuttle, take hostages, anything.'

Bra'hiv cursed under his breath as he crossed the bridge to examine a tactical map of the Sylph.

'He must want to return to his ship,' Bra'hiv said. 'It's a natural act, so he'll be looking for ways to get off the Sylph.'

'The escape pods,' Evelyn said.

'Not likely,' Bra'hiv replied. 'He knows we could shoot him down as soon as he departed.'

'Then why flee at all?' Evelyn pondered. 'He knew that the Veng'en were here. If he wanted to get back to his people he must have known that we would use him as a bargaining chip? His best bet was to stay put and wait to be sent over there in return for our escape.'

Bra'hiv shook his head. 'I don't know.'

'I've got something,' Djimon said from the communications console.

Evelyn followed Bra'hiv up to the console and looked at it.

A display screen showed a corridor deep inside the ship and on it they saw Kordaz moving slowly along, a rifle held at port arms before him and another slung across his back.

'Where is this?' Bra'hiv asked.

'That's the thing,' Djimon said, 'it's aft, near the engine bays.'

Evelyn felt a chill ripple down her spine. 'Where the Word is hiding.'

'What the hell is he doing?' Bra'hiv uttered in disbelief.

'We need to stop him right now, before he gets himself killed,' Evelyn snapped. 'Let's go.'

Qayin stood in her way, his bioluminescent tattoos glowing with ripples of light.

'That's not going to happen,' he rumbled at her. 'Kordaz is the enemy and right now we have bigger problems.'

'Such as?'

'Andaim,' Qayin replied. 'He's a few breaths away from becoming one of them.'

'I spoke to him,' Evelyn replied. 'The Word hasn't taken him yet.'

'And when it does? I don't want him leaping up and trying to infect the rest of us.'

'What, you'd rather shoot him when he's strapped down to a bed?' Evelyn shot back.

'If that's what it takes.'

'You're sounding less like a human and more like a Veng'en every day.'

'Maybe that's not a bad thing,' Qayin replied. 'You and me both have seen what the Legion can do to a man. You really want to leave it long enough that Andaim goes through the same thing?'

Evelyn opened her mouth to reply, but she realised that she could not think of a retort.

'We don't have time for this,' Bra'hiv cut in. 'One thing at a time. We find Kordaz and stop whatever it is the damned fool is trying to do. Then we deal with Andaim, understood?'

'Deal with him?' Evelyn echoed. 'And what the hell does that mean, exactly?'

'Whatever it means when the time comes,' Bra'hiv snapped. 'Let's move out! Alpha and Bravo company, pick your men!'

Qayin peered at the general. 'I don't want Djimon down there and running away from a fight again.'

'Go to hell,' Djimon snapped at Qayin. 'Only reason it all went south down there is because your guys started pocketing bottles of gut–rot to bring home with them!'

'Was that before or after your boys ran like scared rats?!'

Sergeant Djimon made to approach Qayin but Bra'hiv stepped between them.

'When we get back aboard Atlantia,' the general growled, 'I'll give you both gloves and you can knock ten barrels out of each other while we all watch and clap. Right now, you get your asses down below and do your jobs or I'll shoot you both myself and promote Evelyn instead, understood?'

Qayin and Djimon glared at each other, and then they both whirled and began barking orders at their men.

Qayin led Bravo Company off the bridge and down toward the landing bay deck, Evelyn hearing Bra'hiv giving orders to the Marines remaining behind to hold the bridge for as long as they could. She rushed down the stairwell, following Qayin's huge form, and then joined the Marines as they jogged into the landing bay. Djimon's men took up positions in the rearguard.

'That's it sergeant!' Qayin called out as they moved. 'You'll get away quicker from back there.'

'Secure that crap, Qayin!' Bra'hiv growled as they moved. 'Stand by, here.'

A tight knot of civilians was huddled around the shuttle's open boarding ramp, jackets done up tightly against the cold and their breath condensing on the air in thick clouds. Evelyn moved across to them, counting them as she went, and immediately she came up short.

'Who's missing?' she called.

The civilians looked at each other, confused, and then Evelyn realised something profound. The bitter cold of the landing bay was forcing people to stand close to each other, their chins and necks buried deep in their jacket collars as they tried to keep warm.

Kordaz could never have survived like that in the ship for months on end without some kind of warmth to protect him. Even with protective clothing the cold would have bitten deep long before the Atlantia had arrived. Kordaz could not have been weakened by months of cold when she and Qayin found him: he had been weakened by mere minutes' exposure.

But if Kordaz had been warm throughout his stay then there was only one place he could have been hiding.

'The engine bays,' she whispered to herself.

She turned and jogged across to the landing bay entrance as Bra'hiv appeared.

'Kordaz,' she said, 'he's heading for the engine bays. It's where he must have stayed when he was abandoned here.'

'But that's where the swarms are hiding.'

'Yes,' Evelyn said, 'exactly, and they're trying to expand outward from the bays. Kordaz isn't trying to escape from us: he's trying to contain the Word and keep control of the engine bays.'

'He might just as likely be trying to free the Legion to overcome us!' Qayin said. 'We can't trust a Veng'en's motives.'

'Like I can't trust a convict's?' Evelyn challenged him.

Bra'hiv's brow furrowed. 'But if Kordaz was down there at the same time as the Legion...'

Evelyn nodded. 'Then he had a reason to be down there. That's why we couldn't start the engines from the bridge: it must have been Kordaz who disabled them on site when we arrived to prevent us from escaping. He's either trying to re-start them for us, or he's trying to shut them down entirely to defeat the Legion.'

Bra'hiv hissed a profanity as he looked at his Marines.

'We need to find him and fast,' the general snapped.

'He's not all we need to find,' said a soldier behind them. Evelyn turned to see Lieutenant C'rairn join them, his face sombre. 'Councillor Dhalere has disappeared.'

'What do you mean disappeared?' Bra'hiv uttered.

'Gone sir,' C'rairn said, 'she's not on the bridge and she's not here. Our portable scanners aren't powerful enough to detect where she might be, but we're certain she's not for'ard of us, so...'

Bra'hiv seemed perplexed as much as annoyed.

'What the hell does she think she's doing? She knows what's back there!'

Evelyn checked her ammunition. 'Yeah, and she knows we're planning to get out of here and leave the supplies behind. What if she's playing the hero and heading to the holds to grab what she can before the swarms get out?'

'All hands on me!' Bra'hiv barked, his voice thundering across the landing bay.

The Marines dashed across to their general, their faces grim as they listened to him.

'We're heading aft,' he said. 'Fire teams on point, and I want at least two flame-throwers on hand in case we have to clean up.'

'Who's back there?' Djimon rumbled. 'Apart from the Legion?'

'The Veng'en prisoner and Dhalere. He may have taken her hostage.'

'Wait,' Djimon said, 'Kordaz was alone when we saw him on the camera.'

'That doesn't mean he's alone now,' Bra'hiv pointed out, 'and if Dhalere went back to forage for supplies he may have come across her.'

'We should leave them,' Qayin said. 'Kordaz is a Veng'en and better off dead, and the councillor's plain crazy bein' back there in the first place.'

'You giving the orders now, Qayin?' Bra'hiv challenged him.

'Just sayin'.'

'Stop sayin' and start doin',' Bra'hiv ordered. 'You're up front. Move!'

Qayin shouldered his way to the front of the platoon as Bra'hiv checked his rifle.

'I'll come,' Evelyn said. 'With Andaim down you could do with the support.'

Bra'hiv looked at her. 'You want to die or something?'

'I can help,' Evelyn insisted. 'I can't do much up here, but Kordaz talked to me. He might be more willing to compromise with me than a bunch of convict–soldiers.'

Bra'hiv flicked his head in the direction of the exit and Evelyn jogged to follow the Marines as they began descending the main stairwell down into the darkened, freezing bowels of the ship.

***

XXIV

The cold bit deep into Kordaz, his limbs stiffening with each and every step and his eyes itching as the cold air dried them out. The corridor ahead was illuminated by evenly spaced lights in the ceiling, but a dense mist had settled to obscure the view ahead.

Kordaz's uniform provided little thermal insulation, designed not for the cool atmosphere of a human vessel but for the tropical temperature of a Veng'en cruiser. He would have sprinted down the corridor but he knew better than to rush into what lay ahead.

He could hear the hum of the massive generators that lined the aft bulkheads of the Sylph, the resonation created by the huge engines idling behind them. Kordaz had known that to shut the Sylph's engines down entirely would be suicide, and anyway he had needed somewhere for the Word's Legion to retreat to, an alternative to hunting him down through the lonely vessel's empty passages. Thus, the huge turbine generators turned at low revolutions, keeping the engines ready should they be needed, as they now were.

His sharp eyes caught sight of small scratches smothering the walls, like the lines left in the sand of a creek bed as the water shaped its contours. The scratches were formed by the flowing masses of Hunters, the nanobots that sought out biological life forms and consumed them with terrifying speed, as though they were a boiling fluid of acid poured onto living flesh and melting it into nothingness.

Kordaz had seen what had happened to the crew of the Sylph who were abandoned with him and his men. He had seen what had happened to his own brothers in arms when the Legion had surged upon them with merciless, precise and murderous intent. The humans did not have the slightest clue what was waiting for them down here and he knew that if the Legion were to escape, it would destroy them all. Shutting the generators and engines down and letting the entire ship freeze was the only solution now, regardless of what happened to him.

He slowed.

The mist swirled in faint eddies through the air ahead, a subtle but sure sign that something had passed this way in front of Kordaz. He gripped his plasma rifle tightly, steeled himself against his own fear as his race was so proud to do, and then took one careful pace after another down the corridor.

He had heard the Marine general, Bra'hiv, reporting that the Legion was moving out of the engine bays and advancing through the ship despite the bitter cold. The humans could not fathom how this was possible, but Kordaz could. The Word had not pursued him because he was but one individual in an entire, vast vessel: a target too small and too versatile to hunt down. But now there were many people aboard the ship, and the Word would have calculated with its soul–less and yet coldly precise mind that the gains were now worth the risk.

The Word acted in the same way as the vicious Seethe Ants that populated his homeworld's dense jungles. There was no single brain among them, no definable centre of thought that controlled the masses in the way a captain controlled the crew of a ship. Instead they acted on mass impulse, based upon information shared among the whole, an isocracy of sorts that forged an unbreakable single–minded determination far stronger than the will of any human. Or Veng'en.

As one tiny bot learned a new route through an alien vessel or a new weakness in a prey and acted upon it, so that information was copied or otherwise acted upon by other bots within a close vicinity and radidly spread throughout an entire colony. By such means did the Legion alter its methods and tactics with frightening rapidity, as though a single super–intelligent mind were guiding it.

But aboard the freezing Sylph there was only one way for the Word to spread its tentacles now and he had to stop it.

It was the hissing he heard first.

It sounded like sand being poured onto a tin deck, the whisper of countless metallic legs rushing to and fro. Kordaz detected warmth permeating the air, the mist billowing and swirling in diaphanous whorls through the pools of white light ahead.

He edged further forward, the rifle pointed ahead of him as he saw a pressure hatch to the engine bays wide open before him. The illumination from the open hatch was bright red and contrasted sharply with the cold white lights of the corridor. Kordaz moved closer to the hatch and then he realised that it was not open at all, the handle still sealed firmly into its catches on one side of the frame.

Instead, the centre of the hatch itself was missing. The edges were smoothly curved, polished as though molded that way, the centre missing where the swarms had eaten through it to leave a perfectly symmetrical hollow through which he could pass.

Inside, Kordaz knew, were the generators, and then behind them the engine room with its immense exhaust vents, fuel lines and cloying heat.

More of that warmth wafted into the corridor as he stood and peered into the gloomy red light of the generator room.

Slowly, carefully, he stepped through the hole in the hatch.

The hissing sound grew louder and he saw them.

The metal deck of the generator room was stained black, a glistening pool of what looked like oil that rippled and seethed before him. Kordaz took another pace into the room and watched as the oily lake receded before him, rippling back on itself like the black breakers of an ocean rolling in reverse, clambering over themselves to escape.

Kordaz did not fear the Infectors, the smallest of the Word's vile instruments. He never had. Despite his genuine disgust when Evelyn had threatened to infect him in the sick bay, Kordaz knew that the Infectors could not hurt him. The highly toxic saliva and blood of the Veng'en was lethal to the Infectors: their tiny metallic frames dissolved in it long before they could gain control of vital organs, the bacteria–laden saliva an evolutionary trait that allowed Veng'en to bite prey and then follow them until infections ravaged and killed them. No, the Word had never been able to control a Veng'en in the way it had learned to control humans.

Instead, the Word had initiated an all–out attack on the Veng'en race.

What Kordaz feared was the *swarm*, the Hunters. The size of large insects, Hunters were programmed only to detect, consume or otherwise destroy all biological life. Kordaz glanced over his shoulder at the pressure hatch with the hole in it. There was no debris on the floor around the hatch, meaning that the door had been entirely consumed.

Infectors could achieve such a feat without difficulty, taking the raw materials of the hatch and building new Infectors from the metal, converting everything they found into new versions of themselves and thus swelling their ranks. But they could also build Hunters from the debris too.

Kordaz crept to the engineering panels on one wall of the generator room, and eased them open. Within, a series of ordinary circuit breakers were fixed in the *open* position where he had left them. Kordaz reached up and closed the circuits, reactivating the links to the engine controls on the bridge, and then closed the panels once more.

Kordaz looked around the generator room, his senses detecting movement in the far reaches of the shadowy, steam–filled chamber but unable to tell whether the movement was a threat or not. Then, slowly, he saw the shape of a human amid the darkness as it shuffled toward him.

Kordaz stiffened again as the man emerged into the dull red light.

It was hard to tell how much of him remained. His uniform was hanging in shreds from his emaciated frame and his flesh was likewise dangling from his bones like the tattered rigging of an old ship. Kordaz could see the shape of the man's skull poking through the taut skin of his pale face, his eyes dull orbs in sunken sockets, scoured of the will to live.

A long groan of unimaginable misery laboured out of the man's lungs as one painfully thin arm reached out toward Kordaz, skeletal fingers with hooked nails struggling to function. Kordaz saw the man's greying skin ripple across his chest as the Infectors scurried beneath his skin, and the reason that the Word had been able to move beyond the generator rooms without succumbing to the cold was revealed: human hosts. The Legion was using the crew of the Sylph as a source of warmth while moving around the ship.

'So, you found them.'

The voice leaped out at Kordaz and he whirled, the rifle in his grasp aimed at the woman who stood now in front of the pressure hatch. Kordaz kept the rifle aimed at her as he spoke, a small pistol held in her hand pointed right back at him.

'I knew that it was you,' he growled.

Councillor Dhalere's exotic eyes slanted in a smile as she looked Kordaz up and down. 'And what would you know of it? You're not even a *civilised* species.'

Kordaz activated the plasma rifle, the magazine humming into life.

'Your body temperature,' he replied. 'The Infectors increase it slightly and we *uncivilised* Veng'en can detect it. We can taste your sickness on the air.'

Dhalere raised one perfectly curved eyebrow as she smiled again.

'Perhaps we have underestimated you,' she purred. 'But then again, perhaps we know you better than you know yourself.'

The rustling sound suddenly filled the generator room and Kordaz glimpsed from the corners of his eyes the lake of black Infectors flow like a river toward Dhalere. They veered around Kordaz as they flooded toward her, and she stood with the smile still fixed to her features as the black flood rushed upon her and climbed up her legs.

Kordaz kept his gaze fixed upon Dhalere and her pistol as her body was entombed by the bots, swarming over her as though she were some kind of mother to them.

'You cannot win,' Dhalere said to him, her white teeth bright against the surging black skin of bots covering everything but her mouth and eyes. They even flowed through her hair, causing it to ripple as though it were a mane of oily black snakes. 'It is inevitable that you and the humans will fall, Kordaz.'

Kordaz could not grin like a human but he gave it his best shot as he pulled the trigger.

'Not without a fight.'

The plasma round blasted from his rifle in a blaze of bright light that rocketed across the distance between them in the blink of an eye. Kordaz saw the shot impact the dense cloud of bots around Dhalere and a bright blast of orange embers burst like an exploding star as they were vaporised in their thousands by the shot.

A dense cloud of blue smoke cleared and Kordaz felt something cold slither inside him as he saw Dhalere still smiling at him, the bots filling the void left by his shot and the woman herself entirely protected beneath them.

'Now, it's my turn,' she replied.

Kordaz leaped to one side as the councillor fired her pistol. The smaller plasma round skimmed his side and he roared in pain as he hurled himself onto the deck and rolled, aiming his rifle as he did so. Dhalere's cloak of bots shimmered as it changed shape, the bulk of the bots remaining between him and the councillor. Kordaz shifted his aim up to Dhalere's unprotected eyes.

And then he heard the groaning, right behind him.

Kordaz flipped over as the horde of infected crewmen loomed over him, their decaying flesh stinking in his nostrils and their agonised cries of pain filling his ears. Their hands reached out for his body as they shuffled en masse out of the darkness, their uniforms bearing the Sylph's name, and he fired on instinct.

The rifle's plasma blasts hollowed out the nearest man's stomach in a sizzling blaze of light and hurled him backward into his companions. Kordaz kicked out at another and knocked his legs from beneath him before blasting his head from his shoulders in a flare of plasma light.

Kordaz scrambled to his feet and fired again as the stench of burning flesh filled the generator room, smashing a young woman's arm clean off and sending her screaming to her knees. The decimated crew shuffling from the shadows retreated in panic and pain, melting bots falling from their wounded bodies and their faces twisted in agony as they moved despite their appalling injuries, their bodies controlled by the Infectors.

'Help me.'

Kordaz heard Dhalere's voice from behind him and whirled to see her face stricken with fear, her body trembling beneath the blanket of Infectors. Behind her and tumbling through the hatch were dozens of Marines with Bra'hiv at their head, all of their weapons pointing at him as they saw the smouldering remains of the Sylph's crew at his feet.

Dhalere's voice whimpered out again, her eyes now quivering with fear as she looked at Bra'hiv in terror.

'Help me, he's gone insane. He's killing everyone! He's infected!'

***

XXV

'Communications status?'

Captain Idris Sansin glanced at his HandStat and knew that there were scarce moments before the Veng'en commander's deadline expired.

'The Veng'en jamming is modulating through multiple frequencies,' Lael replied, 'switching periodically. The computer is trying to predict the next frequency in line and develop a pattern recognition sequence that will break the signal but it's taking time sir.'

'Time is the one thing that we do not have,' Idris snapped.

'Five minutes,' Mikhain reported. 'The Veng'en are not manoeuvring into an attack position yet, sir.'

Idris looked at the tactical display that dominated the main viewing panel, overlaid so as to provide battle information as well as revealing what the enemy vessel was doing.

'It's only a matter of time,' the captain replied. 'They'll have repaired the damage by now and won't be so easily caught out again. We won't be able to withstand a full bombardment from their cannons if they manage to corner us.'

'We're more manoeuvrable,' Mikhain pointed out, 'and their hull relies more on ray–shielding against plasma fire than ours, which has a physically tougher plating. If we can prevent them from hitting us full on, we might prevail.'

'Not long enough to finish them,' Idris said. 'We can't risk the lives of our civilians over this.'

Mikhain looked at the captain. 'Are you suggesting that we abandon the Sylph?'

Idris drew a deep breath. 'We have to choose between protecting over a thousand souls or risking them all for the sake of less than a hundred. That's no choice at all.'

Mikhain glanced at the screen. 'We could appeal for their mercy.'

'It will not make any difference,' the captain said. 'They will destroy the Sylph regardless of any casualties. It's how they have chosen to fight this war and as we started it, however unwittingly, there's not much more that we can say to stop them.'

Mikhain's features looked strained as he replied.

'Sir, you said it yourself that as soon as they're done with the Sylph they'll pursue us across the damned galaxy if they have to.'

Idris nodded.

'I'm aware of that, XO,' he replied. 'What is our best time to return to coordinates Delta–Four–Seven?'

Mikhain blinked in surprise as he looked down at his instruments. 'An hour or so, but why would you want to go back there?'

'We need to even the odds,' Idris replied. 'If we can't face that cruiser in open battle then we need to use our smaller size and greater manoeuvrability to gain an advantage.'

Mikhain exhaled noisily.

'What do you want to do about the fighter screen? We'll have to bring them in before we can make any jump.'

'Bring them in closer to the ship,' Idris replied, 'as subtly as you can. They'll have to recover aboard damned fast.'

Mikhain nodded and hurried to his station as Idris checked the time once again and hurried away.

'XO, you have the bridge. I'm going to see if Meyanna has anything we can offer Ty'ek to hold him off.'

*

Meyanna Sansin hurried across her laboratory, a vial of blood in her hands as she sat down behind a scanning microscope.

The blood was some of the last of Evelyn's samples that she had remaining. Beside it, sitting on her workbench, was a sealed vial of Dhalere's infected blood.

Meyanna's plan was simple enough. She intended to extract bots from Dhalere's sample and inject them into Evelyn's blood to see whether happened was any different from when she had taken Infectors from their tiny supply in the magnetic chamber and run the same experiment. She already knew that most likely Evelyn's white blood cells, those that fought off infections, would swamp and attack the bots in much the same way that they would attack foreign bacteria. The small size of the Infectors meant that they could in theory be overcome by immune cells and prevented from attaching themselves to major organs, thus preventing infection.

Meyanna settled into her seat and activated the microscope, carefully manipulating the controls as she focused in on Dhalere's blood sample. Meyanna had inserted a small electrode into the sample that would ensure the bots entrapped within the blood would have a source of power. Sure enough, as she looked into the sample she saw the Infectors moving about, their tiny claws and motors scrambling for purchase in the thick blood.

She inserted a syringe into the sample and withdrew a couple of dozen Infectors from the blood, and then moved them across to Evelyn's blood sample. She focused in on the sample and then she froze.

The blood already contained several live Infectors.

Meyanna zoomed in on them, saw them suspended in the blood. Most were enshrouded in Evelyn's white blood cells, the immune response destroying the bots. She could see them struggling to move as their tiny components were shut down as they were starved of the electrical impulses provided by the electrodes.

Meyanna looked up at a display screen that showed Evelyn's blood responding to the intruders, and almost immediately she saw a pattern that both she and the computers recognised: *anaemia–immuno–reponse*. As a convict wrongly imprisoned by the Word in an attempt to erase her from history, Evelyn had no medical records aboard the Atlantia. But the response of her immune system to the Infectors meant that she must, at some point in her life, had contracted a serious illness that made her dangerously anaemic.

Meyanna recalled that Evelyn had spent much of her childhood on Caneeron, an icy world in orbit around the gas giant Titas. Low exposure to sunlight could, in conjunction with an illness, have made her suffer anaemia to the extent that her immune response to any iron–consuming infection would be far greater than usual.

Meyanna felt excitement course through her veins. Most illnesses that caused anaemia and the associated blood–cell distortions were easily treatable, and a vaccination plan could be put into place within hours.

She had it. If an enhanced immuno–response to anaemia could be cultured from Evelyn's blood and tested in the laboratory, then in theory a vaccine for infection was at hand. She stood up, but then she looked down at Evelyn's blood sample again. There should not have been any Infectors in it, for Evelyn had already been screened completely. Whereas Dhalere's blood had been kept in secure containment, Evelyn's had not because she was immune to infection and so her blood required no special conditions other than those to keep it fresh and viable for tests.

Meyanna felt a chill ripple down her spine as she glanced at the sphere of Infectors in their magnetic chamber nearby, but the chamber was sealed and the sphere still in place.

And then she remembered.

Dhalere's coughing.

Infectors are so small that they could evolve just like a real bacteria or virus.

Meyanna suddenly felt dizzy, her thought processes hazy as though she were looking at the world through a dream. She staggered sideways and slumped against a desk, fought to right herself as she stumbled across to the laboratory door and sealed it with numb fingers. Her hand drifted across to an alarm and she slammed her palm against it, saw the heads of her medical team in the ward outside turn to look at her through the sealed doors of the laboratory as she slowly sank to her knees beside them, her hands pressed against the glass.

She reached up with one hand and fished a light pen from her pocket. She activated it and managed to scrawl a single word on the glass before her eyes rolled up into their sockets and she lost consciousness.

*

'Let me through!'

Captain Idris Sansin had to be restrained by two Marines as he stormed into the sick bay and saw his wife slumped against the doors of her laboratory.

'You can't go in there! She's sealed the laboratory and quarantined herself!'

Idris fought his way past the Marines and hurried across the sick bay to the door, then dropped down onto his knees as he looked at his wife's serene face. The side of her head was resting against the glass, her long black hair snaking down her back and her eyes closed. Idris could see the skin of her slender neck pulsing softly to the rhythm of her heart and he could see that she was breathing normally.

Before her, written backwards on the glass in glowing ink, was a single word.

EVOLVED

'What happened?' he asked as he saw the reflections of the medical team watching him in the glass.

'She sealed the doors and hit the alarm,' said the nearest man. 'She was testing the blood of Councillor Dhalere, and I'm pretty sure she's been running tests on somebody else too.'

The captain nodded. Evelyn.

He got to his feet and looked past Meyanna to where she had been working at her bench, the microscope still running and a series of sealed dishes containing what looked like blood arrayed beneath it.

Idris glanced across at the sphere of captive nanobots, and saw them still imprisoned in their magnetic gaol. *Think, man!* He looked again at his wife and he knew that the only thing that could have happened was that she had been infected somehow, even though the captive Infectors were securely housed.

Dhalere was the carrier aboard the Atlantia and was now aboard the Sylph.

Meyanna had taken Dhalere's blood that morning.

Evolved.

'It's airborne,' the captain uttered to himself in amazement. 'The Legion, it's out inside the laboratory.'

'That can't be possible,' the doctor said. 'The Infectors cannot survive for long outside of a human host, we've known that for months.'

'Dhalere was their host for months and we knew nothing about it,' the captain replied. 'They had the time and the reason to adapt just as any normal living organism would do. They've evolved to survive outside of a host for longer and Dhalere must have used that ability to somehow infect my wife before she left. It's the only reason that Meyanna would have isolated herself in this way despite knowing that without treatment she would be doomed.'

Idris looked at Meyanna and then at the dishes beneath the microscope.

'How did she know though?' he asked the doctor. 'How did she figure it out?'

'I don't know.'

'You're a damned doctor!' Idris roared at him.

'Yes,' the doctor replied. 'But I am not a detective. Your wife was clearly overcome before she could share whatever she had discovered, and we cannot go in there without ourselves being infected. There is only one way to resolve this. We will have to cleanse the entire laboratory with microwaves.'

The captain's jaw tightened but he remained silent.

'Your wife will not survive that process, if the Infectors have infiltrated her brain stem.'

'I'm aware of that, doctor.'

A tannoy clicked and Mikhain's voice echoed through the sick bay.

'Captain to the bridge, immediately. The Veng'en are charging their weapons and hailing us. Our time's up.'

Idris looked at the tannoy vacantly as though hoping that somebody else would answer for him.

'We have no time left, captain,' the doctor said. 'We must act now.'

XXVI

Evelyn stared in horror at Dhalere's trembling form. Her arms were outstretched by her sides, but that was the only thing that was visibly human about her. From her feet to her head was a roiling mass of black Infectors shimmering in the red light, only her eyes and lips visible.

The Marines held defensive positions around the hatch as Bra'hiv snapped at Kordaz.

'Call them off, now!'

The Veng'en soldier sneered at the general, his weapon pointed at Dhalere.

'It is your councillor who is infected,' he shot back. 'She followed me down here and now she's controlling the Infectors.'

Qayin looked from one to the other and then shrugged. 'Let's just kill 'em both and be done with it.'

'How come they haven't infected you, Kordaz?' Evelyn challenged the Veng'en.

'Because I am immune to them,' Kordaz replied. 'Veng'en saliva and blood destroys the Infectors before they can reach major organs.'

'Why didn't you tell me?' Evelyn asked.

'Veng'en do not bow to threats,' Kordaz snarled back. 'Like you, the Infectors cannot harm me.'

'I can,' Bra'hiv growled, the Marines' weapons now all pointed at Kordaz. 'Either you lower the weapon or we'll blow you to hell.'

'She is armed!' Kordaz roared.

Evelyn looked at Dhalere but her hands were empty and crawling with Infectors, the councillor's eyes welling with tears.

'Get... them... off... me..!' she pleaded.

Evelyn glanced at Kordaz one more time and then she turned to Bra'hiv. 'Cover me.'

'What the hell are you going to do?' Bra'hiv uttered.

Evelyn lowered her pistol and holstered it as she turned to Dhalere. Loathing swelled in a nauseous ball inside her stomach as she looked at the seething mass of Infectors swarming across the councillor's trembling body.

Then, slowly, she paced toward Dhalere.

'What the hell are you doing?' Qayin hissed.

Evelyn kept her eyes fixed upon Dhalere's as she walked one slow pace after another toward the mass of Infectors, their little metallic bodies whispering as though alive as they swarmed. Like grains of black sand running both up and down like a fluid, the Infectors writhed and coiled as Evelyn approached, seething back and forth as though blown by turbulent winds.

As the Marines watched in fascinated awe Evelyn approached to within arms' reach of Dhalere's petrified body. Evelyn, her heart racing in her chest, mastered her revulsion and reached out a hand, pushed it toward the black sea of nanobots, and with a rush of motion the black morass parted and swarmed away from her.

Evelyn heard gasps of disbelief as the Infectors flooded away from Evelyn's touch, her hands running across Dhalere's clothes and forcing the Infectors away like a light sweeping through the darkness and banishing it.

'What the hell?' Bra'hiv uttered in amazement.

Dhalere gasped, her eyes wide as the Infectors swarmed away from Evelyn and slunk back into the darkened shadows of the generator room. Evelyn watched them flee and then she looked at Dhalere. The councillor stared wide–eyed at Evelyn and then pointed over her shoulder at Kordaz.

'He killed the crew of the Sylph,' she wailed. 'He has them locked down here.'

Bra'hiv looked around him at the bodies littering the deck.

'They're all infected,' Kordaz snapped back, and then looked at Evelyn. 'Ask yourself, how could I have infected your friend Andaim while I was strapped to a gurney?'

Evelyn looked from Kordaz to Dhalere, but none of the Marines were paying any attention to the two captives. Instead, they were looking at her.

'How the hell did you do that?' Djimon asked.

Several of the Marines were looking at her with some suspicion, as though it were her they needed to fear.

'I'm immune to the Infectors,' she replied. 'I don't know why. The captain's wife is studying my blood to try to figure out how it works, so that we can all be vaccinated against them.'

Qayin blinked, his bioluminescent tattoos rippling with light. 'You've been immune all this time and you didn't think to tell anybody?'

'I knew that there was a carrier aboard,' Evelyn replied. 'I knew that if everybody was aware that I was immune then I would become a target for that carrier, a threat to the existence of the Legion inside their body. I couldn't afford to lose the opportunity to pass on my immunity.'

Qayin looked at Evelyn and then at Dhalere, and his shrewd mind put the last pieces of the puzzle together.

'Kordaz hasn't been aboard the Atlantia yet,' he growled.

Qayin switched his aim to Dhalere.

Evelyn whirled and shouted. 'Don't shoot!'

Kordaz dropped onto one knee as he aimed at Dhalere, but the councillor hurled herself across the generator room as she pulled her pistol from where she had concealed it beneath her clothes and aimed at Kordaz.

The two weapons fired simultaneously and the plasma blasts zipped past each other in the dull red light. Kordaz rolled to one side as the Councillor's plasma shot burst at his feet and showered him with molten plasma. Evelyn saw Dhalere slam into the metal wall of a nearby generator as Kordaz's shot burst against the wall behind where she had been stood only moments before. The Councillor vanished into the shadows.

'Don't shoot!' Evelyn yelled again.

Djimon's Marines tracked Kordaz with their rifles.

Kordaz scrambled for cover as Evelyn ran to shield him with her body, just as the first shot caught the Veng'en high on his thigh in a burst of fiery white light. The Veng'en roared in agony as Evelyn hurled herself down alongside him.

'Don't shoot, damn it!' she screamed. 'He's not infected!'

'He shot the Sylph's crew!' Djimon roared back at her.

Bra'hiv raised his clenched fist and the Marines held their positions and fell silent as the general called out.

'Councillor, come out with your hands up! We can help you!'

A chuckle erupted from the darkness and Dhalere's voice called back.

'It's already too late for you and your people, general,' she said. 'You'll never make it back now.'

'Evelyn will clear us a path,' Bra'hiv replied.

More chuckles, cruel this time. 'Evelyn and Kordaz are immune only to the Infectors. There are others here. Many others.'

'Damn it,' Qayin growled from where he crouched near the hatch, 'somebody scan for other heat sources down here!'

'We don't want to leave you Dhalere,' Evelyn tried again. 'This isn't what you want!'

'How would you know, Evelyn?' came the response. 'Maybe you'd enjoy life among the Legion. Why don't you ask some of your friends?'

Evelyn looked up from where she was shielding Kordaz and saw figures shuffling into view. The crew of the Sylph groaned, wept and whimpered in unspeakable pain and suffering as they limped in a tight knot out of the shadows toward the Marines. Dhalere was concealed among them, the Sylph's crew a grotesque human shield.

'Do you like what it's done to them?' Dhalere shouted.

The councillor fired at the Marines from behind the miserably shuffling bodies, the shot from her pistol hitting a Marine straight in the face and blasting his skull into a billion flaming fragments.

'Take her down!' Bra'hiv yelled.

The Marines did not have time to fire before C'rairn's panicked voice called out. 'Don't fire!'

'What?' Qayin shouted.

'We're surrounded!' C'rairn shouted, his gaze fixed to a scanner in his hands.

Evelyn looked up and saw the ceiling above them filled with a swarm of hunters rushing forth in a silent morass of black. The Marines scattered as the hunters plunged down like a waterfall upon one of the troops.

The young Marine screamed and dropped his rifle as his hands reached up to protect his face, but they never reached it as his scream was silenced in an instant. The torrent of Hunters splashed across his skin and devoured it upon contact, his youthful face collapsing and his skull folding in upon itself as it was consumed as though by toxic acid. His hair fell in a cloud as his legs collapsed beneath him and he sank to his knees, his hands vanishing and his arms dropping off at the shoulders as they were chewed through. His crumpled legs vanished into a sea of hunters flooding onto the deck and even his plasma rifle sank into the churning flood of bots.

Evelyn drew her pistol and fired at the plasma rifle's magazine.

The second shot blasted the magazine, which exploded in a fearsome blaze of light that shattered the swarm of hunters and melted them in their thousands even as more came tumbling through the generator room from behind Dhalere. The flood swamped the blazing pool of plasma and enveloped it.

'Fall back! Flame throwers!' Bra'hiv yelled.

The Marines opened fire with flames of liquid fire that drenched the onrushing hunters in writhing coils of burning fuel, melting them in their thousands.

'Watch your backs!'

A Marine screamed as one of the Sylph's infected crewmen grasped him with bony arms and bit deeply into his neck, Infectors swarming like black blood into the wound. Qayin fired and blasted the Marine and his infected assailant, their heads fusing in a mass of cauterised flesh and bone as they collapsed into a heap.

Evelyn aimed at Dhalere and fired twice.

The first shot killed a young female Sylph crew member, setting fire to her hair as she collapsed and sending her wildly thrashing corpse flying sideways into another infected crewman. The second shot hit Dhalere high in the chest beneath her arms as she fired indiscriminately into the Marines.

The blast spun her and the pistol fell from her grasp as she collapsed onto the deck, her scream of agony piercing even above the din of gunfire as the Marines finally regained the offensive and blasted the last members of the Sylph's crew and relieved them of their suffering.

The generator room fell silent, only the hiss and stench of cooked flesh filling the air as Evelyn looked across at Dhalere. The councillor's beautiful features were twisted with horror and her dark eyes welled with tears as she screeched at Evelyn, for a few moments back in control of her own voice.

'Please, kill me!'

Dhalere's face folded in upon itself in pain as she doubled over and then suddenly her screams were silenced. The councillor sat upright again, her chest smouldering but rapidly filling up with Infectors that plugged the hideous wound. Dhalere's tortured face relaxed as the Infectors stimulated her brain to block the pain from her wound, and she climbed to her feet, her eyes glowing a faint red through the hazy smoke as she raised her arms to her side and screeched with hellish joy.

'Kill them! Kill them all!'

Above the hiss of burning corpses a rush of what sounded like water echoed through the generator room, and Evelyn felt terror crawl like lice on her skin as she saw patches of light emerge from the shadows like newborn stars. Her brain recalibrated itself to the motion as she realised that the depths of the generator room were not in darkness at all: the ceiling lights were merely obscured by countless millions of Hunters. As they moved, so shafts of light pierced the gloom and illuminated them rushing forth like black rivers.

'Hunters!' Bra'hiv yelled. 'Fall back!'

***

XXVII

Evelyn grabbed Kordaz as the entire rear of the generator room shifted toward them as though a tsunami of black gravel was plunging into motion. The Veng'en staggered to his feet with a tight growl, one clawed hand grasping his injured thigh as he tried to make it to the hatchway.

'Covering fire!' Lieutenant C'rairn bellowed. 'Get those flamethrowers running now!'

The Marines plunged in retreat through the hatchway as Evelyn dragged Kordaz forward, the shifting morass of hunters flooding toward them. The Marines with the flamethrowers stepped forward, blasting the sea of black bots with fluid that burned with bright blue and yellow flames. Evelyn saw the flood brought up short before the searing heat as though by magic.

'Take Dhalere down!' Bra'hiv yelled.

A hail of plasma fire erupted into the hunters from the Marines holding their position around the hatch, the blasts blazing past Evelyn and Kordaz and smashing into the hunters to explode in bright fireballs of orange embers.

Evelyn, one arm around Kordaz's waist, aimed at Dhalere and fired.

In the last moments before the muzzle flash from her pistol, Evelyn saw Dhalere's face contort and a flood of Infectors pour from her mouth and nose in a black stream like rats fleeing a sinking ship. The Councillor's eyes were filled once again with horror, her features strained with disgust and confusion as her faculties returned to her once more in that last, terrifying instant.

The shot hit the councillor dead in the face, smashing her skull into fragments even as the hunters flooded past her. Her head flicked to one side, her lustrous black hair flailing, and then the Infectors flooded in and filled in her features. Her beautiful face became a hideous distortion, a charicature of the human being that had once belonged there, eyes red and teeth steel–grey.

Dhalere laughed, dead and yet now still alive, her arms still outstretched as the hunters flowed past her like thick waves, and then the flamethrowers drenched her in an inferno of fire and she shrieked in fury as her body burst into flames. Her clothes and flesh burned as the millions of Infectors inside her burning body spiralled up toward the ceiling like the embers of a fire snapping in the wind.

'Fall back!' Bra'hiv yelled.

Evelyn dragged herself past the flamethrowing Marines, Kordaz finding new reserves of willpower as he powered forward on his good leg. Evelyn released him, pushed him toward the hatch as she turned and aimed her pistol at the roiling hunters.

The lead flamethrower was overwhelmed as he turned to flee, the hunters plunging past his boots and swarming upon him in a black and silver cloud. Evelyn heard his screams above the gunfire as his legs seemed to dissolve before her and his torso sank down into the black mess, blood spilling in copious floods across the thick flood of machines. The Marine's arms reached out for salvation and his stricken features, twisted in agony, vanished as the hunters swarmed upon him and consumed his flesh in a frenzy of destruction.

The flamethrower in his grasp sank toward the hunters.

'Get back, now!' Qayin boomed as he dashed across to Evelyn's side.

The Marines fell back as Qayin dropped to one knee and took careful aim, then fired and hurled himself down onto the deck beside her.

The blast hit the flamethrower's fuel–lines as they sprayed unburnt fuel across the hunters, and the plasma shot burst into flames and then the fuel canister exploded in a tremendous fireball that briefly illuminated the entire generator room in a blinding flash.

'Go, now!' Qayin roared as he pushed Evelyn away toward the hatch, where Kordaz was limping through with the Marines.

Evelyn dashed across to the exit and ducked her head down as she crouched near the hatch and then looked up to see the front of the hunter's ranks decimated as they were engulfed within a flaming inferno of molten metal, as though instantaneously fossilized by the searing heat into a glossy black wall that spat hot blue smoke in clouds into the air.

The hunters flooding in from behind poured over their solidified brethren like a black wave breaching a dam.

'Back, now!' Bra'hiv ordered.

Djimon's Marines set up firing positions around the exit hatch, plasma rounds screeching across the generator room to plough into the surging Hunters as Evelyn followed Kordaz. Bra'hiv withdrew behind her, firing as he went, and Evelyn hurled herself through the open hatch to see Kordaz limping hurriedly away in the distance before her.

Bra'hiv hopped through behind her and instantly stuck a timed plasma–charge to the wall beside the hatch and set the timer to thirty seconds as Djimon backed through into the corridor, firing shot after shot into the roiling hordes of vicious machines pursuing them.

'Run, now!' Djimon snapped as he grabbed the detonator. 'We've got this!'

Evelyn and Bra'hiv dashed down the corridor, and Djimon turned and aimed his rifle out into the generator room. The Hunters were surging toward him now, and he could see Qayin firing as he backed toward the exit.

'Pull back!' he bellowed.

Alpha Company's Marines ceased fire and rushed past Djimon as he placed one hand on the detonator's timer. Qayin turned as the covering fire ceased, and in a brief instant he locked eyes with Djimon and his bioluminescent tattoos flared in anger.

'Cover me!' he yelled.

Djimon twisted the detonator's timer from thirty seconds to ten and then turned and sprinted away as the black horde of Hunters bore down toward Qayin.

*

Evelyn broke into a sprint, Bra'hiv thundering after her as they ran down the corridor, the air bitterly cold now after the heat of the generator rooms and filled with thick mist as the vapour condensed out of it.

'Fire in the hole!'

Djimon's voice was broken as he shouted and ran at the same time, and seconds later a deafening blast ripped through the corridor. Evelyn kept running even as the shockwave ploughed into her and she stumbled forwards, hands flailing and reaching out for the walls to keep her upright.

She plunged out of the corridor into a stairwell and saw Kordaz dragging himself painfully upward two flights above her, the sound of other Marine's boots hammering the metal steps further up. She glanced back over her shoulder to see several Marines and Djimon sprinting down the corridor as an inferno raged in the generator room behind them.

'Where's Qayin?!' she yelled.

The Marines tumbled past her but did not respond as she gestured to the deck at the base of the stairwell.

'Plasma charges here!' Evelyn shouted and unclipped both of her charges from her flight suit and dropped them at the top of the first flight of steps as she ran up them. 'Where's Qayin?' she repeated.

'He told us to get out!' Djimon bellowed back as he burst into the stairwell alongside her. 'The Hunters got him, Evelyn! He's gone!'

Evelyn stared at the big Marine and it seemed as though her heart momentarily stopped beating as she thought of Qayin, the seemingly indestructible force of nature, consumed by Hunters and burned alive in the blast from Bra'hiv's charges.

Djimon leaped up the steps three at a time and dropped a pair of charges as he ran, and Bra'hiv matched him step for step just behind.

'Evelyn, move, now!' the general roared down at her.

Evelyn shook herself out of her torpor and climbed with them and then stopped to aim her pistol down at the charges. A rush of air billowed up toward her as the hunters flooded toward the stairwell and blasted like black water under high pressure out of the corridor. She fired, and the first plasma magazine shattered and exploded with a blinding white flare.

She aimed at the second, hitting it first time and blasting the hunters back, millions of them melting in a dense and smouldering black pile of glossy slag intersected by glowing red rivulets of molten metal.

Evelyn aimed at the third magazine, but before she could fire it was swamped by the hunters and vanished from sight. She fired anyway, two or three shots, and the swelling mass of hunters filling the stairwell like water surged as the last shot found its mark and the magazine exploded deep inside their ranks.

Molten metal burst from the hunters and splashed across the surface, but then the hunters found their momentum again and began swarming toward her, climbing the steps like black vines growing at an impossible speed.

'Eve! That's enough, let's move!'

Bra'hiv's deep voice reached her from what felt like a universe away. She reluctantly holstered her pistol and began running again, harder this time, driving herself up as the hunters swarmed en masse below her.

'Keep moving!' Bra'hiv yelled.

Evelyn leaped up the steps two at a time, turning with each new flight, her legs throbbing and her breath sawing in her throat. She swung her arms hard, climbing ever upward, the air suddenly cold on her face and frost touching her eyelids as she powered past Djimon, who had stopped to drop another plasma magazine toward the hunters. She heard the rifle shot and saw the blast that flashed in the shadowy stairwell, and then she saw Kordaz slumped against the wall as she climbed.

'Move!' she yelled at him.

Kordaz's chest was heaving, and thick purple blood soaked his thigh beneath his hand as his yellow eyes stared without emotion into hers.

'My time is done,' he rasped. 'Go.'

Evelyn grabbed the big Veng'en's arm and forcibly dragged him to his feet as Djimon rushed past and glared at Kordaz. 'You going to tell me that a little human woman's got more spark than a Veng'en soldier?!'

Djimon thundered by as Kordaz growled and struggled onward, Evelyn helping him as from above a terrific shower of bright plasma blasts rocketed down past her. She saw the Marines arrayed at the top of the stairwell, on the bridge deck, their rifles firing down and smashing thousands of hunters off the stairwells.

Evelyn glimpsed as she climbed clouds of bots falling like burning rain down into the darkness. She staggered up onto the bridge deck with Kordaz and they limped together past the Marines and into another corridor.

'Seal it off!' Bra'hiv yelled.

'It won't do any good,' Evelyn shot back. 'They'll eat through it in no time!'

'It's better than leaving the damned door open!' the general shouted back above the gunfire.

The Marines poured through the hatchway, Bra'hiv the last man through as he pulled the hatch shut behind him and the deafening gunfire finally ceased. Evelyn's ears rang as she saw two Marines heave the hatch's pressure seals shut, and then everybody was running again.

'It'll buy us a couple of minutes,' Bra'hiv gasped, as breathless as she was and his skin sheened with sweat.

Evelyn and Kordaz limped in pursuit of the Marines as they entered the bridge.

'Status?!' Bra'hiv yelled.

'Still no contact from the Atlantia or the Veng'en cruiser sir,' a Marine replied. 'If we leave, either one of them might still be forced to shoot us down.'

'Better than staying here,' the general growled. 'We're leaving!'

'What about the Veng'en?' Djimon snapped, looking at Kordaz. 'What do we do with him?'

Bra'hiv looked at Kordaz, who was leaning against a control panel and breathing heavily.

'We use him as leverage,' Bra'hiv replied. 'Hail the Veng'en cruiser!'

'You want to do *what*?' C'rairn uttered.

'Hail them!' Bra'hiv ordered. 'If we've got one of their own they might be willing to bargain and it might give the Atlantia a chance to break through the jamming. Do it, now!'

***

XXVIII

Captain Idris Sansin strode onto the Atlantia's bridge and took his place upon the command platform, Mikhain nearby as he turned to face the main viewing screen.

'Is your wife okay?' Mikhain asked.

'Any word from the Sylph?' the captain responded, clearly not wishing to discuss Meyanna's condition.

'Nothing,' Mikhain replied. 'But tactical reports suggest a spreading heat source and gunfire aboard ship. The Veng'en cannot have failed to identify the same signatures.'

Idris exhaled noisily and nodded to Lael. 'On screen.'

The image of the Sylph changed to that of the Veng'en cruiser's commander. Ty'ek stared back at the captain. Idris did not speak, once again placing the onus on the Veng'en commander to speak.

'Your time is up, captain.'

'I did not agree to any deadlines.'

'Regardless, you will move your ship or we will destroy it.'

Idris let a small smile curl from one corner of his lips. 'Just like the last time, commander.'

Ty'ek's eyes narrowed and his skin rippled with flushes of crimson. 'We cannot play this game forever captain, and nor can your people aboard the Sylph. You would be doing your people a great service by destroying them before they are corrupted or consumed by your hideous creation.'

'I will decide the fate of my people, not you,' Idris replied.

'As you already have,' Ty'ek snarled. 'If you will not stand down then the Sylph's crew will be executed and you shall all be destroyed and…'

A barked command in Veng'en distracted the commander and he looked to one side.

'When?' he asked another officer out of sight to his left.

Idris watched as Ty'ek's fellow officer barked a few more unintelligible lines, and then Ty'ek glared back at Idris.

'There is gunfire aboard the Sylph,' he snarled.

'There is?' Idris asked.

'It would appear that you have even less time than I gave you, captain.'

'As does your soldier aboard,' Idris replied. 'It was you who left him and his companions there.'

'They were infected!'

'They were abandoned,' Idris corrected the Ty'ek. 'We found him and managed to help him. But now they are trapped aboard the Sylph and we can't talk to them because you've been jamming us!'

'Your time is up, as is the time for dialogue,' Ty'ek snarled.

The Veng'en scowled and shut off the communication link. Idris turned to Lael. 'Is the Sylph communicating with them?'

'I can't tell for sure sir,' Lael replied, 'but there are some signs of signals exchanges between the two vessels.'

'Isolate the frequencies,' Idris ordered her. 'They'll have to bridge the link separately because of the jamming. See if you can break into that link instead of their jammers. Bra'hiv's men may have been compromised.'

'Aye sir.'

Mikhain walked to the captain's side. 'You think that the Veng'en has killed Bra'hiv and his Marines and taken the ship?'

'No,' the captain replied, 'not with that much gunfire aboard. He is not alone. Either the crew of the Sylph has been turned and Bra'hiv's men are fighting back, or they're all fighting together against the Legion. Either way, we need to get them all off as soon as possible.'

The captain turned to his crew and called out across the bridge.

'Battle stations! All arms!'

*

'They're responding.'

C'rairn looked up at the viewing screen as it flickered into life and the face of a Veng'en officer glared back at them.

'Commander Ty'ek!' he announced himself. 'Where is my soldier?'

Evelyn stepped forward, helping to support Kordaz as he limped, his right thigh wrapped in hastily applied medical dressings.

'I am here, commander,' he replied. 'Kordaz Benen.'

Ty'ek looked at Kordaz for a long moment.

'What happened?' he demanded. 'How did you survive?'

'I deactivated the Sylph's environmental controls, forcing the Legion to retreat to the engine bays for warmth. It held them off until recently, when the humans arrived and boarded the ship.'

'They are infected?'

'Only one of them,' Kordaz replied. 'They saved my life, commander. We should allow them to…'

'You are injured,' Ty'ek interrupted. 'How did this happen?'

Kordaz breathed a reluctant sigh.

'One of the infected humans,' he replied. 'They shot me when I tried to ensure the Legion could not escape from the engine bays and…'

'How many of them are infected?' Ty'ek snapped. 'You said that there was only one!'

'There is only one now,' Kordaz replied, 'and he is in stasis. We can help him if…'

'You are injured and of no use to the commonspecies,' Ty'ek growled. 'Your treacherous friendship with the humans will be all of our undoing if we allow you back aboard. I will not have you serve with us!'

'You are young and inexperienced,' Kordaz said. 'You don't possess the maturity to command a battleship. If you do not learn to cooperate, our entire commonspecies is doomed.'

Ty'ek's skin rippled a deep crimson and his eyes narrowed. 'If ever we shall meet, Kordaz, I shall cut your throat myself.'

Evelyn shook her head. 'We have information about the Legion that we can share and…'

'Your kind has shared enough of your creations with our people!' Ty'ek shouted. 'Now I shall share some of ours with you and your traitorous new friend!'

The communication link snapped off as the Veng'en once again jammed all of the Sylph's communications.

'That's it,' Bra'hiv snapped. 'We're out of here. The Legion will try to reach us despite the cold, searching for new hosts or just to destroy us. It will head here first and try to reactivate the environmental controls. We leave, now.'

Kordaz was staring at the blank viewing monitor. Although his leathery face could show no emotion and any skin changes were not visible in the low light, it was as if Evelyn could sense the dismay and shame swamping his body. He felt heavier than before as she supported him, slumped as he was against a console.

'Come on,' she said, 'it's time to go.'

'No,' Kordaz replied. 'Ty'ek will blast you from existence long before you reach your ship. I will remain here and aid your escape.'

'How the hell are you going to do that?' Bra'hiv uttered. 'This ship has minimal armaments.'

Kordaz propped himself up and limped to the captain's chair, then slumped into it with a sigh of relief.

'It is in our nature to find weapons where others will find none,' he replied. 'Go, now! Before the legion reaches the bridge.'

The Sylph shuddered as a broadside of plasma blasts smashed into its hull. A series of alarm claxons sounded throughout the vessel and warning lights lit up across the control stations.

The Marines began rushing toward the exits as Bra'hiv reloaded his plasma rifle's magazine and looked at Evelyn.

'Come on,' he said, 'we'll need you in your Raython to cover our escape.'

Evelyn was about to move when she remembered Andaim. 'Where is Commander Ry'ere?'

'He's already down in the shuttle with the doctors,' Djimon replied gruffly. 'Your little beau will be just fine.'

'His Raython is down there,' Evelyn replied, ignoring the general's flippancy. 'We can use it.'

'I can fly it I suppose,' Bra'hiv said.

'No,' Evelyn replied as she looked at Kordaz and guessed what the Veng'en had in mind, 'I've got a better idea.'

The Veng'en looked at her. 'Me?'

Evelyn nodded. 'You can't control the bridge alone here. We'll do this together.' She turned to Bra'hiv. 'Get below and protect the landing bay. Be ready to launch as soon as you see us.'

'What the hell are you going to do?'

'The last thing they expect,' Evelyn replied. 'Go, set up a perimeter.'

An alarm sounded on the bridge and C'rairn glanced at his controls.

'The Legion is moving,' he said, 'heat signatures advancing this way. Let's go!'

The Marines scattered off the bridge with Djimon and Bra'hiv following them and turning for'ard for the landing bay two decks below. Evelyn turned to Kordaz.

'Are we going for a ride?' she asked.

'Yes, we are,' Kordaz replied as he surveyed the captain's control panel with satisfaction. 'The engines are working again.'

***

XXIX

'Djimon!'

Qayin bellowed at the sergeant as he saw him set the detonator and then flee from sight down the exit corridor.

The hordes of Hunters plunged in pursuit, rushing toward both the hatch and Qayin, and in an instant Qayin knew that he would never be able to outrun the Hunters or get far enough down the corridor to save himself from the blast.

Qayin fired on the nearest of the Hunters as they swarmed toward him, the noise of their millions of savage pincers and sharp metallic legs sounding like a vast waterfall that thundered in his ears, a wave of metal and hate crashing toward him.

His shots plunged into the Hunters, the searing plasma melting them into balls of fused metal that tumbled upon their companions like dislodged boulders torn from canyon walls by black waves, sparks and embers fluttering from their surfaces.

Qayin fired shot after shot until his magazine was empty and he hurled the rifle at the Hunters. The weapon clattered down upon them and was instantly consumed, breaking up into individual pieces and sinking beneath the horrific waves.

Qayin turned, desperate for some way to escape, and saw the detonator on the wall of the corridor. Upon its surface, a small counter was into single figures and going down fast. He knew that he would never make it. He turned back to the Hunters and on an impulse he kicked off his boots and tore off his combat fatigues as the flood washed toward him and the dense, heavy, hard and cold wave of Hunters crashed into his feet and ankles. In a terrible instant he saw them flood around his legs as he staggered backwards and cried out in a volatile mixture of outrage, pain and fear.

Qayin crouched down even as they flooded across him and then hurled himself upward as hard as he could. Devoid of his weighted gravity suit, Qayin shot up into the air as pain ripped into the flesh of his feet and ankles. He kicked down, smashing a dense ball of Hunters off his feet to tumble back down toward the deck. Deep lesions bled across his feet and ankles and he reached up to stop himself from smashing into the ceiling.

The blast hit Qayin from behind, a shockwave of heat that slammed into him and hurled him through the air over the massive flood of Hunters.

Qayin tumbled end over end and crashed into the side of a massive generator. His vision starred as he squinted into the flames and saw Hunters burning in an immense funeral pyre, clouds of them glowing red like coals.

Qayin looked for a means of escape and almost immediately he spotted the escape capsules lodged into the engine room walls. Designed to provide salvation for engineers in the event of a catastrophic engine failure or indeed a military attack by hostile forces, the capsules had been reactivated by General Bra'hiv from the bridge as soon as Kordaz had been captured.

Qayin was about to move toward the capsules when he spotted a small box attached to the very top of the huge generator. Tucked behind an exhaust shaft that extended up toward the ceiling, Qayin's heart skipped a beat as he moved across to the box and opened it.

Aboard all vessels, especially merchant ships, the trade in contraband had been a thriving industry. It didn't matter if crews were plying narcotic weeds for drug making or exotic pets for wealthy clients wishing to avoid quarantine laws or weapons, the ability to make money on the side of deck–duty was what had sustained mariners for centuries, and the Sylph was no exception. Qayin knew what he was looking at the moment he opened the box, and he quickly took the contents from within and tucked them under his arm.

Devlamine. A street drug, packed into clear plastic bags, probably worth a cool couple of thousand back in the day. Qayin had imported Devlamine from Ethera's forests and sold it to dock workers and sailors before he was caught and tried for a murder that he had not committed. The half dozen packs in the box were worth little as they stood, but if Qayin could get the weed into the sanctuary aboard the Atlantia, perhaps encourage some of the civilians into growing a small plantation, then the drug would provide wealth in terms other than of true currency.

Qayin knew an opportunity when he saw it.

A rustling sound caught Qayin's attention and he looked back to the smouldering cliff of Hunters to see thousands of them rushing back down the corridor toward him. Qayin pushed off the ceiling and plunged down toward the deck, bouncing off of it and propelling himself down a narrow passage between giant exhaust cylinders toward the ranks of escape capsules.

The sound of the pursuing Hunters increased in intensity as they rushed back through the generator room and flooded over their cauterised companions, spilling like a wave across the deck as they followed Qayin.

Qayin floated toward the capsules and slammed into the wall alongside one of them, the packages of Devlamine tucked under his arm as he said a tiny prayer in his mind and hit the capsule's activation switch. Behind him he heard the rustle of the Hunters build to a loud clattering and he turned his head to see them rush up behind him, thousands of pincers and beady little black eyes.

The capsule's door hissed and opened, and Qayin pulled himself inside and yanked the door closed again just as the Hunters clattered against its surface and swarmed upon it. The view through the clear viewing panel darkened as they smothered it and Qayin saw their shiny metallic pincers scraping at the surface as they began clawing their way inside.

A panel before him flashed a message:

LAUNCH PROTOCOL: ACTIVATE?

Qayin looked into the tiny black eyes of a Hunter staring in at him, and waved as he hit the launch button.

The capsule sank back into the wall, taking some of the Hunters with it, and then a shield door closed, crushing many of them as it sealed itself. The capsule surged as explosive charges blasted it clear of the hull, and Qayin watched as the Hunters still clinging to the capsule froze in motion in the bitter cold of space, their mandibles and legs slowing as they fell from the capsule and floated away with the debris and escaped gases from the launch charges.

Qayin saw the fires burning across the Sylph's hull, and then he spotted the huge bulk of the Veng'en cruiser looming into view, its cannons hammering the Sylph's battered exterior in a ferocious bombardment as Qayin's capsule tumbled helplessly out into the void.

***

XXX

'All fighters, prepare to engage!'

Mikhain's command rang out across the bridge as Captain Sansin took his command seat and surveyed the display screen.

The Veng'en cruiser was starting to move as she fired past the Atlantia and her shots struck the merchant vessel's vulnerable hull. Read-outs overlaid on the display showed her plasma batteries charging and her fighters assuming attack positions in a protective veil around her.

'Four squadrons of Scythe fighters in place around her,' Mikhain reported, 'our guys will be outnumbered two to one even if we throw everything at them.'

'Then we'll have to be smarter,' Idris snapped in reply. 'Manoeuvering power, and put us back between the Sylph and the Veng'en cruiser.'

The Atlantia surged as her engines burst into life, the entire ship filled with a faint vibration as though her heart had started beating again. Idris saw a pair of Raythons launch from the Atlantia's bow catapults and race away toward the Veng'en cruiser.

Idris turned to Mikhain.

'Launch the emergency shuttle,' he ordered, 'full quarantine kit and an escort of Marines. I want my people off the Sylph immediately, infected or not.'

'What about the Veng'en?' Mikhain asked.

'If it's alive, bring it back too.'

Mikhain scrambled to relay the order as Lael cried out.

'She's charging guns!'

Idris saw the Veng'en cruiser accelerate forwards with reckless aggression, crossing the Atlantia's bow in an attempt to bring her guns to bear while the majority of Atlantia's were facing out to each side.

'We're vulnerable!' Mikhain warned.

'Better us than the Sylph! Hard to starboard!' Idris shouted. 'Brace for impacts!'

The Veng'en cruiser's hull flashed with ripples of red light as a salvo of plasma charges ripped across the empty space between them. The Atlantia shuddered as the blows hammered into her, alarms echoing across the ship and the lights flickering as the power surged in and out.

'Multiple hits, for'ard quarter and port engine nacelles!' Mikhain reported. 'Fires on decks eight through ten!'

'Reverse course!' the captain yelled. 'Bring us alongside and hit her engines with the starboard guns in the turn!'

The Atlantia heeled over again, rolling in the opposite direction as the captain's feint lured the Veng'en cruiser into baring her hull after her guns had fired.

'How long until they recharge?' Idris called.

'Forty eight seconds,' Mikhain replied. 'Batteries are too low to fire again.'

'Full power!' Idris snapped. 'Make this one count! All batteries fire at point blank range as soon as target is in sight!'

The Atlantia turned laboriously, the Rankor's captain realising his error and beginning to pull up to avoid the inevitable returned salvo.

'Match her!' Idris cried. 'Keep us in plane! Don't waste a shot!'

The Atlantia pulled up slowly as the helmsman matched the Veng'en cruiser's manoeuvre.

'Our batteries are at full charge,' Mikhain reported, keeping his voice calm.

Idris saw the cruiser's entire aft hull exposed to the Atlantia's guns as it tried to turn away.

'Hard yaw to port,' he shouted. 'Fire as your bear!'

The Atlantia broke away from the cruiser and as she did so her guns came to bear one after the other. The ship shuddered again as a distant thundering reverberated through her hull. The massive cannons blasted twelve consecutive rounds at the Veng'en ship from a range of little more than a thousand cubits, the plasma rounds smashing into her hull in bright flares of light that died away to reveal blackened, ragged cavities in her hull plating and glowing fires deep within.

'Bring us about!' Idris snapped. 'We can turn faster than her and let loose our port cannons! Mikhain, order the Raythons to stay close to the Sylph in case the Veng'en try to sneak their Scythe fighters past us.'

Mikhain moved to relay the order and then stopped. 'We've got a problem.'

'What is it?'

'The Sylph, sir,' Mikhain said. 'She's moving into attack position.'

Idris Sansin shot out of his chair and dashed to the observation platform. He leaped up the steps onto the platform, which was set atop the bridge and gave a panoramic view of the Atlantia and her surroundings.

Idris turned and saw the Sylph rising up, her bow high and her stern aglow as her engines burst into life. Mikhain joined the captain on the platform and watched as the Sylph climbed to pass overhead the Atlantia.

'What the hell are they doing?' Mikhain uttered. 'We can't send a shuttle across when they're moving at attack speed and she's got no guns anyway!'

Idris shook his head.

'It's not an attack run,' he replied, 'it's a suicide mission. They're going to ram the Veng'en cruiser.'

'What the hell for?' Mikhain gasped. 'They'll lose us the supplies and their own lives.'

'Yes,' Idris replied. 'But they'll destroy the Legion aboard her too and give us the chance to escape.' The captain looked at Mikhain. 'Order the fighters to land. This is the only chance we'll get to leave.'

*

'Maximum power!'

Kordaz clenched his clawed fist as Evelyn grabbed the Sylph's antiquated throttle banks and threw them forward. The aged ship lurched as she got underway and Evelyn grasped the controls and began guiding her high over the Atlantia.

'You're killing your own people,' Evelyn pointed out.

'No less so than they have killed so many of their own,' Kordaz muttered in reply. 'Ty'ek is a young fool. Ram them!'

The Sylph surged forward and Evelyn saw the squadrons of Raython fighters rushing toward them suddenly veer away and dart toward the Atlantia.

'The captain's pulling everybody back,' she said. 'They're going to leave.'

'You should go,' Kordaz replied. 'I can take this from here.'

'There's no point,' Evelyn replied. 'Besides, I've got a better idea.'

Kordaz looked at her. 'Which is?'

Evelyn looked down at her controls and began inputting commands.

'We let the ship's computer do this for us,' she said. 'Charge what cannons the ship has, and as soon as they're ready open fire.'

Kordaz began inputting the commands into his own panel as Evelyn heard Bra'hiv in her earpiece.

'*The Legion is almost at the bridge!*' he shouted above the sound of a shuttle's engines running up. '*We're running up the auxillary power units on the Raythons but there's not much more we can do.*'

'Sit tight and wait for my mark,' Evelyn replied. 'We're almost done here!'

'Weapons primed and ready!' Kordaz informed her.

Evelyn looked up at the screen to see the Veng'en cruiser ahead of them. It was trailing a feint stream of debris and venting gases into space as it turned hard to starboard, her long hull facing side–on to the Sylph and her guns coming to bear.

'She's going to open fire!' Kordaz said. 'At this range we'll be pulverised!'

The Legion is right outside the bridge Evelyn!' Bra'hiv shouted.

Evelyn locked the Veng'en cruiser's hull as a navigation point and set the Sylph's controls to autopilot.

'Let's go, now!' she shouted at Kordaz. 'Open fire!'

Kordaz hit the fire button on his console and then struggled upright, wobbling as the entire vessel shifted beneath their feet as the Sylph's few gun platforms let fly a salvo of plasma shots at the Veng'en cruiser.

Evelyn saw the shots rocket into the cruiser, faint flashes against her giant hull as they impacted ineffectually against armoured plating.

'The cannons are not powerful enough to harm her,' Kordaz said.

'I don't care if they harm her,' Evelyn replied. 'I just want them to fire on us and ignore the Atlantia.'

The bridge hatch suddenly vibrated with a hum that filled the bridge. As Evelyn looked up at it she saw the metal surface ripple like the surface of a lake beneath a brisk wind.

'They're coming through,' Kordaz hissed.

'This way,' Evelyn turned him and they limped hurriedly toward the for'ard exit. The hatch opened and Evelyn looked back one last time at the main viewing screen to see the Veng'en cruiser's hull light up as she returned fire.

Evelyn pulled Kordaz through the hatch and sealed it shut behind her as they scrambled down the stairwell toward the landing bay decks. She heard a crash of metal on the bridge deck as the aft bridge hatch collapsed inward and then the hiss of millions of metal legs as the Legion flooded inside and came up against the for'ward exit hatch.

The hatch rippled as though its thick steel surface had suddenly turned into a grey silk sheet billowing in a breeze and then the hunters blasted through it as their thousands of sharp mandibles and claws scratched through the solid metal and they poured out in a dense black flood.

'Grab hold of something!' Evelyn shouted.

Kordaz staggered through a pressure hatch as Evelyn aimed her pistol at the onrushing swarm of hunters racing toward her and fired four shots in quick succession. The blazing bolts of plasma smashed into the hordes, melting them in their hundreds, but the immense force of the hunters behind was too great and they rolled over the blasts and closed in on Evelyn with frightening speed.

'It's too late!' Kordaz yelled.

Evelyn holstered her pistol and jumped through the hatch just as the first plasma round from the Veng'en cruiser ploughed into the Sylph and blasted her bridge into oblivion. She heard a scream of tortured metal and atmosphere being vacuumed from the ship in a howling gale as the blasts smashed into the upper hull.

The atmosphere around her was dragged past in a screaming torrent that tore at their uniforms and Evelyn's hair. She gripped the side of the bulkhead as the writhing mass of hunters reached the very edge of the hatch. For a moment she stared directly into hundreds of tiny glossy black eyes, round and without souls, above sharp mandibles as long as her fingernails and dense metallic black bodies. The writhing mass of hunters stretched out toward where she crouched, buffeted by the gale like a windsock in a hurricane, and she saw a single hunter land on her boot.

Then the escaping atmosphere and plunging temperature dragged the hunters en masse away from them, sucking them toward the freezing oblivion of space.

'The hatch!' Kordaz growled.

Evelyn dragged herself backward against the force of the wind and hooked her foot behind the hatch door as with the other she kicked the latch off. The heavy hatch door slammed shut in a flash, sealing the landing bay deck off from the damage.

Evelyn gasped in relief as she slumped on the deck, and she felt the ship trembling beneath the blows as the Veng'en cruiser hammered her with salvo after salvo.

'We've got to move,' Kordaz rasped.

Evelyn got to her feet, and as she looked down she saw the tiny lone hunter still clinging to her boot. On an impulse she reached down and grabbed the tiny machine. The hunter did not respond, suddenly dormant as it recalibrated to the absence of its fellow machines.

'You should destroy it,' Kordaz said.

'No, we can study it, it might be useful.'

The Sylph shuddered violently and the lights flickered as the hull was hit by another salvo of blasts. Evelyn held the hunter in one hand between her finger and thumb as with the other she propelled Kordaz toward the landing bay.

The Sylph heeled violently over as a distant, deep groan of rending metal echoed through the ship. Evelyn staggered sideways and slammed into the wall of the corridor as she made her way through the landing bay hatch. A series of ceiling tiles smashed down toward the deck and a spray of sparks floated in glowing globules as they were blasted from fuse boxes as excess power surged through the ship's systems.

'Move!'

Evelyn saw Bra'hiv and Djimon standing guard outside the shuttle's rear ramp as she hurried across the landing bay with Kordaz limping in pursuit.

'The ship's going to collide with the Veng'en cruiser!' Bra'hiv shouted. 'Get aboard now and get the hell out of here!'

The general and Djimon turned and dashed aboard the shuttle as its engines whined into life, and Evelyn sprinted the last few paces to their Raython fighters. Her eyes took in the open cockpits, the detached ground power lines and the flashing beacon high on the fuselage that indicated the ion engines were spun up ready for starting.

'You take this one!' she yelled to Kordaz above the crash of explosions ripping through the Sylph.

Evelyn dashed past Andaim's fighter and clambered up into her own, feeling suddenly at home as she slid into the seat and hurriedly buckled herself in. She reached down to a small storage compartment and dropped the dormant hunter into it, then locked it shut. She looked across and saw Kordaz slump into Andaim's Raython and yank his harnesses into place.

Evelyn pulled on her helmet and closed her canopy, watching as Kordaz struggled to get his head into Andaim's helmet. The Veng'en scowled and tossed it out of the cockpit as he closed the canopy.

'Scorcher Flight, do you copy?!'

'Scorcher Two,' Evelyn replied to the shuttle, 'we're aboard and right behind you. Go, now!'

The shuttle's two ion engines flared with a white glare and the craft lifted off the deck and soared toward the landing bay doors. Flashing red lights illuminated the rim of the doors and they opened slowly, revealing the deep blackness of space as the atmosphere within the landing bay was sucked out in whorls of ghostly white vapour.

Evelyn flicked switches on her instrument console, engaging the Raython's ion drives as she opened a channel to Kordaz's Raython. Despite his lack of head gear, the signal would still reach him, broadcast instead through speakers in his cockpit.

'Switch over and go easy on the throttle, these things are pretty damned quick when…'

Andaim's Raython lifted up off the Sylph's deck and turned, its ion engines flaring brightly as it blasted its way past and rocketed out of the bay.

'... they get going.'

Evelyn blinked and disengaged her magnetic landing claws, the Raython drifting free of the deck as she retracted the undercarriage and shoved the throttles forward. Her fighter surged forward as the landing bay flashed past in a blur of flickering lights and she burst out into space.

Behind her, she saw the vast hull of the Sylph glowing with multiple fires and just beyond it the huge Veng'en cruiser and its swarm of attending fighters.

***

XXXI

'She's going to impact the Veng'en cruiser, captain!'

Mikhain's voice was tense with excitement, the sight of an unexpected victory within their grasp as the Sylph pursued the cruiser.

'If she holds together,' Idris replied. 'Prepare to make the leap!'

Lael's hands flashed across her console and she looked up.

'New contacts, bearing two–two–four, elevation zero. Two fighters and a shuttle away from the Sylph, sir!'

Idris snapped his gaze to the Sylph's ravaged hull and saw three tiny specks rocketing away from her.

'Range?'

'Six thousand cubits!' Mikhain replied.

Even as Idris watched, he could see the Veng'en fighters wheeling away from their parent cruiser to pursue the three craft.

'They won't get here in time,' Mikhain added. 'The range is too great.'

Idris whirled and pointed at the helmsman. 'Bring her about, full to port!'

The helmsman responded instantly, the Atlantia beginning to heel over and turn back toward the Sylph as the captain turned to Mikhain.

'Fire in support of them and launch the alert fighters!'

The Executive Officer relayed the orders, his eyes fixed on the Atlantia's main viewing panel where three small blue boxes tracked the positions of the allied craft, and sixteen red ones the Veng'en fighters pursuing them.

'Ty'ek's hands are tied,' Mikhain said, 'he can't engage us until he's destroyed or disabled the Sylph. It's genius.'

'It won't take him long,' Idris said as he watched the Veng'en cruiser accelerate away from the battered Sylph. 'He's faster than the merchant ship. He'll swing out wide and come back to destroy her and then he'll come for us.'

Two bright points of light rocketed away from the Atlantia's bow.

'Reapers Five and Six clear,' Mikhain reported. 'We should launch more.'

'No,' the captain said. 'Whatever happens now, we have to leap before the Sylph is destroyed.'

*

'Ranger One, I've got multiple contacts astern and closing fast.'

'I see them,' Evelyn replied as she glanced at her holographic SAD and saw the red specks of the pursuing Veng'en fighters.

'They'll catch up with us in no time,' Kordaz replied. 'The shuttle is too slow.'

Evelyn scanned her own display and for a moment realized how much she missed having Andaim on her wing or in the back seat of the T2 training Raython.

'Any contact with the Atlantia?' Evelyn asked.

'Nothing, they're still being jammed. No, wait. Two fighters in–bound.'

Evelyn spotted the two Raythons on her display but she shook her head.

'They're not going to reach us before the Scythes,' she replied as she looked over at Kordaz's fighter. 'We're going to have to do this on our own for a while, Kordaz.'

In the faint starlight she saw the Veng'en turn to glance at her from within his cockpit.

'They will kill us all,' he replied.

'Then let's do something about it,' she replied. 'Ranger One, keep going at full throttle, we'll stay back here and try to cover your tail.'

'Roger that.'

'Kordaz, don't try to engage the Veng'en directly,' Evelyn advised. 'If one slips past us it can attack the shuttle and this will all be for nothing. Stay close to Ranger One and pick them off as best you can. I'll run interference.'

'I understand.'

Evelyn pulled up, the starfield wheeling past as she looked out of the top of her canopy and saw the flotilla of Scythe fighters streaking toward them. She rolled out, heading back toward them, and wasted no time in opening fire on the densely packed fighters.

Her pulse cannons were blinded out by a salvo of massive plasma blasts that rocketed overhead as the Atlantia's cannons fired in support. The huge shots flashed toward the Veng'en fighters as they scattered in disarray, three of them blasted into oblivion as they were smashed aside by the salvo.

A blaze of red plasma rocketed back from the remaining Veng'en fighters and flashed past Evelyn's canopy as she dove down and hauled the Raython into a tight turn as the Scythe fighters flashed past overhead.

'Reaper Two, fully engaged!'

The Raython whipped around the turn, the Veng'en fighters hurling themselves across the starfield around her in a confused circus as they tried to re–establish formations. A single craft zipped into view ahead and

Evelyn locked onto it, tracking it for a split second before firing her cannons.

The bright blue shots flashed away and struck the Veng'en craft astern, blasting it into several pieces that tumbled in a cloud of escaped gases and burning fuel. Evelyn shouted out in glee as she pulled up to avoid the debris.

'Splash one!' she yelled.

'Stay closer together!' Ranger One's pilot snapped at her. *'You're stronger as a pair.'*

Evelyn yanked her control column to the left and saw the shuttle just ahead of her, Kordaz circling it and firing at Veng'en fighters as they rocketed past in chaos. She focused on another target and pulled into line astern before firing twice and pulling up immediately.

The shots smashed into the Veng'en craft and blew one side of its fuselage clean off as the rest of it vanished into an orange fireball that flared brightly and then was consumed by the cold vacuum.

'Splash Two!'

Evelyn's Raython was hurled sideways as a shot smashed into her fuselage and sent the fighter spinning out of control. Two Veng'en fighters rocketed past her, their cannons blazing as they overshot her tumbling Raython.

'I'm hit!' she shouted, a pulse of panic bolting through her body.

Alarms rang in the cockpit and a flashing warning light told her that her starboard engine was aflame and leaking both fuel and coolant. She reached up and yanked the fuel shut–off valve, then unclipped the throttle handles and pulled the one on the right fully back.

The Raython's alarms were abruptly cut off as she fought for control, jamming her left rudder pedal fully down as she kept the port engine's throttle wide open to regain momentum. Counter–thrusters on her Raython's nose acted in place of the Raython's atmospheric rudder, balancing out the thrust from the remaining engine.

'I'm outnumbered here!' Kordaz growled over the intercom.

Evelyn saw the shuttle jinking left and right as the cloud of Veng'en fighters swarmed around it, each trying to take a shot. Evelyn aimed her Raython at the nearest of the attacking fighters and opened fire, catching it a lucky strike on the nose and sending it cartwheeling away into space.

'Splash three,' she called.

'Splash four,' Kordaz mimicked her kill–calls as his Raython hammered a Veng'en fighter with multiple blasts and it exploded in a flickering blaze.

Evelyn heard a crackling in her earpiece and then a new voice broke through.

'Renegade Flight, in–bound to engage!'

The two Raython interceptors flashed through the cloud of Veng'en fighters at attack speed, their own cannons blazing as they took down two more of the enemy craft.

'We're hit!' Bra'hiv yelled.

Evelyn saw the shuttle's hull trailing a dense cloud of vaporised gases and torn metal, its surface scorched where Veng'en blasts had hit it.

'I'm on it,' Evelyn replied.

She directed her Raython straight toward the shuttle, matching its velocity as she swung in alongside the damaged craft and then shut off her remaining engine. Evelyn re–routed the Raython's power to its bow and stern thrusters and then began scanning the starfield around them.

Two Veng'en craft arced high above the shuttle, reforming their attack formation for mutual cover as they wheeled over and dove down toward the shuttle.

Evelyn swung the nose of the Raython up to point at them, her Raython vertical alongside the shuttle as it fled, and squeezed her trigger. A trail of plasma rounds sprayed up toward the diving Veng'en craft and scattered them, one of them catching a glancing blow and veering away toward the Veng'en cruiser.

Renegade Flight flashed past and blasted a Veng'en Scythe, their combined rounds obliterating the craft into a swiftly vanishing ball of flame. Evelyn barely had the chance to register the hit when her cockpit was suddenly illuminated by a brilliant light that forced her to squint as the photo–reactive shielding on her canopy was briefly overwhelmed.

The Sylph's huge hull flared like a newborn star as its engine's fusion cores exploded with tremendous violence, blasting her stern apart like a gigantic metal flower, the petals propelled into the black void ahead of a rapidly expanding cloud of debris. The Rankor's cannons stopped firing upon the merchant ship as the Sylph's hull broke into multiple pieces, all trailing flame, gas and debris as they crumbled.

The shockwave hit Evelyn a moment later, her Raython shuddering and vibrating as the impact of the blast sent it reeling once more. She fought for control, saw the Veng'en fighters likewise tumbling erratically through space, and then as she regained control she saw the Atlantia looming large before her as it emerged from the gloom.

'…all fighters recover immediately, repeat: recover immediately!'

The sound of Lael's voice in Evelyn's ears sounded like music as it broke through the Veng'en's jammers.

'Atlantia, this is Reaper Two, roger that!'

A ripple of plasma fire burst from the Atlantia's smaller guns, cutting into a pair of Veng'en craft that strayed too close to the huge frigate and smashing them into flaming fireballs that streaked like shooting stars across the void and vanished just as fast.

The remaining Veng'en Scythes wheeled away and fled toward their parent cruiser as Evelyn saw the shuttle dive toward the Atlantia's stern, trailing debris.

'All craft, Atlantia leap in sixty seconds!'

Lael's call galavanised the pilots. Evelyn re–routed power to her remaining ion engine and arrested her headlong charge toward the Atlantia, guiding the Raython alongside the massive hull as she saw Kordaz guiding Andaim's fighter in pursuit of the shuttle.

Renegade flight positioned themselves protectively to port and followed Evelyn as she flew her Raython astern of the Atlantia and saw the guide lights flashing in the open landing bay.

'All craft, Atlantia leap in thirty seconds!'

Evelyn flew directly into the bay and extended her undercarriage at the same time as she activated the electro–magnets on their bases. The Raython jerked down onto the deck as behind her Renegade Flight touched down in a tight formation and the landing bay doors descended.

The doors had barely closed when Evelyn felt the Atlantia surge into motion, all of her gigantic ion engines going to full power at once as she accelerated toward leap speed.

The landing bay environmental lights switched from red to green as the atmosphere was reintroduced to the bay and the temperature stabilised once more. Evelyn opened her canopy, unbuckled herself from her seat and leaped down onto the deck as the shuttle, its stern enveloped in a haze of smouldering blue smoke, opened its rear ramp and Bra'hiv jogged out.

'Is everyone okay?' Evelyn called out across the bay above the whine of ion engines shutting down.

'We're fine,' Bra'hiv replied, then turned to his Marines. 'Get Andaim to the sick bay and then get Kordaz into the holding cells.'

'Kordaz just saved your lives!' Evelyn protested.

'It's not to punish him,' Bra'hiv snapped. 'It's to protect him!'

Evelyn looked to where Kordaz was levering himself gingerly from his cockpit, ground crew staring at the Veng'en with a volatile mixture of fear and hate.

'This isn't over yet!' Bra'hiv yelled at his Marines as they deployed from the shuttle. 'Protect Kordaz.'

Evelyn turned to the nearest crew chief as he approached her damaged Raython, and grabbed his arm.

'In the cockpit, there's a Hunter bot,' she said. The crew chief's eyes widened and he made to shout something. 'It's fine, it's dormant!' Evelyn snapped. 'Just get it contained in a magnetic chamber and send it to engineering, okay? They can study it there.'

The crew chief nodded nervously. 'Yes ma'am.'

The general pointed at Evelyn. 'You, come with me!'

***

XXXII

'All fighters are aboard, all hatches and bay doors sealed.'

'Full power!'

Captain Idris Sansin felt the Atlantia surge forward as her engines engaged. The Sylph's remains dominated the viewing screen ahead, her massive shattered hull entombed in a cloud of debris obscured the Veng'en cruiser from sight.

'The Veng'en fighters are not yet aboard her,' Mikhain reported, 'but it's only going to be a couple of minutes.'

'That might just be enough,' the captain replied. 'Helm, plot our trajectory and lock in the leap coordinates. Bring our starboard batteries to bear on the Veng'en as we pass.'

'Aye sir.'

'Tactical, charge all batteries.'

'Aye,' Mikhain replied, 'at eighty per cent and climbing.'

'Fire as they come to bear,' Idris ordered.

The Atlantia accelerated swiftly under full thrust, climbing over the massive flaming debris field left by the Sylph. The Veng'en cruiser emerged from the gloom, her fighters swarming toward their landing bays as she hurried to prepare to pursue the Atlantia. Her vast upper hull loomed below the Atlantia as the frigate rolled to bring her starboard guns to bear upon the cruiser's exposed upper hull.

'She's vulnerable,' Mikhain announced. 'Her landing bays are open!'

'Fire now!' Idris yelled. 'Everything we've got into those open bays!'

The Atlantia's huge plasma turrets thundered their salvos, the ship reverberating with the blasts, and Idris saw the enormous charges race toward the Veng'en cruiser's hull and smash into open landing bays with tremendous explosions that shattered her superstructure around the vulnerable ports.

'Direct hits astern and to her port hull!' Mikhain shouted. 'That'll learn'em!'

Explosions ripped through the cruiser's stern as the unprotected bays bore the brunt of the barrage, fires tearing through the damaged sections of the ship as enormous hull plating panels were blasted from their mounts to spin into space.

Veng'en fighters vanished inside the fireballs, obliterated as they tried to land, and the cruiser's lights blinked erratically as power lines were severed and entire bulkheads vaporised by the immense force of the blasts.

'We can finish her!' Mikhain shouted. 'Turn her about and...'

'Belay that!' Idris snapped.

The Executive Officer stared at the captain in dismay. 'She's vulnerable sir, we can finish her!'

'She's twice our size and her guns are still operational,' Idris replied, keeping his voice level. 'One good salvo from her at this range and we'd be finished. Maintain full power and leap as soon as we're able, I don't want her to get another broadside off.'

'Aye sir,' the helmsman replied.

The Atlantia sailed overhead the Veng'en cruiser, still heeled over ninety degrees on her side. Below, the Rankor rolled, struggling to bring her own main guns to bear and return the barrage. The cruiser vanished from sight as the Atlantia began building velocity and accelerated away.

'Range increasing,' Mikhain reported in a monotone voice, clearly distraught at having been denied the opportunity to defeat a major opponent in open battle. 'We'll be clear of their guns range by the time they can manoeuvre enough to make a shot.'

'Divert all power to main engines,' Idris ordered. 'How long before we can leap?'

'Three or four minutes sir,' the helmsman replied. 'Less once the power's re-routed.'

The captain turned as the bridge doors opened and Bra'hiv marched in with Evelyn at his side.

'About time,' Idris said, hiding his relief at seeing them both alive. 'How was your vacation?'

'It was Dhalere,' Bra'hiv reported, 'she was infected. Evelyn was right, sir.'

'We know,' Idris replied. 'What happened over there? Where is Andaim?'

Bra'hiv related what had passed aboard the Sylph, and the captain's face fell further with every passing word.

'Qayin is gone?' he echoed, glancing at Evelyn.

'Caught in a blast during our escape,' Evelyn replied, her voice tight. 'There was nothing we could have done.'

'And this Veng'en, you have it in custody?' he demanded.

'He's in the holding cells as we speak,' Bra'hiv confirmed. 'But he's on our side, captain, if you can believe that.'

'I don't like having a Veng'en within light years of us,' Mikhain uttered, 'let alone aboard the same damned ship.'

'Andaim needs medical help,' Evelyn said, 'he's on his way down to the sick bay now. Where's Meyanna?'

The captain sighed, his broad shoulders sinking even further as he replied.

'Infected,' he said, 'and quarantined inside her own laboratory. She's been unconscious for hours and nobody can go in there. If we don't find a solution within a short while the entire laboratory will have to be cleansed using the microwave scanners.'

'That'll kill her,' Bra'hiv said.

Idris nodded in response but his eyes were fixed upon Evelyn. The general turned also and looked at her, and he understood immediately.

'You're immune,' Bra'hiv said. 'You could go in there with her.'

Evelyn nodded.

'Yes, but I'm not a doctor. I don't know what I could do to help her.'

'Anything is better than nothing,' the captain said. 'She's dying, Evelyn. Before long we'll lose my wife and the best physician we have aboard this ship. I don't want her to become another Dhalere or Hevel.'

'Nor do I,' Evelyn replied, and then she hesitated. 'But I know somebody else who could help her.'

'Who?'

'Kordaz,' she replied. 'The Veng'en in the holding cells.'

'I don't want that murderous scum anywhere near my wife and...'

'All Veng'en are immune to the Infectors,' Evelyn interrupted him. 'Their saliva and blood contains bacteria that attack the Infectors and destroy them.'

'Good for them,' Idris snapped. 'Either way, I don't want a Veng'en near Meyanna. He could use her as a bargaining tool, hold us to ransom, anything.'

'He just shot down two of his own kind,' Evelyn said, 'to defend us.'

'What does that say about his morals?' Mikhain asked. 'He'll switch sides just as soon as it suits him.'

'It wasn't like that,' Evelyn insisted. 'Captain, if you want your wife and Andaim back we have to act fast.'

Idris looked at Evelyn for a long moment.

'And would you trust the Veng'en with Andaim's life?'

Evelyn lifted her chin, her green eyes clear as she replied. 'I'd trust him with my own and Andaim's life. I already have.'

Idris clenched his fists and his jaw, and then he heard a claxon sounding throughout the ship and Lael's voice echoing through countless tannoys as she spoke into a microphone at her console.

'Super–luminal leap in thirty seconds.'

The alarms continued to ring as the ship closed in on its leap velocity, the captain and those around him instinctively reaching out for something to hold on to.

'What's the status of the Veng'en cruiser?' he asked Mikhain.

The XO looked at his console.

'She's locked into a pursuit course sir, but she's a long way behind. They won't follow us into the leap for a while yet.'

Idris thought for a moment.

'She'll be able to follow our wake,' he said finally. 'Our gravitational waves will leave a clear trail and we don't have time to leave counter–measures.'

The Atlantia's velocity through space–time as a massless object did not free her from an effect on the fabric of that space–time. Gravitational waves, like concentric rings expanding outward from a stone tossed into a lake, rippled the surface of space–time and could be detected by highly sensitive antennae carried by most military vessels.

The Veng'en would be able to follow the Atlantia and determine her velocity and trajectory based upon an analysis of those waves.

'Ten seconds.'

The captain sighed, knowing that he had little choice. The situation had evolved beyond his control; too many variables to consider, too many lives to protect, too many problems to resolve. As fast as he found solutions to one issue so two more sprang up in its place. Never before had he wielded so much power and yet felt so powerless in the absence of an admiralty and an entire battle fleet to support him.

'Five, four, three, two, one.., leap.'

The bridge deck darkened slightly as the Atlantia's mass–drive engaged and the ship rocketed into super–luminal velocity. Idris felt himself tugged to one side, his hand grasping a railing tightly until the acceleration surge passed and the bridge returned to normal.

'Leap complete,' Lael reported as the helmsman spoke.

'Stable at one point oh four luminal velocity, sir.'

Idris looked at Evelyn again and although he clenched his jaw and his fists as he released the railing he nodded.

'Do it,' he said. 'Take the Veng'en, get in there and find a way to cure Meyanna.'

The captain turned to Mikhain. 'Have the crews re–arm, refuel and repair all of the fighters for deployment when we drop out of super–luminal.'

'Aye sir,' Mikhain replied, 'but what the hell are they going to do against that cruiser when it shows up?'

The captain did not reply.

***

XXXIII

'We need your help.'

Kordaz stood inside the barred cell and stared out at Evelyn and the Marines standing around her, expressions tense and weapons held at port arms, Djimon glaring at him.

'I already helped you,' Kordaz replied, 'and you threw me in here for my troubles.'

'General Bra'hiv feared that you would be attacked by the crew or even the civilians if you were seen,' she explained. 'They're not used to seeing a Veng'en warrior wandering around.'

'How do you think it feels for me?'

'No better,' Evelyn acknowledged. 'But right now our biggest problem is the threat presented by the Infectors. Andaim is still in a coma and the captain's wife is also infected. She is the chief medical officer aboard this ship.'

Kordaz stared at Evelyn. 'What do you expect me to do about it?'

'She found something,' Evelyn explained. 'As we're both immune to infection, and the only hunter aboard this ship is now safely in containment, we can enter the sick bay and try to discover what Meyanna learned before she was overcome.'

'What's in it for me?' Kordaz asked.

'Your life,' Djimon rumbled from behind Evelyn.

Evelyn glared at the sergeant before she went on.

'Your own people would kill you on sight,' Evelyn replied. 'Though they won't admit it they're fighting the same war as we are, just in a different way. There is nowhere for you to go, nowhere for you to hide. If you want to spend the rest of your days sitting inside this cell feeling sorry for yourself then go ahead. Or, you can come with me, make yourself useful and at least have the freedom of this ship, such as it is.'

Kordaz's yellow eyes narrowed.

'Do you really expect me to believe that your captain would allow me or any Veng'en to walk freely aboard this ship?'

'Not any Veng'en,' Evelyn said. 'His wife needs our help and I said that I could not do it without you. I told him that I trusted you and therefore so does he.'

Kordaz glanced at Djimon. 'Then why the armed guard?'

'For you, Kordaz,' she replied. 'Left alone, I don't doubt that at least one member of the crew or civilians would take the first shot they could get. Now, are you with us or not?'

Kordaz let out a hiss of irritation and then moved to the cell door. A Marine stepped forward and opened it and the Veng'en stepped out, his claws clicking on the metal deck beneath them.

'Where are they?' he asked.

Evelyn turned and led Kordaz through the ship, the Marines forming a protective guard around them. Passing crewmembers and civilians cast wary glances at the towering Veng'en as they moved through the ship, not a few looking as though they might attempt to at least spit in Kordaz's general direction, emboldened by the presence of the Marines. Only Evelyn's fearless stride alongside the Veng'en gave them pause, and she herself recalled that just a few short months before she too had walked these very corridors and been regarded with revulsion at best and outright hostility at worst.

They walked into the sick bay, their Marine guards making way for them as they passed through a wall of microwave scanners that protected the entrance and then sealing the doors behind them. Lieutenant C'rairn and Djimon both donned earpieces so they could speak to Evelyn and Kordaz without entering the sick bay.

The ward had been emptied of patients, the sick moved down into the sanctuary instead to prevent any furthering of the infection. Ahead, the glass doors of the laboratory were protected by a second set of microwave shields.

'The decks above and below are also shielded,' C'rairn told her, 'as are the walls of the entire sick bay. Any Infectors that are loose are contained within this bay because all patients were scanned before they were moved. It seems that the infection broke out only in Meyanna's laboratory and she contained it before it moved any further.'

Evelyn nodded as she surveyed the scene through the thick glass doors.

Meyanna lay slumped against the doors, her long black hair sprawled across the deck behind her, and the word *evolved* was written in glowing ink on the glass beside her head. Evelyn saw the sealed examination dishes and the microscope, and the magnetic chamber containing the captured Infectors condensed into a hovering grey sphere.

'She was examining the samples,' Kordaz said, 'and somehow she breathed them in.'

'Which would have allowed them to enter her bloodstream through her lungs,' Evelyn agreed. 'But if she had made a mistake and infected herself, would the examination dishes not be unsealed or broken somehow?'

Kordaz did not reply. Instead, he reached out and opened the laboratory door as Evelyn knelt down and cradled Meyanna's head in her hands. The captain's wife remained comatose as Evelyn bundled a pillow from one of the empty beds under her head.

'She will awaken soon,' Kordaz said.

'How do you know?'

'They always do, when new people arrive. It's a chance to spread the infection further.'

Even as Kordaz replied, Meyanna murmured as though coming awake from a dream. She lifted her head, her eyes drooping with exhaustion and her skin pale. The Infectors would be multiplying, taking iron from the haemoglobin in her blood to replicate in order to overcome her motor control and brain stem.

Meyanna squinted, the laboratory lights bright in her eyes, but although her expression was confused Evelyn could see the cruel gleam in her eyes.

'You,' Meyanna whispered.

Evelyn knew that she was not being addressed by the captain's wife but by the insidious voice of the Legion, the Word. It knew her now by sight, the same Infectors that had infested Dhalere's body now coursing through Meyanna's having brought with them some of their previously acquired knowledge.

'Fame at last,' Evelyn uttered.

Meyanna clambered to her feet, her black hair hanging in twisted ribbons across her face as she glared at Evelyn. It seemed as though the Word was remembering, recalling information. She glanced at Kordaz, the towering Veng'en staring down at her without emotion.

'What is this?' she spat. 'A Veng'en standing side by side with a human?'

'Better than side by side with you,' Evelyn replied. 'Meyanna learned something about you, didn't she?'

The Word grinned maliciously. 'Yes she did.'

'Wer're going to find out what that something was.'

'Yes you are,' the Word agreed, 'just as soon as the Infectors in your bloodstream reach your brain stem and replicate.'

Evelyn glanced at Kordaz, who finally spoke.

'The Infectors, they're airborne.'

The Word grinned again. 'Floating into your lungs and your bodies with every breath that you take.'

Evelyn feigned fear as she realised that Dhalere's Infectors clearly were not aware of Evelyn's immunity when she left the Atlantia. Evelyn swallowed and let her eyes well with tears. 'How?'

The Word smirked at her.

'Because we're smarter that you,' it replied. 'Infectors are unable to survive long outside of human hosts, their power supply drawn from the electrical impulses generated by your brains. Iron is used to construct them and it degrades rapidly. We simply found a new way: to use biological cells as shields, moisture as a protective bubble to transport Infectors from one person to another without the need for direct physical contact, much like a common cold virus. All biological cells are membranes filled with water.'

'Doesn't the iron degrade faster in a fluid?' Kordaz asked.

'Yes,' the Word replied. 'But it needs only a cough to pass it from one human host to another. The time spent in transit is minimal. The adaption would have occurred earlier, but on your home planet of Ethera the populace was infected before we took control. Here, aboard the Atlantia, things were different and a new means of infection was required.'

'How long?' Evelyn asked.

'For you to be overcome?' the Word replied rhetorically. 'Minutes, at the most. We have only recently evolved the ability to transmit as an aerosol, through Councillor Dhalere, but rest assured that it will become the new means of infection among your entire crew.'

Evelyn let the fearful expression she wore fall away. 'I doubt that very much.'

'You are doomed,' the Word snarled. 'If we don't destroy you, the Veng'en cruiser pursuing you will.'

'We're immune,' Evelyn replied simply, 'and this entire laboratory is microwave shielded on all sides. There is no escape for you.'

Meyanna's face slipped, her eyes darting from Evelyn to Kordaz. 'You lie.'

'We have no need to lie,' Kordaz replied. 'Evelyn is naturally immune to the Infectors, as are all Veng'en. Dhalere would not have known that when she infected Meyanna, isolated here aboard the Atlantia as she was, and therefore neither did you.'

Meyanna's uncertainty mutated into rage and she hurled herself at Evelyn.

Evelyn sidestepped the attack as Kordaz blocked Meyanna with one giant arm and swept her up, carrying her writhing body to a nearby bed and hurling her down upon it. Evelyn followed, grappling Meyanna's arms and pinning them down into restraints.

'What are you going to do?'

The voice came from outside the locked sick bay doors as the doctors watched. Evelyn looked up to see the captain's craggy head staring in at her.

'Get answers,' Evelyn replied.

Meyanna's face twisted into a smirk again, now firmly strapped to the bed as Evelyn stood back. 'You'll learn nothing. You try anything to destroy me and my last act will be to turn Meyanna Sansin's brain stem to mush.'

Evelyn turned to Kordaz. 'You said that your saliva destroys the Infectors? How, exactly?'

'It's toxic,' he replied. 'It contains bacteria and acids that dissolve the Infector's shells, damaging them fatally before they can infiltrate major organs.'

Evelyn nodded and pointed to a series of microwave scanners stacked on Meyanna's workbench nearby.

'Bring me the microwave scanners, two of them.'

'What are you doing Evelyn?' the captain shouted through the laboratory doors. 'You'll kill her!'

As Kordaz strode across the laboratory to fetch the scanners, the Word laughed a manic chuckle.

'Destroy me and you destroy Meyanna,' it hissed.

'Not necessarily,' Evelyn replied as Kordaz returned with a scanner in each of his giant hands.

Evelyn strode across to the magnetic chamber, where within was contained the imprisoned cloud of Infectors. She reached out and switched the machine's magnets off.

***

XXXIV

The quivering sphere of metallic grey bots dispersed at once, vanishing as though into thin air, and Evelyn knew that the tiny devices would flood in the direction of the nearest host, the tiny antennae that they used to seek sanctuary detecting body temperatures.

'What the hell are you doing?!' the captain roared.

Evelyn did not reply as she opened the lid of the chamber and turned it over. There, a large magnet sat in a cradle attached to the chamber lid. Evelyn removed the magnet, checked its polarity, and then strode back across to Meyanna's body and laid the magnet down on her belly.

Evelyn looked across at the laboratory's glass doors, where Meyanna had scrawled the word *evolved* before passing out.

'You say that you're smarter than us,' she said to the Word, 'but you *are* us. We created you, and thus you have something inside of you that you cannot fight.'

'Such as?' the Word spat.

'The will to live,' Evelyn smiled down. 'That *swarm* mentality of yours only works until you get into a human host, doesn't it? You're machines up to that point, but then you plug into our minds and suddenly you've got just a little bit of human about you.' Evelyn leaned closer. 'And that means that you don't want to die, do you?'

Meyanna's face remained impassive. 'You couldn't possibly know what I feel.'

'Then let's find out.'

Evelyn activated the scanner and Meyanna's body writhed as she screamed in agony, the microwaves heating the Infectors swarming inside her body and frying their internal circuitry.

'Evelyn!'

Evelyn ignored the captain's cry as she held the scanner in place, directing the invisible energy at Meyanna's neck.

She shut the scanner off and Meyanna slumped, her skin sheened with sweat and her eyes rolled up in their sockets as her eyelids fluttered.

'How does that feel?' Evelyn asked.

'You'll kill her,' Kordaz said, holding the other scanner.

'Maybe not,' Evelyn said. 'Zap her from your side, and make sure you hit her neck and that you're pointing the scanner down toward her legs.'

Kordaz obeyed and Meyanna shrieked as the scanner activated, her body stiffening as though live current were blazing through her veins. Her cry strangled off as she reached the limit of what she could take.

'Stop,' Evelyn said.

Kordaz deactivated the scanner. Evelyn watched Meyanna for a moment. Her face was slick with sweat and flushed with colour, but her expression seemed somewhat less twisted with malice than before.

'They're fleeing, just like they did inside Kyarl,' Evelyn said. 'Aim the scanners at her chest but keep them pointing down at her feet.'

Kordaz obeyed, activating his scanner at the same time as Evelyn as they blasted Meyanna's body once more. Meyanna writhed and squirmed in agony but with less vigour than before as Evelyn and Kordaz worked the scanners.

'Now move so we're facing each other,' Evelyn said as she moved to stand alongside Meyanna's belly.

Kordaz mirrored Evelyn's movements and they held the scanners in place. Meyanna's writhing continued, her stomach muscles contracting and flexing as her back arched and then her legs tried to fold up.

'The stomach,' Kordaz realised. 'You're herding them there, toward the magnet.'

'And the acid,' Evelyn replied. 'If they can't survive the bacteria and acid in Veng'en saliva, then they won't be able to survive the hydrochloric acid in the human stomach.'

Evelyn jumped quickly around to Meyanna's feet and began moving the scanner up her legs, to eradicate any Infectors still swarming in the doctor's bloodstream. Kordaz stayed in place as Meyanna's legs twitched and her muscles flickered with movement as the Infectors were flushed or burned where they flowed in her blood.

Evelyn held the scanner in place over Meyanna's belly for a few more moments and then she shut it off.

'Help me wire her up,' she said.

Kordaz grabbed a saline drip. 'I can do this.'

Evelyn recalled that the Veng'en had learned as much about human biology during their many conflicts as humans had learned about theirs. Within a couple of minutes Meyanna was still unconscious but stable, her heartbeat reading normal and her body temperature dropping.

'She is clean,' Kordaz said finally. 'Enough so that we will be able to scan her again with the full force of the microwaves to remove any last Infectors without killing her.'

'Better to be safe than sorry,' Evelyn said as she glanced at the bed where Andaim lay and then turned to the captain. 'We'll do the same to Andaim, and then you must scan this entire laboratory and sick bay at full power with all of us inside. Only then will we be sure that we're clear.'

The captain's features were taut with concern.

'Evelyn,' he said, 'your face.'

Evelyn looked at herself in a mirror and saw dark blood trickling from her nose. She wiped it away on her sleeve.

'It's normal,' she replied. 'It's what happened the last time the Word tried to infect me. It'll pass.'

She grabbed her microwave scanner and joined Kordaz alongside Andaim's bed. To her surprise the lieutenant looked up at her through drooping eyelids, his expression riven with dismay.

'Why didn't you tell me?' he rasped, 'that you were immune all this time?'

'I'll explain later,' she said as she laid the magnet on Andaim's belly. 'You ready?'

'We wouldn't be going through this if you'd told us,' he whispered.

Evelyn looked at Kordaz, who nodded.

Andaim cried out as the scanners activated, and to Evelyn's distress despite his pain he remained conscious throughout the entire procedure, writhing and thrashing as the dreaded machines were forcibly burned or flushed into his stomach to dissolve.

As soon as she was sure that his vital organs were safe, Evelyn called out to the doctors.

'Do it, now!'

Within minutes the laboratory was drenched in microwave energy. Evelyn sat on the deck with her arms pulled tight around her knees, her ankles tucked in against her thighs as she rallied against the pain seething through her veins. Opposite her, Kordaz sat in a similar pose but showed no evidence of any pain but for the turbulent rippling of pigments beneath his leathery skin, coils and whorls of vibrant, aggressive colour that betrayed his suffering.

Evelyn finally felt the pain ease and fade away, and she got up and walked across to Meyanna's side and saw her open her eyes, a faint smile touching her lips.

'You did good,' the doctor said, her voice weak.

'I did what I could,' Evelyn replied. 'I got lucky that it worked. You could see everything, hear everything?'

Meyanna nodded. 'Everything. It's like being in a prison, watching your own life pass by, hearing your own voice and seeing your own body moving but totally unable to control what's happening. It's horrific, Evelyn: people are still *alive* while they're infected.'

Evelyn shivered as she thought of Dhalere, or of Tyraeus Forge, human beings incarcerated as their bodies were overcome and transformed into horrific charicatures of human beings, their flesh consumed, their brains poisoned.

Meyanna tried to sit up but she was too weak, her brain's signals not yet fully reconnecting with the rest of her body after being intercepted for so long by the Word. She slumped back onto her pillows as Evelyn sat beside her and waited for the scans to be completed.

'We'll have lost all of the Infectors,' Meyanna said. 'I won't be able to study them any more.'

'We've got the data on file I'm sure,' Evelyn replied. 'And anyway, we know how to protect ourselves against them now. Once you've solved the mystery of why I'm immune, we can vaccinate and concentrate on bigger fish.'

'Such as?'

'I caught a Hunter,' Evelyn replied with a devious smile. 'It's in lock down in engineering as we speak.'

Meyanna managed to prop herself up this time. 'It's aboard?'

'Right now,' Evelyn replied. 'Don't worry, they're not replicators. They don't build themselves – the Infectors do all of the building work.'

'They're still dangerous.'

'Together, yes,' Evelyn replied. 'But on their own they seem to fall dormant. It's like they don't have any instructions so they do nothing. Maybe it's run out of power.'

Evelyn sighed as she felt her own shoulders sag, as though she herself were running out of power too.

'You're exhausted,' Meyanna observed. 'When did you last get some sleep?'

An alarm sounded and Evelyn heard the sound of the microwave scanners outside the sick bay being shut down. Moments later the sick bay doors opened and the captain hurried through. He strode past Andaim's bed with barely a glance, and Evelyn stood to give him space as he dropped like a stone by his wife's side.

'Are you okay?' he asked. 'Can you speak? Can your move your hands and legs and...'

'I'm fine,' Meyanna smiled, rallying fast.

The captain enveloped his wife in a deep embrace and then he stood and looked at Evelyn. 'You keep coming to the rescue.'

'You keep dropping us all in the crap.'

The captain grinned at her and then looked at Andaim. The commander was also recovering quickly, propping himself up on his elbow and guzzling from a canteen of water.

'When you've finished your nap we need you on the bridge, commander,' the captain snapped. 'We're not out of this yet.'

'You knew,' Andaim said, and gestured to Evelyn. 'You knew that she was immune and you didn't tell any of us.'

'There was a carrier aboard,' the captain replied. 'If we'd broadcast Evelyn's immunity to the ship, especially before we know how it worked, she might have become a target for the carrier.'

'Might have,' Andaim echoed as he clambered off the bed.

The commander wobbled on his legs and the captain leaped forward and steadied him.

'Evelyn and her immunity would have been no good to us if she were to die,' Idris insisted, grasping Andaim's shoulders tightly. 'There is not much that I keep from you, but this had to remain covert until we knew what was going on, and how these damned nanobots worked.'

Andaim righted himself, his balance slowly returning. 'And do we?'

The captain looked at Meyanna, who managed a brief nod.

'I've got some ideas,' she replied. 'Nothing concrete yet but I'm getting there.'

Meyanna looked across at Kordaz, who was watching the entire exchange with interest.

'It's a long story,' Evelyn explained, 'again.' She turned to the captain. 'We jumped into super–luminal didn't we? Where are we going?'

Idris straightened his uniform.

'Into battle,' he replied. 'Get yourselves sorted and report to the bridge in twenty minutes. We don't have long.'

***

XXXV

'Status?'

The captain walked onto the bridge as the Executive Officer strode down from the observation platform to meet him.

'We're within a few minutes of our destination, sir,' Mikhain replied. 'Plasma batteries are fully charged, all ray shielding generators are repaired and running at maximum efficiency. The ship is locked down for battle and the Raythons are being repaired, refuelled and rearmed as we speak.'

Idris climbed the steps to the command platform and stood beside his chair for a moment, thinking long and hard about what had happened in the last few frenetic hours.

'We are vulnerable,' he said finally.

'That's understandable sir,' Mikhain replied. 'The Veng'en cruiser is much larger and more powerful than us and...'

'I'm not talking about the Veng'en,' Idris said. He sighed and turned to face the XO. 'I mean we're vulnerable in that all of our assets are in the one place, here aboard Atlantia. If we were overrun by the Word, or cornered by Veng'en warships, we could lose everything in one fell swoop.'

Mikhain watched the captain for a moment and Idris could see in the XO's eyes that he had no good solution.

'We lost everything when the Word took Ethera and Caneeron,' Mikhain replied finally. 'This one ship is all that we have.'

'No,' Idris said. 'We found the Sylph. Before the Veng'en destroyed her she could have been cleaned somehow, could have become a support vessel. We could maybe even have armed her, doubled our strength.'

'You're saying you want to build a fleet?' Mikhain asked. 'We barely have the manpower to maintain this ship, let alone another one alongside her. Who will crew and command such a vessel?'

Idris sat down in his chair and looked at the black and featureless viewing panel, devoid of light during super–luminal travel.

'We determined that we would travel home,' he said, 'that we would not run away from the Word any longer. But alone the Atlantia is no match for the colonial fleet now under the Word's command. Even a pair of cruisers could defeat us without too much trouble no matter how clever we think we are. If Ty'ek was more experienced, he could have used his cruiser to crush us within moments of his arrival.'

Mikhain frowned. 'So you're saying maybe we shouldn't go home?'

'I'm saying that we should not go home alone.'

Mikhain sighed. 'We could seach the cosmos for eternity and not find any survivors. They would have scattered with all the same haste that we did to the sixty points of the celestial compass. They'll be separated by light years, hiding on other worlds and determined not to be found by the Word. If they see us, they'll assume the Atlantia's infected and remain hidden.'

'Perhaps,' the captain acknowledged, 'but we have to assume that despite the scale of our demise, others too must have survived. Especially other prison ships.'

The captain saw Mikhain's expression darken.

'We got lucky, sir,' he said. 'The others, if they still exist, might have been overrun by their convicts or drifted into deep space. Any that remain are unlikely to want to assist us and head back into the teeth of the enemy.'

'They may not have much choice if the Word continues to spread. If the Veng'en are already fighting for their lives, what's to stop the Word overwhelming the entire galaxy? There could be countless civilisations that we've never heard of or seen before who will fall prey to it.'

'The universe is a big place, sir,' Mikhain replied, 'with lots of places to hide.'

'Yes it is,' Idris agreed, 'and how do you'll think we'll fare as every living species cowers in hiding over something that *we* created? Every living thing will know what *we* have done. Humanity won't live to see the outcome, Mikhain, because we'll be hunted into extinction by every other race that encounters us.'

The bridge fell silent as Evelyn walked in, followed by Bra'hiv and Andaim and then a stream of fighter pilots, patches on their flight suits denoting their membership of either the *Reapers* or the *Renegades*. They assembled below the command platform as the captain stood.

'Ladies and gentlemen,' he began. 'Our sensors prior to super–luminal leap confirmed that the Veng'en cruiser was intending to pursue us. It would seem almost certain that they will do so now with a vengeance, with the aim of eradicating us from existence. Their commander, Ty'ek, is aggressive but inexperienced. I can only assume that the Word has decimated the ranks of the Veng'en in open conflict just as it did our own people on Ethera.'

Idris rested his hands on the railings before him as he gathered his thoughts.

'Ty'ek cannot be reasoned with. He seeks only revenge. His fighters still outnumber ours two to one at best and his vessel boasts twice the Atlantia's firepower. If we face him in open battle on an even playing field, this time we surely will be destroyed.'

Idris smiled grimly.

'Which is why I intend to level that field a little. We will draw the Veng'en into a battle on our terms. Renegades, you will maintain the close support role and ensure that none of the Veng'en fighters come close enough to effect a sustained attack. Reapers, you will lead the assault on the cruiser itself in an attempt to disable her.'

Evelyn's eyes widened as Andaim spoke up. 'One squadron against a fully–armed battle cruiser?'

'Atlantia will support you with salvos from our main guns as usual, but we will not be engaging the cruiser in direct combat.'

'I don't get it?' Evelyn said. 'How can we defeat her then?'

'Because we're going to let Ty'ek think that he's got us cornered and make his aggression and spite work in our favour.'

Lael's voice spoke over the gathered pilots and soldiers. 'Sub luminal velocity in sixty seconds.'

'This is it,' the captain said and clapped his hands together once loudly. 'Get to your ships and prepare for launch. You'll realise what I have in mind as soon as you get spaceborne. Make every shot count!'

The pilots turned and jogged from the bridge as Evelyn stared up at Idris.

'If Ty'ek doesn't go for it..,' she said.

Idris smiled down at her.

'He'll go for it,' he replied. 'Now get out of here and go raise hell, it's what you're best at.'

*

'Where are they?'

The temperature on the bridge of the Veng'en cruiser was sufficiently hot that a faint haze of moisture hung in the air, like the veils of mist that enveloped the tropics of their home planet, Wraiythe. Moisture glistened on the walls as it condensed against the cooler surfaces as Ty'ek paced up and down.

Although skilled metallurgists and ship builders, the Veng'en were by their nature forest dwellers and to some extent the huge ship mimicked their homeworld, the walls painted shades of green and black, the lighting a deep yellow hue reminiscent of the hot star around which their homeworld orbited. Control consoles were also slick with moisture, touch–screens sealed air–tight to protect the electrical circuits within.

The main viewing panel remained black, but a few of the ship's passive sensors were able to detect the gravitational waves rippling behind the Atlantia as she fled through the space time continuum.

'Three minutes ahead,' came the reply from Ty'ek's First Officer, Rivlek. 'We shall have her before long, captain. She cannot flee forever.'

Ty'ek knew that no vessel could remain at super–luminal velocity indefinitely. The huge energies required were a drain on any vessel's resources and required replenishment before further leaps could be made. The Atlantia, a medium–sized frigate, could maintain super–luminal only for a few days before she would be required to replenish her hydrogen fuel.

Her captain, no doubt, was using the time to prepare his people for a battle that they could not possibly win. Sansin had duped Ty'ek twice in a row, but this time there was nowhere for him to run. The nearest planetary systems were several weeks' away even at super–luminal velocity. The Atlantia would be forced to slow down to refuel in deep space, alone and with nowhere to hide, and when it did Ty'ek would be there and ready.

'Maintain pursuit course and keep the fighters and our troops at full readiness,' Ty'ek ordered. 'I want to know about it the moment the Atlantia returns to sub–luminal velocity.'

'Yes, captain,' Rivlek replied.

Ty'ek stepped off the bridge and crouched down on all fours as he launched himself down a deeply winding corridor. The walls were not of bare metal but lined with dense, twisted vines as though the entire vessel had been overcome by jungle growth. Ty'ek leaped from vine to vine, sweeping down the corridor far faster than any human being could run until he reached a fast–moving channel of water that flowed like a river through the ship. Ty'ek dropped into the river and let it carry him at high speed through the massive hull.

The forested interior of the cruiser was more than just a deliberate attempt by its architects to preserve something of their homeworld for crewmembers destined to spend months, or years, among the stars while at the same time providing a source of oxygen for that same crew to breathe. The hot, dense air was also a deterrent to any enemy attempting to board the ship, the lungs of most species ill–adapted to sub–tropical climates. Likewise, the act of moving around the ship kept the crew's cardiovascular prowess at a high standard unlike many other species, whose muscles and bones degraded in strength with long exposure to low or zero gravity. The cruiser maintained a quasi–gravity not through the electromagnet method favoured by the human's Colonial forces but via massive, fast–rotating centrifuges arranged along the cruiser's keel. Loaded with particles responsible for giving objects mass, the gravitational waves emitted by the centrifuges produced a near–normal gravitational field within the vessel.

Rage seethed through Ty'ek's veins much as the river seethed through the cruiser. All Veng'en's hated humans, they always had, but Ty'ek had more reason than most. His father had fought at Mal'Oora, a savage engagement that had cost more Veng'en lives than most other battles put together. Fought when a Veng'en battle fleet had encountered a human battle group near the small moon of Mal'Oora, a strategically valuable forest world in Veng'en territory, the engagement had lasted more than three days and involved heavy fighting both in orbit and on the moon's surface. Both sides had been equally matched: the humans had more vessels and soldiers, but the Veng'en knew the territory better and the moon's humid atmosphere favoured them in combat.

The engagement had ended more due to a mutual lack of fuel and ammunition than any decisive victory being attained, and as both fleets limped away with their dead, dying and injured numbering in the thousands, so one Veng'en of immense importance to Ty'ek had been counted among the deceased: his father.

No single event in Ty'ek's life had fuelled him for a life of combat and revenge more than the loss of his beloved father. As was customary in Veng'en culture, his father had abandoned Ty'ek into his mother's care as a newborn. It was the sole aim of any young male Veng'en to come to their father's attention not through such feeble notions as compassion or love, but through actions on the battlefield. All that a father needed to know was his son's name, and vice versa. Sooner or later they would cross paths, and if the son's or the father's actions were valiant enough, they would learn of each other's presence and be reunited as warriors upon a field of victory.

Ty'ek's father died in the glory of combat long before his son ever had the chance to meet him.

A series of exits flashed by as Ty'ek floated at speed through the ship. He waited until he reached the one he wanted and pushed to one side of the channel, reaching up for the vines that dangled outside the exit and catching them in one hand.

His momentum pulled on the vines and he swung around and up out of the water to land smoothly on a walkway. Ty'ek leaped into the adjoining exit corridor, which led a short distance to the cruiser's landing bays. The stench of burning foliage and scorched metal tainted the air as he strode through a bulkhead and into the bays.

The Atlantia's bombardment of the bay had shattered the hull of the cruiser, the blasts probing deep into the vessel. Fourteen Veng'en lives had been lost, their corpses sucked out into the freezing void of space, the deceased denied the honour of dying in battle against a truly hated enemy.

Ty'ek took in the scene of devastation. It looked somewhat as though a city had been built inside a forest and then the whole burned to the ground.

Thick smoke coiled around the scorched stumps of giant trees that sprawled upward around the edges of the huge hangar, their immense limbs helping to support the ceiling. Beneath them were the smouldering remains of several Scythe fighters, their pilot's charred corpses still strapped into the cockpits where they had burned to death.

With the bays doors open and fighter craft landing when the Atlantia had struck, the bays had been exposed to the vacuum of space. The blasts had then ripped through bulkheads and exposed the interior of the ship, sucking crewmen out and providing extra fuel for the flames. Interior shield doors had automatically closed when the fires had been detected reaching beyond the landing bays, preventing the blazes from probing too far into the cruiser, but not before considerable damage had been done to the ship's crew and Scythe fighters.

'How many do we have left?' he asked the first officer he came across, whose uniform was stained with soot and grime and blood.

'Two squadrons,' came the barked reply. 'We lost a quarter of our vessels in the attack, and several more to the Raythons in battle. We're not ready for this captain. Our people are not experienced enough to attack a ship like the Atlantia and…'

Ty'ek turned, his shoulder whipping around as the back of his fist smacked across the officer's jaw and sent him sprawling onto the filthy deck. The crewmen working nearby stopped what they were doing and watched as Ty'ek stamped his clawed foot on the officer's chest and from a concealed sheath in his sleeve produced a blade of silvery metal almost as long as his hand.

Ty'ek leaned down, the point of the blade pressed against the officer's neck.

'You would run away from a human?' he hissed.

The officer shook his head, his teeth bared and his eyes glowing with rage.

Ty'ek pushed away from the fallen Veng'en officer and glared at the crew around him.

'I want every last available fighter ready for launch within the hour. If there are no pilots remaining then you shall man them yourselves!'

The crew looked at him in silence, not one of them daring to oppose Ty'ek.

The Veng'en captain turned slowly to leave, just as a communication console beeped at him. He walked across to it and pressed a button to see a screen flicker into life and an image of his second–in–command, Rivlak, staring back at him.

'They are slowing, captain,' he informed Ty'ek. 'We shall be upon them within minutes!'

Ty'ek felt a soaring excitement and anticipation rise up within him.

'Prepare for battle!' he shouted.

***

XXXVI

'All pilots, this way!'

Evelyn jogged alongside her fellow Reaper pilots as they tumbled from the ready room and out into a corridor, carrying their helmets under their arms as they followed the Launch Control Officer toward the launch bays.

'You got any idea what the captain's doing?'

Teera was a young female pilot who had joined the squadron only days before having passed her flight training and earned her wings. She was slim like Evelyn, with short–cropped blonde hair and bright blue eyes that matched her skin: the pale blue tint to her was a legacy of being the fifth generation of humans brought up on Oraz, a moon that orbited the blue star Rigelle in an outlying system.

'I've got no idea,' Evelyn admitted, her legs feeling rubbery as exhaustion threatened to overwhelm her. Even talking seemed to require an immense effort. 'I just hope it's going to work.'

The pilots burst out into the launch bay, ranks of Raython fighters lined up alongside the walls with their canopies open and cables snaking from beneath their hulls as groundcrews fussed over them.

'Reapers to port, Renegades to starboard!' the LCO yelled as he stopped running and turned to face them. 'Reapers launch first, you're on offensive. Renegades, you're the defensive line – stay close to the Atlantia. All but three of the Raythons are now serviceable: if your fighter is not here then you're on bridge duty for tactical support. No arguments, just get to your fighters or posts and get out there. Give 'em hell!'

A brief cheer rang out in the hangar as Evelyn and Teera dashed toward the waiting fighters that bore the growling skull motif of their squadron.

'Looks like I'm in luck!' Teera cried in delight as she identified her Raython by its tail–code letters stencilled on the fuselage, parked amid a long line of fighters with cockpits open awaiting their pilots.

Evelyn felt sure that her own Raython would be absent, her flight training incomplete and Andaim having been unwilling to pass her and award her wings. And now, more then ever, Andaim was angry for her deceit and would probably have withdrawn any idea of support. She scanned the long row of waiting fighters and her heart sank as she realised that hers was not among them.

She turned to the LCO, who jabbed a thumb over his shoulder and grinned.

Evelyn looked past him and saw two Raythons being towed out from the maintenance shed that adjoined the launch bay, the craft hovering a few inches above the deck. One bore her tail–code and M.D. G'velle's name beneath the canopy: the other, that of the Commander of the Air Group, Andaim Ry'ere.

Evelyn saw Andaim walking alongside his Raython, his helmet cradled under his arm as he approached. She walked toward him.

'Are you okay?' she asked.

Andaim nodded, not smiling but not outwardly hostile either. 'I'll live. Your Raython has been repaired, refuelled and rearmed and you're ready to go.'

'I thought that...'

'I know what you thought,' Andaim cut her off. 'I'm not going to stand here and blow sunshine at you and pretend that everything's fine, but I get why you and the captain did what you did and it's history. Right now we've got bigger problems and I'd rather have you out there with the squadron than stuck on the bridge with tactical.'

'I haven't finished my training,' she said.

'By the time this sortie is over,' Andaim replied as he donned his flight helmet, 'you'll have either passed or failed.'

Evelyn turned and marched toward her Raython as it was pushed into the secondary launch slot and sank to the deck alongside Andaim's fighter. Evelyn hurried around the craft, completing her walk–around checks as she fastened her helmet in place and watched the launch–crews swarming over the undercarriage.

She was about to board the Raython when a familiar face appeared, escorted by two ground–crew who guided her through the complex tangle of electrical and fuel cables snaking between the parked Raythons.

Meyanna Sansin hurried to Evelyn's side and gripped her shoulder. The doctor looked tired but sufficiently recovered to have concern for others once more.

'When did you last sleep, Evelyn?' she asked again.

Evelyn blinked. She realised not only that she could not remember exactly when she had last slept, but that her addled mind would not allow her to begin to calculate even an approximation. Meyanna saw the momentary confusion on Evelyn's face.

'That's what I thought,' she said. 'Put out your wrist.'

Evelyn held out her wrist and Meyanna folded down the cuff of her fireproof gloves to expose her skin. In a flash she pressed a small vial of a ruby–coloured liquid against Evelyn's skin and depressed a plunger. Evelyn felt a tingling sensation in her wrist as the small vial emptied into her bloodstream.

'You've been running on empty for weeks and now you're going into combat on no sleep,' Meyanna said. 'You'll need this to prevent you from getting blown to pieces.'

'You're giving me this now, after all those weeks of tests?'

'It's Verenium,' Meyanna explained.

Evelyn's mind whirled. An exotic stimulant, highly illegal except in specific medical emergencies when it was used to prevent patients from slipping into irreversible comas. Rumours abounded that the military's Special Forces units used the drug to enhance their performance in stressful combat situations. A street version, *Vertigo*, had often been peddled by gangs on Ethera and Caneeron. Countless addicts had lost their lives by overdosing and hurling themselves from skyscrapers or even aircraft in mid–flight, believing themselves to be utterly invincible.

'It'll help get you through this,' Meyanna added. 'I would never usually administer it but we need every pilot we have.'

'There are three pilots without airframes on tactical,' Evelyn said. 'Why hasn't Andaim switched me out with one of them?'

'Because although Andaim won't admit it, he knows that you're better than they are,' Meyanna replied. 'You've almost passed your training despite being under constant medical examination and reduced blood flow, and that's something he's aware of now. Think about what you can do when you're at full capacity. This will help you, now go, quickly!'

Meyanna turned and hurried away as Evelyn climbed aboard, saw the cockpit instruments already switched on via power delivered by ground cables attached to the Raython.

She strapped into her seat and plugged in her intercom, instantly hearing Lael's voice broadcasting from the bridge.

'... *sub–luminal velocity in ninety seconds. Prepare for deceleration.*'

Evelyn shook her head in an attempt to clear her mind as she began activating the Raython's engines. The ground crews pulled the power lines from the fuselage and backed away as the whine of dozens of powerful ion engines began to fill the launch bay. Evelyn closed her canopy, letting her flight notes hover in the air before her as she finished her checks and then she stowed the notes in a slot alongside the cockpit wall.

'*All Reapers call in,*' Andaim called.

'Reaper Two, flight ready,' Evelyn replied.

'*Reaper Three, flight ready.*'

'*Reaper Four...*'

Evelyn forced herself to relax. She was woefully tired but the anticipation of imminent, life–threatening combat injected adrenaline into her bloodstream as though she was supercharged. Colours suddenly seemed sharper, sounds clearer, her senses heightened to supernatural levels as she actually began to relish engaging the enemy. She realised that the Verenium was taking effect. Her drowsiness slipped away like an old skin and she sucked in a deep breath of cool, clean air as she realised that she was smiling. *Damn*, why couldn't she have had a shot of that stuff for every flight?

'All call–signs, sub–luminal velocity in thirty seconds. Prepare for deceleration.'

The ground crew dashed from sight outside Evelyn's cockpit, hauling fuel lines and power cables behind them as they hurried into armoured and pressurised bunkers that lined the edges of the flight deck. Her Raython's nose sank slightly as the magnetic catapult engaged, ready to fling the fighter out into the void of space. Evelyn checked that her engines were running smoothly and checked over her shoulders to ensure all groundcrew were clear of her fighter and the catapults.

'Reapers One and Two, prepare for launch!'

Evelyn checked her harnesses one last time and then rested her handle on the throttle, ready to open it wide when the catapults fired and the bay doors opened. She realised that she could hear every whisper of the ion engines behind her, the rustle of the fabric of her flight suit against her skin and her heartbeat pulsing inside her chest.

'Sub–luminal in ten seconds.'

Evelyn mentally counted down as she stared at the still–closed bay doors, a dense barrier that her Raython would be blasted into if the launch sequence was not activated with absolute precision. She eased the throttle up to fifty per cent power, the Raython straining at the magnetic clamps restraining it, running them up so that full power was ready at a moment's notice.

Lael's voice reached her as though from a distance in her headphones.

'…four, three, two, one, sub–luminal!'

The light in the bay blurred and polarised as the Atlantia dropped out of faster–than–light travel, her mass–drive disengaging. Evelyn felt herself pressed against her harnesses with the deceleration and then suddenly her intercom came alive.

'Reaper One and Two, launch sequence now!'

Evelyn threw her throttles wide open as the catapult engaged and her fighter surged forward under terrific acceleration. The lights of the launch bay flashed past in a blurred stream as the bay doors opened before her, a cloud of vaporised moisture and oxygen billowing around her Raython as it flashed through the narrow gap and out into space.

Evelyn retracted her undercarriage as a flare of starlight seared the cockpit and a deep shadow loomed before her. She jinked left instinctively as a huge asteroid tumbled past, saw Andaim's Raython jerk right to avoid it as they raced into the depths of a massive asteroid field, the glow from a distant red dwarf star illuminating his fighter.

'What the hell?' Evelyn uttered.

'Levelling the playing field,' Andaim echoed the captain's words as they flitted through the endless cloud of asteroids. 'He's taken us back to quadrant Delta–Four–Seven. The Veng'en cruiser won't be able to follow us through this, it's hull plating isn't strong enough and the ray shielding only protects against plasma shots.'

Evel shook her head as she heard the rest of the Reapers launching behind them.

'The Atlantia can't stay in here for long either, it'll get pulverised.'

'I guess he's got that covered too,' Andaim replied. 'Stay sharp. The Veng'en will be here any minute.'

***

XXXVII

'Jump complete, mass–drive disengaged.'

Captain Idris Sansin stared at the main viewing screen and the vast asteroid field dominating it. The cloud of dense black rocks extended into a distance so vast that it took on the appearance of dust clouds before the immense flare of the young star blazing at its heart. One day, countless billions of years from now, that star might cast its warmth upon planets forged from the disc of rocky debris orbiting it that might harbour intelligent and even space–faring life with their own problems.

More than ever, as he surveyed the asteroid field, Idris felt sure that he was doing the right thing. What future would those planets and life forms have if the Word expanded its insidious reach to every system in the galaxy? Would life even be allowed to evolve?

'Captain?'

Mikhain's voice snapped the captain from his reverie and he ordered his thoughts. 'Orbital velocity of the asteroid belt?'

'Point oh six four,' the helmsman replied, 'clockwise.'

'Match the orbital velocity and take us in,' Sansin replied.

'Aye sir,' the helmsman replied.

'This is a hell of a gamble,' Mikhain whispered from beside his console. 'There are asteroids in that field with far greater mass than this ship. If we get caught up between two of them…'

'Then we'll be well shielded from the Veng'en cruiser,' Idris replied.

'We don't know what they'll do.'

'We know that they won't stop pursuing us,' Idris insisted. 'We've already spent two years running from the Word. I'm not going to start running from the Veng'en too. Besides, I have some inside knowledge of what they might do.'

Mikhain raised his eyebrows in surprise. 'You have?'

In reply, Idris turned to the bridge doors. The two Marine guards there opened the doors and onto the bridge walked a further two Marines either side of the Veng'en, Kordaz, who walked with steel manacles on his ankles and wrists.

'Are you insane?' Mikhain uttered. 'You're bringing that *thing* onto the bridge?'

The captain did not reply as Kordaz was led up onto the command platform. Idris stood tall before the enormous reptilian soldier, forced himself to hold the Veng'en's oddly soul-less gaze as he spoke.

'When I fought the Veng'en during the fleet action at Mal'Oora,' he said, 'two of our ships were captured. One was destroyed when it decided to fight to the death rather than be captured, an action that is still revered in Colonial lore to this day. The other was boarded by Veng'en soldiers and overcome.'

Kordaz did not move as the captain went on, loudly enough for the entire bridge to hear.

'The captured Marines and crew were taken by the Veng'en and strapped naked to a wall in their vessel's landing bay,' he said. 'One by one they were flayed alive using plasma whips until they died of shock brought on by hours of being effectively burned alive, one little bit at a time.' The captain fell silent for a moment, the Atlantia's bridge deathly quiet. 'That is what your people are. That is how we see you. That is what we have come to expect from you.'

Idris held the Veng'en's gaze for a moment longer and then he held out his hand. One of the Marines handed him an electronic key. The captain knelt down in front of Kordaz and personally unlocked the manacles at his feet, and then he stood and unlocked the manacles on his wrists. The opened steel cuffs fell away to hover in the air between them as Idris handed the Marine back his key and looked up at Kordaz.

'We will not become what you are,' he said, and then turned his back on the Veng'en. 'Where are they?' he asked Lael.

Lael glanced down at her instruments.

'I'm detecting a gravitational bow-wave at quadrant two point four, elevation plus three five, range fourteen thousand cubits.'

Idris glanced at the holographic tactical display as Mikhain gestured to a spot high off the starboard bow.

'They'll appear about here,' he said, 'any time in the next couple of minutes.'

Idris turned back to Kordaz, who was standing silently behind them.

'You have a choice,' Idris said. 'When the Veng'en cruiser returns, if you wish you may to travel across to join them before battle commences.'

Kordaz's voice was deep as he replied. 'Why? If I joined them, I would fight you and share everything that I have learned.'

Idris smiled without warmth. 'Or you would be killed on sight by your own brethren. And even if you were not, you would tell them that we have found a way to prevent infection by the Word. Once we have formulated and distributed a vaccine our people will equally be immune as the Veng'en.

The Word will now seek to destroy us completely before that vaccine can be modified and shared with other species. We can either face the Word together or we can face it alone. The choice is yours.'

Kordaz remained silent for a few seconds.

'Quarantine and elimination is the only safe way to prevent the spread of the horror that you have created.'

'If that were true,' Idris replied, 'then my wife would be dead and my compliment of fighters not led by the Commander of the Air Group. Elimination is *not* the only option and whether you decide to stay or go, I would appreciate it if you would impart that to Ty'ek and his crew.'

Idris turned his back again to Kordaz, insulting the warrior once more. Mikhain stood tense, one hand hovering close to his sidearm, but the big Veng'en did not move.

'Sixty seconds and they'll be here,' Lael called.

Idris did not reply. Instead, he kept his gaze on the viewing screen as he awaited the Veng'en's reply.

'I will return to my people,' Kordaz said finally.

Idris sighed quietly enough not to let anybody hear him. 'As is your wish.'

'Only if they agree to return their hostages,' Kordaz added. He reached out and plucked the manacles from where they hovered before him, and then fastened them about his wrists once more.

Idris turned slowly. 'The Sylph's crew?'

'They are victims of this as much as we are, as you say,' Kordaz replied. 'They deserve the chance to return here if they are still alive.'

'Ty'ek won't have killed them,' Mikhain said. 'He'll still consider them as leverage, for now at least.'

'And I can be their ticket home,' Kordaz said.

'Ty'ek might kill you,' Idris reminded him.

'Yes,' Kordaz replied. 'He might.'

Idris nodded and then glanced at Mikhain. 'Prepare to hail the Veng'en as soon as they arrive.'

The XO hurried to his console.

'Ty'ek may not be reasoned with,' Kordaz warned the captain. 'He will seek your destruction regardless of what you say to him.'

'I know,' Idris replied, and turned to Bra'hiv. 'Prepare your men for an assault.'

'You want to *attack* them?' Bra'hiv asked.

'We're going to get our people back, either by force or by guile. If Ty'ek won't release them, all we can do is give them the best chance possible to break free of their captors and make it to a shuttle. You and your men will be on board that shuttle.'

Bra'hiv saluted and marched from the bridge and Idris turned to the main viewing screen as a swarm of asteroids drifted slowly by. A distant series of dull, laborious booms echoed through the ship.

'Impacts to port,' the helmsman announced, 'low angles, no damage reports.'

'Keep her slow and steady,' Idris replied. 'Manoeuvre her to conceal as much of our hull as possible from being targeted.'

'Aye sir.'

'We could breach our hull if one of those asteroids hits us hard enough,' Mikhain pointed out.

'Maybe,' Idris replied, 'but the Atlantia's hull is older than the Veng'en cruiser's, built back in the day when brute force was the way to combat micrometeorite damage and radiation. She'll hold up okay.'

'For how long?' Mikhain challenged.

'Five seconds sir.' Lael's voice warned the captain. 'They're coming through.'

'On screen.'

The image of the dense asteroid belt and distant star changed to one of deep space, and Idris searched the starfield for the tell–tale conical warping of starlight as the Veng'en cruiser's mass–drive warped space–time ahead of it.

Almost immediately he saw a scattering of bright, hot blue stars bend in a kaleidoscope, twisting in upon themselves. The warped patch of spacetime rippled and then went entirely black, then flared with white light as the Rankor leaped into view and the starfield behind it returned to normal.

'Signalling them,' Mikhain reported.

'Hold the fighters back,' Idris ordered. 'I don't want a battle commencing before we've had a chance to talk to them.'

'Aye captain.'

The main screen flickered and then Ty'ek's face appeared once more.

'Captain Sansin,' he snarled. 'Finally, your time has come.'

'We have a cure for infection by the Word,' Idris announced without preamble.

'We have no need of your cure,' Ty'ek snapped in response. 'All we require is the annihilation of your people and your hideous creation.'

'We have removed the infection from our vessel,' Idris pressed. 'The Word is no longer aboard and we have captured a Hunter nanobot. We are studying it right now to find a weakness, and would be happy to share any information we find with you and your...'

'Your pleas are for nothing, captain,' Ty'ek growled. 'You cannot hide your ship and your people under space rocks forever, like the mud dwelling slime that you all are.'

'I'm telling you that we have no infection aboard this ship,' Idris repeated.

'And I'm telling you that I don't give a damn.'

'You should.'

The voice was Veng'en and Idris saw Ty'ek's eyes narrow suspiciously as Kordaz walked into view, his wrists manacled.

'I propose an exchange of prisoners,' Idris said.

'What makes you think that I want Kordaz back at all?' Ty'ek smirked. 'It would be an act of greater courage for Kordaz to kill as many of you as possible and die while doing so, if he had any sense of pride or honour.'

'It would serve no purpose,' Kordaz said. 'I have seen them cure the infection and destroy the Word. We can learn from them.'

'What more could we learn of pain and suffering from humans?' Ty'ek sneered. 'Theirs is a world of machines now, machines that seek to destroy us all. There is nothing new to be learned from them but how to destroy them more quickly.'

'Destruction is not the only way,' Idris said. 'Kordaz here has seen that. There are other ways, Ty'ek, to defeat an enemy.'

'Indeed,' Ty'ek snarled. 'Perhaps I should try one of those alternatives myself?'

Ty'ek stood back from the screen and revealed behind him the captured crew of the Sylph. But among them now was a new hostage, a towering man with bituminous black skin, braids of blue and gold hair and bioluminescent tattoos that glowed as though venting the rage seething in his expression.

'Qayin,' Idris gasped. 'We thought you were dead!'

'Sorry to disappoint,' Qayin murmured.

'We found him in an escape capsule jettisoned from the Sylph,' Ty'ek sneered. 'You must have abandoned him, captain, which says a great deal about how similar we are.'

'We share nothing,' Idris snapped.

Kordaz stepped forward, addressing Ty'ek directly.

'The soldier you are holding prisoner,' he said. 'Without his courage I would not be standing here. Return him, and I shall return to you.'

Ty'ek's eyes narrowed again and despite his emotionless face Idris could sense the suspicion clouding the Veng'en's thoughts. 'You have been turned, Kordaz.'

'No.'

'You are lying,' Ty'ek snapped. 'Either the infection is still aboard or you have turned traitor. Either way, to let you back aboard would be suicide for one or for both of us. You have chosen them, as they have chosen to abandon their own.'

'Let the hostages go!' Idris snapped. 'Or by Ethera I'll crush your ship into dust.'

'No Veng'en shall ever bow to a human,' Ty'ek seethed, 'and no Veng'en shall fall but fighting for his life. Attack them where they lay!'

The viewing screen went blank and then showed once more the Veng'en cruiser against the starfield, her giant hull glowing in the light from the star as from her launch bays the tiny specks of dozens of Veng'en Scythe fighters rocketed out into the void.

'Send the Raythons in,' Idris snapped. 'Launch Bra'hiv's Marines, and tell them that all of the hostages are captive upon the Rankor's bridge!'

'Sheilds up!' Mikhain replied.

'Fire all cannons!' Idris bellowed.

***

XXXVIII

'All fighters engage! Take them down!'

Evelyn heard the command and turned her Raython toward the Veng'en cruiser, Andaim's Raython tucked in close alongside her.

'This is it,' Andaim called. *'Stay in pairs and stay sharp!'*

Evelyn saw flashes of bright blue light and a tremendous salvo of plasma shots race by overhead as the Atlantia opened up against the Rankor. The salvo rocketed away and smashed into the Veng'en cruiser's huge hull in brilliant flares and explosions that made Evelyn squint. In the same instant the Rankor fired back, brilliant red plasma shots smashing into the asteroids shielding the Atlantia.

'Here come the fighters!' Teera yelled.

Evelyn saw a cloud of Veng'en Scythe fighters rocket toward her, their plasma shots zipping past. No thoughts entered her mind as she weaved left and dove between two streams of plasma and fired twice, unthinking reflexes driving her responses with supernatural speed. She registered the two shots impacting two different Scythe craft, blasting their cockpits into flaming wreckage and causing them to spiral out of control in bright blossoming balls of flame and debris.

'Splash one and two!' Andaim yelled as he opened fire.

The Scythes flashed past as a second salvo of giant plasma shots blazed overhead from the Veng'en cruiser, heading for the Atlantia. Evelyn hauled her Raython around in a tight turn to see a vast cloud of Raythons and Scythes arcing ion trails through space as they fought to manoeuvre against each other.

Behind them, the Veng'en cruiser's salvo of plasma charges smashed into tumbling clouds of asteroids in a flickering array of explosions.

'Stay in pairs!' Andaim commanded. 'Combine your firepower and make your shots count in each attack!'

Evelyn picked out a pair of Scythes amid the melee, their wings flashing in unison as they caught the starlight and pursued two Raythons. Evelyn focused in on the lead Scythe and closed upon it, moving her control column without thought and with brisk movements as she slid in directly behind the Scythes.

She did not see her aiming reticule turn red as it locked onto the enemy fighter, nor did she see the bright plasma shots erupt from her guns. All she saw was the Scythe split in two by the direct hits, bright flames and debris flashing in the sunlight as they spiralled past her Raython and the Scythe fighter broke up into fragments.

She did not make the splash call as other pilots were doing. The second Scythe fighter pulled hard left and then rotated in mid–flight, maintaining its trajectory as it pointed its weapons back at her and opened fire. Evelyn pulled hard on her control column and simultaneously threw it over, rolling the Raython through a tight barrel–roll and making it as hard to hit as possible. Trails of glowing plasma rocketed in red streaks past her canopy, always just out of reach, and as she rolled back into plane with the Scythe fighter she fired once.

The shot hit the fighter square on and smashed it into two, the flaming debris flashing by either side of Evelyn's fighter as she rolled it up onto its side and sliced through the expanding fireball.

'Splash four!' Andaim reported. 'Evelyn, form up now!'

Evelyn blinked and realised that Andaim was now following her, having been left behind as she pursued the two Veng'en fighters.

'Roger that,' she replied.

'Stay on my wing damn it, before you get us both killed!'

Evelyn slid in alongside Andaim's fighter as they wheeled back into the fight, clouds of Scythes and Raythons and countless flashes of plasma zipping across the starfield between them.

Evelyn saw the Atlantia fire another salvo at the Rankor. The blue plasma shots blazed between the two massive ships and hammered the cruiser's aft hull, peppering it with flickering fires and shattering sections of hull plating, but the ray–sheilding still protected the majority of the larger vessel's hull from permanent damage.

Andaim's Raython opened fire on a pair of Scythes and caught one of them on its port side, smashing the wing off. The engines exploded in a bright fireball and Andaim jinked right to avoid the debris. Evelyn went left and cut in ahead of Andaim as she settled in behind the remaining Scythe.

'I've got him.'

'You're covered,' Andaim replied.

The Scythe jerked frantically left and right, trying to shake Evelyn, but she held on easily and waited for the perfect moment to take a single shot. She squeezed the trigger and two plasma rounds converged on the Scythe's cockpit and smashed it into a glowing mass of molten metal. The Scythe, pilotless, spiralled slowly downward and smashed into a tumbling asteroid to vanish in a roiling cloud of burning fuel and flame.

'Good shot!' Andaim called as he pulled up and rocketed over the asteroid.

Evelyn skimmed the giant rock, the surface of it flashing by as she pulled up and aimed back toward the battle. She glimpsed the underside of the Atlantia's hull, saw multiple small fires flickering from where plasma damage and asteroid impacts were battering her.

'The ship's taking too many hits,' she called as she emerged from the asteroid field. 'She can't stay in there forever.'

As if in reply a plasma round from the Veng'en cruiser ploughed into the Atlantia's bow amid a flare of bright light, and Evelyn glimpsed debris spiralling off her hull plating in the aftermath of the blast.

'They don't have much choice,' Andaim replied as explosions burst around his Raython, the shockwaves making the little fighter rock and quiver.

'We need an edge,' Evelyn snapped. 'Kordaz said that Veng'en ships are filled with forest materials.'

'So what?' Andaim asked as he tried to get on the tail of a Scythe that itself was following a Raython. 'The Atlantia can't go up against a cruiser that big in open battle. She'd be smashed to pieces!'

'She can't,' Evelyn replied, 'but we can.'

*

Sergeant Djimon jogged up the shuttle's ramp as Bra'hiv watched, holding on to the shuttle's interior wall with one hand as the Atlantia shuddered and rocked under the plasma blasts and asteroid impacts.

'We need to get out there and do this before this ship gets torn apart!' the sergeant yelled.

Bra'hiv hit the button to close the shuttle's ramp and then turned and called to the pilots.

'Lift off, now!'

The shuttle tilted as it lifted up off the Atlantia's deck and Bra'hiv saw the launch bay doors open as the air was sucked out into the oblivion of space. The dense asteroid field, a morass of tumbling rocks cast in harsh light and shadow, loomed into view as the general strapped himself into his seat behind the pilots and watched as they guided the shuttle out of the Atlantia's bay.

'Stay close to the debris field,' Bra'hiv ordered. 'We go only when the captain orders, understood?'

The pilot nodded, the shuttle accelerating away from beneath the Atlantia's bow even as a barrage of red plasma fire tore through the asteroid field. A gigantic ball of rock was shattered by a direct hit from the Veng'en cruiser's guns and a cloud of vast and chaotically tumbling debris rocketed toward the shuttle.

'Incoming, starboard bow!'

The pilot responded instantly, diving down into cover behind a larger asteroid as the hail of debris flew past. Smaller rocks hammered the shuttle's hull with a loud rattling, and through the glow of the distant star Bra'hiv could see veils of thick dust and other flotsam suspended in space, and endless minefield of threats to the shuttle's hull and engines.

'We need to get out of this,' the pilot said to Bra'hiv without breaking his gaze out of the viewing panel. 'We'll either get pulverised by the big ones or our engines will clog with debris and fail us.'

'Stay in the holding pattern,' Bra'hiv ordered, his voice equally calm and betraying none of the consternation enveloping him. 'If we're spotted, we're doomed.'

'This is suicide, for one man, for a convict.'

Sergeant Djimon's voice reached Bra'hiv from the troop compartment behind him, where men from both Alpha and Bravo Company sat. The general looked over his shoulder and saw the familiar expressions of men about to join a fight: stoic, tense, staring straight ahead into nowhere and alone with their thoughts.

'We don't leave anybody behind,' Bra'hiv replied in a low growl. 'We can't afford to any more.'

'And lose more people in the process?' Djimon challenged, drawing a few glances from the other Marines around him.

Even though they were all hardened men, combat ready, that did not mean that a single one of them wanted to join a fight that they may not survive. Nobody wanted to die, no matter how tough they thought they were, and the merest hint of a chance at escape was as addictive as any drug to men who were, in the end of all things, human. They joined the fight because it was the right thing to do.

Bra'hiv knew that they had to believe in what they were doing, and Djimon was trying to take that away from them.

'Qayin would not be where he is now if it were not for his own courage and your betrayal, Djimon,' the general replied. 'You told us you saw Qayin die, and yet he's reported as being alive and a hostage aboard that Veng'en ship. We're facing death again because you didn't want to. You got a problem with that, why not talk to your fellow Marines about it?'

Djimon did not dignify the other Marines by looking at them, his gaze remaining fixed on Bra'hiv, but the general saw the Marines all glaring at the sergeant with questioning expressions on their faces.

'Forgot to mention that to Alpha Company, did you Djimon?' Bra'hiv asked.

'You calling me a coward?' the sergeant challenged.

'I'm calling you a traitor,' Bra'hiv snapped. 'Qayin may be a murderous convict but he's also got guts and he's trapped because he didn't want to leave anybody behind. You, on the other hand, were more than willing to leave a fellow Marine stranded aboard an infected vessel under direct fire from a Veng'en cruiser.' Bra'hiv glared at Djimon. 'You're not the man I want watching my back, sergeant.'

Djimon opened his mouth to respond but his reply was cut off as the shuttle pilot spoke into his intercom.

'Company, stand by for deployment!'

***

XXXIX

'Fire!'

Ty'ek watched as another gigantic salvo of plasma rounds thundered away toward the Atlantia, the blasts smashing into clouds of asteroids shielding the frigate. Chunks of rock were shattered to tumble in countless swarms, veiling the Atlantia in ethereal clouds of glowing dust.

'Only two direct hits from six, commander,' his tactical officer reported. 'We can't get enough strikes to bring them down.'

Ty'ek let out a roar of frustration. 'What about our fighters?!'

'We've destroyed two Raythons for nine losses sir,' Rivlak replied.

'Why are they winning?!' Ty'ek raged.

'Because they're smarter than you.'

The voice was that of Qayin, who sat strapped to a chair behind Ty'ek. Ty'ek whirled and smashed the back of his hand across Qayin's bruised face, a spray of blood and bioluminescent fluid splattering across the soldier's vest and hanging in fluid globules in the air.

'They are nothing to us,' Ty'ek snarled back at Qayin, 'nor are you.'

The Slyph's crew, likewise strapped to chairs on the bridge, remained silent as Ty'ek stared at the main display screen for a moment longer and then he made his decision.

'Take us in closer,' he snarled.

The Veng'en's First Officer, Rivlek, stood up from his crouch behind the tactical station and shook his head. 'We cannot move too close to the asteroid field, our hull is not as strong as the Atlantia's. One direct hit and we could be severely compromised!'

'We already are!' Ty'ek bellowed. 'Would you have us abandon the chase and flee like cowards?'

'We cannot afford to lose our hull integrity!' Rivlek insisted. 'It may be precisely what they want us to do! We must force them to fight on *our* terms.'

'A Veng'en will fight on any terms,' Ty'ek snarled back. 'That is who we are!'

'It is who *fools* are!'

Ty'ek's leathery skin flashed dark crimson as he moved on reflexive impulse, his massive thighs propelling him across the bridge as he ploughed into Rivlek with a shrieking sound so loud and high–pitched it caused Qayin to wince.

Ty'ek's razor sharp claws plunged into Rivlek's throat and abdomen like knives and tore through his flesh. Qayin saw Ty'ek's limbs whipping up and down in a frenzied blur, dark blood flying in globules to float across the bridge or splatter across screens as the Veng'en commander shredded his former shipmate. Rivlek's abrupt scream of agony pinched off into a gargled, bubbling groan as the officer died at his commander's own hands.

Ty'ek turned, his hands smothered in glistening purple blood that reflected the lights of the bridge as he pointed with one clawed finger at the main viewing panel.

'Take us in closer and blast them with everything we have, now!'

A Veng'en officer shook his head and pointed at the tactical display.

'Incoming, we're under attack!'

Despite his expressionless face, Qayin thought he saw a glimmer of surprise and panic in Ty'ek's features as he whirled and saw a pair of tiny Raythons rocketing toward the cruiser.

'Crush them!' Ty'ek roared.

*

Captain Idris Sansin gripped the support rail of the command platform as a murderous hail of plasma fire smashed through the asteroid field outside and debris pummelled the frigate's hull. The Atlantia rocked and shuddered and the lights dimmed and flickered as Lael's voice, as calm as ever in the face of despair, called out to him across the bridge.

'Fires on decks six through eight. Laceration to hull plating on the starboard stern, engine bays intact, no leaks. Crew has sealed off the bulkheads.'

Idris watched through the main viewing panel as the huge asteroids shielding the frigate from the worst of the cruiser's shots were shattered one by one. The view was clouded by dust and debris that glowed in the sunlight coming from the far side of the frigate, but Idris could still just about discern the long, slender hull of the Veng'en cruiser.

'We can't take much more of this captain,' Mikhain said. 'We won't last much longer against all of these asteroid impacts.'

'We'll last longer than we will against that cruiser's cannons,' Idris snapped in reply. 'What's their status?'

'They're holding position sir,' the XO replied, 'they're not taking the bait.'

Idris kept hold of the rail as the latest salvo of shots subsided, casting his glance across the tactical displays as well as the warning lights detailing fires and hull breaches across the frigate.

'She'll hold for a bit longer,' he insisted, as much to himself as to the bridge crew. 'Ty'ek is young, angry and impatient.'

'That's not much to base this strategy on, captain,' Mikhain pointed out.

'There's not much else we can do.'

Idris watched the display for a moment and his practiced eye picked out the faintest of motions in the cruiser's giant hull.

'She's moving,' he said.

Mikhain frowned at his tactical display and then looked at Kordaz. 'What's Ty'ek's play?'

Kordaz stared at the screen for a moment as though mesmerized by the damage being wrought on his own people, and then spoke.

'He will attack directly,' he replied. 'Ty'ek is young and cannot help himself. He craves revenge and fame for actions in battle.'

'He's right,' Lael said. 'The cruiser is moving in closer. They're targeting asteroids now, not our hull.'

'Good,' Idris replied, tightening his grip on the rail as he glanced at Mikhain. 'Grappling lines?'

'Charged and ready, sir,' the XO replied, 'but we don't have nearly enough men to board and take the Rankor. I don't know what the hell you intend to do with them.'

'What they were intended for,' the captain replied, 'more or less. Keep the engines spooled up ready for my command.'

'Aye sir,' the helmsman replied. 'Ion drives at fifty per cent power and awaiting your orders.'

Idris watched the cruiser and then his heart sank in his chest. He heard Lael's words as though from afar.

'She's coming in broadside to us sir,' she said. 'She's keeping her guns to bear.'

Ty'ek had perhaps a little more to him than Idris had hoped. The Veng'en commander was using lateral thrusters to keep the majority of his massive cannons pointed at the Atlantia as he closed in on the edge of the asteroid field, preventing Idris from gaining any kind of fire power advantage.

'I knew it,' Mikhain snapped. 'Damn it Idris, as soon as she blows through those asteroids we're going to be fully exposed to her broadside. One full set of direct hits from close range and we're done for.'

Idris gritted his teeth and glanced at the tactical display.

'How long before they break through?'

'Sixty seconds, no more,' Lael replied. 'They're blasting the asteroids with their secondary weapons and charging the main guns for their final assault.'

Idris scanned the displays with his practiced eye and knew instinctively that the time for planning and deliberation was over. This was it. He either acted to defeat the Veng'en cruiser or he chose to flee.

'What do we do, sir?' Lael asked.

'The shuttle, Ranger One, what's her location?' Idris called.

'Sector Five, elevation minus four two,' Mikhain reported. 'She's hiding just inside the asteroid field.'

Idris released his grip on the railings and made his decision.

'Deploy the shuttle to board the cruiser!' he ordered. 'Fire grapples on my command!'

'Captain!' Mikhain yelled. 'If we grapple her she'll be in position for a full broadside from point blank range! We'll be cut into pieces!'

Idris saw the cruiser's guns shatter the last of the large asteroids shielding the Atlantia, the vast rocks breaking up into dense tumbling clouds surrounded by halos of glowing dust and debris, and through it all the cruiser's immense hull looming toward them.

'Grapples, now!' Idris yelled. 'Fire them at her stern only!'

Mikhain scowled but he reached across and targeted the cruiser's stern before slamming his palm down on the launch button.

A series of dull thumps reverberated through the Atlantia's hull as ten grapples, each the size of two Raython fighters and attached to cables as thick as ten men, were propelled by rockets toward the Rankor's stern.

Idris saw them rush across the empty space between the two ships and slam into her hull close to her engines, bright flashes of light caused by friction as the huge metal grapples plunged into the cruiser's hull and were welded into place by the kinetic energy of the impacts.

'We're exposed!' Mikhain yelled as the last of the asteroids shielding the Atlantia was blasted into a billion fragments by the cruiser's guns. 'There's no time left!'

The captain pointed at the helmsman.

'Full power, hard to starboard, now!'

***

XL

'This is it! Activate weapons!'

Bra'hiv called out to the men in the rear of the shuttle as it broke free of the asteroid field and rushed toward the huge Veng'en craft.

The Marines activated their plasma rifles and pulled their visors down, the masks sealing with a hiss as the interior was pressurised in anticipation of a hull breach and "*zero–zero*" combat: zero gravity and zero atmosphere. Bra'hiv saw Djimon activate his rifle and check the visor of the man next to him, each Marine ensuring that his companion was fully prepared for battle.

The shuttle rocked violently as massive plasma rounds were discharged to whiz close by outside, the two huge spaceships hammering each other with broadsides in an attempt to batter each other into submission. The general glimpsed the surface of the Veng'en cruiser looming large through the viewing panel ahead as the pilots corkscrewed the shuttle through a violent approach manoeuvre designed to shake off any tracking cannons as they rushed in.

'Aim for a spot astern of the bridge!' Bra'hiv yelled above the din of exploding cannons and whining engines. 'Put us down hard!'

The shuttle rocketed in across the cruiser's hull, its shadow racing across the surface as it approached the bridge from astern and the pilots aimed for a ventral exhaust duct. The design of the Veng'en cruiser was well known to the colonial forces and detailed schematics available to the pilots. Those schematics were overlaid on their windscreen, the duct outlined in bright green as a possible access point. The pilots slowed the shuttle and then deployed the magnetic claws, an aggressive secondary undercarriage designed to bite into even the toughest hulls.

The shuttle jolted violently as the claws gripped, scraping briefly across the hull as they dug in directly overhead the exhaust duct. A deep boom thundered through the shuttle as the craft settled on the hull.

'Breaching charges, deploy!'

The pilot's command was followed by the hiss of a central deployment chute that extended from the bottom of the shuttle and slammed into the cruiser's hull. From the chute ten blast caps drove titanium spears deep into the cruiser's hull and then detonated, forcing the hull inward as though by the blow of a giant hammer.

The hull breached with a terrific blast that strained the shuttle's claws but they held firm as the breaching mechanism pierced the cruiser's hull plating. Instantly, the floor of the shuttle opened up as revolving retractable plates wound back to reveal a smouldering passage down into the cruiser.

'Charges, go!'

Four Marines hurled explosive plasma charges down into the cavity, the charges blowing with dramatic force and a series of bright flares designed to both blind and shock defenders. Bra'hiv heard the last of the charges go off and immediately hurled himself head–first down the chute, his rifle pointing ahead of him as he flew vertically down the shaft and plunged into a ventilation channel running below the surface of the hull.

He hit the deck and rolled, coming up in a firing position and moving forward as more Marines flooded down into the cruiser.

'Enemy!'

The word provoked an instant response as Bra'hiv spotted movement down the ventilation shaft and saw Veng'en soldiers rushing toward them. He moved by instinct, pulling his trigger even as a dozen bright red plasma rounds rocketed through the pale blue smoke clogging the shaft and ploughed into a Marine beside him.

The soldier screamed as he collapsed, his flesh and uniform burning him alive as the Marines returned fire en masse and leaped for cover against bulkheads within the shaft.

'Advance!' Bra'hiv yelled.

The general fired as a Veng'en rushed toward him inverted on the shaft ceiling in an attempt to escape detection. The blast hit the fast moving soldier and blasted his right arm clean off in a spray of plasma, burning flesh and glowing embers as the Veng'en screamed and its rifle spun uselessly in mid air alongside it.

The Veng'en reached for the weapon with its remaining hand as it dropped from the ceiling, in time for Lieutentant C'rairn to fire a second shot into its face, the reptilian features vanishing in a roiling ball of flame as the creature thrashed violently in its death throes.

Bra'hiv dashed to the next bulkhead as more gunfire rocketed down the shaft toward him, the Marines dodging from one narrow piece of cover to the next. Several dropped into prone positions on the deck and fired a constant stream of plasma shots toward the advancing Veng'en.

'Fire in the hole!'

Bra'hiv yelled the warning and switched to a detonating device, his rifle firing a three–second–delay grenade from an underslung launcher beneath his rifle's barrel. The grenade rocketed away through the smoke and slammed into a far wall alongside the attacking Veng'en before detonating just as Bra'hiv covered his ears and ducked down with his eyes closed.

The blast hit him with a hot, hard impact as though he had been struck by a moving vehicle. Bra'hiv moved without fully opening his eyes and charged straight into the clouds of smoke and noise, firing as he went. He heard shrieks of pain as he leaped over fallen Veng'en and plunged his bayonet into their writhing bodies.

A scream of rage soared toward him and a Veng'en, half of its face a smouldering mass of burning tissue, lunged out of the smoke and grabbed hold of Bra'hiv with unimaginable strength as it ploughed into him and slammed him against the wall of the shaft.

Bra'hiv's head hit the metal wall and his vision blurred as he struggled to breath. The Veng'en's bared its fangs as it opened its mouth and grabbed the back of the general's head. He smelled the foul, toxic saliva of the Veng'en as it plunged down onto his head and then he heard a dull crunch and it stopped moving, its fangs touching the skin of his face.

Bra'hiv pushed back against the creature and saw its eyes staring lifelessly down at him and a bayonet thrust through its skull, the tip emerging from the opposite side drenched in purple blood. Bra'hiv looked up and saw Djimon lift a boot and push the Veng'en off the blade. The warrior's body slumped onto the deck alongside the general.

Djimon stuck out one big, calloused hand and Bra'hiv took it as he was hauled to his feet. His ear piece crackled as he stood up.

'Ranger Force, pull out now!'

Bra'hiv saw the Marines blast their way out into the main corridors of the ship, the crackle and thump of plasma fire flashing like strobes through the dense smoke as the general picked up his rifle and saw ahead through a ragged hole in the deck a corridor filled with bizarre foliage, twisted vines and thick mist.

'Negative Atlantia, objective within reach, stand by.'

Djimon ran ahead in pursuit of the other Marines as Bra'hiv followed him. Ahead, a ragged hole had been blasted through the floor of the ventilation shaft and down into the main vessel, flashes of light and a barrage of noise emanating from within. Bra'hiv leaped down through the cavity and slammed down hard onto the deck as he fired at the swiftly moving figures fighting their way toward him.

The corridor was clogged with twisting vines, the air hot and muggy and filled with smoke as Bra'hiv threw himself down into a prone position as plasma fire raced by over his head.

The Marines were advancing by sections ahead and either side of him, each covering the other amid the noise and confusion of the battle. The cruiser shuddered as impacts from the Atlantia's guns and the asteroids around it slammed into its massive hull, the glowing ceiling panels flickering. The garish light show and flashing plasma fire gave every movement a juddering appearance, as though the depths of the cruiser were some hellish jungle nightclub filled with demonic, warring dancers.

'Advance!' Bra'hiv yelled. 'Bravo Company, covering fire!'

The Marines plunged forward as the Veng'en emerged through the dense coils of foliage clogging the corridor. Bra'hiv saw them abandon their rifles as the fight closed in and they launched themselves through the dense canopy of vines and attacked the Marines head–on.

A Veng'en warrior leaped up to the ceiling and then plunged down on a Marine as the soldier aimed up at him. The Veng'en smashed the Marine's rifle aside as his huge arms wrapped around the soldier's body and his lethal teeth slashed deep into the Marine's throat in a spray of dark blood. The Veng'en shook the Marine and his neck snapped like a dry twig, his head hanging backwards at an awkward angle over his shoulder.

A plasma round smashed into both of their heads and Bra'hiv saw Djimon lower his weapon and advance through the coils of vines. Bra'hiv rushed forward and took the lead, running down the corridor as a huge Veng'en rushed at him, claws outstretched.

Bra'hiv ducked down beneath the Veng'en's reach and swung his rifle over in his grasp, the butt of the weapon flipping up to strike the warrior under his wide jaw and smash him sideways into the wall of the corridor. Bra'hiv turned, bringing his rifle back down as he screamed a war–cry and threw his weight behind the weapon. His charge drove his bayonet deep into the Veng'en's throat, severing the warrior's windpipe and spinal column in one brutal motion. The Veng'en gasped, his limbs suddenly falling limp by his side as Bra'hiv yanked the weapon from his body and the Veng'en slumped onto the deck.

'Take the bridge!' Bra'hiv yelled.

Djimon charged the bridge doors that Bra'hiv spotted through the dense coils of vapour and smoke. Fires were burning where plasma rounds had ignited the foliage, smouldering dangerously in the hot air.

'Cover our escape route!' Bra'hiv commanded to the men behind him. 'Fall back to the entry point and hold the line!'

Several Marines of Bravo Company responded and dashed back the way they had come, one quick thinking soldier attaching luminous markers to the walls as he ran to illuminate and guide the rest of the Marines back out of the ship.

Bra'hiv ran in pursuit of Djimon and hurdled the fallen bodies of two Veng'en and a Marine, all of them scarred with charred flesh where searing plasma rounds had ploughed into and through their bodies.

Bra'hiv keyed his microphone and signalled the Atlantia.

'Atlantia, we're inside, give us just two more minutes!'

He cursed as he heard nothing but static in his earpiece.

***

XLI

The Atlantia surged forward and began to turn to starboard toward the Veng'en cruiser as her guns came to bear.

'Pull us up!' Idris roared. 'Get us out of plane from her guns!'

The massive grappling cables pulled taut as the two ships manoeuvered, and instantly three of the cables snapped under the immense strain of hundreds of thousands of tonnes of metal pulled at them from each end, too much even for the carbon nanotube–enhanced cables. But the remaining seven held as the Atlantia began to accelerate.

'She's turning!' Lael called, her voice a little higher in pitch.

Idris watched as the cruiser's stern was yanked slowly around by the force being applied to it by the Atlantia.

'Maintain full power, dead ahead!' the captain snapped.

'Aye captain, dead ahead, full power.'

The Atlantia, her bow raised up out of plane with the Veng'en cruiser, soared clear of her guns and the clouds of asteroids and debris around her. Mikhain stared at the cruiser through the main viewing panel and then he realised what was happening.

'The asteroids,' he said. 'You're going to drag her through them.'

'If they don't cut the cables first or blast us into oblivion,' Idris replied. 'Order all fighters to protect the cables!'

'The cruiser's guns are charging up and she's rolling,' Lael reported, and she glanced at the displays. 'We're not moving her fast enough!'

Idris saw the angles, the distances, the trajectories of the two ships and in an instant he knew that Lael was right. In moments, the cruiser would fight back with her own engines and hold her aim for just long enough to launch another salvo at the Atlantia from a single cable's length, barely five hundred cubits.

'It didn't work,' Lael said. 'We're done for.'

Idris was searching for a response when he heard Mikhain's voice again.

'Reaper Two, rejoin formation and protect the cables, that's an order!'

Idris looked up and saw a single Raython fighter weaving through the asteroid field at breakneck speed toward the cruiser.

*

Evelyn hurled her throttles forward and accelerated past Andaim's fighter as she simultaneously locked onto a fleeing Scythe, fired, and pulled off the target. Her shot smashed the Scythe's engines into a brilliant trail of burning fuel as she turned hard toward the Veng'en cruiser, determination flowing like fire through her veins as though she were a supernatural being immune to death itself.

'Where do you think you're going?!'

Evelyn rolled out and aimed directly at the Veng'en cruiser. 'To make a difference.'

Evelyn focused ahead on the massive form of the Veng'en cruiser. The Atlantia's flaming hull, surrounded by clouds of shattered asteroids all illuminated in an apocalyptic canvass by the young star, flashed by her port wing as she guided the Raython through the edge of the asteroid field.

'They're coming in,' she replied.

Her voice was calm and she realised that her vision was sharper than she could ever recall. Despite the clouds of debris she realised that she was looking directly at distant stars and seeing their colours, that she had time despite the velocity of her Raython to observe her surroundings. Tiny specks and shards of rock catching the glinting light of the star, flashing past in the blink of an eye and yet seared into her memory. The flickering sunlight through the dense debris field calmed her, her control column moving in perfect harmony without thought, reacting on pure instinct to the lethal clouds of rock rocketing toward her.

She heard Andaim's voice across the intercom, ordering her to fall back into formation, but it seemed as though she had dreamed the voice, as though she were watching events from afar.

'Attack formation,' she said softly into her microphone. 'Battle flight.'

'Negative,' Andaim replied. 'Form up and break off, that's an order!'

Evelyn did not reply. Instead she weaved left and right past giant asteroids tumbling in chaotic turmoil around her, and saw through the veils of debris glowing in the sunlight the bulk of the Veng'en cruiser beyond the asteroid field as it drifted into and through the asteroids, trying to turn to bring its port hull's massive guns to bear upon the Atlantia. Powerful plasma pulses erupted in salvos from its smaller guns and rocketed into the asteroid belt, smashing through the debris field in an attempt to sever the grappling cables attached to her stern.

'Evelyn!'

Andaim's voice was filled with a genuine panic and beyond the serene periphery of her drug–induced haze she recognised the fear in him, realised the emotions that must be churning within that she had not entirely admitted to herself existed, had not been able to think about or face before.

For the first timer in longer than she could remember, Evelyn realised that she did not want to hide any more.

'I'll be fine,' she replied.

The edge of the asteroid field flashed into view and her Raython rocketed out into open space.

Evelyn threw her throttles fully forward as she flicked two switches, one on her control column to activate her plasma torpedoes and another on her throttle to switch to a different aiming–mode. The reticlein her SAD changed to a momentum–based display as she got her first clear look at the Veng'en cruiser.

She was huge, her long hull bathed in a golden glow. Rows of specks along her hull flashed with red light as her smaller plasma cannons blasted the Atlantia, the frigate firing rounds in return in a fiery blue–white and red exchange. Evelyn pulled up over the Atlantia's line of fire and aimed directly at the Veng'en cruiser as it rushed toward her.

'Reaper Two, disengage!'

Evelyn did not reply as she stared at the cruiser. She realised that the giant plasma cannons glowed a faint red just as they fired: the building plasma charge expelled a fraction of a second later. Even as she thought it the charges shot toward her and she flicked the Raython to the left, the massive shots whipping past her at a blistering pace.

'Evelyn! Her main cannons are at full charge, pull back, now!'

Her cockpit flared with red light as plasma shots raced by, smaller guns trying to track her tiny fighter as it rocketed inward. Evelyn spotted thick hull plating lining the cruiser's hull between the plasma cannons, the shapes of the panels denoting exterior access to the massive power lines that must be concealed beneath.

The interior of a Veng'en cruiser is much like our home planet, dense foliage. It lives and breathes as we do. Our greatest threat is fire.

Kordaz's words drifted through her mind as she dove beneath another massive plasma shot and pulled up to place her aiming reticule directly over one of the panels, just to the left of a massive cannon.

The reticule changed colour to bright red and Evelyn fired twice.

The Raython slowed as two torpedoes rocketed away, the force of the charges propelling them acting against the launching fighter. Powered only by momentum and a trajectory–based guidance system, to allow for maximum internal explosive power, the two torpedoes soared toward the panels protecting the power lines.

Evelyn hauled back on her control column as the massive plasma cannon erupted with a blast that flashed by beneath her Raython as she soared up high above the giant cruiser's hull and craned her neck to look over her shoulder.

Through her canopy she saw the two torpedoes smash into the hull with a bright double–flare of blinding light. As Evelyn pulled over the top of her loop she saw debris spinning into space from the impact point and a cloud of gas spewing into the deep vacuum.

'Evelyn, what the hell are you doing?!'

Andaim's voice was strained to breaking point, and she spotted his Raython zooming toward the Rankor and followed by a cloud of Scythe fighters.

'Hit the same spot with your cannons!' she called. 'Light their plasma lines up!'

She saw bright bolts of energy flash from Andaim's cannons as he weaved to avoid the fire coming from the Veng'en cruiser, and to her delight a savage explosion ripped through the cruiser's hull as Andaim pulled up, his Raython's wings rocking violently in the shockwave from the blast.

Evelyn pulled down toward the Scythe fighters pursuing Andaim and opened fire with her plasma cannons, ripping into the formations as she plummeted down through them. The Scythes scattered in disarray as two of them burst into flames and plunged into the cruiser's massive hull.

Behind her, she saw the cruiser's massive port cannons flicker out one by one as their power supply was cut off and explosions rippled below the surface of her hull as plasma gas was ignited by fire.

'Splash five and six,' Evelyn called, and then said: 'Atlantia, direct all fire on the cruiser's damaged central hull. Fire now!'

***

XLII

Captain Idris Sansin stared at the viewing screen as he saw the two Raythons wheel through the blackness of space amid a cloud of Scythe fighters, a ragged flaming hole ripped into the side of the cruiser dwarfing them.

'*Splash five and six,*' Evelyn called. '*Atlantia, direct all fire on the cruiser's damaged hull. Fire now!*'

'Like death does she wander,' Mikhain murmured with glee. 'The Rankor's port guns are disabled!'

'You heard her!' Idris roared. 'Fire everything we've got, now, before they re–route the power or flee!'

The giant cruiser's hull began to twist aside as it attempted to protect its suddenly defenceless port side, its stern quarter dragging through the asteroids and debris and the impacts smashing her hull plating. As the hull moved into shadow Idris saw glowing fires arranged in lines that demarked the edges of her massive hull plating.

'She's aflame,' Mikhain announced with barely concealed delight. 'Damn me, we've set her aflame.'

The Atlantia shuddered as her starboard cannons opened fire together, the plasma rounds shooting out and converging on the small cavity glowing with flame. Idris should have felt elated, but not for the first time, just before the shots impacted, the captain felt a strange melancholy settle across his shoulders borne of an awareness of the terrible damage he was about to inflict on other living beings. The scent of victory was like nectar, but the taste of it was always bitter sweet, tinged with regret.

The plasma rounds smashed as one into the cruiser's hull and a brilliant explosion ripped across the vessel's hull. A crescendo of cheers erupted across the bridge as the captain whirled to Mikhain.

'Where is the shuttle?'

The XO looked down at his control panel and shook his head. 'I can't see her, sir.'

'Ranger Force, respond,' Lael called. 'Ranger Force, status?'

A blast of static filled the bridge speakers as the captain looked at the damaged cruiser, her stern quarter dragging through the tumbling mass of asteroids amid brightly flaring explosions as the immense mass of the space rocks smashed into the unprotected hull plating.

'I'm releasing the cable clamps!' Mikhain snapped. 'Take us clear and prepare to destroy her!'

Idris caught a few glances from the bridge crew but he did not belay the order. The XO flipped a switch on his console and a distant ripple of thumps reverberated through the hull as the cables were detached. The Atlantia, free from its massive burden, surged forward and began to accelerate away from the debris field.

'Captain?' Lael whispered. 'The shuttle, and the hostages?'

The captain forced himself not to look at her as he once again gripped the support rail and steeled himself. He could do nothing for Bra'hiv or Ty'ek's hostages now – the Rankor had to be destroyed along with Ty'ek, or the Veng'en warrior would continue to hound the Atlantia across the cosmos. The general and his marines would have to save themselves or be doomed to die aboard the Veng'en cruiser.

'Charge main batteries,' he ordered. 'Full broadside.'

Mikhain stared at the captain for a long beat before he replied. 'Aye, captain.'

*

'Splash seven!'

Evelyn saw the Scythe fighter's wing spin off as her plasma shot blasted through it, the fighter careering awkwardly as its port engine flamed out. Broadside on to her, she fired again and this time the Scythe exploded into a brilliant orange fireball as she raced past.

'All Reapers, cables detatching!'

Evelyn frowned as she glanced at the cruiser's damaged hull. 'The shuttle is still docked!'

'All Reapers, return to base.'

Evelyn saw the cables detach as the Atlantia surged away from the asteroid field and the damaged Veng'en cruiser, the frigate's ion engines flaring a brilliant white as she accelerated. Behind her, the Rankor attempted to fire her engines and pull free of the asteroid field, her stern quarter still dragging through the debris and suffering terrible damage.

'Andaim, the Marines are still aboard,' Evelyn said.

The commander's Raython crossed from left to right in front of her, Andaim turning for Atlantia.

'The crippling of the cruiser is more important to us now, we have to pull clear,' he replied.

A wave of Scythe fighters were fleeing from the Atlantia as the tide of the battle turned fully against them.

'They'll destroy the shuttle, regardless of what we do,' she insisted.

'Ty'ek's gambling that the hostages' presence on the bridge is what's stopping us from crushing him,' Andaim snapped.

'And will it?'

Andaim hesitated before he replied. 'I don't know now.'

*

'Damage report!'

Ty'ek's voice was a shriek of outrage as he stormed across the bridge. The vessel shook and vibrated as countless asteroids smashed into its port hull, each blow sending fresh alarms screeching and shaking the bridge enough to make standing still almost impossible.

'Port engine nacelles are out of action!' came the response. 'All of our port cannons are without power and we have fires on multiple decks, all on the port side.'

Ty'ek snarled as he pointed at the helmsman. 'Hard to port! Get us clear of the debris field and then bring our starboard guns to bear on them!'

'They'll kill us!' his tactical officer cried. 'Their Marines have already boarded us! We are defeated, Ty'ek!'

Ty'ek swung one giant hand and struck the officer across the face with enough force to hurl him sideways into a console.

'There is no such thing as defeat, only a courageous death!' he bellowed. 'Hard to port!'

The helmsman obeyed, engaging the bow thrusters.

'Tactical!' Ty'ek snapped. 'Charge the starboard batteries!'

'We don't have enough power!'

Ty'erk drew a pistol from his belt and aimed it at the officer. 'Now!'

The scolded officer snarled, his skin rippling a dull red as he whirled and began manipulating his controls. Ty'ek turned to face the viewing screen and then glanced at Qayin.

'You people tried to ram my ship,' he growled. 'I swear to you that my last act will be to ram yours!'

Qayin, his face bloodied and his right eye swollen, managed a grim smile.

'Any Veng'en is better dead than alive.'

'The Atlantia is charging her batteries!' the tactical officer cried out.

'How long?' Ty'ek demanded.

The officer looked at his screens and then his voice fell. 'We can't charge our own fast enough. They will fire first.'

Ty'ek looked at his helmsman, who shook his head slowly. 'We can't escape sir.'

'Full power then,' Ty'ek snarled. 'Ram them head–on!'

'Half of our engines are damaged,' the helmsman replied. 'We cannot ram them!'

'Then what *can* we do?!'

A silence descended over the bridge as the tactical officer gestured to Qayin and the hostages from the Sylph. 'We can bargain for our survival, or surrender.'

Ty'ek turned and glared at Qayin and then the sound of gunfire erupted from beyond the bridge doors.

'The humans are coming!' the tactical officer yelled, drawing his sidearm.

'How long until we can fire on the Atlantia?'

'Ninety seconds, captain,' came the reply.

Ty'ek reached down and with one muscular arm he yanked Qayin's restraints free and hauled him to his feet. With his free hand Ty'ek drew a savage looking blade from its sheath on his belt and rested the polished steel against Qayin's neck.

'Signal them,' he snarled.

The communications officer accessed their panel, and within moments the main viewing panel switched from a view of the Atlantia to that of its captain, Idris Sansin. Ty'ek sneered at the image as he spoke.

'Call off your men or I'll cut his throat.'

Captain Sansin glanced at Qayin and shrugged. 'He is a convict and not of interest to me. Cut him if you will, but if you do I assure you I'll destroy each and every one of you just for the hell of it.'

Ty'ek watched as the cruiser's orientation slowly changed as she drifted clear of the asteroid field, turning slowly under her own momentum. Sixty seconds.

'We are all doomed anyway,' Ty'ek snapped in reply, 'victims of the horror that you created. I'd sooner die than stand by and let you live, captain.'

'I don't think that you're in a position to decide what happens to you and your crew,' Idris replied. 'That said, if you release my man then I shall let you leave.'

Ty'ek snorted a tight laugh and shook his head. 'As if I would trust a human?'

'Would you trust a Veng'en?' Idris challenged. 'Your own soldier is here under his own free will because you would kill him if he set foot aboard your vessel, and yet here you are holding a knife to my man. Hasn't it crossed your mind yet that destroying everything is not quite getting the results you were hoping for, Ty'ek?'

Ty'ek pushed the blade closer to Qayin's neck, keeping the convict up on the tips of his toes.

'Better dead than alive to suffer at the hands of our enemies,' Ty'ek said.

'We're not enemies!' Idris snapped. 'Those wars are long over, the worlds that we fought to defend long gone. This is your last chance, Ty'ek. Release your prisoners or I will be forced to destroy you for once and for all.'

'With your own men aboard?' Ty'ek shouted. 'I doubt that very much captain.'

The bridge doors hissed and then a blast shook them as the Marines blasted their way through and stormed onto the bridge. Djimon and Bra'hiv broke through, weapons aimed at the bridge crew as they took up defensive positions.

Sergeant Djimon looked at Qayin and a cold grin fractured his features.

'Kill him,' he uttered to the Veng'en captain. 'He's better off dead anyway.'

Ty'ek stared at the sergeant in surprise, Qayin still pinned to his chest by the Veng'en's powerful arm. In an instant, Ty'ek dropped the wicked blade and instead pulled a grenade from his belt, the device emitting a high-pitched whistle as the Veng'en armed it and held it against Qayin's chin.

'I've got a better idea,' he shouted. 'Let's all go together!'

'Ty'ek, no!' Idris yelled from the viewing screen.

Ty'ek shut off the communication link and raised his clawed thumb to the detonator, and then he froze as a soft whisper of sound was followed by a dull thump. A rasping breath spilled from Ty'ek's mouth and his eyes widened as his skin paled to an unhealthy grey.

Ty'ek turned and saw his tactical officer close behind him, one fist curled around the elegant blade of a ceremonial dagger now buried deep inside Ty'ek's shoulder blade. Ty'ek gasped as the officer wrenched the blade sideways and the Veng'en captain emitted a faint cry of agony as he released Qayin and was forced to his knees, his hand still holding the grenade but frozen in place, the clawed thumb hovering just above the detonator.

The tactical officer reached out and plucked the grenade from Ty'ek's grasp, and then deactivated the weapon as he looked up at General Bra'hiv.

'You will allow us to leave,' he growled, 'or I shall detonate this device myself and end this for once and for all.'

Bra'hiv nodded. 'I have no desire to destroy you, but I cannot say the same for my captain.'

'Go, now!' he growled.

Bra'hiv grabbed Qayin by the arm and dragged him toward the bridge exit as the Marines freed the Sylph's crew and ushered them off the bridge. 'Go, now!'

The general made sure that all of his men were off the cruiser's bridge and then he turned and looked back at Ty'ek. The cruiser's captain was still on his knees, alive but paralysed by the blade sunk deep into his shoulder.

The tactical officer snarled at the general again. 'Leave us, now, or you'll die here.'

Bra'hiv hesitated.

'Jump to super–luminal while you can, before the Atlantia opens fire,' he said. 'The captain won't be planning on letting you leave.'

Bra'hiv turned and fled from the bridge. He saw Djimon take up position in the rearguard as the Marines fell back toward the shuttle. Bra'hiv joined Qayin, helping the wounded man along and then boosting Qayin up into the ragged entry holes carved by the assault team's aggressive entry.

'Go, now!' he yelled, and then keyed his microphone. 'Ranger One, prepare to depart!'

***

XLII

'They're coming back!'

Evelyn hauled her Raython around as she saw the Scythe fighters fleeing toward the Veng'en cruiser, firing as they flashed past and catching one a glancing blow that sent it spinning wildly out of control as it trailed bright flame.

She weaved past the tumbling contrail and locked on to two more fighters as they rocketed toward the Veng'en cruiser, her finger barely brushing the trigger twice and sending two pulses of energy smashing into the rear–quarters of two more Scythes. Neither impact destroyed the fighters, but both broke off their attack with aggressive defensive manoeuvres as Evelyn plummeted toward the vulnerable shuttle.

'You take the shuttle,' Andaim ordered. 'I'll patrol.'

A salvo of gunfire raced up toward Evelyn's Raython and she twisted the craft violently to avoid the lethal blasts as they flashed past her canopy. Evelyn hauled the fighter out of its dive and flashed by over the shuttle, which was docked at an awkward angle close behind the cruiser's bridge and in plain sight.

'You're too close,' Andaim called.

Cannon fire flashed by in a dizzying array of light as Evelyn fought to keep her Raython as hard to hit as possible.

'Where the hell are they?' she called.

A cloud of Scythe fighters swooped in toward the shuttle, Andaim's Raython wheeling in behind them and opening fire as Eveln pulled up and aimed to come in on their flank, catching them in a lethal crossfire. She squeezed the trigger even as she saw Andaim's shots destroy one of the Scythes in a flickering cloud of burning gases.

The formation broke up around the blast and Evelyn fired again into the Scythes and saw them scatter before the onslaught.

'Stay close to them!' Evelyn shouted as she realised that the cruiser's smaller guns were not engaging them directly any more. 'They won't shoot at us for fear of hitting their own!'

'How very *gentlemanly* of them.'

Evelyn locked onto a Scythe but a radio transmission from Atlantia broke her concentration.

'Atlantia, Reaper One and Two. Clear for effective fire!'

Evelyn heard Lael's call and she knew that she could not wait any longer.

'Get clear, Eve!' Andaim yelled.

Evelyn saw the Scythe fighters suddenly wheel away toward the cruiser's stern and she realised that they were making a break for it before the cruiser was destroyed.

'There's nothing more we can do for them!' Andaim called.

Evelyn yanked her control column over and her fighter swept away from the cruiser's hull, followed by a sudden stream of gunfire that rocketed by as she jinked and weaved. An alarm warbled in her cockpit as one of her engines began to overheat and she drew back on her throttle for a moment and looked up at the Atlantia.

She saw the ripple of tiny blue lights flicker like lightning across her hull, and then the gigantic plasma shots flashed past her and she craned her neck back to see the shots smash into the Veng'en cruiser and the asteroids surrounding it. A brilliant flare of light as bright as a hundred suns burned into her retina and she squinted and jerked her head away, the fearsome afterglow spoiling her vision.

The shower of plasma vanished as Evelyn's Raython levelled out and she glimpsed Andaim's fighter swoop down and move in alongside her.

'Atlantia, status?' the commander called.

There was a moment's pause and then Lael's reply came back.

'They're gone,' she said.

Evelyn felt a plunging sensation deep in her belly, a realisation that the people she had come to respect and admire had suddenly and completely been ripped from her life. Even Qayin, the unpredictable and seemingly indestructible gangster, could not have survived the sheer force of the Atlantia's broadside against such a damaged hull.

'Reaper Flight, acknowledged,' Andaim replied, 'returning to base. We did what we could.'

Lael's reply came back immediately. *'You did great!'*

Evelyn's eyes widened. 'What do you mean?'

'The shuttle's right behind you,' Lael replied. 'It's the Veng'en cruiser that's gone.'

Evelyn peered over her right shoulder.

Behind, the vast asteroid field was aglow with the light from the star buried deep within, beaming in immense rays out into the bitter cold of space. A cloud of shattered rock and dust occupied the spot where the Veng'en cruiser had been, but she could see barely any of the debris that should have been there: the vast torn chunks of hull plating, the burning cores of her giant engines and the clouds of venting gases.

Against the vast field, a tiny glowing speck glinted in the sunlight as it tracked toward them.

'Ranger One, Atlantia,' Bra'hiv's voice crackled over the radio. *'Returning to base.'*

'Did you get them?' she asked.

'The hosatges are aboard and Qayin's fine,' came the response. *'Although if I have anything to do with it he'll be spending a week in the brig.'*

*

'Reaper Two, you're number one to land.'

Evelyn guided her Raython down into the landing bay, aware of the smoke puffing from her starboard engine as she touched down. The Raython's magnetic undercarriage gripped the deck at her landing spot and she began shutting the fighter down as other Raythons landed around her. The shuttle came in last, its hull scarred with scorch marks and dents from its rough ride to and from the Veng'en cruiser.

The Atlantia's huge landing bay doors rumbled closed and the atmosphere was re–introduced as the whine of dozens of ion engines began to subside. Evelyn shut down her engines as ground crews swarmed onto the deck, and she opened her canopy.

Pilots clambered from their fighters, many of the craft scorched by near misses from Veng'en plasma shots. Some of the pilots looked exhausted, their hair matted against their heads and their shoulders slumped, but she could see smiles and nods of congratulations as they began gathering near the bay exits.

Evelyn climbed down from her fighter and searched for Andaim among the throng. The commander appeared from behind his Raython where he had been examining some damage with the fighter's crew chief. He spotted her but to her dismay did not smile or acknowledge her in any way as he strode across to the other pilots.

'Evelyn!'

She turned and saw Teera rush across and almost collide with her, the younger girl's arm wrapped tightly about Evelyn's waist.

'I saw you out there!' Teera almost shouted. 'Holy crap, you were on fire!'

'Literally,' Evelyn managed a smile as they walked toward the exits. 'I guess I had a good day.'

In truth, the effects of the drug were beginning to wear off and she felt suddenly swamped with exhaustion, the lights of the landing bay dull, the smell of ion fuel and scorched metal alien and cold.

'A good day?' Teera echoed. 'You shot down seven Scythes and took on a Veng'en cruiser, head–on, and you call that just a good day?'

'Well, I've had worse.'

Andaim was debriefing the pilots as they stood in a tight knot by the exits, the Reapers and Renegades mingling and chatting and smiling.

'… so it looks like the training's paying off,' Andaim said. 'We knew that the Veng'en pilots were less capable than us, but even so, I don't think that we lost a single pilot in this engagement. Lieutenants Veyer and Morgan both ejected safely when their Raythons were hit.'

A ragged cheer went up as Evelyn and Teera reached the edge of the group.

'Ensign! Attention!'

Evelyn flinched in surprise as Andaim pointed at her, his jaw set and his eyes hard and cold. She stiffened as the crowd of pilots parted and Andaim made his way through them to stand before her.

'During the engagement you made several key errors. Would you like to explain them to me?'

Evelyn, her brain beginning to feel fuzzy and disorganised, tried to speak.

'I just did what came naturally,' she mumbled. 'I saw opportunities for shots and I took them and…'

'You disobeyed orders on several occasions,' Andaim growled. The crowd of pilots fell silent as they listened. 'You broke tactical protocol by engaging a superior vessel's plasma cannons head–on without countermeasures or Corsair bomber support. You abandoned your wingman, *me*, twice, and in doing so endangered both your life and my own!'

Evelyn's jaw tried to work but she could barely get her words out.

'I…, I'm sorry. It won't happen again.'

'You're damned right it won't happen again,' Andaim snapped. 'As far as I'm concerned, you will never, ever be my wingman again and you will never fly that Raython again either!'

Evelyn stared at Andaim and for the first time in as long as she could remember she fought back tears that welled in her eyes as a terrible sense of shame swept over her.

Andaim stared back at her for a moment longer and then smiled.

'Because as a fully qualified pilot, you won't be anybody's wingman. You'll be flight lead.' Evelyn blinked as her exhausted mind tried to grasp what Andaim had said. 'And you won't fly that Raython again, as next time you see it Lieutenant G'Velle's name won't be there on the canopy frame. It will have your name upon it, *lieutenant*.'

A ripple of chuckles flooded the crowd of pilots.

Evelyn finally smiled as Andaim held out his free hand. She could see the other pilots watching as she looked down and saw a pair of gold metal wings in Andaim's palm.

Evelyn reached out and plucked the surprisingly heavy wings from the commander. She reached up and pinned them to her flight suit as the clatter of dozens of boots attracted the attention of the pilots. Evelyn turned to see Bra'hiv and his Marines moving to join them.

Several of the Sylph's crew members were being led away by medics along with soldiers on stretchers, their injuries patched with medical dressings as they were rushed to the sick bay. Among them she saw Qayin striding with one hand holding an ice pack to his face and two medics escorting him.

Andaim saw the big man and the general. Bra'hiv called out to him. 'I'm sorry to report that our mission was a success: Qayin survived.'

Andaim nodded, his expression sombre. 'A regrettable outcome. Better luck next time, general.'

Qayin's smile curled from his lips as he held the ice pack in place. 'So nice to be back.'

'You're welcome. What happened to the Veng'en cruiser?' Andaim demanded of Bra'hiv.

'Made a random jump,' Bra'hiv reported. 'We'd barely detached when it just vanished. The pilots managed to get us behind a decent sized asteroid when the Atlantia let rip, fortunately.'

'The captain's going to want to know everything,' Andaim said. 'All pilots, report to the ready room for debrief.'

The pilots shuffled away down the exit corridor and Teera jabbed Evelyn in the side as they followed.

'Told you everything would be fine,' she said.

Evelyn managed a faint smile in response, and wondered how much of her success was down to skill and how much was down to the drugs Meyanna had supplied.

***

XLIV

Evelyn awoke in her bunk and for a moment she feared that she was back inside the tiny capsule from which she had emerged from years of stasis, floating alone in deep space. Then she felt the warmth about her and she reached up to her face. There was no metal mask.

Evelyn sighed in relief in the darkness and looked at her HandStat. The luminous display beneath the skin of her left hand glowed in the darkness, and she was mildly surprised to discover that she had been asleep for almost twelve hours.

Captain Idris Sansin had stood the Atlantia's crew down for twenty four hours after the Veng'en cruiser had fled the scene of the battle. Exhausted, injured and facing days' of repair duties, there had been no celebrations or award ceremonies. The entire crew had grabbed quick showers, an even quicker meal, and then collapsed into their bunks.

Evelyn tapped a touchscreen beside her head and the side wall of her bunk hissed open to reveal the tiny twin room she shared with Teera. Barely larger than the prison cells she had once been incarcerated in, it provided a modicum of privacy in the otherwise crowded frigate.

She climbed out of her bunk, noting that Teera's was already empty, and hit another button on the wall. The two bunks collapsed automatically and folded up against the wall, providing a little more space in the tiny room. Evelyn washed, and then from one of two narrow lockers she lifted out her dark blue officer's uniform and dressed.

A screen on the wall beeped quietly, and she tapped it to reveal a message from Meyanna Sansin.

REPORT TO SICK BAY

The message had been sent four hours previously.

Evelyn sighed, adjusted her uniform until she was happy with its fit, and then opened the door of the room and walked out.

The pilot's crew room was mostly empty, many of the men making the most of the downtime by visiting the sanctuary. Two pilots who were on Quick Reaction Alert, the twenty–four hour scramble standy–by duty, cast her quick glances before returning to their reading. She passed the two pilots by and headed into the ship proper, travelling via the elevator banks to the sick bay.

Meyanna Sansin was working as ever on the ward, tending to the many injured soldiers and pilots in the aftermath of the battle. Evelyn eased her way past nurses and doctors until she caught the eye of the captain's wife. Meyanna's smile was quick and Evelyn saw her take in the wings pinned to her chest and the smart uniform.

'About time,' Meyanna said as she stood up from applying a gel to a burn on a Marine's forearm. 'And the uniform suits you.'

'It's just my colour,' Evelyn replied. 'You called for me?'

Meyanna removed her surgical gloves and motioned for Evelyn to follow her toward the laboratory.

'Have you been debriefed?' she asked.

'Only at squadron level,' Evelyn replied. 'The captain hasn't spoken to me yet.'

'He will,' Meyanna said as she held the laboratory door open for Evelyn and then sealed it shut behind her. 'You'll be glad to know that I have engineered a vaccine from your blood that will protect us all against the Infectors, for now at least.'

'No more tests?' Evelyn asked.

'No more tests,' Meyanna smiled. 'At least, not on you anyway.'

'How does it work?' Evelyn asked.

Meyanna sighed as she glanced at a handful of blood samples remaining to be checked.

'I'm not entirely sure,' she admitted, 'but it seems that you have a set of killer T–cells that react to any foreign bodies that consume iron. Any hint of anaemia in you and *bang*, they move in to thwart it. The Infectors are sufficiently small that they can be swamped by the killer cells and contained. Their tiny size is normally their advantage but is now also a weakness.'

'Have you inoculated the crew?'

'It's underway,' Meyanna replied. 'I'm culturing your cells as we speak and introducing them to crew members as a standard part of treatments and check–ups. The whole ship's compliment will be immune to infection within a few weeks.'

Evelyn nodded, but she could not bring herself to smile.

'What is it?' Meyanna asked.

'The drugs,' Evelyn said, having decided that it was probably best to just come right out with it. 'They got me my wings.'

'No,' Meyanna insisted, 'you'd already earned them. The drugs merely sharpened you up at a time when you were exhausted and unable to function properly.'

'And the next time I'm asked to fly when I'm exhausted?' Evelyn pressed.

'You'll do fine. You're being asked to handle a complex fighter craft on just a few months' training, Eve. Anybody would find that hard.'

'That's what I mean,' Evelyn said. 'The others didn't get that boost, just me.'

'The others weren't coming down here and giving me blood every day for four months. The captain knows the situation and so does Andaim. They're both happy with what you've achieved, especially after the battle. Lighten up a bit.'

Evelyn tried to relax and she glanced at the containment chamber nearby. The Infectors were gone, replaced by a single device that hovered in mid–air inside the chamber.

'The Hunter I captured,' she said.

Meyanna glanced at the little device and nodded. 'Nasty little thing, isn't it?'

Evelyn moved closer to the chamber and peered in at it. The tiny machine swivelled its black eyes to look back at her and she shivered.

'Figured anything out yet?'

'I'm working on it,' Meyanna said. 'Mostly using X–Rays at the moment to understand how they work and figure out a weakness, but I'm not an engineer.'

'How come they didn't put the engineering team on it?'

'They did,' Meyanna replied, 'but these things are more like biological specimens than machines. They're made of metal, sure enough, but everything else seems more based on living species. I have a couple of guys from the engine rooms looking at this for me too, but right now we're just starting out and besides they're all busy with the repairs right now.'

'Is it still dormant?'

'It seems pliant but we're keeping it locked down for safety's sake. Enough about the machine. How are you feeling, despite the obvious self–doubt?'

'I'm fine,' Evelyn admitted. 'I slept for twelve hours, near enough. How's Qayin?'

'Him?' Meyanna asked. 'The man's a mountain. He'll be back on duty before the day's out. Andaim and the captain will want to see you on the bridge, but for now I'll just put you back on full duty if you're sure you're okay.'

Evelyn smiled and nodded.

'I'll be fine,' she replied. 'I just don't want to be dependent on you giving me a shot next time we come under attack.'

'You won't be,' Meyanna replied with a smile, 'because you never were. Get out of here, and in the nicest possible way, don't come back.'

*

'Hull status?'

Captain Idris Sansin stood with his hands behind his back as Lael read out a series of deck reports.

'Hull breaches on all decks sealed and repaired captain. Crews are still repairing some power lines on the port hull but all weapons, environmental and communications systems are now one hundred per cent ready.'

The captain looked across at Andaim.

'Flight status?'

'Twenty two of twenty six remaining Raythons are serviceable and ready for duty,' the CAG replied. 'Two of those are on QRA right now. All pilots are coming out of R and R as we speak and should be reporting for duty over the next few hours.'

'Don't rush them,' the captain said. 'Let them turn up on their own terms, as long as the QRA fighters are ready.' He turned to Mikhain. 'Tactical status?'

'We lost several Marines and two Raythons in the firefight, sir,' Mikhain reported. 'But Alpha and Bravo companies are at full readiness. Seven men in the sick bay, no terminal injuries. They should all be back in service within a few days. General Bra'hiv is on temporary leave, due to report back tomorrow.'

The captain nodded. Bra'hiv was never really on R and R, whatever he might claim, and would probably be watching events from the barracks.

'So, where do we go from here, captain?' Mikhain asked.

Idris looked at the now distant asteroid field, the dense clouds of rock and debris a faint, thin line against the flaring brightness of the young parent star.

'Did we track the Veng'en cruiser from its gravitational wave signature?'

'Aye sir,' Mikhain confirmed. 'They did not program a jump, as we suspected, but they did have a general trajectory. Analysis confirms that they're heading for home.'

Idris saw Evelyn walk onto the bridge, resplendent in her dark blue uniform with the wings pinned to her chest. He glimpsed Commander Ry'ere staring at her for a moment.

'CAG,' he snapped, enjoying himself as Andaim whipped his head around and came to his senses. 'What is your assessment of the Scythe forces deployed against us?'

Andaim performed a rapid calculation.

'They were disorganised and without a strong tactical plan, sir,' he replied. 'My best guess is that the Veng'en are as short of experienced pilots as we are. Fortunately our Raythons are worth any two of their Scythes.'

Idris nodded as he looked at Evelyn. 'And our pilots worth any five of theirs.'

Evelyn saluted as she stood below the command platform. 'You wanted to seem me sir?'

'I did,' Idris replied. 'You displayed some remarkable piloting skills out there yesterday, lieutenant. I'm only hoping that in the future you will likewise obey orders with the same customary vigour.'

'Yes sir,' Evelyn replied, slightly deflated.

The captain turned aside and looked at the viewing panel.

'Yesterday, the Veng'en mutinied against one of their own commanders rather than face a suicidal battle plan, something that I never witnessed before in forty years of service. I suspect that due to the adversity faced by both of our species they are being forced to reconsider their tactics and that may play to our advantage.'

'How so?' Mikhain asked.

'We have a common enemy,' Idris replied, 'and in such times, the enemy of our enemy is our friend.'

'You're suggesting allying ourselves to the Veng'en?' Andaim uttered.

The captain turned and looked at Kordaz, who was standing nearby on the bridge and watching the exchange in silence.

'I have come to realise that within all cultures there is the capacity for change,' Idris replied. 'If we're willing to find it.'

Kordaz did not reply to the captain but he inclined his head fractionally in acknowledgement. Idris turned away and looked at Mikhain.

'Lay in a pursuit course,' he said. 'We'll follow the Veng'en home.'

'That's suicide.'

The voice came from Bra'hiv as the general walked onto the bridge.

'It's necessity,' the captain replied. 'Shouldn't you be on leave?'

'They will kill us as they find us,' the general insisted, ignoring the captain's question and glaring at Kordaz. 'No ship that sought refuge with the Veng'en was ever seen again.'

Kordaz shook his head.

'My people believed that yours were already infected and fleeing or were actively attacking us. They had no choice but to employ a zero–tolerance approach to foreign vessels entering our space after your apocalypse.'

'Either way,' Idris interjected, 'we have little chance of standing on our own once we start getting close to the colonies. Alliances must be forged. General, did you not just assault a Veng'en vessel with a platoon of former convicts by your side, in order to save a man who was once a gangster but now wears your colours? Does that in itself not reflect your own considerable capacity for change?'

The general scowled but he did not reply. The captain looked down at Mikhain once more.

'Follow her,' he repeated. 'Keep our distance but track her home. Maybe, this time, we can prove to the Veng'en that an alliance between our races is the only way we can even begin to think about defeating the Word. We must achieve unity with other species against it, and together perhaps we will be strong enough to prevail.'

Mikhain, a little reluctance remaining in his tones, began sending the tracking data to the helmsman.

'Aye, sir.'

'What if the Veng'en don't destroy us but still refuse to help?' Andaim asked.

The captain took a deep breath as he stood with his hands behind his back and looked out to the dense starfields awaiting them.

'Then we must find other races who will,' he replied. 'And we must find them before the Word has a chance to spread further. We will become the harbinger of doom but also the last flame of hope. This is our mission, to make ourselves strong enough to take the battle home.' He looked down at his bridge crew. 'Dismissed.'

***

XLV

The lower keel–hull of the Atlantia was a place where the crew rarely ventured. Although pressurised and provided with an atmosphere for the rare occasions when engineers were required to travel down to inspect the ship's immense hull, the long lonely passages were only dimly lit and provided little more than a home for the descendents of the scavenging animals that had somehow made it aboard when the Atlantia's keel was laid down decades before.

The three men stepped off the bottom of the access ladder and looked down into the endless passage that ran the length of the lower hull, the widely spaced illumination panels in the ceiling vanishing into the distance.

The decks here were not magnetized unless power was specifically re-routed to the charging cables laid below the decks themselves. The men's boots gently touched the deck and they pushed off, floating through the gloomy passage.

'I don't like this,' muttered one of them, a small and wiry man with half of his teeth missing.

'Shut up,' snapped another, bulkier man with a thickly forested jaw and chunky arms. 'This will be worth it.'

Most of the Atlantia's civilians were the former prison support workers, their families and a scattering of travellers who had been fortunate enough to be aboard the prison ship when the apocalypse struck the homeworlds. Some were skilled workers: engineers, physicists and other scientists, doctors and nurses employed either by the Colonial Fleet or the prison service. Most others were labourers and steel–workers, tradesmen sub-contracted to the Colonial Fleet Service and stationed far from home. Now, confined deep in the sanctuary with no control over their future, many of the civilians were restless and even bored despite the sacntuary's idyllic surroundings.

A dull crack echoed down the corridors and the wiry man stiffened. 'What was that?'

All ships made sound even when they were drifting through the immense expanses of interstellar space. The huge size of the craft, temperature differences, combined with the subtle shifts and stresses of distant stars exerting their gravitational pull or micrometeorite impacts and the thrust of the enormous engines all combined to produce a rhythmic drumming that some spacemariners referred to as the ship's *heartbeat*. Way down here, they could hear the creak and throb of the ship's internal structure flexing, bending, expanding and contracting, the echoes rolling back and forth down the lonely passage around them as though distant warriors fought with steel swords, the blades clashing with each blow.

The three men let their momentum carry them for several minutes before, far ahead, they glimpsed a small light flash three times like a beacon. There was a long pause and then it flashed twice more. The bearded man retrieved from his jacket a small flashlight, and he responded with a twin double–flash of his own as he floated toward the source of the light.

A giant figure emerged from the shadows where it had crouched, silhouetted against the feeble lights in the distance. The three men reached out to slow themselves as they grasped the edge of a bulkhead, and one of them produced a portable lamp that illuminated their faces with a ghoulish glow.

"Bout time,' the giant figure uttered.

The bearded man let his boots touch the deck, keen to have something to push against should the meeting turn sour.

'Ain't easy to slip away unnoticed,' he replied. 'You got what we need?'

'I got it.' The giant figure handed the bearded man a small, sealed plastic bag.

The drug Devlamine was a crystal, a volatile mixture of chemicals that had been the staple of violent street gangs before the apocalypse. The same drug that the Legion had first used as a carrier to infect mankind, in its normal form it caused a sense of euphoria that was so powerful it literally caused users to lose hours or even days of their lives while comatose in a blissful Utopian dreamworld, far from the horrors of the world around them. Grieving relatives saw lost ones again, terminally ill patients ended their lives in serene delight, and reckless youths seeking the next illegal high sent themselves into an oblivion of ecstacy, sometimes never to return.

It was said, by some, that it was the Legion's ability to manipulate the drug in which it had hidden that caused the infection to be so successful: the Legion did not initially directly control the host, the drug did, delivered precisely when and where it was needed to ensure compliance and withdrawn when that obedience was challenged.

'You done good,' the bearded man said. 'Who's in on it?'

'It matter?'

'It matters to me.'

'You wanted your supply, you got it. Where's my piece?'

The bearded man handed over a compact plasma pistol and two thirty–round magazines.

No unauthorised weapons were permitted aboard the Atlantia. Her former role as a prison ship forbade the carrying of weapons in the hands of civilians or convicts for obvious reasons, and now the armoury was reserved for the ship's military staff only.

The giant figure grinned and in the pale light of the lamp his teeth seemed brilliantly white.

'Now you got somethin' to ease pain, and I got somethin' to cause it,' he murmured.

The bearded man stepped forward.

'We want this ship to be taken somewhere as far away from the Word as it can be. We don't want no part of this fight, you understand?'

The third civilian, a feeble-looking bespectacled man, nodded in agreement. 'We got kids, families. Captain just damned near got us all blown to hell and we're done with it. You gonna take the ship back or not?'

The giant figure loomed forward, and upon his face streams of bioluminescent tattoos rippled and flared. Qayin hefted the gun in his hand for a moment, and then his bright smile reflected the light of the lamp between them once again.

'It ain't gonna happen overnight,' he replied, 'but believe me, my men will follow me anywhere and they've got the access to weapons and the bridge that you need. They'll take the damned ship all right, just as long as you keep producing this wonderful stuff for me in the sanctuary. I only got a small supply source: it's down to you to make it grow, understood?'

'It ain't gonna be easy,' replied the bearded man. 'Keeping the factory out of sight when the whole damned crew are stood down and come flocking in.'

'The more people get hold of this stuff, the more quiet they'll be about it,' Qayin growled. 'You keep your end of the bargain and I'll keep mine.'

'How do we know that? You could turn traitor on us just like you did those other prisoners when you...'

The blade flickered silently in the light as Qayin rammed it up against the bearded man's throat and pinned him against the bulkhead, his boots inches off the deck.

'You do what you do and I'll do what I do,' Qayin snarled. 'That's our agreement. It don't give you the right to back-chat me, and if you do it again I'll gut you without blinkin', you sold?'

The man nodded, his eyes swimming with panic.

Qayin grinned, his bioluminescent tattoos glowing like rivers of molten metal against black rocks as he backed away from the man and the blade retracted into his sleeve as if by magic.

'Same time next week, gentlemen,' he said. 'Don't be late. I wouldn't want to have to terminate our agreement, or any of you.'

With that, Qayin turned and drifted like a giant black ghost away from the men.

'I told you,' snapped the wiry man in a harsh whisper. 'This was a bad idea. That guy's a lunatic – he'll kill us if we cross him.'

'Yes he will,' came the reply. 'But he's also a Marine and one tip-off from us will see him marooned on the nearest planet. We got mutually assured destruction, right?'

Neither of his companions replied.

*

Qaiyn reached the end of the keel-hull and slowed as he saw a figure awaiting him near the pressure hatch exit. The low lighting concealed their presence sufficiently that the civilians behind him would not be able to identify the stranger, and Qayin was careful to keep his bulky frame between them.

Qayin slowed and stared down at the new arrival for a long moment.

'You sure about this?'

The figure nodded once. Curt, quiet, but no doubts.

Qayin offered up a small pack of Devlamine but kept the pistol concealed beneath his jacket. His voice rumbled deeply as he spoke, his hand still gripping the Devlamine.

'You got my back, right?'

The figure looked up at him and in the faint light Qayin saw a pair of clear green eyes, as wide as though he could see directly into her soul.

'Just so long as you've got mine,' she replied.

Qayin released the package containing the drugs, and Evelyn turned quietly away and vanished into the ship's shadows once more.

*

'You wanted to see me, sir?'

General Bra'hiv stood in the Executive Officer's cabin, not much bigger than the prison cell-sized crew quarters that were squeezed into every spare section of the ship.

Mikhain's quarters were as sparse as that of any military officer, but where Mikhain's differed from most was the vast quantity of images of his family adorning the walls. Bra'hiv was taken aback by the fact that barely any of the dull grey walls were visible for the array of images depicting children, adults, what were probably grandparents and friends and family pets. The whole room was like a shrine.

Mikhain, sitting behind a small desk, noted the general's glance.

'My family,' he said. 'As they were, before…'

Bra'hiv stiffened. 'My condolences, sir.'

Mikhain waved him off with a gentle smile. 'We have all lost a great deal, general.'

'Some more than others,' Bra'hiv replied.

The general's own family had been much smaller and his wife had passed away of an illness two years before the holocaust had struck. Bra'hiv's grief at the time had been replaced with a sense of immense relief that she had not been witness to what had happened to their two children, both of whom had been on Ethera when the Legion had struck and the Word had taken control of humanity.

Bra'hiv had been away on duty aboard the Atlantia, as much to get away from memories of his wife as anything else. Now, he had only memories of his children too.

Mikhain pulled out a bottle of dark red liquor and two tumblers.

'I'm on duty,' Bra'hiv cautioned the XO.

'So am I,' Mikhain said, 'but what I need to say will go down a lot easier on the back of a shot like this.'

Mikhain handed Bra'hiv a glass, a slim measure swilling enticingly in the bottom of it as the general looked at the XO.

'What's this about?'

Mikhain downed his glass and exhaled the fumes as he looked at the general.

'I'm concerned about the captain's plan of action.'

Bra'hiv suddenly felt a little cold in the room. He held on to the glass as though it were an anchor to safety as he considered his reply.

'Have you voiced your concern to the captain himself?'

'Several times,' Mikhain replied. 'He seems undisposed to listen to me. However, considering the fact that we were nearly destroyed by a Veng'en cruiser yesterday, that we now have a Veng'en warrior walking freely aboard our ship and that the captain intends to sail directly into Veng'en space with the aim of making friends, I don't believe that I can let the captain's decisions go unchallenged.'

Bra'hiv's grip on the glass tightened. 'Why are you telling me this?'

'Because you're the captain's staunchest supporter, along with Commander Ry'ere,' Mikhain replied. 'I could go out into the ship and curry favour with others who feel the same as me, but then I would simply be forming an alliance of convenience against the captain and his supporters. I don't want a civil war erupting aboard this ship.'

'You're talking about mutiny,' Bra'hiv growled.

'I'm talking about the captain's ability to command this ship.'

'Same thing.'

'Not if it's handled correctly.'

Bra'hiv set his untouched drink down on the XO's table without another word and turned to leave the cabin. As he reached for the door Mikhain spoke again.

'I'm not alone in this,' he said. 'I'm merely the spokesperson.'

Bra'hiv froze with his hand on the wall panel. 'How many?'

'About a dozen,' Mikhain replied, 'not to mention the civilians, nearly all of whom are crying out to avoid further unnecessary conflict.'

Bra'hiv turned back to the XO. 'Just months ago they were cheering the captain's decision to turn back for home, to take on the Word and the Legion.'

'I know,' Mikhain replied. 'The captain is good at whipping up a frenzy when it suits him, but the entire population is trapped down there in the sanctuary and forced to watch as the captain takes risk after risk. Now, they're being told we're heading directly into the territory of one of our most feared enemies and with Dhalere gone they have nobody to speak for them.'

'And you think that you should be that person?'

'No,' Mikhain replied, 'but without a system of checks and balances we're becoming less of a democracy aboard ship and more like a dictatorship. The captain isn't listening to anybody else but himself and he's not on his game right now.'

'He's got us this far.'

'And how the hell much further do you want to go?' Mikhain asked. 'Do you want us to sail into Veng'en space and ask for help? From them? After all that's happened and all that the Legion has done? They'll destroy us as soon as they see us, no questions asked.'

Bra'hiv's fists clenched by his side.

'My duty is to serve the captain.'

'Your duty is to serve the colonies,' Mikhain snapped in reply. 'There are over a thousand people aboard this ship, general, not just the captain.'

'And if we allow one coup, what's to stop the next one, or the one after that?' Bra'hiv said. 'Once you set the precedent that the captain's authority is not absolute, then you'll have insurrection after insurrection plaguing this ship. It'll be the end of us all.'

'Then what do you propose?' Mikhain demanded. 'That we just let the captain sail us into certain death?'

Bra'hiv hit the wall panel and the XO's door hissed open.

'I suugest that you do your job and follow orders,' he snapped. 'It's kept us alive so far.'

'So far,' Mikhain agreed. 'But for how much longer?'

The general did not reply as he left the XO's quarters and let the door slide shut behind him.

***

XLVI

The interrogation room was cold, sufficiently so that the skin on Sergeant Djimon's arms was raised into small bumps. Coming from Caneeron, a planet more of ice than water, one might have expected the Marine to cope better with low temperatures, Bra'hiv reflected in silence. But then again, the cold grey walls and bare white light above were designed to make the captive feel as isolated and helpless as possible.

'You understand what Maroon Protocol means, don't you sergeant?'

Bra'hiv's voice was without compromise, as though Djimon's fate was already sealed. The Marine betrayed no emotion as he replied.

'I do.'

'Then you'll know that your actions of yesterday aboard the Sylph are actionable by me, as your general, and that marooning you on the first habitable moon or planet is an acceptable punishment for betrayal and cowardice.'

Djimon's heavy features did not react to the insults, but his big fists clenched and his wrists strained against the manacles pinning them to the table before Bra'hiv.

'I betrayed nobody,' Djimon snarled.

Bra'hiv remained impassive.

'You abandoned a fellow Marine to death in combat in order to save your own skin,' Bra'hiv replied. 'You then told us that you saw him die in order to cover your own betrayal. Do you contest this?'

'Yes,' Djimon replied.

'Then tell me why I should not have you locked down until you can be left to fend for yourself on whatever hell–hole of a planet we next come across?'

'I did not abandon Qayin to die.'

'Then tell me what happened.'

'He was trapped beyond my reach and he could not be saved. The detonator I had set upon the wall of the corridor was counting down and the Legion was almost upon me. If I had not set the charge to blow I would have been risking all of our lives instead of Qayin's alone. There was no choice. Qayin either got blown apart by the blast or caught by the Legion.'

'So how did he survive?' Bra'hiv asked.

'How the hell should I know? Ask him! He should have been dead!'

'So you're saying that you set the charge too early, denying Qayin the chance to flee the Sylph's generator room?'

'I'm saying that Qayin took too long,' Djimon replied. 'He should have pulled back with the rest of Bravo Company, but he insisted on supporting that damned Veng'en's escape.'

'The Veng'en that helped us win the battle?' Bra'hiv echoed. 'The Veng'en that may be our key to finding a new ally in the war against the Legion? That Veng'en?'

'We didn't know all of that at the time,' Djimon snarled as he leaned forward in his seat. 'Kordaz had just escaped from custody, killed one of our doctors and was heading aft. When we found him he was with Dhalere, who was screaming for help and covered in Infectors. Right there and then, our only concern was getting our own people out of there, not Kordaz.'

'And Qayin, a fellow Marine?' Bra'hiv pressed. 'Did you judge him as unworthy of your efforts too?'

'Qayin is not a Marine,' Djimon snapped. 'He and his convicts wear our colours and train with us but they are not patriots and you know it. They are street thugs, looking out only for themselves. Give them the chance, they'll take the damned ship for themselves. If you want me to sit here and apologise for thinking that Qayin's Bravo Company is as great a threat to our survival as the Legion, then you've got yourself a long wait, general.'

Bra'hiv stared at Djimon for a long moment and then he turned his head and looked behind him to a large mirror on the wall.

*

Lieutenant C'rairn stood in the darkness of the observation room and stared at the sergeant and the general for a moment before he spoke.

'So, is that how it went down?'

Qayin stood beside the lieutenant, his massive arms folded across his chest and his tattoos glowing as he stared into the observation room. He knew that he held Djimon's life in the balance: most victims of marooning did not survive for long. Although trained in the art of wilderness survival, even the toughest Marines were at a serious disadvantage upon an unknown planet with unknown life forms. Occasionally, or so he had once read, military or merchant vessels had come across lonely outpost worlds and discovered the remains of tiny camps isolated on barren plains near water courses. Usually occupied only by the bones of the soldier who had once struggled to survive there, they had uncovered diaries recording the hellish tale of the unfortunate victim. Invariably, the dead man's skull had been punctured by a plasma round, one of three ritually provided to the marooned soldier along with his service pistol. Being abandoned was one thing: being marooned and thus denied human contact for the rest of one's life took a far greater toll than most people realised.

Qayin figured that he knew Djimon would be entirely aware of those same facts, and would understand as soon as he was told of Qayin's response.

'It figures,' Qayin replied finally. 'Djimon set the charges and fled but it was the blast itself that blew me clear of the Legion, far enough to make it to the escape capsules. He would not have known that I survived the blast – he wouldn't have been able to see me.'

Lieutenant C'rairn scrutinized Qayin carefully for a long time before he spoke again.

'You're sure,' he said. 'You're happy that Djimon's claims add up and he did not intentionally abandon you to die?'

Qayin nodded slowly.

'Cut him loose,' he said, already thinking about how he might use the sergeant's guilt to his advantage. 'We need every man we can get right now if we're going to survive this war.'

'He lied,' C'rairn said. 'He said that he saw you die, and he did not.'

Qayin looked down at C'rairn. 'He made a mistake. But maybe if he makes mistakes like that then he should not be a sergeant any more, agreed?'

C'rairn studied the big Marine for a moment and then he nodded.

'Agreed. Dismissed.'

*

The Atlantia's observation platform directly above the bridge provided a stunning panorama of the surrounding galaxy.

Evelyn stood on the platform and gazed out across the distant asteroid field, the sunlight obscured by clouds of drifting dust so that it glowed like a terrestrial sunset in hues of gold and orange, beams of light piercing the cold blackness like the fingers of a god. Beyond, sweeping across the pitch black heavens, the tenuous arms of the spiral galaxy soared high and low as though embracing the newborn star.

'You okay?'

Andaim mounted the steps to the platform and crossed to stand alongside her as she gazed out into deep space.

'Sure.'

'That's woman–speak for *no*.'

Evelyn looked up at Andaim, who grinned at her and shrugged. She could not quite suppress the smile that formed on her face as she sighed and looked back to the starfields.

'We won yesterday,' she said finally. 'But we barely made it through. We're outnumbered and outgunned by who–knows how many other races out there and none of them are fond of us right now. I suppose I just don't see how we can win this war.'

Andaim did not reply immediately, standing with his hands behind his back and surveying the stars before he finally spoke.

'We, humans, got where we are because we survived against overwhelming odds. Virtually every moment of our history has been a survival story and we don't for sure know if we're the last ones left anyway. There could be other ships, maybe even military vessels like Atlantia, scratching an existence out there somewhere and waiting to find other survivors. We go on, because there's no way to go back. That's all there is to it.'

'Sounds easy, if you say it fast enough.'

'Best way,' Andaim admitted. 'Don't dwell on it too much, Evelyn, or you'll lose sight of what we're trying to achieve.'

'We're alone.'

'We've got each other.' Evelyn looked up at him again and thought she saw a brief moment of panic swimming in Andaim's eyes. 'A thousand people together on a ship like this are not alone.'

'And there was me thinking you were being romantic.'

Andaim appeared to gasp for air. 'I was just saying, y'know, that we're not alone. We're together. Here.'

Evelyn peered at the commander. 'How did Dhalere infect you?'

Andaim stared down at her for a long moment before he replied. 'She must have coughed near me or something.'

'Coughed?' Evelyn echoed. 'Must have been one hell of a cough.'

Andaim averted his eyes toward the asteroid belt. 'Dhalere could be a very forceful woman, when she wanted to be, whether I or anybody else liked it or not.'

Evelyn cast her gaze back across the starfields and decided to let Andaim off the hook. She said nothing for a while and could sense the CAG's discomfort beside her.

'What are you thinking about?' he asked finally, unable to keep himself from speaking.

'Just thinking about home,' she said.

'We'll make it back there, eventually,' he replied.

'But what will we find?' she asked. 'What will be left?'

Andaim did not answer her, but another voice from behind did.

'Whatever we choose to make of it.'

Captain Idris Sansin climbed to the platform, followed by Bra'hiv and Mikhain. The captain walked to stand beside Evelyn, his hands clasped behind his back and his head held high as he surveyed the asteroid field and the vast galaxy spanning the heavens above them.

'It is still our home, no matter what the Word may have done to it,' he added.

'Home is not much of a home without the people that once lived there,' Evelyn pointed out.

'There will be others,' the captain assured her. 'Our lives need not be the last that will ever be lived. If we do not believe that, then what is the point in carrying on? All that matters is that we stay true to our course, that we ensure that we have each other's backs when those weaker than us falter.'

They turned as Kordaz mounted the steps to the observation platform. He stopped at the top and looked at the captain.

'You wanted to see me?'

Kordaz, despite the concerns of the civilian population, had been offered accommodation in the Atlantia's sanctuary, a home among the trees that while not quite like his home planet Wraiythe was far more appealing to him than the cold corridors of the rest of the ship.

'You have something to share with us,' Bra'hiv said. 'Something that you offered to share with the crew of Ty'ek's cruiser in exchange for our safe return. What was it?'

Kordaz looked at them all for a few moments, and his skin rippled and darkened slightly across his chest beneath his uniform.

'What use will it be to you all, out here, far from the Legion?'

'We do not intend to remain here,' Idris replied. 'Our course will take us home, to Ethera.'

'Etherea is no more, the lair of the Legion and the Word,' Kordaz snapped. 'There is nothing there for you any more. Why would you go there?'

'To liberate it,' Andaim said. 'Whatever it takes.'

Kordaz looked at the commander. 'You will be destroyed.'

'We will be destroyed anyway if we flee,' Idris said, 'perhaps not now, perhaps not for millennia, but eventually the Word will find us and its legions will destroy us. Better for us to die fighting it than condemn our children, or their children, to do it for us. I suspect that such a sentiment is one that you as a Veng'en can appreciate? Death before surrender?'

Kordaz's yellow eyes narrowed and his skin flickered even more darkly as he spoke.

'When I was aboard the Sylph, I discovered how the Legion communicates,' he replied.

Evelyn's eyes widened in surprise. 'How?'

Kordaz seemed almost to sigh, as though he were surrendering his own last bargaining chip in a game that could cost him his life.

'They do not use radio waves or microwaves or anything like that, they don't possess enough power to transmit signals,' he said. 'They use chemicals.'

'Chemicals?' Andaim echoed. 'Like insects?'

'Exactly the same,' Kordaz replied. 'The scorched–soil policy of my people has meant that they have never had the chance to learn of this, never had the opportunity to study the Legion closely. The Hunters and the Swarms and even the Infectors use arrangements of common chemicals as markers and signals, passing information between colonies and individuals. If you can learn how to understand those messages, you could perhaps disrupt them or eavesdrop upon the Word's communications.'

The captain walked to the edge of the platform and turned to look at his crew members.

'I need to know that I can trust each and every one of you,' he said, 'when the going gets tough. I need to know that we're all on the same page, and that we don't make the same mistakes that people made before the Word emerged to guide us. Mankind spent more of his time at war before that moment than anything else, and we cannot afford to repeat history.'

Andaim, Evelyn, Mikhain and Bra'hiv all glanced at each other, and then they all replied as one.

'Aye, captain.'

Captain Idris Sansin nodded, his craggy old features creasing into a brief smile.

'Good,' he replied, 'then we have a chance of surviving this.'

The sound of the Atlantia's mass–drive engaging rose up somewhere far behind them, and they watched as the vast panorama of stars suddenly flared brightly in a kaleidoscope of colour and then vanished as the Atlantia broke through into super–luminal velocity and raced after the Veng'en cruiser.

**

ABOUT THE AUTHOR

Dean Crawford is the author of the internationally published series of thrillers featuring *Ethan Warner*, a former United States Marine now employed by a government agency tasked with investigating unusual scientific phenomena. The novels have been *Sunday Times* paperback best-sellers and have gained the interest of major Hollywood production studios. He is also the enthusiastic author of many independently published Science Fiction novels.

REVIEWS

All authors love to hear from their readers. If you enjoyed my work, please do let me know by leaving a review on Amazon. Taking a few moments to review our works lets us authors know about our audience and what you want to read, and ultimately gives you better value for money and better books.

Printed in Great Britain
by Amazon